BOOK THREE

BLOODLESS TIES

KATIE WISMER

For more information visit: www.katiewismer.com

Cover design by Seventhstar Art
Proofreading by Beth Attwood

Paperback ISBN: 978-1-7346115-9-5

Hardcover ISBN: 978-1-958458-01-3

First Edition: November 2022

10 9 8 7 6 5 4 3 2 1

for my "we want more spice" readers

ALSO BY KATIE WISMER

The Marionettes Series

The Marionettes

Wicked Souls

Bloodless Ties

Ruthless Ends (Coming September 2023)

The Pact Series

The Anti-Virginity Pact

The Anti-Relationship Year

Poetry

The Sweetest Kind of Poison

Poems for the End of the World

Breakable Things

SIGN UP FOR MY AUTHOR NEWSLETTER

Sign up for Katie Wismer's newsletter to receive exclusive content and be the first to learn about new releases, book sales, events, and other news! Signed books can also be found on her website.

www.katiewismer.com

THE ESTATES

New York City, United States
Carrington Estate

Prince Rupert, Canada
Auclair Estate

São Joaquim, Brazil
Queirós Estate

Stockholm, Sweden
Olofsson Estate

Rjukan, Norway
Botner Estate

Dikson, Russia
Vasiliev Estate

Utqiagvik, United States
Locklear Estate

Chongqing, China
Wénběn Estate

Tórshavn, Faroe Islands
Jógvan Estate

Hat Yai, Thailand
Suksai Estate

PLAYLIST

Listen on Spotify: shorturl.at/eimyz

Come Back When You Can — Barcelona
In My Veins — Andrew Belle
Insomniac — Justus Bennetts
DRUGS — lil aaron
Casanova — Blake Rose
The Tradition — Halsey
Easier than Lying — Halsey
Hate You For A Lifetime — Connor Kauffman
Missing My Soul (you won't find it) — Cameron Sanderson
Healing — FLETCHER
better with you — Virginia to Vegas
getting low - Ziggy Alberts
Paralyzed — Sueco
buzzkill — MOTHICA
Nightmare — Halsey
Pumpkins Scream In the Dead of Night — Savage Ga$p
I Believe — Jonas Brothers
It Is What It Is — Lifehouse
Bloodstream — Stateless
I Need To Know — Kris Allen
Xo — Nightly
Safe Place to Land — Christian Burghardt
Delicate — Damien Rice
Getaway Car — Taylor Swift
Go On Then, Love — Said The Sky, The Maine

FOMY (Fear Of Missing You) — [SEBELL]
Anchor — Novo Amor
Cruel Melody — Black Light Burns
Cupid Carries A Gun — Marilyn Manson
Lipstick on the Glass — Wolf Alice
I'm Not A Vampire — Falling In Reverse
Freak Like Me — NoMBe
she calls me daddy — KiNG MALA
honey — Halsey
Wrong Places — Libby Larkin
Sick — Barcelona
Breakdown — Barcelona
Numb — Barcelona
It's About Time — Barcelona
Lesser Things — Barcelona
I BELIEVE — Ziggy Alberts
Ode to a Conversations Stuck in Your Throat — Del
Water Gap
Easy — Troye Sivan
There's No Way — Lauv, Julia Michaels
Beyond — Leon Bridges
hate u love u — Olivia O'Brien
Hanging By A Moment — Lifehouse
All In — Lifehouse
Dancing With Our Hands Tied — Taylor Swift
Damage — The Band CAMINO
I Only Wanna Talk to You — The Maine
maybe — Machine Gun Kelly, Bring Me The Horizon
Happier Than Ever — Billie Eilish
Wherever You Will Go — The Calling
Feelings — Lauv

PROLOGUE

No one told me it would hurt. But somehow, what came after was worse.

First, there was the severing. The bond snapped like a bone in my chest, splintering and shattering and *aching.* The kind of pain that blotted out the rest of the world. Nothing else mattered. Nothing else existed.

Then, in the place it had been, was a void. I could feel where it was supposed to be, but instead of my body stitching itself back together, growing over the space it no longer needed, the absence erupted inside of me like a black hole.

I waited for the pain to ease, for the hollowness to fade, but it never did. If anything, it grew stronger with each passing moment. Like I'd lost a limb, a fundamental part of myself.

Did it feel the same for Reid? The gap between his ribs? He must have felt the bond break.

But would he believe the lie?

That seemed the worst of all.

A cloth covered my face, the ether-like odor flooding my senses, and the darkness inside of me grew and grew until it swallowed me whole.

PART I
VALERIE

CHAPTER ONE

THERE ARE others in the room. I feel them before I hear them. Their body heat brushes against my senses, and the blood pulsing through their veins filters in next, the scent faint but clear.

Humans. Two, by the smell of it.

Whatever is beneath me is soft, warm. A bed. I remain lying on my back, eyes closed, listening and checking my body for injury. But honestly, I might be the most well rested I've been in a while. I curl my fingers and toes beneath the blanket, noticing immediately that my fingers are bare—my ring is gone.

After everything, it's a dumb detail to get caught up on, but...

Glass clangs together somewhere in front of me, followed by a sharp intake of breath.

"*Hush*," scolds a feminine voice. "You'll wake her."

"Is she meant to sleep this long?" replies a second, softer voice.

I definitely don't recognize the sound of either of them. The drowsiness is slow to fade, my eyelids heavy and my words rough as I squeeze out, "Who are you?"

I manage to sit up in the bed, though my head spins as I do.

Both women gasp and clutch their hands to their chests. They're in white dresses with red aprons—a maid's uniform, if I had to guess. Pretty much everything else about them looks the same too—sharp noses, bright orange hair pulled back in a bun. Sisters, probably. It's not even their appearances that give it away. It's the familiar way they lean into each other, clutching one another's hands, still staring at me like I've just risen from the dead.

They're standing in front of a small table at the foot of the bed, a tray with food and tea propped on the edge. That explains the noise.

They blink at me as if stunned.

"Well?" I prompt, a hint of irritation creeping into my tone. They must have known I'd wake eventually. I glance down at myself. I'm in a white nightgown that's not my own, my hair loose and wavy. And...*clean*? I inhale through my nose, picking up notes of a lavender soap. Did someone bathe me?

I comb through my memory. The last thing I remember is being in a cell in the estate's basement, dirty and starving and decomposing. How did I get here? *When* did I get here?

And where is *here*?

I squeeze my eyes shut, trying to make sense of the memories, but they're fragmented and spliced, flying through my mind like a movie too fast for me to see. The colors are too bright, the sounds too loud.

"I'm Orla, miss." My eyes fly open as the rounder of the two dips into a curtsy. "At your service."

"Sienna," says the other, mirroring the movement. An accent pulls at their words, curling their letters into something heavy and thick. Scottish, maybe?

My eyebrows inch up, and I take in the rest of the room. It's a far cry from the cell I'd just spent weeks—months?—in. The bed is massive, covered in fluffy white blankets and an array of decorative pillows. Windows take up the majority of the far wall, but I can't see past the maroon drapes to whatever is outside.

My gaze lingers on them a moment too long. The red is deep, dark. Almost the same shade as the blood coating my hands in every other scrap of memory currently on a loop in my head.

"Shall we start a fire for you, miss?" says one of the girls. As she stares at me with her big, round eyes, I realize she probably *is* just a girl. She can't be older than sixteen.

What the hell is going on?

The girl who spoke—Sienna, I think—turns for the fireplace in the corner when I don't respond and starts arranging the logs.

"You must be hungry," says Orla. "Would you prefer to take your breakfast in bed?"

My stomach growls at the mention, so I give her a slow nod. She slips the tray into her hands and brings it to my side. An array of meats, cheeses, bread, and jam is spread out, along with a bowl of fruit and a teapot. She pours a cup and holds it out for me. My hand shakes as I reach for it.

"Where am I?" I ask.

She giggles as if I've made a joke and exchanges a glance with her sister over her shoulder. Flames leap into the air, warming the room as Sienna rises to her feet and dusts off her hands.

"Oh! Don't forget this!" Sienna grabs a tall mug left on the table and adds it to my tray. The scent hits me immediately, and I sit up straighter, eyes darting to the cup.

"We'll come back in a bit," says Orla, taking a slow step away from the bed.

Finally managing to pry my eyes away from the mug, I look up to find a hint of uncertainty pinching her brow.

"Enjoy your meal," Sienna says with another curtsy, then the two of them turn and disappear into the hall. I squint, trying to see what's outside the door, but they close it before I get the chance.

I eye the food on the tray warily but don't have enough resolve to hold back from grabbing the mug. It's warm in my hands, and the blood is equally warm as it slides down my throat.

The moment the coppery taste floods my mouth, images assault me, too many to count. Blood on my hands, in the water, pouring from wounds, dripping down my chest, splattering against walls—but nowhere, not in a single memory, can I remember the face of the person the blood belonged to.

I drink every last drop, trying to bury the feeling threatening to emerge in my chest, and my body relaxes as the blood courses through me. The relief is sweet, but not as desperate as it had been the past few months.

It must have worked then, right?

I dig through my last memories again, trying to put the pieces together.

You have a deal.

The smile James Westcott had given me will forever be seared into my brain, but everything after that is dark. Did he even follow through with his part? Am I cured, or is it only a matter of time before the hunger comes raging back?

Sliding my legs out from under the blankets, I grab a piece of bread from the tray and shiver as my bare feet hit the cold hardwood. The fire crackles and spits in the corner as I stand and test my weight. It's nothing compared to what I'd felt in the cell, but the weakness is still there. I shuffle along, forcing myself to chew and swallow as I survey the rest of the room. There's a door beside the fireplace, likely a bathroom. I reach for the door the maids left through, unsurprised to find it locked.

I let out a huff through my nose. Not only is my ring gone, but they also trimmed my nails. None of them are long enough to break skin anymore.

No matter. Shoving the sleeve of my nightgown up, I wrap my arm around my body and bite down hard on the fleshy part of my biceps. My teeth break the skin easily, and blood trickles to my elbow, a few drops falling to the floor. It's then that I notice the red salt embedded in the wall above the molding.

Tilting my head back, I let out a long, slow breath. There goes any attempt to get out. It won't stop me from doing magic *in* here, but nothing that crosses the line. I grab a piece of cheese off the tray, then venture to the window. Shoving the curtains aside also proves to be a fruitless endeavor. The windows are blacked out. They are, however, cold as I lay my hand against the glass. Nearly frozen.

Wherever the hell I am, it's not New York. There's no way it would be this cold there already. Either that or a lot more time has passed than I realized. I run my fingers along the edges of the window, but there's no latch or way to open it. I'm about to give up and crawl back into bed when my gaze snags on the chair in the corner. My clothes are folded in a neat pile, Reid's jacket sitting on top, the one he'd wrapped around me in the cell.

My lungs constrict. The suede is smooth beneath my fingers as I pick it up, and the woodsy scent of his after-shave washes over me.

My hand drifts to my stomach, finding that hollow feeling in my gut where the bond used to be.

What had he found in my cell? James Westcott—I can't even bring myself to think the word *Dad*—said he'd fake my death. Had the cell merely been empty when Reid returned, or had Westcott done something more elaborate?

The door handle turns, and I drop the jacket and slide into bed, taking the teacup in my hands as it opens.

"Oh, good!" Sienna pops her head inside, then the rest of her body follows. I glance behind her, but her sister is nowhere to be seen. "You're up and moving. Come along." She heads for the bathroom. "Let's get you washed up and ready."

"Ready for what?" I ask, my hands tightening around the cup.

She glances at me over her shoulder and waves impatiently for me to join her. "You'll see soon. Now come along."

I set the cup on the tray but don't move any closer to the bathroom. Is she intending to help me bathe? Maybe she's the one who did it before. She sighs and ducks through the door without me. A moment later, a faucet sputters to life.

"I'll be back in twenty minutes," she announces as she steps into the room. "And I'll be right outside if you need anything." With another curtsy, she excuses herself, and I wait for the door to click shut before venturing into the bathroom.

It's nearly as big as the room itself. A large clawfoot tub sits on the opposite end, where water is rushing from the faucet and sending steam into the air. White towels are neatly folded on a bench beside it, along with a change of clothes. I busy myself rustling through the different drawers as I wait for the tub to fill, finding soap, a hairbrush, razors, and lotion, and pointedly avert my gaze from the mirror that stretches the length of the wall. After spending however long I'd been in that cell, I have no desire to see what I look like.

As I pull the nightgown over my head, I can already tell I've lost a significant amount of weight. My hips and thighs have always been the fullest parts of my body, but now my hip bones are plainly visible, as are my ribs.

Wrapping myself in a towel, I head into the room, scoop up the plate of food, and shove a few more bites in my mouth. My appetite is nonexistent, and I hold back a gag as I force the food down, but if I want any hope of getting my strength back, I need to eat. Once the plate is empty, I finish off the tea and pad to the bathroom.

The water is so hot it burns my skin as I slide into the

tub. I relish the sensation as I lean back and let the water rush over my head. I scrub at my skin and hair for a few minutes, images assaulting me every time I close my eyes.

Blood coating my skin as I woke up in Central Park.

The dead witches in the field.

A young boy begging for his life.

The look on Monroe's and Daniel's faces when they found me.

I force my head under the water and don't surface until I feel like I can't hold my breath for another second, then sit up, gasping for air. No amount of soap is going to get me clean. The blood might no longer be caked under my fingernails, but I can still feel the ghost of it there.

Maybe I always will.

I pull the plug from the drain and step out of the tub. As I stand naked and wet, the full extent of the coldness of the room registers, even with my vampire body being less affected by it. The hairs on my arms rise as I quickly dry off with a towel, wrap it around my hair, and pull on the clothes they laid out for me—shapeless trousers and a button-up blouse.

Who the hell chose these?

Tucking the shirt into the too-big waistband, I hurry to the fireplace to stoke the flames, willing them to warm the room faster. I jump at a knock on the door. It couldn't have already been twenty minutes. I wait for the maids to walk in, but the door doesn't open.

A second knock sounds as I rise to my feet. They hadn't waited for an answer either of the other times they barged in, so why now? Plus, the door is locked. I couldn't open it if I tried.

A third knock.

I test the knob. Still locked.

"Who is it?" I call.

"Honestly, Valerie?"

What little warmth was left in my body chills. I stumble back a step. Surely I'd heard wrong. Surely—

The door swings open, and the girl on the other side smiles. She looks nothing like the last time I saw her. Now, her dark hair is soft and full of volume, the large curls well past her shoulders. Her face is round and full of color again, the light back in her eyes as her smile twists into a smirk.

"You look like hell," says Calla.

CHAPTER TWO

THE ONLY LOGICAL explanation is I'm still in the cell. Reid never came. James Westcott never came. This room and the maids and the food—none of it's real. It's all been an elaborate hallucination my delirious and deteriorating mind concocted to cope with what's happening to me. Which means I'm still dying.

But dreaming up my dead sister? That's cruel, even for me.

Shaking my head, I step back from the door, unable to look at her face for another second. Her footsteps follow me as I retreat into the room.

"Valerie—"

"No," I snap. Her voice is exactly how I remember it. Raspy and low. Just like her face, somehow my brain held on to every detail. Even now that years have passed, the memory is perfectly intact. Or maybe it's not. Would I know if my memories warped over time? Would I be able to tell?

"I know what you're thinking," she continues.

"Do you?" I demand, and it comes out like a harsh laugh. "Please, enlighten me."

The door clicks behind her, and she leans against it. I consider going back to bed, but now my body is thrumming with restless energy, and I pace the length of the room instead. I can't look at her. When I do, my mind dips with vertigo, momentarily confused about *when* I am. Looking at her, I'm eighteen again, and none of this has happened.

My entire world hasn't fallen apart yet.

How many times over the past few years have I wished she were here? To think she's been alive all this time, maybe even witnessing everything that's happened back home without her...

It's unthinkable. Because the Calla I knew never would have let us suffer like that.

"Knowing you, you're in some kind of denial spiral in your head right now."

I say nothing, my feet moving faster, each step eliciting a hollow thud against the wooden floor. The chill from before is nonexistent now. Heat engulfs every inch of my skin.

This isn't happening. *This isn't happening.*

"But that'll pass. Once you get over that, I'm guessing you'll be pretty mad. So when you get to that point, can you give me a heads-up before you, like, throw something at me?"

I turn, and her next words die on her lips as she sees whatever is on my face.

This can't be real. But it can't be a dream. I've never had a dream feel like *this*. The colors this bright. Her face this clear. My body this exhausted.

15

Which would mean…

"I mourned you," I whisper.

She flinches, her gaze dropping to the floor between us.

"Adrienne mourned you," I add, my voice rising. "Even *Mom* was so broken up about it that we didn't see her for *weeks*. Adrienne never got over it. Not even a little bit. Do you have any idea what this did to us?" I'm shouting by the end, my hands shaking at my sides.

"Val—"

"They told us you overdosed! All this time, I've been wondering how I missed it, if there was something I could have done…" Her expression pinches together, less pained and more guilty now. My throat thickens, and my voice drops to a whisper. "The venom. The addiction. None of that was real, was it?"

The utter terror I'd felt every day since that the same thing would happen to me…the nights I'd lost sleep…the nightmares I couldn't wake up from…and it was all a lie.

"Val, please—"

I let out a bitter laugh. "That was your cover story, wasn't it?" She opens her mouth to respond, but now that the words have started coming out, I can't stop them. "And you've just been, what? Out here alive all this time? And you never thought to *tell us*? How could you—"

"I know you're upset." She takes a step closer, and I lurch away before she can touch me.

"How could you do that to me?" I demand through my teeth, my voice breaking in the middle. At some point, tears must've escaped because my cheeks are covered in them now.

"Would you let me explain?" she pleads.

"You know when a good time for that would've been? Two years ago."

"Valerie—"

"Just get out."

She takes another step, and I flatten myself against the back wall, not caring that I've spent every day the last two years wishing that she was alive, not caring that I have no idea where I am, not caring as a tear falls down her cheek, because all that matters is I can't stand to look at her, not for another second. Not when the person I thought she was has been overshadowed by whoever the hell was willing to do this to us.

"I swear to God, Calla, get the fuck out of my face—"

"Or what?" she demands, her voice suddenly hard. "What are you going to do, Valerie? You can be hurt. You can be pissed. You can even hate me. But right now, you're going to sit your ass down, shut up for once in your life, and listen to what I have to say to you."

My jaw snaps shut with an audible click. She lets out a long sigh, and her black dress swishes around her legs as she grabs a chair and sits beside the bed. I remain standing by the window and cross my arms over my chest as she chews on her lip and considers her hands in her lap.

"They faked your death too, you know," she says quietly. "Just like mine. Did *you* feel like you had a choice?"

I don't respond.

"Do you think it was any easier for *me* being away from the rest of you? I didn't ask for this, Valerie. Just like you didn't."

"Where are we?" I ask, my voice cold and flat.

She winces and pinches her lips together. "I can't tell you that."

My eyebrows shoot up.

She holds up her palms. "I don't make the rules. I'm sure they'll tell you once they're sure they can trust you."

Once *they* can trust *me*? The person they essentially kidnapped? "Who is *they*?"

The same look passes over her face.

I scoff. "Let me guess, you can't tell me that either?"

We stare at each other, and I lean against the wall, dizzy. I try to hold on to the anger—to whatever other hot, screaming emotion is rattling around in my chest right now —but there's no hiding the tears dripping down my chin, or the way my chest starts to shake.

Calla's eyes glisten, and she moves like she's going to come to me, but I hold up a hand to stop her, somehow simultaneously unable to bear the thought of her any closer and needing to wrap my arms around her and never let her go.

"I'm—" Her voice breaks, and she clears her throat. "I'm so sorry, Val."

Every night I'd sat in front of her grave, the pictures I'd had to delete on my phone because I couldn't look at them anymore, the nights I cried myself to sleep, agonizing over if I could've done something to help her, to save her...

And all this time, she's been here.

"That's not good enough," I whisper.

"I know." She calmly crosses her legs. Somehow the gesture is simultaneously familiar and formal. The carefree, fluid way she moves. The twitch of her mouth when she's uncomfortable that scrunches her nose.

But she's older now. There are lines around her eyes that weren't there before and a heaviness behind them. If she wound up in the same place I did, does that mean she went through all the same things during her initiation? Does that make her a…?

She meets my eyes like she can tell what I'm thinking and gives me a humorless smile. "We have a lot to talk about."

Slowly, I sink onto the edge of the bed. When it becomes clear I'm not going to break the silence, she sighs.

"For what it's worth, it's really good to see you, Val. I've wanted to reach out so many times. You have no idea. But Dad—"

"Don't." My blood pressure spikes at the word. "Don't call him that," I add more quietly.

She presses her lips together, then gives a small nod. "He convinced me to wait. That once you reached your initiation, you'd join us, and we'd be together again. So I just had to wait it out. And—"

"So you knew this was going to happen to me?" I demand, anger sending me back to my feet. "You knew about what would happen when I got paired?"

The way she can't meet my eyes at all now tells me everything I need to know.

"You didn't think to warn me?" I mean for the words to come out sharp, hard, but my voice barely manages a whisper. "And Adrienne? Will the same thing happen to her?"

"Valerie, it's not that simple. It's not that I didn't *want* to, but—"

"Did you know what he was planning? How he had that thing *attack* me?"

"No," she says, voice suddenly fierce. "I had *no* idea about the wendigos, I swear to you. I thought he was going to fake your death and take you away after your initiation like he did for me."

"Then why didn't he? Why make me..." I trail off, my throat thick. My skin burns where its claws had torn through my chest. *Why make me go through that? Why make me kill all those people?*

"The plan with the wendigos has been in motion for a long time," she says quietly. "He didn't tell me what he was planning to do with you. I didn't even know about it until recently. I think he saw you as an opportunity to get inside the walls of the estate. Especially once you were paired with the prince, I think he was hoping you'd..."

Realization washes through me like ice water. "He was hoping I'd kill Reid."

Calla looks at her hands in her lap.

"And everyone else at the estate?" I demand, my voice rising. "You didn't care if any of them were collateral damage? What about Adrienne?"

Calla flinches. "He swore he'd protect her—"

"She almost *died* in that bunker."

Calla's head whips up. Either she's become a better actress from the last time I saw her, or this really is the first she's hearing of this. She opens and closes her mouth a few times like she can't decide what she wants to ask, but I see it in her eyes the moment she figures it out.

That *I* was the reason she almost died.

I tighten my jaw and turn away, wishing the windows weren't blacked out so at least I'd have something to focus on.

"Was it during the blood exchange?" I ask, still staring at the glass. "Is that when you turned?"

"Yes," she whispers.

"So the venom addiction—that was your cover story."

"Yes."

"And you've been with *him* all this time."

"Yes. Listen, Valerie, I know you're angry. You have every right to be. But there's so much you don't know. Just hear us out, please. You might be surprised."

"Us?" I ask through my teeth.

There's a moment of silence, and then: "Well, I'm supposed to escort you to D—to his office once we're done here."

"And if I refuse?"

She doesn't respond. The floor creaks behind me as she gets up from her chair, but I still don't turn. Her footsteps draw closer, and my shoulders tense. Without warning, she throws her arms around me from behind, pulling me against her chest. I don't return the hug, but I don't pull away. I stand stiffly until she's done and finally releases me, holding my breath so I don't have to breathe in her scent.

"I think you'll actually find that there's a lot going on here that you agree with," she whispers, and then the distinct tingle of blood magic dances across my skin— somehow familiar, but not my own. My vision swims, and I feel her hands catch me before everything goes black.

CHAPTER THREE

I STARTLE, and my head twitches against my chest. It takes a moment for the room to come into focus, and when I realize who's sitting across from me, my entire body recoils.

James Westcott's elbows are propped on the massive wooden desk between us, his hands interlaced. His only reaction to me waking is a flicker of his eyes up and down my face.

"Where am I?" I demand, gripping the arms of the leather chair beneath me and looking around. The office is massive, with the entire back wall covered in windows. The thick, red curtains, of course, are drawn so I can't see whatever is outside. A fire roars in the fireplace beside us, and the portrait hanging over the mantel makes my blood run cold.

It's a painting on canvas, the brushstrokes delicate and precise. But the face staring back at me is...me. A younger version of me, granted, but the resemblance is undeniable.

I look five, maybe six. Around the age I was when *he* left. A slightly taller Calla is painted standing beside me, her hands around my shoulders. Baby Adrienne rests in my arms, her face tucked against my chest.

I whip my head to look at him, but he hasn't moved, his face the picture of calm.

"I do apologize for Calliope's methods to bring you here. I've spoken to her. It won't happen again."

I glance behind me as if she might be standing there, but the rest of the room is empty.

"You are not a prisoner here, Valerie."

"I just can't leave and had no choice but to come," I snap.

He opens his mouth to respond, then closes it, but I can already tell what he was going to say. *You had a choice.* "I trust you found your accommodations comfortable?"

I can still taste the blood from earlier in my mouth. My jaw clenches. I don't want to ask him anything. To give him even that smallest amount of power over me. But I have to know. I keep my gaze focused on his desk as I grit out, "Is it —did you—am I—?"

"Are you cured?" he asks, voice utterly calm, as if I'd asked if it was raining outside. "Yes."

"How?" All the research Reid and I did brought us to the same conclusion: there is no cure.

Just thinking his name hits me like a punch to the stomach.

Where is he now? Is he okay? The hole in my stomach where the bond used to be tightens, as if searching for him, but there's no one on the other end of the line anymore.

"That's unimportant." Westcott's voice draws me back to the room, and I frown.

"Why can't you just answer the question then?"

He gives me a humorless smile but says nothing.

There are a million other things I could ask, a million other things I'm dying to know, but instead, what comes out is: "What do you want?"

He spreads his hands in front of him as if the answer's obvious. "I want to talk."

"Then talk," I bite out, my fingers tightening around the chair's arms. "You want me to trust that I'm not a prisoner? To trust *you*? Then give me a reason why I should."

He sighs and shakes his head a little, but he's smiling. "You were always the most like your mother."

I jerk my head as if he slapped me. "I am *nothing* like her."

He laughs, the sound low and gravelly. "You'd be surprised. Though I suppose she does put on a good mask for the world."

I don't react to his words because I know that's exactly what he wants. He's been gone for the last fifteen years. He hasn't been living with her. He hasn't seen the things she's done. I know good and well who she is. Mask or not, no one is that good of an actress one hundred percent of the time. No one can fake that kind of cruelty.

I grind my molars for a moment before gritting out, "What am I doing here?"

"That"—he pushes his chair back and stands—"will depend on if I decide you can be trusted."

"*I* can be trusted?" I demand.

He continues as if I hadn't spoken. "In the meantime, Calliope has volunteered to show you around and help you get settled into the routine here. I know right now you look at me and you see the enemy, Valerie," he adds as he paces over to the window. "It can be difficult to see the bigger picture from within the walls of the estate. And if you don't trust me, I hope you'll trust your sister's judgment. She was a lot like you when she first came here, and it took some time for her to reconcile with the idea that her loyalties may have been in the wrong place. So if it takes you some time to come to the same conclusion, I am prepared to wait."

"How am I supposed to trust you after all you've done? After what you did to *me*?"

He doesn't blink. If he feels guilt over it—if the words affect him in any way—he doesn't show it. "Would you have agreed to leave under any other circumstances?"

No.

He gives me a small smile when I don't respond. "In time, you'll understand."

I scoff and shake my head. "You're so sure you're right."

"I am," he says simply. "But I know how difficult it can be to break free from their manipulation. Especially when it's all you've ever known."

"Coming from the man who forced me into a position where I couldn't refuse his help in order to get what he wanted."

He sighs.

"You won't even tell me where I am," I continue.

"A safe house. One of many." He pauses, then adds, his

voice quieter, "You're in Canada, Valerie." Something shifts behind his eyes, as if he's hoping offering this small piece of information will somehow get me on his side, will somehow be enough to forget everything he's done.

I realize then having this conversation in here was an intentional move. He probably doesn't even have that painting up normally. This is all a carefully orchestrated routine. Some warm food, a picture from another lifetime, and a small piece of information thrown out as bait.

But the only things I see when I look at his face are all the bodies I'd left strewn throughout New York. The blood on my hands. Daniel in a hospital bed. Adrienne's hair gripped in my fist. The panic in Reid's face.

When I meet Westcott's eyes, my jaw locks so hard the bone threatens to break through skin. He must see the shift in me too, because he returns to his chair and lets out a long breath.

"We'll talk more another time," he says. "Calliope is waiting out in the hall to show you around."

I rise from the chair, my legs weak from exhaustion and malnourishment, but I force myself not to stumble as I head for the door.

"They would've killed you if you'd stayed," he adds quietly as I grip the doorknob. "You know that, don't you? Those people you gave your entire life away to, they would've put you down like an animal. I didn't kidnap you, Valerie. I brought you here to save you."

I yank the door open without a word.

Calla is sitting against the opposite wall with her knees tucked into her chest. The moment she sees me, she jumps to her feet. "How'd it go?"

"You ever use your magic to knock me out again, and I'll fucking kill you," I mutter, turning away from her. I don't know where I'm going—if I'm even pointed in the direction of my room, seeing as I'd been unconscious on my way here—but I keep walking.

Calla's slippers smack against the floor as she jogs to catch up with me, then falls into step at my side.

"You can *try*," she singsongs, as if everything is fine. As if nothing between us has changed.

I glare at her. She's always been one to pretend problems don't exist, as if that will make them disappear. But now? With this?

"Okayyyy." She blows out a breath. "Well, can I show you around? This place is huge, and there's some people I want you to meet, and—"

"Is one of these doors mine?" I ask, pointing at the various rooms on our left.

She snaps her mouth shut and nods, pointing at the door two down from us. I quicken my pace until I reach it, then wrench it open.

Calla's eyes widen as I step inside. "I—"

I slam the door in her face and lock it. The silence of the room crowds in around me. Now without Calla or *his* face in front of me, the anger tightening my chest ebbs away and melts into something else.

I back away from the door, my breaths coming in hard and fast, and I turn for the bathroom, hesitating only a moment before grabbing Reid's jacket to take in with me.

Odds are the lock on that door won't keep anyone out if they really want to come in. I lock the bathroom door behind me too, then grab the chair by the tub and jam it under the knob. That, too, won't stop anyone, I know this, but it eases the pressure in my chest, just a little.

I sink onto the floor, the cold tiles pressing into my legs, and grip Reid's jacket tightly in my hands as my head spins. My fingers trace over the zipper. There are spells to contact people through personal objects, though I don't know any. Not to mention the red salt. But even if I reached Reid through the jacket somehow, if he knew where I was, he'd try to find me. And I don't know how many people are here, how many ways out there are, what he'd be facing. Considering Westcott had apparently been hoping I'd take him out in my Wendigo Psychosis stupor, I doubt he'd hesitate in killing Reid if he showed up here.

I gently set the jacket beside me. I can't do that to him. I won't have him dying for me. I won't.

I need to at least figure out what I'm dealing with, get as much information about this place as I can. If I can somehow convince them they can trust me, that I'm coming around to their ideas, maybe they'll let some information slip. That's my best chance—my only chance—of getting out of here.

But Calla knows me better than anyone. My tells. My cues. If I'm lying, she'll be the first to see right through it. She'll be the hardest to convince, and no doubt she's reporting all her observations to *him*.

A small, traitorous voice in the back of my mind echoes the sentiment he pointed out in his office. *If you don't trust me, I hope you'll trust your sister's judgment.*

At one point, I did. I trusted her more than anyone. But how can she support this man who left us all those years ago? Someone who's done so many terrible things, not just now, but for decades? How can she possibly think he's on the right side? I don't know how he's done it, but he's brainwashed her.

I push myself off the floor, turn for the sink, and fill it with cold water to splash on my face. My reflection stares back, barely recognizable. My eyes are sunken into my face, the bags beneath them so dark they look like bruises. My cheekbones are too sharp, my jaw too defined.

"You can do this," I whisper.

My gaze flickers to my arm. The sleeve of the blouse covers the majority of it, but a few black tendrils whisper along the side of my wrist and the edge of my palm. When I run the pad of my thumb across it, the skin feels different now. Firm. Stiff.

Even if I did manage to find a way out of here, I can't leave. Not unless I want this mark to kill me the second I violate the terms of our deal.

The memory is blurry, the edges hazy from the exhaustion and weak state I'd been in. The light behind his head had flickered, casting his face into shadow as he spoke.

"I'll heal you, but you have to come with me. You cannot return to your old life or the estate until I release you from your deal."

"And will you? Ever release me?"

"I'm not a monster, Valerie. And I have no interest in taking you as a prisoner. If you come with me, give it a chance—a real chance— and listen to my side of things, and then still decide you want to leave, I will release you."

"And I'll just have to take your word on that?"

"Yes."

I've gone through the words a million times, trying to find a loophole, to gauge exactly where the line is. *You cannot return to your old life* is so vague, it could apply to anything. But it's too risky to test it. If I assume wrong, I'm dead.

I will release you. He had to have been lying. Why would he go through the trouble of getting me here in the first place just to let me leave? Unless he's really that confident that I'll end up wanting to stay.

A knock on the door to the room startles me out of my thoughts, and I blink back to my reflection in the mirror.

"Valerie!" calls Calla. "I'm not leaving. We can wait like this as long as it takes."

I guess it's good to see she's as strongheaded as I remember. And her weird, deluded way of handling problems—as in, pretending they don't exist in the hopes they'll go away—is clearly still intact.

"You can't seriously want to stay locked in here all night!"

Though that's exactly what I want to do, I know it won't help me get out of here any faster. So I grab Reid's jacket off the floor, slip it over my shoulders, and sigh as I pry the chair out from under the door. Calla knocks again as I cross the room.

"Honestly, Valerie! Since when are you a fan of the silent treatment? Can't you yell and bitch at me already and get it over with? I'll even let you get in a good hit. Just not in the face, okay? Or, if you have to, just not the nose—"

"If I agree to come with you, will you *shut up*?" I snap.

She grins as I swing the door open. A single eyebrow lifts at the jacket that definitely doesn't go with the outfit—which was probably picked out by her, I realize—but she doesn't comment on it. She steps aside and gestures for me to join her in the hall.

A jolt pierces my chest as I look at her face, as if I'm seeing her for the first time again. It almost makes me dizzy, like the borders of reality are no longer distinct. But still, I steel myself with a breath, and follow after her.

CHAPTER FOUR

"WHAT TIME IS IT?" I ask, squinting at the sun. Floor-to-ceiling windows span the walls, and I can't peel my gaze away as we walk. They must be UV-blocking like at the estate because it doesn't bother my skin. Snow-capped mountains surround us in every direction. The drop beneath the windows is steep, disappearing down a snowy path. The sun glints off a frozen body of water at the bottom of the hill, surrounded by small smudges of white that must be trees.

"Oh, yeah, it's pretty much sun around the clock this time of year," says Calla. "We only get about seven hours of actual darkness a day. Don't worry, it'll only last another month or two."

My stomach sinks at the implication. That I'll still be here months from now. It isn't until she steps beside me that I realize I stopped walking.

"It's quite the view, isn't it?" she says softly.

I cross my arms and turn away. The hallway curves and

disappears around a corner. Everything here is so…shiny. The polished floor, the figurines set out on pedestals every few feet.

"*So*," says Calla behind me, her voice light, "I heard you got paired with the prince…"

I glare at her over my shoulder. "Don't."

Her eyes drop to the jacket, then back to my face. She holds up her hands. "Okay. So that's off-limits. I just want to know about your life, Valerie."

I look away and head in the direction we'd been walking. "Can we get this tour over with?"

"You know you can't stay mad at me forever."

"This isn't a joke to me, Calliope."

"I know that."

"No, I don't think you do," I snap. "You want to laugh and joke like nothing's changed. Like you haven't been *dead* to me for the past two years. Like I didn't just get my entire world ripped out from under me and brought here against my will. Like I didn't—" I break off, my jaw aching from how tightly I'm clenching it. I don't know how I would've finished the thought anyway.

Like I didn't just kill an unknown number of innocent people. Like everyone I love doesn't think I'm dead. Like I didn't just lose my bond with Reid, and it still feels like there's a gaping hole in my stomach without him.

"You're right. Valerie, wait." She grabs my arm and pulls me to a stop. "I have no idea what you've been through. I've just been waiting for you to get here for so long, and I was so excited to see you. I'm sorry. I just—I missed you."

She meets my eyes, and stupidly, I feel like I'm going to cry.

She wraps her arms around herself, momentarily lacking all her usual confidence and ease. I clear my throat and look out the window.

"I get it," she says softly. "The way I had to leave everything behind was hard enough. I can't imagine how much worse it's been for you. I'm sorry."

"And yet…" I gesture around us. "You're…working with him?"

She grimaces. "It's complicated."

"You can't do better than that? *It's complicated?* Really? You know what? I can't do this." I turn back the way we came, but she grabs my arm before I can take a step.

"There's a lot I can't tell you. I want to, but I can't." She gives me a knowing look—and there's something there, the way she's trying to tell me more with her eyes than her words, that makes me pause. "But I promise to tell you everything that I can."

I study her face, the familiarity still making my head spin. Quietly, I ask, "Do you actually trust him?"

She loosens her grip but doesn't let go. "I know you don't want to hear this, but yes."

I extract my arm from her grasp.

"Mom and Adrienne are okay," she offers. "From what I've heard, everyone at the estate is."

I don't know who *everyone* encompasses for her. Reid, Monroe, Daniel—is Kirby back yet? I hope so. Monroe will need her now.

"Why me?" I murmur. "Why bring *me* here? Why not Adrienne? Or Mom?"

Calla presses her lips together and sighs. "I'm sure he'll talk to you about that." I roll my eyes, but she keeps talking. "There's a very specific timeline for everything. He's assured me he's getting them too."

She continues down the hall before I can respond. "Now, come on! There's lots to see. This is the east wing. It's off-limits for most of the residents here. Just for our family, Dad's—uh, James's office—some conference rooms, that kind of thing. Most everyone else lives on the lower floors, or in the extra accommodations out back." She checks her watch. "It's almost 7:00 p.m., so my guess is people are in the training rooms or at their posts by now. There might be some stragglers outside."

Training rooms? Posts?

"Exactly how many people are here?" I ask slowly.

She shrugs. "It changes all the time. People coming and going. Right now, probably a few hundred. Though, I think Dad—James—sent a few packs off right before you got here, so it might be a little quieter now."

Packs? As in *wolves?*

"But what's cool is we recently added a screen around the field outside—kind of like a net. It has the same UV-blocking technology as the windows, so the vampires and halflings can be outside during the day, at least in that part of the grounds. Aha! Here we are." The hallway comes to a wall of shiny gold elevators. Calla punches the down arrow, and the numbers above the door tick up until finally resting on ten.

Ten floors?

The door slides open, revealing a petite brunette girl in

twin French braids and dirt-covered overalls. Her entire face lights up when she notices us standing there.

"Callie!" she screeches and shoots forward. I barely manage to step out of the way before she leaps into Calla's arms for a hug. Calla grabs the girl, giggling and spinning her in a circle, as if this were expected.

Callie? She's never, not once, gone by *Callie.*

"Oh my God!" shrills the girl as Calla sets her back on her feet. The top of her head skims Calla's shoulder. At first, I'd thought she was just short, but upon further inspection, she's *young.* Maybe not even yet a teenager. "Is this Valerie?" she asks, bouncing on the balls of her feet.

"The one and only," says Calla.

I don't have time to react before the stranger is now barreling at me. She collides against my chest with more force than I would've thought her small body capable of, and she knots her arms tightly around my stomach.

"*So* glad you're here. Oh my God." She releases me. "We should have a slumber party!"

Calla laughs and pulls the girl away from me. "Run along, okay? Valerie just got here. I still have to show her the ropes. We'll find you later."

"Okey dokey!" She sprints off down the hall, her arms pumping at her sides and braids trailing behind her.

I turn to Calla for an explanation, and a sheepish expression takes over her face as she shrugs.

"Who was that?"

"How many surprises do you think you can handle today?"

"Calla."

"Well," she starts, wringing her hands together. The

elevator dings as the doors close and it heads back downstairs. "That's Ollie. Short for Olive. She's kind of, well, one of our half sisters."

I stare at her, not sure which words to latch on to first, *one of* or *half sister.* "Come again?"

"Yeah." She shrugs and pushes the button for the elevator to come back.

"How many are there?" I demand when she doesn't elaborate.

She continues facing the elevator and crosses her arms over her chest. "In total? I'm not sure. Ones who are here? Well, with you now, there's nine of us."

"*Nine?*"

The doors slide open, and Calla hurries inside. I stare after where the girl—Ollie—disappeared. A half sister...? One of many, apparently.

"Come on, Val. Get in." Calla sighs as she reaches forward to hold the door, as if she didn't drop a huge bomb. She smiles as I step in and the doors close, the mirrored insides reflecting my scowl back at me.

"You don't find that odd?" I demand.

She shrugs. "Dad's been around for over a century. Don't *you* think it would be odd if we were the only children he had?"

My skin bristles at that word, every alarm in my body screaming *wrong.* I don't care who he is biologically. The man who came to visit me in that cell was not the same one from when we were children.

Or maybe the version I remember never existed at all.

He has also been Xavier Hearst, Nathaniel Strand, Christian Mazar... That's what Magnolia had said. I guess I shouldn't be surprised that he'd had entirely different lives with those identities—different families. And according to Reid, if he really was behind the wendigo attacks that happened in the past, the first did happen nearly a century ago.

I can't fathom how life must look after that much time has passed. No wonder he sees me as expendable—sees us all as expendable. We're blips on his radar…and just a few of God knows how many children. Who cares if you lose one if you have a dozen to replace them?

The heat filling my veins isn't anger, no matter how much I want it to be. Instead, I keep seeing that moment he got on his knees to give me the violin. I'd felt like the most special kid in the world—the most special kid in *his* world.

"Where are you taking me?" I mumble as the elevator plunges down.

"It's nice out today, so I'm guessing most people are in the training yard. We'll head over to the mess hall later for lunch. Meal times are strict. If you don't show up on time, you don't eat. Here we are."

The elevator dings, and noise floods inside as the doors slide open. We step out into a glossy, hotel-esque lobby with towering marble pillars framing sliding glass doors on the opposite side. I look back and forth as Calla leads us through the streams of people moving past, nearly giving myself whiplash.

Probably a few hundred. That's how many people Calla said were here. They can't all be like me—brought here against their will. So then where are they all coming from?

My head pulses as a million scents assault my senses at once, and I immediately know the bodies brushing past me aren't all witches. From the smells of it, there are humans, wolves, witches, and *others* mixed in. Things I've never smelt before. The combined energy buzzes in the air, raising the hairs on the backs of my arms.

"You get used to it," Calla murmurs as she loops her elbow through mine and steers me toward the doors.

Cold air gusts into my face as we step outside, carrying with it the bite of ice and snow as the wind scatters it on the ground. There's a fine layer of it, and it doesn't seem sticky enough to last. Calla continues around the corner of the building, her steps quick and sure, like she's traveled this path a million times. It's nearly transparent, the net Calla was talking about, but there are flickers of it as it shifts in the breeze. Somehow I can feel the sun directly on my skin, but none of the uncomfortable effects.

"There she is!" calls a deep voice.

Every muscle in my body tenses as an earsplitting growl rips through the air. I hurry around the corner of the building looking for Calla and stumble to a stop as a field swims into view.

A man jogs toward us in nothing but a pair of black sweatpants. Snow falls onto his exposed chest, but he doesn't seem to notice.

"Leif!" Calla holds her arms out as he reaches us, and he scoops her up and spins her around, his gigantic build making her look like a doll.

He turns to me as he sets her back on her feet and shakes his head to get the sweat-drenched, black hair out of his face. Perfectly white teeth flash as he smiles. "You must be Valerie."

Before I can react, he lifts me up like he did Calla and

39

spins me around until I'm dizzy. The musky scent of wolf seeps from his pores, and I stiffen in his arms.

"This is Leif," Calla explains as he returns me to the ground, and my pride alone keeps me from wobbling.

"What is with everyone here and hugging?" I mutter.

Leif chuckles, the sound low and surprisingly warm. "You were right! She is like the grumpy version of you."

I scowl at Calla. Of all the ways she could've described me, *that's* what she chose?

Another growl reverberates through the air, and I look up as two men lunge for each other, shifting midstep. Large, gray wolves take their places right before they clash in a flurry of claws, fangs, and spit.

Calla doesn't react to the display, nor does the group of onlookers. A few others linger by some equipment on the opposite end of the field, doing push-ups and pull-ups, but they don't turn at the sound of fighting.

"Coleman's totally going to get his ass handed to him," Leif says.

"I don't know," singsongs Calla. "Saint's been quite fond of Sherill's desserts lately. He's looking a little slow."

Leif barks out a laugh as the larger of the two wolves pins the other and bares its teeth. Snow mats against the smaller one's fur as it thrashes on the ground and maneuvers itself out of the hold.

"Well." Calla claps Leif on the back. "We'll see you at lunch? I want to finish showing Val around."

Leif salutes her, then gives me a little bow. "Wonderful to meet you, Valerie." Still stunned, I don't respond, but he just turns and jogs over to rejoin the rest of the crowd.

"So, yeah, this is the training yard," Calla says, opening

her arms wide like she's presenting something. "But people mostly use it to mess around. I'll take you around the rest of the grounds once the sun goes down, if you'd like. Come on. I'll show you how to get to the mess hall from here."

"How do you know them...?" I ask, eyes lingering on the wolves.

Calla shrugs. "Everyone here knows everyone, pretty much. Leif's cool though. He's a good buddy."

A few heads pop up and watch us cross the edge of the field. Calla waves to them before leading me to a side door. I crane my neck before stepping inside, taking in the towering structure. On the outside, it almost looks like it's entirely made of mirrors. The sun reflects off the snow and the building, casting everything in a golden glow.

"So food is here on the first floor," Calla says, the heat blasting from the overhead vents washing over us. "Most of the middle floors are housing, so you probably won't ever find yourself on them, but you're welcome to explore if you're curious! Anything with limited access is clearly labeled and locked, so you wouldn't be able to get in there anyway—"

"Calliope! *There* you are." A willowy redhead skitters out from behind the front desk in the lobby, waving her arms like she's trying to signal a plane. "Wait!" Her high heels click against the floor as she hurries toward us with tiny, quick steps.

"Valerie, this is Sutton. She's basically the concierge around here," Calla explains as the woman reaches us, slightly out of breath. "Sutton, this is my sister, Valerie."

The woman glances at me for half a second. "Hi. Calliope." She grabs Calla's arm in a way that makes me clench my teeth. "Rome needs to see you in Control Room 1."

"Right now?" asks Calla.

Sutton huffs. "Actually, he asked for you like half an hour ago, but I haven't been able to—"

"All right. All right." Calla takes me by the arm. "We'll stop by on our way."

"I don't think he'll want to be kept waiting!" Sutton calls.

Calla flicks her hand over her shoulder. "Thank you, Sutton."

The sound of her high heels fills the lobby again as she heads to her desk. We turn a corner into a wide hallway, and Calla erupts in laughter, pulling something out from under her shirt as she walks. The leather string around her neck is thin, with a key card attached at the end.

"We call her Chicken Little," Calla explains. "The sky is always falling for her." She pauses at a door in the middle of the hall and swipes her card along the keypad. The red light flashes green.

I move to follow her inside, but she just cracks the door and pokes her head in. "Sutton said you were looking for me?"

Luckily, Calla is a full head shorter than I am, so I back up a step and rise on my tiptoes. Lights flash on various monitors—dozens of them, by the looks of it. I squint, trying to get a look at one, and a jolt goes through me as I recognize the image. The video shows the back of the Carrington estate with the pool in the foreground. Where could the camera possibly be to get that angle?

How the hell did they get a camera on the estate's grounds undetected?

And *why*?

My gaze shifts to the monitor beside it as a man steps up to the door, blocking my view. A single dark eye and thick beard are all that's visible through the crack as he holds out a folded piece of paper with two fingers. "Get that to your dad, ASAP."

Calla sighs and reaches for it, but the man tightens his hold and raises it a few inches higher.

"It's urgent, Calliope."

"Yeah, yeah, Rome, I got it."

The man's eye narrows, but he doesn't resist as Calla snatches the paper and shoves it down the front of her shirt alongside the key card.

Rome glances up, noticing me behind Calla.

"Bye, Rome," Calla says, then turns, grabs my arm, and pulls me down the hallway. Several seconds pass before I hear the door click shut, followed by a beep as it locks.

It's hard to say with that brief glimpse, but the estate seemed relatively the same as when I left—as in, still in one piece. So at least that's a good sign. Is everyone out of the bunker now then? Maybe they already were by the time Reid found me in that cell. My head spins, momentarily disoriented.

"Why are you watching the Carrington estate?" I ask.

Calla's eyes cut to mine, a clear warning in them. And there's something about the furrow in her brow that seems like concern. For me or for the estate, I'm not sure. After a moment, she says, "There are cameras on all the estates."

But she doesn't answer the question.

"We'll drop it off to him on the way," she continues, indicating the message, as if the previous conversation never happened. "Don't mind Rome. He's locked in there all day. It's bound to make a person antisocial. *Anyway.* What do you want to see next? We have a gym, and a weapons room, and an indoor training room. There are some lounges on the upper floors with *killer* views, and a library—"

"How long has this place been here?"

"A few decades, at least. I'm not sure. It's just one of many too. This one's a little more out of the way, and it's mostly used to house human refugees from the nearby regions. More important personnel are usually at the other ones. Dad says this one is his favorite, though, so he comes back here when he can."

My mind trips over her words, struggling to decide what to focus on first. *Human refugees? One of many? Important personnel?* She makes this sound like a military operation. I'd known James Westcott had a following, but I had no idea the extent. If there are hundreds of people in this one alone, how many people does he have on standby? And for what?

"I've kind of turned into his personal assistant over the years. Which sounds totally boring, but I like it. Well," she snorts, "except when they treat me like a carrier pigeon. Val?" She steps in front of me, stopping me in my tracks. "You good?" Her eyes sweep my face, and her expression softens. "I'm sorry. I know I keep throwing a lot of information at you at once. How are you holding up?"

How am I holding up? My mind is spinning a mile a minute, and it's so exhausting trying to untangle it all that I feel like I could sleep for the next week straight and it still wouldn't be enough. "Processing," I say.

She nods slowly, then hooks her elbow through mine. "You know what? I know exactly what room you should see first."

CHAPTER FIVE

THE ELEVATOR TAKES us to the ninth floor, this time with far more people crammed inside. I take deep breaths through my nose, trying not to feel claustrophobic as strangers' shoulders nudge me on both sides. Most of the others get off before we reach our floor, a few trickling out at a time.

Once it's just me and Calla left, she flashes an apologetic smile. "As well designed as the rest of this place is, you'd think they'd have more than a handful of elevators."

The ninth floor looks identical to the tenth in décor, though the layout is entirely different. I'm expecting the doors to slide open to another hall full of doors, but we step out into wide-open space, the entire floor a single room.

The far walls are curved and made up of floor-to-ceiling windows, looking out at the surrounding snowy mountain peaks. Plush carpet sinks under my feet as I follow Calla inside. Leather couches and chairs sit across from each other with a massive black piano in the corner.

There's also a raised platform with a bar in the back and a handful of tall tables and stools.

"We call this the piano room," Calla explains. "It's usually a lot livelier later in the night or early morning. On weekends the kitchen caters so you can get food up here with your drinks. And if I'm correct, I could've sworn we had a…" She heads for the corner with the piano and ducks behind the bench. A moment later, she reappears with a triumphant smile and a familiar-looking case in hand.

My stomach bottoms out at the sight of it.

"I know it's not yours, and I don't know—I feel like musicians are weird about that kind of thing," Calla continues, oblivious to the growing nausea in my stomach as she sets the case on a nearby couch, pops it open, and pulls out the violin. "But you're welcome to use it!" She grins up at me, but I can't bring myself to fake a smile back. "Or not," she says quickly, putting the instrument back in its case. "Bad idea? Do you still…? I just thought…"

"Thanks, Calla. I appreciate the gesture," I mumble, my voice coming out flat and monotone. Suddenly, stupidly, I feel like I'm about to cry, and I don't even know why.

"Val, I—" She reaches out like she wants to touch me even though several feet of space are between us. "You know what? Why don't we take a beat? The tour can wait. We have so much to catch up on from the past few years. I want to know everything!"

"No offense, Calla, but I don't really feel like talking to you about a life you've all made it very clear I'm never going to get back."

Her face falls as the elevator dings behind me.

"What's this I hear about an emergency? Why didn't you come find me right away?"

His voice sends ice down my spine, and I whip around as James Westcott steps into the room.

"I'm sorry!" Calla rushes forward, pulling the slip of paper out. "I was about to come find you, I swear. I just wanted to show Valerie…"

He snatches the paper out of her hand and opens it. Either whatever he reads isn't as much of an *emergency* as Rome had made it out to be, or he has a very good poker face because his entire body seems to relax as he folds the paper and stuffs it in his pocket. He almost looks bored.

"Calliope, why don't you head downstairs and help the others prepare. We have a new batch coming in tonight."

A new batch?

"Oh." She straightens, her eyebrows arching in surprise. "Sure." She starts to step toward me, but he holds up a hand. "I'll send Valerie down later. I'd like to have a word with her first."

A hint of uncertainty creeps into Calla's face, but she nods and slips from the room wordlessly. Westcott doesn't say anything until the elevator's doors slide shut behind her and the glowing numbers overhead tick down.

He ambles toward the windows and sinks into a chair. "Why don't you have a seat, Valerie?"

"I'm fine standing."

There's no warmth or amusement on his face. "Have a seat."

I hate that I obey, but my feet move forward almost of their own accord. I take the seat facing him, then cross my arms over my chest. "Another chat so soon?"

A thin, humorless smile rises on his lips. "I wanted to give you some time to process. Adjust. Have a look around. Spend some time with your sister. But you and I still have several things to discuss." The harsh lines on his face ease a little. "I want you to be comfortable here. And I want to give you all the information. You might be surprised to find that afterward, this is actually where you want to be."

"There's nothing you could say that would make that happen."

"I'm sure you ran into some of the other residents while Calliope was showing you around," he says. "You saw how many people live here. There are just as many, if not more, at our other facilities. Do you truly believe every single one of the people who believe in our cause is also wrong? Also evil?"

I cross my legs. "Look, I'm not interested in doing this back and forth with you. Whatever it is you want to tell me, can we get on with it? You've given me no reason to believe that anything you say is the truth anyway. For all I know, everyone here is brainwashed or here against their will, just like me."

He leans forward, propping his elbows on his thighs, and nods slowly. "I can understand why you feel that way. And I'd be happy to submit to a truth spell if that would make you more willing to listen. I'm not trying to trick you, Valerie."

I hesitate, my arms tightening across my chest. When I don't respond, he flips a blade out of the large ring on his middle finger, and I start as I realize how similar it is to mine. Without a word, he slices the palm of his hand, then squeezes it into a fist and lets his blood fall to the floor.

"I swear to speak only the truth for the rest of this conversation. No deception. No lies. No half-truths." His blood sizzles as it hits the carpet, then evaporates like smoke. I frown as he rests his hands in his lap. "You're wondering why I used blood if I'm not a blood witch."

I give a single nod.

"I've gained powers over the decades, from other witches, that have allowed mine to evolve. It's not the same as being a natural-born, but it does allow me to have similar abilities."

"Gained them how?"

He doesn't blink. "The witch from whom I absorbed the power either died or became human in order to complete the transfer."

I swallow hard, my hands tightening to fists. I'd read about spells where you could *willingly* transfer your powers to another witch. But to *take* them? Just how powerful is he now then? I guess that explains the skinwalking human forms too. The thought makes my stomach churn. How many other unheard of things can he do?

"So you've been going around murdering other witches for their powers?" I bite out. "And *that's* how you're starting off this conversation to get me to *trust you?*"

"I told you I would not lie to you, Valerie. And I'll admit, I've done things in my past that I look back on with regret."

I'd grown up believing my father was a skinwalker, but everything Reid and I found in our search for information on James Westcott described him as a vampire. I narrow my eyes.

"Did you even have any magic of your own to begin with?"

A smirk pulls at the corner of his mouth. "Unfortunately not. But we can't all come from such distinguished bloodlines."

I bristle at the tone of his voice. As if we're not related. As if my blood, at least in part, isn't *his*. But I can't quite read the look on his face. He can't possibly be…envious.

"Would it make a difference if I told you the last time was over twenty years ago?"

"Why? Because you already had all the powers you needed?"

A muscle in his jaw flexes, and he doesn't answer right away. "I only ever stole from witches who deserved to die," he says finally.

"And who are you to make that call?"

He spreads his hands out in front of him. "You seem to be fine with your queen making those kinds of calls. Is that any different? I doubt her sentencings have gotten any more humane in my absence." He leans forward, a half smile on his face now. "Has she run out of room in that crown of hers yet?"

"Of course I'm not fine with it," I mumble.

"And yet, you were a loyal servant of the estate, were you not? You might not have worn the same uniforms as the humans, but make no mistake, you were no more important. Can't you see that it's a tyranny? They make these grand claims of safety and protection to keep you all in their grasps, but protection from who? From them?"

"And so your plan is to…what? Kill them all? Or better yet, use people like *me* to kill them all?" I grind my molars so hard pain flares up my jaw, and I curse my voice for shaking.

He lets out a breath through his nose. "You think I wanted it to come to this? You think I didn't try to negotiate with them first? That I didn't try to get them to see reason? But they're not interested in reform. Why would they be, when they have all the power?"

"I don't believe you. I've never heard anything about these negotiations."

He lets out a single laugh. "Of course you haven't. This was years ago—decades, the first time I brought it up. Right around the time dear old Queen Carrington decided to execute me instead. I took that as a no. They weren't willing to listen, so we're simply evening the playing field and weakening them until they do."

"Who is this *we*?"

"You'll find our side to be much more diverse. Wolves, humans, witches, halflings—anyone who has been victimized by the vampires' rule. They may have the advantage with their current standing, numbers, and glamouring abilities, but can't you see, Valerie? We have something much stronger. We have a common enemy and a desire for change that's enough to bring all these different people together. All we want is a voice. A government that looks after the interests of all species—not one that allows one to dominate the rest. You may not agree with my methods, but can you honestly tell me you think everything should stay the same?"

"You know what? No." I rise to my feet. "It's easy for you to sit here in your pretty little castle in the mountains and preach about how things need to change. But that's not what you're doing. You're taking innocent people and forcing them to do your dirty work while you sit back and watch and claim all the glory. I don't think this is about helping people at all. Sure, maybe that's what you've been spouting to get all these people to follow you, but I'm not buying a single piece of this bullshit. What about all the innocents in the estates you've been attacking? The children? The human servants? The families? Your own *daughter*? Do you have any idea—" I break off, my chin wobbling as the memories pour in.

No. I won't let him see me cry. I won't let him see the extent of the damage he's caused.

"Valerie—" He stands, and I retreat, putting more and more distance between us.

"If you truly wanted me on your side, if you truly wanted me to believe you actually gave a shit about anyone but yourself, you never would have done that to me. You could've taken me like you did with Calla. So why? What was the point?" My voice cracks on the last word, and I turn my back to him.

His arms close around me a moment later, and I thrash, trying to break loose, but he tightens his hold.

"Get off of me!" I seethe.

"Listen to me," he says, his voice low and rough. "It was a risk coming back to get your sister, and it was a risk coming to get you. I could've exposed myself. I could've lost everything we've worked for. You were in deeper than Calliope had ever been. I knew it would be harder to convince you to leave. I had to find a way where you couldn't say no, otherwise that risk would've been for nothing. I was doing it to save your life, Valerie. I thought it

53

better to ask for forgiveness than to risk leaving you behind."

"And Adrienne?" I demand, my voice breaking around her name. "You left her behind."

"For now. It's only temporary."

"I don't believe you. I don't believe a single word you say. Now *let me go*."

To my surprise, he does. I stumble away from him, breathing hard. He doesn't move. He just stands there, watching me, every line of his face hard.

"You may not think of me as your father, Valerie, but I am. And it's my job as your parent to protect you. And that's what I've done. If you need to hate me for that, then at least you're alive to do so."

I shake my head. I can't even look at him.

"It's nearly mealtime," he says. "I'll take you down—"

"I can find it on my own," I snap.

A beat of silence passes between us before he finally nods and heads for the elevators. He hesitates before stepping inside and glances at me over his shoulder.

"I'm a patient man, Valerie. Understanding. And if you need to act out as you adjust here, I can take that. But understand this. These are my people here. My responsibility. You may be my blood, but if you become a threat to our cause, you won't be treated any differently than anyone else. So take your time deciding which side you're on. But I hope you choose right when you do."

CHAPTER SIX

THE MESS HALL isn't hard to find. I just follow the noise. Voices layer on top of each other as I draw closer. The lobby is surprisingly empty as I step out of the elevator. I head in the opposite direction Calla and I had gone earlier to get to the training yard, my stomach still churning from that conversation with Westcott. I don't know why I'm bothering to go. There's no way I'll be able to muster an appetite.

The glass double doors are propped open, revealing a room noticeably different from the rest of the building. Warm-toned wood spans the floor and ceiling, with long tables stretched down the middle and smaller round tables scattered throughout. The majority of seats are already taken as I venture toward the line that wraps around the perimeter of the room.

Again with that confusing mix of scents—wolves, witches, and whatever *else* is in here. I'm sure the tang of fried food and grease hanging over the room isn't helping.

But there's blood somewhere too—the scent too sharp and strong to be *inside* someone's body.

The line moves forward quickly, and I blink, momentarily disoriented. For just a second, I could believe I was at school grabbing lunch with Monroe and Kirby. I half expect to see the backs of their heads among the tables, an empty seat beside them waiting for me.

My stomach sinks as it occurs to me I might never get to do that again. I might never see them again at all.

"Next!"

I glance up at the woman in a hairnet behind the counter and slip a tray off the stack, my gaze drifting over the different options. The harsh lines of her face soften as she watches me.

"You're new," she says. "Here." She quickly loads a plate with mashed potatoes, green beans, and a slab of ham. "There's a drink station over there." She nods to the right.

I hesitate, my fingers tightening around the tray. "Um, is there…?"

"Blood?" she offers. "Yeah. There's some over there too. Enjoy, honey. Next!"

Bodies bustle back and forth as I head in the direction she pointed, voices and laughter carrying through the room. A soda machine sits in the center of the table, along with a huge water pitcher, and a second glass case full of a thick, red substance. I grab one of the cups and position it under the tap, wincing as it splatters into the glass. It feels warm to the touch though, so at least I won't have to drink it cold.

56

I'm debating taking the tray and retreating to my room when I hear someone call my name.

I glance around, frowning, as a dark-haired guy at a nearby table rises to his feet. He grins when I meet his eyes, then waves for me to join him.

Not seeing Calla anywhere and not knowing what else to do, I head toward him. The rest of the seats are filled with near-replicas of the first man, all broad-shouldered and sweaty. They must be the wolves from outside.

"Boys, this is Valerie Darkmore," says the first one as I set my tray down.

I glance at him sideways, trying to remember his name.

"Leif," he supplies, then points out the rest of them. "That's Coleman, Saint, and Jones."

They each wave as he says their names, and I slowly sink into the chair. If only my friends could see me now, sitting at a table surrounded by werewolves.

"No pressure or anything," says the blond with dimples across from me. Saint, Leif said his name was. "But we've all heard about your reputation, even all the way out here."

"Badass," says the ginger beside him—Jones—as he nods.

"You should come hang out with us tonight," says Leif beside me.

I quirk an eyebrow. "And what reputation would that be?"

"That you have no soul," Leif says cheerfully.

"Heard you could end a man just by looking at him," adds the larger guy on his left—Coleman.

"Now that you're also half-vamp, I wouldn't mind

seeing you in action," chimes in Jones as he takes a bite of meat.

Now that you're also half-vamp. How does everyone know everything around here?

"Not sure your *leader* would take me killing off his disciples too well," I mutter, fidgeting with my hands beneath the table, but that just draws my attention to the bare place my ring should be.

Leif snorts.

I eye the knife beside my plate. It's a butter knife, barely even sharp, and large and clunky, but maybe...

"He certainly walks around like a drill sergeant," mutters Coleman.

My eyebrows slowly inch up my face as I stuff the knife under my sleeve for later—just in case. The wolves seem too preoccupied to notice.

"Don't tell him I said that," Coleman adds.

"Dude, she's his daughter," Jones mumbles.

"You guys aren't fans of his?" I ask. They exchange a wary glance. Before they can respond I add, "Good. Me neither."

Leif watches me for a moment, considering me. I stare back, unblinking, and he gives me a slow smile. "I knew there was a reason I liked you."

EVEN ONCE THE mess hall starts to clear out, I still can't find Calla. Not wanting to spend the rest of the night holed up in my room, I decide to explore the rest of the building on my own. The wolves disappear somewhere outside, and things are noticeably quieter than they had been earlier—fewer people in the lobby and the halls. Where they all went, I have no idea.

Sutton watches me from behind the desk in the lobby with narrowed eyes as I venture to the windows and peer outside. Calla had mentioned other surrounding structures, but I have no idea where they are. I couldn't see any when we were out in the training yard, and all I can see from here is an endless expanse of snow and more mountains and trees.

"Can I help you find something?" Sutton calls behind me.

I turn away from the windows, my eyes burning from the brightness of the sun glinting off the snow, and it takes them a few moments to readjust to the room. "Where is everyone?" I ask, pacing over to her desk.

She lifts an unimpressed eyebrow. "Their jobs."

I ignore the judgmental tone as I prop my arms on the counter. "So everyone here works?"

She nods. "Everyone does their part."

"What kinds of jobs?"

She lets out a slow breath as if this conversation is exhausting. "Well, there are the maintenance jobs to keep everything running smoothly around here, the cleaning crew, the kitchen teams, the gardeners, the trainers, the engineers, the data analysts, the tutors, the advisors, the security team, the—"

"Okay, I think I got it."

She gives me a humorless smile then looks at her computer, her long nails tapping away on the keyboard, a clear dismissal. Aren't concierges supposed to be, I don't know, friendly?

Not knowing what else to do, I head off to explore. If every other person staying here has a job, odds are I'm going to have to chip in eventually too. Maybe that's where Calla disappeared off to, though I don't know why she wouldn't at least come find me and give me a heads-up first. Or maybe it's self-centered to think that because I've shown up, things should change for her. She's been here for two years without me. She has an entirely new life, new friends, new routines. She probably doesn't have time to hold my hand while I adjust.

The thought makes me recoil. *Adjust* implies I plan on staying.

I start by checking out all the exits and entrances, hoping it looks like I'm going for a casual stroll. Cameras wink at me from every corner in the ceiling, and based on the panels near each of the doors, they have a security system. Same goes for the windows—they all have latches with glowing red lights.

Getting away from this compound would be the least of my worries though. We're clearly in the middle of nowhere. Even on a good day, I don't think I'd be able to teleport myself far enough.

Sighing, I glance at the ugly black mark on my arm again. If I tried to leave, it would probably kill me anyway.

Calla was right. Most of the middle floors have nothing of interest. Well, I'm willing to bet none of these floors will have anything of interest to me. Nothing I have access to, at least.

That control room with the monitors…*that* I would like to see.

I'd only managed to peek at a few of the screens—how many other cameras do they have set up? And where? Is it just the estates, or elsewhere? How long have they been watching them? A shiver runs down my spine at the thought of how many times *I* may have unknowingly been on those monitors.

Which brings me back to thoughts of the estate and the academy. Of everyone I've left behind. My chest aches, and suddenly it's hard to breathe. My feet wind their way to my room, and I lock the door behind me. Whatever had been blacking out the windows before seems to have been removed, the room now full of light. I guess they decided I could be trusted enough to see outside.

I yank my hair back to tie in a ponytail and pause. I'd almost forgotten about the knife in my sleeve. Sliding it out from under the hair tie, I spin it in my hands, considering. I can't keep lugging this gigantic thing around, but for some reason, having a blade on me of some sort, no matter how pathetic, brings me a sense of calm.

I kneel before the fireplace in the corner and get to work. I prick my finger with the knife to get the fire going, not wanting to use too much magic in my weakened state if I don't have to. If I could just melt off the handle and sharpen it…

Sweat beads on my forehead from the heat of the fire, and I close my eyes, dizzy. It brings me back to the days before initiation, the sickness, the weakness. Even once I'd kicked that, I'd traded it for the hunger, and now I'm back to this.

I shake my head at myself. In that cell, I'd thought this was my best option. Making the deal meant coming here, but it also meant finally being free of the hunger. Its absence hasn't brought as much relief as I'd hoped. There might not be bars on the windows or guards at my door, but this feels like more of a prison than that cell ever had.

My eyes fill with tears as I situate the knife in the fire. I may have held on to my humanity, but all I want is to go home.

IT's dark when I wake, the sun having finally set. At some point, I moved to the bed, the covers tucked up around my chin and Reid's jacket clutched in my arms in a ball.

"Come on, Valerie! Open the door!" someone calls and knocks loudly.

I sit up, rubbing my eyes. That must've been what woke me up. The knocking continues, and I groan, roll myself out of bed, and shuffle to the door. When I open it, Leif is standing on the other side, fist still raised. He grins and drops his hand when he sees me, then his eyes flicker to the bed.

"Were you *sleeping*? It's only midnight!"

"Do you need something?" The hallway behind him is empty, so apparently he came up here on his own. When I'd heard the knocking, I'd expected Calla. How had he even known which room was mine?

"Yeah, I need you to put your jacket and shoes on and hurry up. The sun will be up by four, so we don't have a lot of time."

"Time for what?"

Sighing, Leif shoulders his way into the room and searches the ground.

"What are you doing?" I demand.

"Sit down," he says, voice casual, as if this is an everyday thing between us, as he finds my shoes and scoops them up. "Calla said you'd probably be moping," he continues, and when he notices I still haven't moved from the door, he simply kneels in front of me and takes a foot into his hand.

"Leif—" I grab the wall for balance before I topple over as he tightens the laces and goes for my other foot, but I yank it away before he can get it. "I'm perfectly capable of putting on my own shoes."

"Could've fooled me," he says, voice still perfectly cheery.

I rip the sneaker out of his hand and tug it on. "And I'm not moping," I mumble.

"Seem pretty mopey to me."

"Where is Calla?" I ask, glancing into the hall.

"She will be joining us shortly," he says, words crisp and formal like a waiter at a restaurant. He slips Reid's jacket off the bed next and holds it out to me. I quickly snatch it away, for some reason not wanting him to touch it. He raises his eyebrows but says nothing.

"The others are already waiting for us downstairs. I'm just here to escort you."

"The others? Escort me where?"

He sighs and shoos me out the door. "I *told* you at lunch you were hanging out with us tonight. I doubt dear old

James gave you a good welcome, so we've taken it upon ourselves."

I narrow my eyes. "Why? Why do you care? You don't even know me."

He shrugs as we head down the hall, his long legs eating up the distance much faster than mine. "I like you, Dark-more. Plus, you kind of looked like a sad puppy today. What can I say? I'm a sucker for the strays." He nudges me with his elbow as we wait for the elevator. "Get it? Wolf joke."

I cross my arms over my chest.

"I'll grow on you," he adds, still grinning. In fact, I don't think I've yet to see him stop smiling. It's like his face isn't capable of making any other expression.

I say nothing as we climb into the elevator and he jabs the button. I stare straight ahead at the mirror on the back of the door. Leif stands a respectful distance away, his hands together in front of his body, and a small smile on his face. His reflection towers over me by more than a foot, but he somehow manages to make his presence nonthreatening. Even with the broad shoulders and sharp lines of his face, everything about him seems…friendly.

He glances at me sideways, and the amusement in his expression flickers, but the doors slide open before he can say anything.

I follow him through the lobby, squeezing past the crowd that's accumulated. Most seem to be heading in the direction of the mess hall, so it must be getting close to another meal time. At first I think Leif is leading me back to the training yard, but once we step outside, he turns in the opposite direction. Now that the sun's gone down, everything looks completely different. Countless stars shine overhead, piercingly bright, blanketing the entire sky. Insects buzz in the air as Leif pivots and leads us to a hill on the opposite side of the building.

"Where are we going?" I ask, glancing at the fading lights of the compound over my shoulder. Despite the glow of the moon and stars overhead, it's *dark* out here. With my half-vampire side, it's not that bad, and judging by the way Leif navigates through the trees with ease, his eyesight must be heightened too.

The snow slides beneath my shoes as I climb after him, soaking in the sides and wetting my socks. I cringe. Though the cold doesn't bother me as much anymore, it's still not comfortable. I pull Reid's jacket tighter around myself and tug the zipper all the way up to my chin. A hint of his scent hits me as I do, and it's almost enough to stop me in my tracks. The ache in my stomach where our bond used to be pulses.

"We're almost there!" Leif calls without looking back.

The wind whistles through the trees, picking up the snow beneath our feet and scattering it across the ground. The lights of the compound grow dimmer and dimmer behind us as we head deeper into the trees, and it occurs to me I'm heading into the middle of the woods with a were-wolf I barely know in the middle of the night. He could be bringing me out here to murder me for all I know.

At least it's not a full moon.

I smell them before I hear them. The musky scent rises to the forefront of my senses over the woodsy pine of the forest—at least three of them, I'd guess.

I see the fire next. It's small, just a few logs propped

together, the smoke curling toward the starry sky. Laughter ebbs through the trees as we draw closer, and a deep voice lets out a whoop as the figures around the fire turn and watch us approach.

"What took you so long!" calls one of the men, tossing a can to Leif as we step out of the trees.

Leif catches it in one hand and cracks it open. The beer fizzes over the side, and he grins as he brings it to his mouth.

The fire is set up in a small break in the trees, and I realize we're right beside the edge of a cliff. I can't tell how steep the drop is from here, but the view looks out at the surrounding mountains, and the compound glows at the bottom, farther down than I'd expected. How long had we been climbing?

My stomach sinks. Even with my heightened eyesight, there's no other trace of lights or life anywhere. No buildings, no cars. Nothing for I don't even know how many miles.

"For you, my lady." Saint holds a beer out to me. I hadn't realized I'd drifted to the edge of the cliff. The rest of the wolves are still by the fire, talking among themselves.

I take the beer and nod, but Saint doesn't return to the others. He steps beside me and follows my gaze to the horizon. "Your sister should be coming up here any minute now too."

I crack open the beer without responding.

Saint lets out a chuckle and holds up his beer. "Enjoy the view." With that, he heads over to the others.

The wind picks up, scattering my hair around my face. My mind flashes back to another night, somehow simultaneously similar and yet not the same at all. Another fire, another forest. Another life, almost. The night I'd found out about the poison in my blood.

The night before everything in my life spiraled out of control.

The fire crackles behind me, and I take another sip of my beer, barely tasting it as it goes down. What I could really go for is a cigarette. My fingers ache with the need for it.

"There she is!"

"Hello, hello!" Calla's voice breaks through my trance, and I turn as she hurries up the hill, the pompom on her hat bouncing as she goes. "Where's—oh!" Ignoring the beer Jones offers her, she rushes to me and throws her arms around my shoulders without warning. "*So* sorry, Val. I got pulled into something. But I trust the boys have been keeping you company." She shoots a look at them over her shoulder. "And keeping their hands to themselves."

"We've been perfect gentlemen," Leif assures her.

"Uh-huh." Calla hooks her arm through mine and drags me toward the others. "Did you bring everything?" she asks.

Coleman snorts. "You think we're amateurs? Of course we came prepared."

"You'll like it," Calla assures me as she goes for the cooler on the other side of the fire and digs out a beer. "It's fun. I invited some of the other girls too," she adds. "I don't know if they're coming though."

"Here." Leif pulls some keys out of his back pocket, takes the beer from Calla, and stabs a hole in the bottom.

Without missing a beat, she tilts her head, opens the other end, and shotguns the entire thing.

The boys cheer as she drops the can and grabs a second from the cooler.

"Come on, Val!" She grins. "I seem to remember you were always faster than me."

I stare at her, the fire casting shadows over her face. I'd gone to a few parties with her my freshman year at the academy, but honestly, going out with her was exhausting. It seems two years in this place hasn't dampened her enthusiasm in the slightest.

"I'm good," I say.

"Do you guys have everything set up yet?" she asks.

"Been here two minutes and already barking orders." Coleman shakes his head, but he's grinning. "You better finish more of those for us," he says as he and Saint hoist two wooden posts off the ground and carry them toward the cliff. Leif starts handing out more beers as the two of them sink them into the ground.

"Do one with us, Val," Calla says, hooking her arm through mine and pulling me against her side. Leif and Jones are already stabbing holes in their cans, and they exchange a quick sideways glance before popping the cans open and guzzling them down.

The pile of empty cans between us grows quickly, and I sigh as Calla pushes a new one into my hand. She meets my eyes for a moment, a question in hers. And despite the heavy feeling clinging to my skin, the memories and flashbacks that keep surfacing in my mind, the thoughts of everyone who isn't here, I force a smile.

I've spent the last two years of my life wishing I could

get my sister back, and she's standing right here. She's trying.

"Fine."

She grins as I hold up the can. I have the knife I'd made in my pocket, but I'm not sure if I want anyone else to know about that yet. Jones whips out a pocketknife and digs a hole into the bottom for me. "But just the one."

I bring the can to my mouth, open my throat, crack it open, and quickly swallow the beer. Leif lets out a low whistle as I drop the can at my feet, and Calla beams and does a little jump.

"That's gotta be some kind of record," mutters Jones. "She's putting us all to shame."

"What do you need all the empty cans for anyway?" I ask.

"We're ready for you!" calls Saint.

"Me and Valerie first!" Calla grabs two cans from the pile and hurries to the posts sticking out of the ground.

Once the cans are balanced on them, Leif nudges me, holding out a bow.

"I'll show her first," Calla offers, taking the bow from Leif and scooping an arrow from a pile on the other side of the fire. There's something blunt on the end instead of the usual arrowhead. In one swift movement, Calla nocks the arrow, dips the tip into the fire until it lights, and lets it fly toward the posts. It strikes one of the cans, sending a high-pitched metal clink into the air, and the light of the fire flickers out as it disappears over the edge of the cliff.

"This is what you guys do for fun around here?" I mutter.

"Oh come on, Val." Calla hands the bow to me. "You can't tell me you don't want to try it."

I bend and grab an arrow, smirking. "You're littering," I add.

"We clean them up afterward," says Calla. "Now stop stalling. Unless you think you can't—"

Bringing the arrow up, I copy Calla's movements to light the end, close one eye, and let out a slow breath, releasing the string on the exhale. The arrow strikes the second can and follows Calla's over the edge.

"If you miss, you have to shotgun another beer," Calla explains as I hand off the bow to Leif. Saint runs up to replace the cans on the posts as Calla and I drift to the back of the group, her arm linked through mine. I almost forgot how much she used to do this, like she always had to be touching someone else.

"They're obnoxious," she murmurs. "But they can be fun to hang out with."

"We heard that!" Jones calls.

"Good!" she yells, then turns to me. "Are you at least having a *little* fun?"

I smirk and bump my shoulder against hers. "Mountain life has turned you into a hick."

"I resent that! I feel I've always been a hick at heart."

I snort, and she huddles closer against my arm. "It really is good to have you here, Val. I know it's more complicated than that, but I missed you so much."

My throat tightens as I stare at the fire, and the sound of arrows striking metal fills the air. "I missed you too," I whisper.

CHAPTER SEVEN

AT SOME POINT, Coleman and Saint disappear to get more
wood as Leif and Jones situate some logs around the fire to
sit on. Calla and I huddle together on one. Though I doubt
either of us needs the body heat to keep warm, it's nice
being close to her. I'd almost forgotten the smell of her hair
—like honey—but now as she leans her head on my shoulder, I remember all the times I'd crawled into bed with her
at night growing up. How we'd curled around each other,
the smell of her hair filling my head as I fell asleep.

"We're running low on drinks," Saint announces as he
feeds more branches into the fire. "I think we had some
more in the room."

"You left them in the room?" Coleman groans. "I'm not
going all the way back."

"Not it!" calls Calla.

"Oh come *on*." Jones rolls his eyes. "It'll take one of us
like an hour—you could just pop down there."

Calla doesn't blink. "I might make it look easy, but I promise it's not that simple."

What she's not saying is she's had way too much to drink to pull off a teleportation spell right now. And with how complicated they can be...it's not the kind of thing you want to risk going wrong.

"I got the wood. I did my part," adds Coleman.

"Don't get your panties in a twist," Leif grunts as he pushes to his feet. "I'll get them."

"You can't carry them all yourself," Calla points out.

"I'll go with you," I offer. I probably couldn't swing a spell right now either, but I'm pretty much the only one around here who hasn't contributed anything so far.

Leif's eyebrows shoot up as he looks at me. "Really?"

I shrug and untangle myself from Calla. "Sure."

"Hm." Leif gives the others a pointed look as he throws his arm over my shoulder. "She's been here all of five minutes, and she's already a better friend than the rest of you. Take notes, boys."

"Bring food too!" calls Jones as Coleman chucks a snowball Leif's way. He twists us to the side so it doesn't hit me, then flashes Coleman his middle finger.

"You guys bicker like siblings," I mutter as we trudge through the trees.

He snorts. "May as well be. We've all been in the same pack forever."

"Really? How does that work? I'm not that familiar with...uh...werewolf politics."

Leif snorts. "It's not common practice. Cam's just a sucker for strays like me. He takes in wolves with nowhere else to go. Orphans. Kids with parents who *aren't* wolves who kick them out when they turn. That kind of thing. Coleman and Saint have been with him since before they turned for the first time. Cam found me when I was thirteen. And we added Jones to the mix a few years later."

Cam. Why does that name sound familiar? "That's your pack master?"

Leif nods.

"I didn't realize nonwolves could *have* wolf kids," I admit.

"Oh, yeah. Weird how it works. The gene can skip generations, sometimes for so many years that the line isn't aware it runs in the family."

I glance at him sideways, but there's nothing heavy about his expression. He seems as light and carefree as before. But for him to end up in the pack at thirteen, something must've happened.

"You can ask," he says without looking at me. "I don't mind."

"What happened?"

He grabs my arm to help me over a patch of ice as the hill slopes downward, the lights from the compound swimming into view below. "Parents died—both were wolves—executed, actually." He glances at me sideways, then quickly away. "Queen Carrington's orders."

A small jolt goes through my chest. "I'm sorry," I whisper.

He shrugs. "It was over ten years ago. And my life hasn't been bad after that. Cam's a real hard-ass, but he looks after us. Took over the pack from his dad. His dad was still in charge of things when Coleman and Saint joined. I think he was only, like, sixteen when he took over. I can't imagine that kind of responsibility right now, let alone at sixteen. He should be getting back here soon, actually, so you'll probably get to meet him. Don't take it personally if he's a dick."

I frown, trying to do the math in my head. That would make Cam close to Reid's age then. Twenty-six, maybe twenty-seven.

I shove down the pit that immediately opens in my stomach at the thought of Reid.

"So you guys don't live here?" I ask.

"Not usually. We stop by from time to time, help out if we're needed. Cam's got some agreement with Westcott. I don't really know the specifics. But it's nice here. Warm place to sleep. Food. Can't complain. So you grew up at the Carrington estate?"

I nod and glance at him sideways again, but there's no bitterness in his voice as he says it. Despite it likely being the place both of his parents were executed, there's not a hint of tension on his face.

He shakes his head. "That whole system you guys have got is so strange to me."

I frown. "How so?"

"I mean"—he grabs my hand and helps me over another patch of ice—"you grew up there. Then you go to that academy when you're eighteen, right?"

I nod.

"That's like a whole other world though. On the inside. So you never really get to see what the world is like outside of the bubble, so how are you even supposed to know that's where you want to be if you don't know any alternatives?" He gives me a rueful smile. "That's probably the point, huh? They don't want you to think you have options."

My skin burns at his words. At how *right* he is.

His smile softens. "For the record, I'm not, like, judging you or anything. I can't imagine growing up in that kind of environment. Plus—" He breaks off, wincing.

"What?"

"I don't know. Your mom—she's got quite the reputation too."

I snort. "Trust me, there's nothing you could say about my mother that would offend me."

And yet, the mention of her has my muscles tensing like they're preparing to be struck.

"So that much is true, huh?"

I picture her standing outside my cell, the coldness in her eyes despite my tears and pleas. She left me there to die. "Probably worse than whatever you've heard."

"You know," he says, the tone of his voice shifting to something light. "Calla's been talking about you nonstop for the past two years. *Valerie this. Valerie that. This one time, Valerie did this...*" He trails off, smirking. "She's your biggest fan. It's cute."

I ignore the lump rising to the back of my throat. There was a time when we were inseparable, when *I* looked up to *her* like that. But after the past two years of being on my own, that version doesn't feel like me anymore. I clear my throat. "Have I lived up to the stories then?"

"Nah." He glances at me sideways. "You seem much cooler."

By the time we reach the bottom of the hill, my shoes are completely soaked through with snow.

"Aw, shit," Leif mutters as we step into the lobby.

"What's wrong?"

"I think we missed dinner."

"There's still a few minutes before the doors close!" Sutton calls from the front desk.

Leif gives her a tight-lipped smile as we slip past her and into the hallway that leads to the mess hall. Once we're out of earshot, he leans over and murmurs, "I take it you've met Chicken Little."

"Yeah, I don't think she likes me."

"Trust me, she doesn't like anyone."

The mess hall is more packed than it had been during lunch, though by now most people are already seated, with only a few left waiting in line.

Leif piles his tray high with every option they have tonight—biscuits, gravy, broccoli, and a brownie—then heads over for the drink station. After getting my own plate, I grab a glass of blood and follow him to the only table open in the corner.

"Didn't the others ask us to bring food for them?" I say as I set the tray down.

"Pfft. I'm not fetching them food *and* drinks. Do I look like a waiter?" I hesitate before sitting, and he rolls his eyes. "We'll wrap up some brownies before we head back. Happy?"

"You really just volunteered to get the drinks so you could make it back in time for dinner, didn't you?"

He taps his nose, then points at me and winks. "Those guys have no concept of time," he mumbles as he shoves a huge forkful into his mouth. "They're always making me miss mealtimes."

76

I smirk as he shovels more food into his mouth, abandoning the fork and grabbing the biscuit to smear around the gravy on his plate instead. With how much he acts like a golden retriever, I've been having a hard time picturing him as a wolf...until now.

I eat as much as my nonexistent appetite will let me before pushing my plate away. Leif's eyes flicker from it to me.

"Have at it," I say.

He pulls it over and dumps the leftovers on his plate.

Now that we're sitting still, it sinks in how *soaked* I am. My socks cling to my feet, and my pants up to my knees feel damp.

"I think I'm going to head upstairs..."

Leif's eyes snap back to my face. "What? No! We're not done for the night."

"I'm currently walking around with mini puddles inside of my shoes."

"Okay, fine. You can head upstairs to change. But you can't call it a night already." I purse my lips, but he keeps going before I have the chance to protest. "Don't tell the guys, but we can even break out the good stuff before heading back. Deal?"

"And the good stuff entails...?"

He finishes the rest of his plate, stacks our dishes together, and stands. "Guess you'll have to come with me to grab it to see."

ONCE LEIF SNEAKS back into line and wraps a few brownies in napkins, he shoves them in the pockets of his jacket and we head out. He'd told the others he needed to go to *the room*. I'd been expecting the wolves to have rooms on the lower floors, but Leif veers like he's heading for the training yard, then keeps walking. A few others are lingering outside—some throwing around a football, some running laps around the perimeter—and they wave to Leif as we pass. The path circles the building, then disappears into the trees, but the promise of light pokes through in the distance. No wonder I hadn't been able to see the other structures before.

It takes another few minutes of walking before we reach a clearing in the forest, where a series of smaller huts sits in a semicircle. Most of them are dark, though the one in the middle's windows are glowing, and torches flicker along the paths connecting them. Leif heads for the one on the far right and stomps the snow off his shoes before shouldering the door open.

The small action makes me pause, and my fingers drift to the zipper of Reid's jacket. He always used his shoulders to push things open too.

Leif's eyes follow the movement of my hands before he calls, "Come on in," and disappears into a back room.

The inside is bigger than I'd expected. The door leads directly into a living room with a couch, a few chairs, and a TV. I can see the kitchen from here, and a few doors line the right wall—rooms, presumably.

Glasses clank together in the back, and I close the door behind me as the wind picks up so snow doesn't blow inside.

"So, you got a boyfriend back at the estate?" Leif calls.

I stiffen and wrap my arms around myself, my fingers tracing the soft fabric of Reid's jacket. It's cold and wet now from the snow.

Leif's head pops into the hall. "Don't worry. I'm not hitting on you. You're not my type."

I snort as he disappears back into the room. "Thanks."

He reappears with two bottles of a dark liquid in his hands and gives me a half smile. "Girls, I mean."

I blink. "Oh."

He sets the bottles on the coffee table and flips one of the caps off, then glances up at me through his lashes. "Is that a no?"

I shift my weight. "I…don't know."

His eyes flick to the jacket. "An *it's complicated* situation?"

I chew on my lip, my mind going to the last night I'd spent with Reid in the bunker. We'd never talked about what that was, exactly. Never had the chance. I guess I don't even know what I wanted it to be. All the time we'd spent together had been so tangled up in the problems around us. It's hard to imagine what could have happened if things hadn't been so complicated.

"You know what? I think I might have some boots here that'll fit you. Doubt LeeAnn would mind. Hold on." He slips through another door. "It's your partner, right?" he calls, then reappears with thick socks and brown hiking boots in his hands. "He's the complication?"

"Thanks." I take the boots and grab one of the chairs. "Yeah," I say as I pull off my shoes. "He's the complication."

Leif shakes his head, smiling. "It's always the broody ones."

I chuckle and replace my soaked socks with the new ones. Despite not being as bothered by the cold, my feet still feel like ice. I smile a little. Months ago, before I knew him, I would've described Reid the same way. But it's funny how wrong you can be about a person. "He's not that broody."

"Ah, shit."

I look up at him. "What?"

He grabs the bottle from the coffee table and takes a swig. "You're in love with him."

"I didn't say that."

He shakes his head and offers the bottle to me. "You didn't have to."

I yank the laces on the boots as tight as they'll go, shaking my head. They're about half a size too big, but I can make it work.

I don't argue with Leif. The fact of the matter is, I could've been in love with Reid. I know that. I could've gotten there easily. After Connor, I'd thought that wasn't possible. But it doesn't matter anyway, because we'd never had the time, and now we never will. And maybe that hurts more. To know I'd never truly had him. That he'll always be a maybe in my past. An almost. A could've been.

I take the bottle from Leif and swallow a mouthful, wincing as the whiskey burns on its way down and warms me from within.

"You ready to head out?" he asks.

I nod and follow him through the door.

He smirks at me sideways as I swallow another mouthful, the other bottle tucked under his arm. "Try not to drink the whole thing before we get there."

"If you didn't want me to drink it, you shouldn't have given it to me."

"Just looking out for you, Darkmore. You had two beers earlier. Weaker men would puke."

The snow crunches underfoot as we circle toward the training yard. I open my mouth to respond, but screams ahead cut me off. Leif's head whips up at the same time mine does as a large group rounds the corner.

No, not a group. Four men in matching black uniforms are ushering half a dozen people. The ones in front seem to be going willingly, but the one at the rear is clearly *not*. She shrieks and thrashes against the man's arms around her waist, but he hoists her up and drags her forward.

A coldness I haven't felt all night trickles through me as they near and the light falls on her face.

"Winnie," I whisper.

She doesn't notice us standing there as their group heads to the back door of the compound and disappears inside.

"You know her?" Leif asks.

"Yes," I say, my voice barely audible. "What are they doing? Where are they taking her?"

"The humans are going downstairs. But she wasn't, was she?"

"How could you tell?"

He taps his nose. "Can't you?"

I nod.

He chews on his bottom lip. "I doubt they're taking her downstairs then. So your guess is as good as mine."

"What does *downstairs* mean?"

He furrows his brow. "Calliope didn't tell you? She made quite the fuss about it when she first got here."

I shake my head. "We haven't really had all that much time to talk."

He sighs and scratches at the back of his neck. "No one around here really talks about it. No one I know, at least." He glances around, but we're alone. "But they bring in a new batch of humans every once and a while. Though they've been showing more frequently lately."

"Why are they here?" My shoulders tense, as if somehow I already know the answer.

"They're all volunteers, that's what Westcott said. But I —" Leif shakes his head. "I don't know. Maybe I'm wrong and they do know the full extent of what they're getting into. But even with promises of being able to reverse it once this is all over, I don't know how he can make that claim—"

"Leif, what the hell are you talking about?"

He finally looks at me, his expression the most serious I've seen from him. "The experiments. To create the wendigos."

Create the wendigos.

That first night at the academy fills my mind like smoke. The claws tearing through my chest, slicing skin and muscle. And everything that came after.

Everything that brought me here.

And they've been using humans to do it. Nausea twists in my stomach.

I look from Leif to the door they dragged Winnie through. He said they took volunteers. Winnie could not have looked more unwilling. They can't—she can't—

I turn to Leif. "Can you show me where it is?"

He's already shaking his head. "I don't think that's a good idea. We're not supposed to—"

"If you won't take me, I'll find it on my own."

"Valerie—"

"I think it's my fault she's here, Leif." If Daniel hadn't introduced us, if she hadn't agreed to meet with me... "She's been in hiding her entire life, and then she tried to help me, and now she's here."

His face falls as he looks between me and the compound, but then he sets the bottle of whiskey in the snow and juts his chin forward. "I'm so going to regret this."

CHAPTER EIGHT

WINNIE and the others are long gone by the time Leif and I make it inside, so hopefully he's right about where they're taking them. We slip through one of the back hallways, hoping to avoid Sutton's prying eyes in the lobby, and head for a service stairwell. It's cold and dingy, a stark contrast to the rest of the building, and I follow Leif down three floors of the concrete stairs. I scan the ceiling, but it's devoid of the cameras I've seen everywhere.

I doubt it's because the universe is suddenly on my side. Is it because what goes on down here isn't common knowledge? They don't want a record of it?

Or something else?

"If they're still in there, we can't—" Leif starts.

"Just give me a minute to think."

The stairs end at a metal door with a keypad. I frown at the red salt embedded in the wall. So no using magic to get past it either. Otherwise, I'd just teleport us to the other side.

"You think that werewolf strength might come in handy? It's that or…"

The echo of footsteps makes every muscle in my body go rigid. Leif grabs my arm, and I tighten my fist around the knife until blood coats my palm. Voices draw closer, and we hunch in the shadows of the small space beneath the stairs.

I don't think I could make us invisible if I tried. In theory, it wouldn't be that different from teleporting, but I don't know if it's even possible, and right now won't be the first time I try.

Instead, I focus on our scents. Even if by some miracle no one sees us, Leif's wolf odor is hard to miss. If I can manipulate our body chemistry enough to stop emitting any smell, or at least lessen it…

The magic falls over us like a second skin, but I feel the exertion like a weight pressing on my lungs. My chest tightens around it, but I grit my teeth, forcing myself to hold on. I've pulled off harder spells before. I can do this.

The door creaks open.

"What are you doing?" someone calls inside.

"I thought I heard voices."

"Come on, give me a hand."

The footsteps retreat, and I surge forward, trying to catch the door before it latches. Leif gets there first and wedges something small in the doorjamb.

I let out a shaky breath and join him beside the door, trying to see what he used to prop it open.

It's only then that I realize I'm no longer holding the knife. The jagged end points toward us, catching the overhead light.

I raise a single eyebrow at him, and he shrugs, a self-satisfied smile on his face now.

I strain my ear for voices or footsteps before peering through the crack. The small window of space isn't enough to see the room clearly, but there's no one near the door from what I can tell. No scents or heartbeats either.

Holding my breath, I nudge it open, inch by inch, willing it not to make a sound. I twist sideways to squeeze through, grabbing my knife as I go. Once I'm inside, I let out the quietest exhale I can.

It looks a lot like the control room upstairs—a single chair facing a desk full of buttons and gauges. Though instead of a sea of monitors, it overlooks a plane of glass. The room is empty, so the men must have gone through the other door across from us. Leif hurries in after me and slowly eases the door shut.

I inch forward. Lights flicker on the control board in front of us, but the chair for whoever usually sits here is empty.

I choke on my next breath. On the other side of the glass is a small, round room, the floor lower than ours. Harsh lights shine on the five metal tables filling the space, a person strapped to each, gags tied around their mouths.

I search their faces, but none of them are familiar.

None of them are Winnie.

They're also not struggling against the restraints on their ankles or wrists. They don't seem distressed at all.

"She's not in there," I whisper.

"Then let's get the hell out of here."

"No, it has to get done tonight." A door on the other side of the glass bangs open, and a woman I don't know strides into the room, followed by two of the men we'd seen in the training yard. She's as tall as they are but wafer-thin, and she winds through the five tables, inspecting each person as she goes.

She glances up at the glass, and her black eyes meet mine. My blood runs cold, but then she looks away, snapping her fingers at the men beside her.

It must be a one-way mirror.

"My bag?" she demands.

The one closest to her fumbles with a gray duffel bag and hands it to her.

She digs through it for several seconds and huffs. "Imbeciles," she mutters, then stomps from the room...

...toward *our* room.

Leif yanks me down by the arm, shoving both of us under the table. I barely have time to catch my breath before the door on our side flies open and she steps through. Sweat beads on my forehead as I strain to cover our scents.

The woman is still muttering under her breath as she crosses the room, her high heels stopping a pace away, and something beeps overhead as she jabs a button. Static fills the air, and then:

"Control Room 1. This is Rome."

"Your idiots brought down the wrong bag."

Rome sighs heavily on the other end. "I'll see what I can do."

"*Now*, Rome," she snaps. "He wants this done tonight, before the hit on the prince. We don't..."

Whatever she says next turns into a loud buzzing in my ears. Leif tightens his hold on my arm, his nails pinching

87

my skin. The blood drains from my face, and it takes everything inside me to focus on holding on to the magic.

Before the hit on the prince.

Reid.

"Ugh." The woman takes a step back. "It smells like wolf in here."

Leif tenses beside me.

"Someone's coming down with it," says Rome.

"Have you heard from him?" The woman slumps into the chair and rolls it to the edge of the control board. Leif and I flatten ourselves against the wall, her shoes a whisper away from us now. "I haven't been able to get ahold of him all night. Why the hell he wanted to do this the day before, I have no idea."

"I think he's off the grounds tonight."

The woman blows the air out of her cheeks. "First he had to go get the Darkmore, now this. He's getting sloppy."

"Charity," Rome says, his voice hard.

"Oh, that's right. I forgot you were a kiss-ass. Don't mind me. Do you at least know where he wants everything for tomorrow? He gave me a list, but then nothing else. And you know if it's not where he wants it to be, he's going to blame it on me, as if I was supposed to read his mind."

"You can bring it in here," says Rome. "They're taking one of the trucks tomorrow, I believe."

"They're *driving?*" She scoffs. "Glad I'm not on the roster."

"Oh, yeah, maybe not. I don't know. No one tells me anything."

There's a knock, and Charity pushes to her feet. "I'll see you in that poker rematch," she says, then jabs off the microphone. "What took you so long?" She throws open the door and a skinny boy with a face full of freckles pales on the other side.

"I—I got here as fast as I could."

"Stop talking." She snatches the bag from his hands and turns for the other door. The boy stands there for a moment, his eyes locking on us. My heart stops in my chest. I stare back at him, silently pleading for him not to say anything. His expression doesn't change, and he glances the way Charity went. But then he scurries back the way he'd come.

I start to deflate against the wall, but Leif yanks me out from under the table and into the hall before I can protest.

I don't realize how shaky and sweaty I am until we're back in the training yard. I pull in small, uneven breaths. Leif says something beside me, but I don't hear him. He doesn't let go of my arm, and him pulling me forward is the only thing keeping me moving.

The hit on the prince.

"There you guys are!"

"Where the hell did you go? We thought you were bringing beer."

"Is this my whiskey?"

I blink, still trying to catch my breath.

"You've been gone for hours. What happened? Are you all right?"

"What happened? What's wrong?" Calla's face appears in front of me, and she grabs my arms. "Val?"

Leif mumbles something too low for me to hear. I don't hear Calla's reply either. Their voices turn into a vague humming in my ears, and the entire world feels unstable beneath my feet.

Hands brush my arms, turning me.

"Let's get you inside." Calla—Calla's voice. Her hand rubs up and down my arm. Footsteps crunch somewhere behind me. "It's all right," says Calla. "I've got her."

The world blurs. My stomach flips as the elevator surges up, and Calla's arm tightens around my shoulders. She says nothing until we're in my room.

She walks me over to the bed before doubling back and shutting the door.

"What happened?" she asks, coming to sit next to me. "Where did you and Leif go? You were gone for hours."

I grip the edges of Reid's jacket, my fingers cramping around the fabric. *The hit on the prince.* Tomorrow. She said they were doing it tomorrow.

"Valerie, you're scaring me. Talk to me."

I have to do something. To warn him. To stop them. But how? I don't know how to get around this place yet, let alone where anything is. But I can't sit here and do nothing, knowing it's going to happen.

"Okay, okay. How about we lie down, yeah?" Calla pulls back the blankets and ushers me in. I curl into a ball, and she gets to work untying the laces of my boots.

"These aren't my shoes," I murmur.

She pauses, then continues pulling them off my feet. "I noticed that," she says, her voice soft like she's afraid she's going to spook me back into silence. "Here we go." She drops the second boot to the floor, then climbs into the bed beside me, pulls the blankets over us, and wraps her arm around my waist, her face fitting into the space between my shoulder and neck.

I swallow hard, unable to close my eyes, and she reaches around until she finds my hand.

She falls asleep quickly, like she always did, and her light snores fill the room. But I can't sleep. I can't get the muscles in my shoulders to relax. So I lie there, listening to her breathe, and my brain turns in furious circles as it tries to summon a plan before tomorrow.

THE NEXT DAY, I sit at the edge of the bed watching Calla sleep, trying to talk myself into what I need to do. The string attached to her key card is poking out of her shirt and tucked under her cheek, her arm stretched wide like she's reaching for me.

She'll forgive me for this. She has to.

She sucks in a sharp breath and stirs, rolling onto her back. Slowly, she opens her eyes and finds me staring at her.

"What the fuck, Valerie?" She sits up straight, holding a hand to her chest. "You scared the shit out of me. What are you doing?" When I don't respond, she inches closer. "Are you okay?"

"What do you know about their plans to take out Reid tonight?" I ask, my voice entirely monotone.

Her face falls.

And my stomach drops with it. "So you did know."

"I—I didn't know they'd actually made a plan to do it."

I narrow my eyes. "If they were to do it, where would they be leaving from?"

"Valerie…" She shakes her head. "You can't interfere. You can't stop—"

"Where. Would. They. Leave. From?"

She scoots closer, her hands reaching for me. "Look, I know—"

"You don't know," I snap. "Now tell me how to stop them."

She stands like she's going to leave, and I leap up before she can take a step, blocking her path to the door.

"You can't stop it!" She throws her hands up and lets them slap against her thighs. "They could have already left for all you know."

I grab one of her arms, forcing her to look at me. And even though I have no idea what I'm doing, she freezes in my gaze.

"Take off the key card and hand it to me."

She does so without hesitation, and I quickly slip it over my neck. "Now tell me everything you know about the plan."

She doesn't blink, and her voice comes out emotionless and smooth. "They're leaving when the sun goes down at eight."

"From where?"

"I don't know."

"How can I find out?"

"You could go to the control room and access the cameras. You might be able to see them on the monitors."

I tighten my grip on her arm, not daring to blink in case it breaks the connection.

"You're going to forget you and I had this conversation."

"I'm going to forget you and I had this conversation," she echoes, her wide and innocent brown eyes staring into mine. Guilt cuts through me like a knife, twisting and pulling in the pit of my stomach, but I keep going.

"And you are going to cover for me in case anyone asks where I am."

"I'm going to cover for you if anyone asks where you are."

I stare at her for one more second, my grip loosening on her arm. "I'm sorry," I whisper, then I dig my nails into her arm until blood breaks the surface and cut off the oxygen to her brain enough to make her lose consciousness. She goes limp, but I catch her before she can hit the floor, then gently lay her on the bed. "Forgive me," I whisper, then take off down the hall.

CHAPTER NINE

ALL I WANT to do is run, but I force myself to walk so I don't draw attention to myself. People in the halls, the elevator, the lobby, are all a blur. My vision narrows and tunnels in front of me, my pulse thudding in my ears. What I'll do once I reach the control room, I have no idea.

When the sun goes down at eight.

The sun is hanging low in the sky as I cut through the lobby. There's time, but not much.

I feel Sutton's gaze on me as I pass her desk, and I have half the mind to cast a forgetting spell or try another glamour. If someone comes looking for me, she'll be the first to tell. But I don't have time, and with the surrounding crowd, I can't risk anyone seeing. Best to act natural. There are plenty of explanations for me being down here. I could be going to breakfast like the rest of them.

When I reach the control room, I pause and fill my lungs with air. I wait, listening. One heartbeat, slow and steady. I glance around the hall, but I'm alone.

The camera in the corner, however, is pointed directly at me. Can Rome see me standing out here? Can someone else? How long until I draw suspicion?

Sliding the makeshift knife out of my sleeve, I slice my palm, then squeeze my hand into a fist, focusing on Rome's heart on the other side of the wall. I just need it to slow enough for him to pass out. The system beeps as I swipe Calla's card, and I quickly open the door and slip inside.

Rome is sitting in the chair behind the panel, one hand clutched to his chest. His eyes harden as they lock on me. I squeeze my fist tighter, willing him to lose consciousness, and he lurches to his feet. Sweat breaks out along my skin, exhaustion sinking in. He stumbles toward me, his teeth gritted. No, not teeth. Fangs.

He hisses and throws himself forward. The force of his body slams me into the wall, and his hands clamp around my throat. I gasp, clawing at his arms, and he tightens his grip until I see stars. Not knowing what else to do, I stab the knife into the side of his throat. His hold loosens in surprise, and I duck, slipping free. That cut won't kill him. It won't even slow him down for long.

Rome lets out another hiss and lunges for me. I grab the chair and throw it between us, stumbling over my feet and landing on my back. He trips and steadies himself against the control panel as I desperately search the ground for something to use. A pencil rolls from the desk, and I snatch it as he attacks, stabbing it up through his palm as he reaches for my throat.

He roars in pain, his eyes flicking to the control panel for a moment. Can he use it to call for help? To alert someone else that I'm here? I shove myself between him and the buttons before he has a chance, focusing on the energy buzzing in the blood seeping from his hand, using his own power against him. I imagine a fist squeezing around his heart, sharp nails digging in, piercing through the tissue, clamping tighter and tighter until it bursts.

Blood spurts from his mouth, and he collapses on top of me. I wheeze, tasting the coppery tang on my lips as the weight of him knocks the air from my lungs. I shove his body and roll him to the side, waiting for another beat to make sure he's really dead. With shaking hands, I pull myself to my feet.

I turn to the monitors—dozens upon dozens covering the entire wall. My breaths come in short and fast as I scan them, trying to find something useful.

"No, no, no," I whisper, turning to the panel, but the glowing buttons don't make any more sense to me. I didn't get this far to fail now. I squint at the screens, looking for any kind of transportation, any way someone could leave. The cameras are all tuned into the different estates and academies, none focused here on the grounds.

My gaze freezes on the monitor closest to the door—the Carrington estate. The screen is full of movement as servants set up rows of chairs and flower arrangements near the garden. It almost looks like they're setting up for a...funeral.

My heart stops as I study the scene, looking for any hint as to who it's for.

I blink, snapping myself out of it. I don't have time for this. *Reid* doesn't have time for me to get distracted right now. I push buttons at random until I find one that makes the screens change.

There. An exit near the huts Leif took me to last night. There's a separate building with a garage door. There must be vehicles in there, right?

My heart lurches into my throat as the control room door swings open.

"Well, well. What do we have here?"

I stare at the stranger as he steps inside, unable to move. His presence fills the room, his golden eyes freezing me in place. His hair is cropped close to his head, but I can tell it's light, the same shade as the stubble lining his jaw. He sniffs the air, and I catch his scent too—earthy, musky. Wolf.

A half smile plays at his lips. "Halfling. A daughter then, I'm assuming?" He glances from Rome to the overturned chair to the monitors, then back to me. "You've certainly been busy."

I don't—can't—say anything. I can't get around him. His body blocks the entire doorway. And I'm barely keeping myself standing as it is. I won't be able to take him out too. Something tells me he won't go down as easily as Rome did.

He cocks his head to the side, watching me, then slowly, he crosses his arms over his chest and lets the door close behind him. He juts his chin at the control panel. "Go on then."

I don't move.

That same predatory smile returns to his lips. "You didn't know what you were doing in the first place, did you?"

My face burns, but I can't argue because he's right. This was a pathetic, desperate, half-baked plan. And Reid deserves more than this. A more capable partner. If the roles were reversed, he would've come up with something better. Something that *worked*. Now he's going to die, and it'll be my fault.

The stranger takes another few steps and peers at Rome's body. He makes a sound with the side of his mouth. "Did you have to make it so *messy*? There must have been other ways with an easier cleanup. The bloodstains will be hard to hide." His gaze flickers back to me, a single eyebrow raised. "You hadn't thought of that?"

"Who are you?"

He grins as if it's the most amusing thing I could've said. "Cam."

My stomach plummets. Leif's pack master. The one with an alliance with James Westcott.

"Does that mean I get to know your name now?" he asks, nudging Rome's limp arm with his boot. "If I'm going to help you clean this up, I think I deserve that much."

Help me? I stare at him. Is this some sadistic wolf thing? Play with your prey before you kill it? Give me a sliver of hope before calling Westcott and getting me caught? Maybe if I catch him off guard, I can take him.

"You don't talk much, do you? Or are you in shock? This isn't your first kill, is it?" He peers at my face again. "Nah. Can't be. I can see it in your eyes. Well, come on then. The longer you wait, the more likely you are to get caught. You should probably go clean that blood off too. Kind of a dead giveaway."

I wait for the punchline of whatever joke this is.

"Okay, so we'll put a pin in the name. Do you want his feet or head? Or maybe we should start by clearing that security footage, yeah?"

He strolls to the control panel and punches a few

buttons. The screen in the middle pulls up the camera outside the door. And with another few clicks, the screen goes black, then flickers back to life.

"Ah," he sighs. "Like it never happened. Well." His eyes flash to Rome's body, then around the room, focusing on something behind me. "I guess you could put him in the supply closet for now. At least until you have time to get rid of the body. Oh, wait. You were a Marionette, were you not? Can't you…?" He waves his hands in the general direction of Rome, presumably indicating I should use magic to dispose of him.

Footsteps pound outside, and we both whip our heads toward the monitors. Sure enough, bodies are flooding the hall.

"Well." He tsks. "Looks like it's too little too late. Better luck next time, little witch."

The door flies open behind him, and the light from the hall falls on me like a spotlight, illuminating the blood dripping down my face and the dead vampire at my feet.

CHAPTER TEN

"Two DAYS. You have been here for *two days,* and you couldn't follow a *single* rule." His voice is piercing, jagged, like a serrated knife cutting through my skull. I flinch against the leather chair beneath me as he paces the length of his office behind his desk. His footsteps boom against the hardwood. Calla waits quietly against the wall in my peripheral vison, Cam standing on the other side of the room, and half a dozen security guards are behind me near the door.

Westcott stops in his tracks and looks at me for a second, then drops his gaze, shaking his head.

"Rome has been employed here for over a decade," he snaps, then braces both hands on the desk and leans toward me. "What could have possibly possessed you to do this? What was so goddamn important for you in that control room, huh? Make me understand, Valerie, because I'm not seeing the reasoning here."

I stare at my hands in my lap, my fingers tracing along the hem of Reid's jacket. *I failed.*

"Valerie," Westcott barks, but I still don't look at him. "If this is your idea of acting out, you've taken it too far. I will not allow you to be a danger to my people here. Do you understand?"

I failed.

Have they already left? Are they already there? Is he already dead? Even without the bond, I'd know, wouldn't I? I'd sense it somehow.

"I said, do you understand?" Fingers grip my chin, and I flinch. I hadn't seen him come around the desk, but Westcott's nails dig into my skin, forcing me to look at him. He jerks my head so far it strains my neck, and I let out a surprised sound.

The floor creaks as Cam drifts forward, but he stops after a single step.

"Got it," I grit out.

Westcott's nostrils flare as he glares at me. "You are not leaving this room until you tell me why."

I shake out of his grasp, but he doesn't back up. If he thinks he's intimidating, he has another think coming. I didn't spend the last twenty-one years getting slapped and cut and scolded by my mother at every turn just to cower beneath this man.

"Then I guess everyone in here should get comfortable," I mutter.

He raises his hand, and I hold his gaze, daring him to do it.

"It's about the prince!" Calla cuts in. "She heard about the hit on the prince."

I cut my gaze to her, scowling—both for her telling him, but also at my own failure to glamour her properly if she can remember that. She doesn't meet my eyes, her fingers nervously fussing with the key card now back around her neck.

Westcott says nothing, but he steps back and leans against the edge of his desk as he runs a hand along his jaw. I can feel the heat of every eye in the room on me now, but I stare him down.

He sighs. "Tell me that's not what this was about."

I say nothing.

He rubs his eyes and flicks his hand, apparently dismissing the security. He doesn't speak until the door clicks shut behind them.

"I'm afraid your efforts were for not, Valerie." He paces around the desk and sinks into his chair.

I swallow hard. So they've already left then. Are already on their way—

"He's already dead," he continues.

My eyes snap to his face, my blood turning to ice in my veins, freezing my heart and stopping it midbeat. "I don't believe you," I whisper.

He holds up his palms. "Made it easy for us, really. Came to us—looking for you, I expect. I can show you him, if you'd like, before we dispose of the body."

I look between him and Calla, my breaths coming in short, harsh gasps now. He must be lying. Calla keeps her eyes trained on her feet. Cam clears his throat behind me, and I hear him take a step.

"Not just yet, Camden," says James. "It's actually good luck you're here. I'll be leaving the compound tomorrow.

Seeing as you are still in my debt, she is your responsibility until I return."

"I have to get back——"

"To your pack, yes, yes." Westcott waves him off. "I'm not asking you to stay. Valerie will be needing some new accommodations anyway after this stunt. I don't trust her here while I'm gone."

Cam opens and closes his mouth with an audible snap.

His words buzz in my ears like tiny insects, holding no meaning to me because all I keep hearing over and over is *He's already dead. He's already dead. He's already dead.*

"...make the necessary preparations...we'll come get you from your room...we can talk about this more when I return..."

My vision blurs in and out, and hands brush against my arms, but I barely feel them. We're moving, and people are still talking, but I'm just sinking. Floating and sinking and drowning and numb.

When I blink, I'm sitting on the bed in my room, alone.

My hand rests on my stomach, my fingers digging in, as if I can claw my way to where the bond used to be, just to feel that it's not true. It can't be.

The door swings open, and I jerk my head up as Calla steps inside. She doesn't quite meet my eyes as she wrings her hands together in front of her.

"I can take you to go see him, if you want."

I say nothing. I don't think I could if I tried. But I force myself to stand. I half expect Westcott or his security to be waiting for me in the hall, but Calla and I walk alone in silence. I can't feel my legs as they move beneath me, and our surroundings turn into little more than a blur.

As we come to a metal door at the end of a hallway, Calla swipes her key card, but doesn't move forward.

"I'll give you some time alone," she says.

I turn and face her before she can leave, meeting her gaze for the first time since being in Westcott's office. A light sparks in her eyes, a hope.

"You know, I always thought when it came down to it, you'd have my back," I say. "Always."

Her face falls.

"But now? I don't know who the hell you are. The Calliope I knew died two years ago. And I guess she's going to stay that way."

"Valerie—" She stops abruptly and closes her mouth.

Because what can she say? What can she possibly say right now?

I look her straight in the eye, and my brain doesn't register her as the same person from my memories. She could be anyone. Anything.

Everything inside of me is numb and cold and dark, like something snapped, something much deeper than the bond had ever been.

My voice comes out utterly calm, monotone, as I say, "You're dead to me."

Then I close the door between us.

Still, I feel nothing. Nothing but the bone-chilling cold. A single light shines from the ceiling, illuminating the metal table in the center of the room where a black body bag waits. I stand frozen by the door.

The silence crowds in around me, and I force myself to step forward. My footsteps echo in the small room until I reach the table. The bag is zipped shut and so utterly, utterly still. My hand shakes as I pull the zipper down.

A small, inhuman noise sounds in the back of my throat, and it's as if the world has been frozen in black and white until this moment, and then in the blink of an eye, everything snaps into blindingly bright color. I stop at his chin, my breaths coming in short and fast.

His skin looks paler than usual under the harsh light, his eyelashes fanning out over his cheeks. I push the hair away from his eyes, and my lower lip starts to tremble when I feel how cold his skin is.

"Reid," I whisper, as if somehow he'll hear me. As if somehow he'll answer. I squeeze my eyes shut, and tears rolls down my cheeks. "Reid," I say through my teeth, louder this time, and I'm not standing in a cold, metal room with his body.

I'm standing beside him near the river, holding his hand as we spread Quinn's ashes. I'm crying in his arms after my mother told me she wished I was dead. I'm laughing with him in the grass at the estate after the thousandth time I got the names wrong as he tried to help me study. I'm watching his face crease in concentration as he bends over the clay, building something beautiful out of nothing. I'm feeling him through the bond and feeling his hands in my hair as he kissed me and feeling his breath in my ear and feeling his hands on my back as he held me until I fell asleep.

My vision blurs so much with tears that I can't see the room in front of me anymore.

"What did you do?" I whisper, pulling the zipper farther and fisting my hand in his shirt. "What did you do?" I shout.

The tremors spread from my hands up to the rest of my body until my teeth start to chatter, and I fold over him, pressing my face against the side of his neck, but he already doesn't smell like him anymore.

The door beeps behind me, but I don't move. I tighten my hands in his shirt, holding him to me, and an image flashes in the back of my mind.

A bird in a field, one moment lying in the snow surrounded by blood, the next, taking flight.

I can save him. I can bring him back.

"Valerie." Hands wrap around my arms.

"No!" I scream.

"Valerie."

The hands pull harder, and then are joined by a second set, hauling me away. Reid's shirt slips from between my fingers, and I thrash against their hold.

I just need some blood. I just need enough blood. I can do this. I know I can.

"*Valerie.*"

Twisting my head to the side, I sink my teeth into my upper arm until blood rushes to the surface. The hands drag me toward the door as the magic prickles against my skin. I concentrate on Reid's body, willing the blood in his veins to force his heart to pump. Willing him to come back. Willing him to *live*.

We're almost to the door now.

"Stop! No! Let me go!" I scream, trying to break free. I just need a little more time. I just need…

There's the bite of a needle in the side of my neck, and my vision swims. Then the rest of the world goes dark.

PART II

CHAPTER ELEVEN

REID

I KEEP EXPECTING the metal to be cold in my hand, but it never is. The ring is heavier than I would've guessed, but that's probably thanks to the knife hidden inside. It's warm like it just came off her hand, though it's been days now. Days since the blood, and the bone-chilling silence, and me slipping it from her finger right before they took her body away...

I tighten my fist until the metal digs into my skin, then shove it in my pocket, forcing my mind back to the present.

This is one of the biggest crowds I've ever seen for a funeral. And the estate has no shortage of them. Not necessarily because we have so many deaths, but because my mother enjoys the spectacle.

My jaw tightens at the chaos around me—voices, sobs, tears. It looks like most of the academy is in attendance as well, the younger students somehow crying the loudest, despite never once speaking to her.

Her.

I swallow hard. I can't think her name. Not right now.

The cool air breezes through the crowd as everyone finds their seats, their black clothing blending in with the surrounding night. The casket is set up with the gardens as the backdrop.

She would have liked that. She liked it out here more than she cared to admit.

I can almost hear her violin coming through the hedges, the soft, seamless flow of the notes. I can imagine her sitting on the bench by the fountain, eyes closed, that damn scrunch in her nose as she concentrates. Though her fingers would move expertly along the strings, making it look effortless.

She made pretty much everything she did look effortless.

I squeeze my hands into fists until my veins bulge and my fingers ache.

It's a clear night, the stars bright overhead. They've set up torches on the outskirts of the crowd, the flames flickering in the breeze.

I linger toward the back as people fill the chairs. Her friends take up the front row, clinging to each other and crying. Her sister sits in the front on the other side, staring ahead and looking dazed. Her mother's arm is wrapped around the sister's shoulders, but I can't see her face.

Which is probably a good thing. I'm barely holding back from ripping her throat out as it is. I won't do it here. But one of these days.

My mother is also in the first row, the seat beside her empty, waiting for me.

I remain standing in the back as the service begins. This

being the shortest partnership I've had to date, it should be easy. It should be nothing.

It should be.

Coming in the first place was a mistake. I can't stand here and listen to these people talk about her. The theatrical tears and stories that don't even sound like her. These people are so fucking full of shit.

God, she would've hated this.

A door creaks open in the estate behind me, and I can feel who it is without turning. That's more of a punch to the gut than anything else. Because just for a moment, the briefest second, I pretend that tug in the back of my head is her.

The bond with him, it's nothing like it was with her. I can't feel his emotions like I could feel hers, which is for the best. I shouldn't resent it. Not when I'm the reason it's there. No one forced me to turn him. But every time I feel someone else's presence in my head, and it's not her, it makes me want to punch something.

A small part of me had wondered if he would show up. It would've meant a lot to her to see him here, but I honestly couldn't have guessed either way. He steps up beside me as the service continues on. I'm not listening anymore.

"She would've hated this," Connor says lowly.

I don't respond, and I don't look at him. I don't want to see whatever is on his face.

He moves away, sliding into a chair in the back row as another girl takes the podium. At least this one won't be insufferable. She was a friend—Monroe is her name. She looks straight down the aisle and meets my eyes. The muscles in my jaw work, and a tear runs down her face.

I lower my gaze so she doesn't think I'm scowling at her.

Eventually the talking stops, thank God. Then one by one, people go up to the casket. Her friends are some of the first, and they loop toward the back once they're finished. I can feel them looking at me as they approach. They're hooked at the elbow, tears staining both of their faces. The light-haired one—Kirby—looks up as they pass, and there's no mistaking the pity in her eyes. I nod at them, grateful they keep walking and don't stop to talk.

The line slowly works its way through, and it's not until everyone else finishes and spreads out on the grounds that my feet carry me forward. My breaths come in shorter with each step, a solid weight expanding in my chest as I draw closer. When I reach the casket, I don't look down for several seconds.

But no amount of standing here will make me ready.

They put too much makeup on her. That's my first thought when I look down. Her skin is pale, smooth. Too perfect. No trace of the freckles along her nose. And the blush is too low on her face. When she blushes, it hits higher on her cheekbones than that. Her dark hair is straight over her shoulders, missing all of its usual waves.

She looks like a beautiful, dead stranger.

I swallow hard, but I don't look away. Her hands are folded over her chest, and they have her in a red dress with a high neckline to cover where her throat was slashed.

Seeing her like this, it brings back the memory of a few

nights ago as she'd lain in that fucking cell. She'd been cold and unmoving then too.

I'll be right back.

That was the last thing I said to her.

I'll be right back.

She died alone. Alone and waiting for me to come back.

There had been so, so much blood. Splatters on the wall, the floor. It was still warm and dripping down the bars as I rushed down the stairs. And her body, so limp and still on the ground—

My soul *burns*, and my heart feels bloody and raw and useless in my chest. She'd been so weak. Too weak to defend herself. Attacking her when she was like that was so goddamn cowardly. To think of her struggling, trying to fight back—

I suck in a sharp breath. I can't think about this. I won't.

Glamouring the man in the cell next to her for answers had proven pointless. He had a block in his mind, just like Madison had.

Which told me all I need to know about who did this.

I grit my teeth until pain flares up my jaw.

My hand shakes as I reach for hers. Just for a moment. Just to feel her one more time. Her skin is cold to the touch. I run my thumb along the back of her hand and slide my fingers beneath hers—

—and everything inside of me goes still.

My eyes snap to her face, tracing over every detail—her eyes, her nose, her lips. I lift her hand in mine and run my thumb over her fingertips again.

Her perfectly smooth fingertips.

I check her other hand, just to be sure. My breathing quickens, and I glance around before setting her hand back on her chest. No one is looking my way.

I take a step away from the casket, then another, suddenly needing to put as much distance between us as possible. The agonizing ache in my chest eases, the fist squeezing around my heart finally relenting. I pull in what feels like the first breath I've taken in days.

I work my way through the crowd, urgency quickening my pace, now actually looking at those in attendance, really looking at them. Their faces are a flash of tears and flushed cheeks and running makeup. Her loved ones, all the people who've known her for her entire life, how can they not see? How do they not know?

I hesitate once I reach the end of the aisle and look back at the body, so still and beautiful in the moonlight.

But that is not Valerie.

CHAPTER TWELVE

VALERIE

THE FLOOR IS MOVING beneath me. Metal clangs together nearby, and it takes me a moment to realize it's coming from *me*. I try to look down, but every movement is slow, pained, like I'm slogging through wet cement. A car—I'm in a car. It jostles, and something cold bangs against my ankle. I reach down, the pads of my finger running along the lump right above my shoe.

A shackle. I inhale sharply and check my other ankle, but there's nothing around the left one. There also isn't a chain attached to it…so then why is it there?

It's dark, even with my vampire vision. The feeling of fabric against my face registers next. A blindfold. I reach for it, and someone clears their throat across from me.

"I wouldn't if I were you."

I freeze. The voice is unfamiliar, deep. When I search for my magic, nothing answers my call. Not even a ghost of it.

My blood runs cold.

The shackle. There must be red salt or something similar in it. It's not meant to physically tie me down. It's trapping my magic inside of me.

"Might as well relax," says the voice. "We've got a long way to go."

I swallow hard. The musky scent of wolf is thick enough in the air to choke on. How did I get here? How long was I unconscious?

The memories come rushing back. Hands yanking me away. Reid—

I deflate against the seat, the ache in my chest returning full force. I barely feel the pinch of the needle in my neck this time, and the following darkness is almost welcome.

"SHE'S NOT GONNA BURN up in the sun, is she?" asks a muffled voice.

"I don't know. Let's find out," says a second.

"Do *not* open that door. Step away. Get back to camp. Now."

"Good to have you back, Cam," grumbles the second, followed by fading footsteps.

My head lolls against my chest, drool dripping from the side of my mouth. I sit up, wiping it away with the back of my hand. The world is still dark, the blindfold secure across my face, but I can't sense anyone else in the car with me anymore.

Someone bangs on the door, the sound reverberating through the small space.

"Darkmore," calls Cam's voice. "You awake?"

I ease the blindfold off but don't respond. I blink a few times, willing my vision to adjust. If I had to guess, I'd say I was in the back of a van. No windows.

"Darkmore." More pounding on the door.

I glance in the general direction of his voice, but still don't respond. He's worried about opening the door and killing me? Good. Let him worry.

"Jesus Christ." The door slides open, but not as much light falls on me as I'd been expecting.

I blink to find a large blanket coming toward me. Before I can react, he throws it over my head, wraps his arms around me, and tosses me over his shoulder. I grunt as he stands, slamming the door shut behind him, and starts walking. The blanket presses against my face a little too tightly, and I gasp, trying to draw in breath. He might not kill me with the sun, but he's on the way to effectively smothering me to death. My entire body bobs up and down with his paces, and a wave of motion sickness hits me stronger than anything I'd felt in the car.

"Put me down," I grit out.

"Ah, so you can speak. We're almost there," says Cam.

"I can't breathe."

"You'll be fine."

I scowl. His shoulder cuts in above my hip, and I wince. But he carries me like it's nothing. His breathing isn't even altered. I think he might be using one hand.

"Just let go of me."

"Trust me, princess," he mutters, "I'm not any happier about this than you are."

He tosses me up as he readjusts his grip, and I grunt as my stomach lands back on his shoulder.

"You're far too calm," he muses. "You don't even burn in the sun, do you? Kind of wishing you'd responded now, huh? Could've avoided this."

"You're a dick," I mutter.

"So I've been told, but I'm also the only thing standing between you and two dozen wolves who would happily rip your throat out, so if I were you, I'd be nice to me."

I lock my jaw, biting back the response on the tip of my tongue. It would be different if I had my magic, but the feeling of the shackle banging against his thigh threatens to suck the air from my lungs. A feeling I remember all too well from that day tied to a chair with the Russians.

Powerless.

Defenseless.

Human.

I can take care of myself, I'd told Reid after returning to the tattoo shop for information on James Westcott.

Against an entire pack of wolves? No, Valerie, you can't.

And that had been *with* my magic.

And now?

The memory sends another pang through my stomach. *Reid.* I clench my jaw, fighting back tears.

He's dead. And it's my fault.

My fault. My fault. My fault.

"Nothing to say?" Cam muses.

"Fuck you," I spit.

"Is that her?" calls out a voice.

I stiffen, but Cam continues at the same pace. Then without warning, he flips me onto my feet and rips the blanket off my head. Someone gasps near me as I blink, trying to adjust to the glaring sun overhead. I might not burst into flame, but my eyes burn, and my skin prickles. I push the staticky hair out of my face as the camp swims into view.

And *camp* truly would be the best word for it.

Though we're in the center of a clearing, trees surround us in every direction. Large canvas tents that look like they were swiped from the military are spread out in the dirt, more than I can count.

And standing in front of me is a group of at least twenty men, all with their arms crossed and staring at me. My heart stops in my chest at the sight of the man in the center.

The red tattoo on his face seems to reflect the sun, but not as much as his teeth as he gives me a predatory, slow smile.

Terrence McCullough.

The last time I'd seen him—which I'd been hoping would be the only time—was when I was torturing him. Seems he remembers that as well as I do.

"This is Westcott's daughter," says Cam beside me. "She'll be staying with us until he gets back."

"You want to keep a *vamp* in the camp?" someone calls.

"Are you questioning me?" Cam asks, his voice perfectly calm.

There's a pause, and then a quiet "No, sir."

"She'll do her part, just like the rest of you. Speaking of, get back to work."

The group disperses, though several of the men linger behind, shooting second glances at me over their shoulders. There are noticeably no women here. I know that's not a wolf thing. There are plenty of female wolves. So do they just not have any in their pack? Why?

"We don't have any extra tents," Cam says. "So I guess we'll have to…"

"She can take mine." Leif walks up to us, wiping what looks like grease off his hands with a towel. "At least until we get another set up. I'll bunk with one of the other guys." He meets my eyes and smiles, but I don't return it. I can't. The weight in my chest is still too suffocating.

My fault. My fault. My fault.

"I'll show you where it is," Leif says, though his voice is muffled and distant.

"I don't have time for any handholding today," grunts Cam. "So she's with you until sundown. Explain the rules to her while you're at it."

"Got it," says Leif.

I don't realize Cam is gone until Leif gently tugs on my arm, leading me through the camp. The air is full of voices and humidity, tent flaps whipping in the breeze as the wolves come and go. Some of the tents are noticeably smaller than the others—probably the ones for sleeping.

Maybe at one time I would've cared about what's in the other ones. Maybe I would've cared about getting passed off to Cam like an unwanted child. Maybe I would've cared about having no idea how long I'll be in this camp.

But not today.

"Here we are," says Leif, holding open the door to a small tent.

It's tall enough for me to stand, though Leif has to duck as he slips in beside me and immediately starts cleaning. There's a cot on the far end with a lantern beside it and a rumpled pile of blankets on the ground. Leif's clothes are strewn about, along with some books, shoes, empty food wrappers, and old bandages.

"I'll get my stuff out of your way before tonight," he says, piling more of the clothes in his hands.

"You don't have to do this," I mumble.

"It's no problem." He pauses once his arms are full and turns to me. "I'm guessing they didn't send you with any changes of clothes or anything?"

I look at myself, only now realizing. At least I'm wearing Reid's jacket. I don't care about anything else getting left behind—it's not like any of it was mine to begin with.

"I'll leave some of my clean stuff in here," he decides. "And I'm sure Cam will have whoever goes into town next pick you up some stuff."

Into town? So we're not completely in the middle of nowhere.

"Anyway, I'm not sure what kind of work assignments Cam will have you on—since I'm willing to bet he won't take the time to teach you how to do anything—but I'm on laundry duty today, so you can come with me."

He pulls two large white bags out from the corner and starts stuffing his dirty clothes inside.

"You don't have any…sunglasses, do you?" I mutter, rubbing my forehead. A headache is already pulsing there, and my fingers twitch like they want to flip the blade out of my ring before I remember it's not there anymore.

Not that my magic would work if I tried it anyway.

"Uh, yeah." He grabs some off the makeshift desk in the corner, composed of a few overturned cardboard boxes.

He eyes me as I slip them on. "The sun still bothers you, doesn't it?"

"I'll live."

His frown deepens. "I'm sure if you told Cam—"

"I'm fine," I snap. The last thing I need is this entire camp of wolves knowing all my weaknesses when I'm already defenseless.

And if they're allied with James Westcott, they're just as untrustworthy.

They're just as much to blame.

He gives a single nod before heading for the tent's opening. "Right this way."

I shuffle after him as he winds through camp.

"Laundry!" he calls.

One by one, people pop out of the tents with handfuls of clothes and shove them into Leif's bags, though their eyes never leave me. I meet their glares head-on, and silently curse myself when one growls and I stumble. His mouth twists—more baring his teeth than smiling—before turning away.

"This is Ledger," says Leif. The man looks the most like a wolf out of the lot of them, even in his human form. A gray and black beard takes up most of his face, and his hair is long and curls past his shoulders. The thick muscles of his arms threaten to burst out of his T-shirt, but of all the tents we've passed so far, he's the first to smile at me.

"Sorry for the welcoming," he grunts, his voice as low as I'd thought it would be. "Not a lot of manners around these parts."

"This is Valerie," says Leif.

Ledger bows his head. "You let me know if these kids give you any trouble, Valerie."

"Thanks," I murmur.

I count twenty-six wolves in total, including Leif and Cam. I suppose there might be others not here at the moment. It seems small for a pack, though I don't have anything to compare it to.

"River's this way," says Leif as he readjusts the bags over his shoulders.

"Do you want me to carry one of those?"

"Nah. Boys are all telling me I need to bulk up anyway." He pauses like he's waiting for me to laugh.

I keep my gaze focused on my feet. The ground is damp and covered in moss—wherever we are, it's humid and considerably warmer than it had been at the compound.

New Jersey. Reid's voice echoes in my mind. *Camden Farley. He's the pack master for some wolves near the Pine Barrens. And he has quite the reputation.*

For?

Cruelty. But he's also been off the map for years. His whole pack, actually.

I don't know Leif well, and maybe it's stupid to trust him so easily. But when he talks about Cam, the look he gets in his eye, it's not fear. It's respect.

I guess I should know better than anyone about how reputations can lie.

At least I know where I am. If we're in New Jersey, we can't be that far from the estate. Not that I can do anything about it, but there's some comfort in the knowledge. Though I wish I'd looked up the Pine Barrens on a map when I had the chance.

The chatter of camp fades behind us as we snake through the woods, Leif's steps confident and quick despite all the trees looking exactly the same. How many times has he made this trek?

How long have they all been living out here?

And why?

I know it's not a wolf thing. Plenty of packs live together but are integrated in society.

The trickle of water pricks my ears, and we run into a small stream a few steps later. I don't know if it's the sun or the shackle around my ankle dimming my senses, but I should've heard that before now.

Leif follows along the water until the trees thin, opening up to a lake.

"If you want to wash up," he says, "you can do that here too. I just wouldn't drink it. Not until we filter it, at least." He sets the bags on the rocks and pulls out the clothes one at a time. "Soap's in the bottom of that one, if you want to grab it." He nods to the bag he emptied. "And there should be some buckets around here somewhere, unless whoever did this last fucked everything up."

I dig around in the bag as he pushes to his feet and pull out a plastic bag of small tablets. I squint at them. Are they...detergent?

"Here they are!" Leif wrestles two buckets out of the bushes, settles himself on the rocks, and gets to work.

He's fast and efficient, so I sit back, not wanting to get in his way, and find a spot under a tree, trying to get out of the sun. He shoves the clothes in the first bucket along with some of the detergent, then rinses them out in the river, beats them against a rock, rinses them again, wrings them out, then tosses them into the second bucket.

Once I get a feel for the process, I pick up a shirt to join him. He smiles at me over his shoulder as we fall into a silent rhythm.

"I heard about what happened," he says after a few minutes. "I know you probably don't want to talk about it, but I just wanted to say I'm sorry."

I wring out the shirt in my hands a little harder than necessary, and the cold water runs down my arms and drips off my elbows. "Thanks, Leif," I murmur.

What happened. Such vague, general words. Emotionless words. So much softer and simpler than whatever the hell is happening inside my chest.

I'd taken the deal to save myself, yes, but also so no one else I cared about would get hurt. But now...

Westcott is so fucking full of shit. I'd known he hadn't meant any of that sentimental bullshit. I *knew* it. If he really wanted me to trust him, he never would have done this. He never would have taken the one person—

"Anyway." Leif turns back to the bucket and adds more water. I force my hands to relax, my knuckles aching from how tightly I'd been gripping the shirt. "Don't let the guys around camp get to you. They'll come around. Most have family or friends who've...not had the best history with the Marionettes, you know?"

"I get it," I say. And I do. I can't even blame them for hating me because I've seen the way the queen and the estate treats the wolves. How little mercy she shows them. The obvious disdain in her voice when she speaks about them. Of course they hate us.

Of course they hate *me*.

How many of them have we executed over the years? Let alone all the laws in place that won't let them step foot in our cities.

"We don't have a lot of rules around here," Leif continues, "but I wouldn't cross Cam. He's not as tough as he seems, but he *is* the pack master, and he doesn't take insubordination lightly. We all have jobs to do, and if you don't work, you don't eat. But above all, do nothing to endanger the pack. We might not like each other half the time, but we look out for each other. And Cam takes fairness and punishment seriously."

I nod, wondering what *punishment* means around here, but I don't ask.

The weight of the sun only increases as time goes on until I can barely keep my eyes open.

"Leif?" I murmur.

He tosses another pair of clean pants into the second bucket. "Yeah?"

"I'm going to need blood. And consistently. Otherwise I'll start eating you guys."

He pauses. "Noted. I'll talk to Cam."

He still has half of the clothes to do, but I retreat to the shade, hoping getting out of the sun will make my head stop spinning. Maybe the tiredness is from completely swapping my sleep schedule overnight. Resting my forehead against my knees, I close my eyes and pull in a deep breath through my nose.

The water splashes as Leif finishes the laundry, and mercifully, he doesn't try to keep the conversation going.

"We've got lines to hang these to dry at camp," he murmurs.

I look up as he washes out the remaining bucket and tucks it where he found it in the trees. He eyes me on the rock, a line forming in his forehead.

"You good to walk back?"

"I'm fine," I say, but when I push to my feet, I sway.

He reaches out a hand to catch me, but I swat him away and steady myself against the tree.

"You should tell Cam that you shouldn't be out in the sun—"

"I'm *fine*, Leif," I snap a little harder than I intended.

He drops his hands and nods once. "Okay." With that, he hefts the bucket up and heads through the trees.

We don't speak the entire walk back.

———

THE SUN SETS NOT long after we return to camp, but the absence of the sun doesn't bring the relief I'd been hoping for. The hunger growls inside of me, far too reminiscent of the uncontrollable kind that plagued me the last few months. I need blood, and soon. And I doubt Cam will appreciate me drinking from his wolves.

Leif disappears with the clean laundry as a wolf I don't know gets a fire started in the center of camp. I linger on the outskirts, already forgetting which tent is supposed to be mine.

"Hey, princess, you want to give me a hand?"

I jump as Cam steps up behind me with a large contrap-

tion in hand. My eyes fall on the lump beside the fire next—a
deer? Cam props the long rod on his shoulder, clearly meant
for spit roasting. He pauses, his eyes lingering on my face.

"Terrence!" he calls. "Hold on with that. You gut it
yet?"

My stomach bottoms out at the sound of his name. He
grunts something that sounds like a negative.

Another man appears at Cam's side, taking the other
end of the rod, and they carry it to the fire.

"Let Darkmore have it first," Cam says.

Terrence steps out from behind the fire, the flames
dancing across his scowl. "She won't know what she's
doing," he barks.

"Not to prep it, you idiot," says Cam. Over his shoulder
to me he adds, "Hope you're not a picky eater."

The blood, I realize. He wants me to drink the blood
from that dead animal. Just the thought of it makes me
want to gag. A slow smile spreads on Terrence's face.

"Hey, Cam!" someone calls from across the camp.

He sighs, leaves the setup to the others, and jogs off in
that direction.

"Well, come on then," says Terrence, a smile in his
voice, though there's nothing friendly about it.

I glance around and swallow hard. None of the few
wolves I know are around. I slowly make my way toward
him as the others set up logs and chairs around the fire,
paying me no mind. The deer's carcass is lying in the dirt at
Terrence's feet, and I'm sure he's hoping I'm going to get
on the ground to drink from it. Something he'll enjoy the
sight of all too much.

I'm nearly there when he sidesteps in front of the deer,

blocking my path.

Of course he isn't going to make this easy.

Slowly, I look up at his face. The shadows cast from the fire cling to his tattoo, making the lines look thicker and deeper.

"You hungry, little vampire?" he coos.

I stare at him, expressionless, refusing to let him see that *yes*, after being in the sun all day, my body is *aching* for it. Even the thought of sinking my teeth into a dead animal's fur right now isn't as repulsive as it should be. Not as long as it satisfies the hunger.

"Are you going to get out of my way or not?"

He tilts his head to the side. "I want to hear you beg for it."

A few guys around us stop what they're doing, watching us.

I hold Terrence's gaze and keep my voice perfectly even as I say, "Like you begged me for your life?"

Red slowly creeps up his face as a vein bulges in his neck. "I'd watch yourself, little Darkmore."

"Oh, is that not something you want them to know?" I ask, my voice overly sweet as I turn to look at the others, all who have stopped to watch us now. "How it only took a few minutes for you to break and tell me everything I wanted to know—"

It happens too fast for my brain to process. The only things that come through are the sounds. The tearing of fabric, shouts somewhere behind me, a deep, guttural growl.

But what comes next is the pain. Blistering hot and razor sharp, it follows me into the dark.

CHAPTER THIRTEEN

REID

THE SUN SETS LATE this time of year, which couldn't be any more inconvenient. I get up a few hours before sunset, wide awake despite barely sleeping. I spent most of the early evening digging through my old leads. They led nowhere before, but maybe I was looking in the wrong places.

I'd found Westcott in Canada. Though he was posing as the specialist from Auclair, that seemed more a moment of convenience for him rather than an orchestrated plan. He'd already been in Canada—for what, I'm not sure. But it's a start.

Then there's the lead from Madison—Camden Farley. His pack has been rumored to be somewhere in the Pine Barrens. Considering the area spans over a million acres, that hardly narrows it down. I doubt Westcott would be anywhere near the pack either, but Farley must be in contact with him. He must know something.

He has to.

If she's with Farley...

I don't let myself finish the thought.

Her ring drums against my collarbone, now on a cord around my neck, as I jog down the estate's stairs.

So I won't lose it, I tell myself.

The first thing I did was have a witch at the estate try to trace it, but she hadn't seen anything. Based on the look on her face, she definitely thought that meant Valerie was dead.

But no.

I remember the moment the bond broke all too well. The pain was enough to bring me to my knees.

But it was too sudden. Too fast.

If she'd died, if she'd really struggled and fought and bled out like that scene in the cell was meant to lead me to believe, I would've felt that. I would've felt her pain, her fear, before it all went black.

I'm sure of it.

I don't have the first idea about finding a pack of wolves, but I know someone who might. Whether he'll be willing to help could go either way, considering the last time I saw him my mother was banishing him for being in a relationship with one. Tracking him down could be a dead end, but it's better than nothing.

And I need to get out of the region. Tonight. We've been increasing border security with the attacks—more and more every week.

Things have quieted down since the wendigos and the bunker, something my mother has tried to pass off as a victory. But what most of the public doesn't know is she didn't drive them out. They left on their own.

We all know that won't be the end of it.

And I know my mother. Her patience is thin, and appearances are everything. If she can't get this under control, and soon, people will question her. I can't risk getting stuck on this side if she closes the borders entirely.

"I need to talk to you."

I freeze on the estate's front porch, blinking back to my surroundings. A yellow taxi is parked a few feet away, and Connor climbs out of the back seat. The hell is he doing here? I've only seen him a handful of times since he moved out, and *now* he shows up? I don't have time for this.

He waits until the car drives off before adding, "I'm coming with you."

I blink. "What?"

The harsh lines on his face remain. "You're going after her, aren't you? You think she's still alive."

"I didn't—"

"I can feel you."

I stare at him, my protests dying in my throat. "Fine," I finally say. "I think she's alive. But you're not coming with me." I start to step around him, but he grabs my sleeve and pulls me to a stop.

"I'm coming whether you like it or not."

My eyes narrow. "Why do you care?" The last few months he's done nothing but flaunt his indifference toward her, something I felt cut her deeper and deeper every time despite the smile she tried to keep on her face. And now suddenly he wants to… "You care," I murmur, the realization sinking into the pit of my stomach like a rock in the water.

His scowl deepens, and he drops his gaze to the ground between us. Valerie and I had both pretty much given up hope that the change in Connor's personality would fade. Not after all this time. But now, if he's starting to...

Oh, God.

"Look, if this is about whatever's been going on between you two, I don't care. I'm still coming." My eyes shoot to his face, and he gives me a humorless smile. "This really worked out for you, didn't it?"

"I didn't mean for any of this to happen," I snap.

"Save it." He shakes his head. "We both know you didn't turn me for me. You didn't even do it for her. You did it because if you were involved with my death, you knew she'd never forgive you."

I hold his glare, but I don't argue. Because he's right. It wasn't the only reason, but I'd be lying if I said that hadn't been a big part of it. Of course she never would've forgiven me. Never would've trusted me again. But that doesn't mean I *wanted* him to die. To see how much losing him ripped her apart.

He lifts an eyebrow. "You don't even know where you're going, do you? How do you know I couldn't help? I know her better than anyone."

I hate the twinge in my chest the words cause. Because he's right. He *does* know her better than anyone, and I *don't* know where I'm going.

"Don't slow me down," I finally say.

He nods and takes a step back, and I notice for the first time the pack slung over his shoulder. "I'll go get a car."

THE DRIVE IS A QUIET ONE. Connor speeds the estate's car through the city, expertly weaving in and out of traffic. I vaguely wonder how he learned to drive, but maybe the estate taught him in case he needed to run errands for his job.

The thought makes my stomach sour for some reason. The moonlight cuts across his jawline through the windshield as he grinds his teeth. I'd tried to insist on driving, but he'd made a good point. Getting out of the region won't be an easy feat, especially with a face as recognizable as mine.

Much easier to hide from view when you're not in the driver's seat.

Even that might not be enough though. Not if my mother has already noticed my absence and anticipates what I'm doing. If she's called mandatory stops at the border to ensure I can't leave, we aren't going anywhere.

Not through the official points, at least.

"An estate car outside the boundaries will draw a lot of eyes," Connor says without looking at me. "We'll need to switch cars or go on foot."

I'd been thinking the same thing. Getting across the border with it would be a challenge, but it can get us close.

I rub my hand against my chest, fingers pressing into the bone. Ever since the bond broke, that part of my brain has been quiet, but I can feel the place it used to be like an unnatural hole. Today, though, for the first time since it happened, a feeling sparked through. A heartburn sort of ache.

What it means, I have no idea.

Maybe it's psychosomatic. I want to feel her there, so I do—that kind of thing.

Or maybe, just maybe, it's something else.

"There's a good chance this road trip ends with both of us dying, you know," I say lightly.

"I know."

I glance at him sideways, at the utter lack of concern on his face—the same look he'd had when I went to ask for his help before Valerie's final trial all those nights ago. No worry for his personal well-being.

Only hers.

I swallow hard and look away.

I'd felt how much losing him had torn her apart as much as I'd seen it in her eyes. But now? If we find her, and she sees she gave up on him too soon…

"So this has been happening since the wendigo attack at the academy? Val's…condition?"

His voice snaps me back to the present, and I shake my head and rub my sternum. "Yes."

Connor nods slowly, a muscle feathering along his jaw. I don't need to feel him through the bond to read the emotions written all over him. *Guilt.* Because in all that time she'd been struggling, he'd been pushing her away and avoiding her. He was the one person she needed the most, and he wasn't there.

Not that it would've changed anything.

His hands tighten around the wheel until white splits across his knuckles.

"Look," I sigh. "It's not your fault—"

"I really don't need you to talk to me about my girl-friend," he snaps.

I clench my teeth to stop myself from correcting his word choice. We fall back into silence, though the tension between us is twice as thick now.

"Head toward New Jersey," I say after a while.

He shoots me a questioning look but complies.

"And I hope you know how to swim," I add.

His head whips all the way to the side this time. "You can't be serious."

I shrug, my gaze still trained out the windshield. "We'll never make it through the checkpoint."

"And you think they won't notice two guys in the water?"

"Not if they don't see us."

"And how are we going to make sure——"

"By not coming up for air," I say.

He scoffs.

"You're a vampire now," I remind him. "Breathing is a habit, an impulse. It feels unnatural not to, but you don't need it. And it's only about a mile."

"A mile," he grunts under his breath, shaking his head. "You're insane."

I shrug, turning to scan out the window as we near the border. "You insisted on coming. If you want to drop me off and head back——"

"Obviously I'm going to do it." He glances at me out of the corner of his eye. "But I swear to God, if this is your idea of a joke or how you're planning to get me out of the way, I *will* come back as a ghost and haunt the shit out of you."

For the first time since she left, I smile.

CHAPTER FOURTEEN

VALERIE

SOMETHING COLD DRIPS DOWN my face. I jolt upright, and for a moment, I have no idea where I am. My surroundings are not at all familiar. The canvas of the tent does little to shade the sun overhead, and I squint, then gasp as I realize I'm not alone.

Sitting at the foot of the cot is a man with scruff covering his jaw and neck. He's holding a wet cloth in his hands, and it drips onto the cot between us. The water is tinged red with blood. I touch my face, and my hand comes away with a mixture of cold water and blood.

It's only then that I notice the pain.

The ache is bone deep. I reach for my face, but the man grabs my hand before I can make contact and shakes his head.

"I wouldn't touch it," he says. "I need to finish cleaning it."

I narrow my eyes. Leif introduced him to me yesterday, but I can't remember his name.

"Ledger," he says, bowing his head. "I'm the only healer around here, so unfortunately, you're stuck with me." He gives me a slight smile, but I don't return it. "May I?" He gestures to my face with the cloth.

I nod.

Pulling out a bottle from a pack I hadn't noticed at his feet, he wets the cloth, and the sharp stench of alcohol fills the tent.

"Don't want this getting infected," he murmurs as he draws closer to me.

I eye the cloth warily but let him bring it to my mouth. I inhale sharply as it makes contact, and the ache quickly shifts into a burn, so loud it echoes all the way down my body.

"I know," he murmurs as he gently presses the cloth in small dabs. "Almost done. I'm just going to lift your lip to see how bad it is on the inside, okay?"

I give him a little nod and close my eyes. He prods my mouth with one finger. A new wave of pain lances through me, and I clench my teeth, a low moan sounding in the back of my throat. But what really makes my stomach flip is how easily my lip lifts for him as he comes back with a Q-tip and starts fishing around. It feels like my lip is split clean in half.

"How bad is it?" I ask, my voice coming out small as he tosses the bloody Q-tip and cloth in a pile at his feet.

"It'll scar," he says, digging through his pack. "And it'll need stitches. But you're lucky he didn't hit your eye."

I glare at the shackle around my ankle. If I could take it off, my body could have this healed within the hour.

"What happened?" I whisper.

He hesitates with a cream in his hands and chews on his lower lip.

"Terrence has always had a short fuse. It doesn't take much to make him shift." He meets my eyes. "You were standing too close."

His phrasing makes me grit my teeth, as if this is my fault.

Though I suppose it is. I don't know why I'd thought goading him last night was a good idea, but I couldn't stand that smug look on his face. The same look he'd given me in the tattoo shop that day before he'd realized I was an actual threat.

And now with this stupid thing around my ankle, the playing field looks very different.

Ledger smears whatever the cream is across my lips and up toward my cheek, so the gash must be larger than I'd originally thought. Surprisingly, getting the actual stitches doesn't hurt as much as cleaning the wound had —or maybe whatever cream he'd used help numb the area. When he's done, I run my tongue along the inside of my upper lip and wince. The taste of blood fills my mouth, and the entire inside of my mouth feels like raw meat.

"I'll need to come check on you daily, at least for a few days, to make sure it's healing properly and not getting infected. Just try to keep it clean. Cam also asked me to bring you this."

He pulls a blood bag out of his pack, and my mouth waters at the sight of it. My pride apparently nonexistent at the moment, I snatch it out of his hand and tear into it. My lip screams in protest as I wrap my mouth around the plastic opening, but I ignore it. The blood is lukewarm and stale, but I drink every last drop.

Where did he get one of these all the way out here?

"You'll be expected to attend the sentencing as well as everyone else," Ledger adds as he starts packing up his bag. He pauses and checks the watch on his wrist. "Should be any minute now, actually."

"The sentencing?" I ask, attempting to lick the blood from my lips without disturbing the wound. In the end, I have to dab the back of my hand against my mouth instead.

"For Terrence," Ledger says as if it's obvious.

I stare at him. "Because of me?"

Ledger nods. "Cam has a strict policy. No violence against other pack members at the camp. Apparently you're included in that now. And my guess is with the unrest you showing up here caused, he's going to want to set the precedent now before we have any more problems." He pushes to his feet and slings the strap of his bag over his shoulder before looking at me on the cot. "How are you feeling? Any light-headedness?"

I slowly push myself up to standing, the blood I inhaled lifting the exhaustion in my limbs as it works through my system. "I'm all right."

He nods toward the tent's opening. "We should get going then."

I swipe the sunglasses off the top of the overturned boxes and slip them on before following him outside. It's surprisingly quiet as I follow Ledger through the other tents and past where the fire had been set up for dinner last night. My stomach gurgles quietly, and I try to remember the last time I ate something. It was before coming here, and who even knows how long I'd been unconscious in that car on the way. It's been at least a few days.

"Where is everyone?" I murmur.

"Probably already there," he says without looking at me.

Ledger crosses the clearing with the tents and continues through the trees. I hurry my steps to keep up with him, grateful for the cloud cover today. It doesn't completely numb the effects of the sun, but it dilutes it.

Voices carry on the wind the farther we walk until we come to a second smaller clearing, no more than a few minutes away from the first.

Ledger was right; everyone else is already here. He breaks off from me and disappears into the crowd, and I glance around, looking for Leif. I find him near the outskirts of the crowd, and he gives me a grim smile as he sees me approach.

"Hey," he says, then holds out a waterskin.

I immediately accept it, then wince as I try to maneuver it around my injured mouth. I can feel Leif inspecting my mouth as I swallow three huge gulps.

"They wouldn't let me come check on you," he says. "Shit, that looks bad."

"Thanks, Leif." I hand the waterskin back to him.

"You know what I mean."

I try to peer through the crowd to see what everyone is facing, but being at least a full foot shorter than everyone else here, I can't see anything. Well, except for the towering tree trunk in the center of the clearing. A knot forms in my stomach.

"Come on." Leif nudges me. "You'll be expected to be up front."

"What? Why?"

He raises his eyebrows at me as if it's obvious as he hooks his hand through my elbow and leads me through the crowd. Instead of the looks of disdain I'm expecting, everyone steps aside and lets us pass when they notice who it is.

"Because this is for you," Leif says.

My next words die on my tongue as we reach the front of the crowd. Terrence is already there in front of the tree trunk, Cam standing behind him. Cam glances at me for a split second before meeting Leif's eyes over my head and giving a swift nod.

All conversation in the crowd quiets as Terrence fists his hand in the back of his T-shirt and yanks it over his head, revealing the tanned skin of his back. He says nothing. He just leans forward and wraps his arms around the trunk. Another dark-haired man steps forward and binds Terrence's hands with rope.

My eyes shoot from Terrence's back to Cam behind him, a sour taste rising to the back of my throat as I realize what's about to happen.

Another man steps up behind Cam, handing him a whip. Cam doesn't look at him as he takes it, veins bulging in the back of his hand as he grips the leather handle. The whip itself, however, glints as Cam positions his feet, the metal chain catching the sunlight. Just looking at it makes me wince. The edges are jagged, sharp.

I lean closer to Leif. "Why is it...?" I whisper.

"So he won't heal right away."

I swallow hard as Cam raises his eyes to take in the rest of the crowd. "Terrence McCullough, I sentence you to ten lashes for the crime of harming someone under the care of this pack. Unless someone is willing to take on your punishment…?" Cam trails off, his eyes sweeping the crowd.

I glance sideways at Leif.

"Proxy law," he murmurs with a shrug. "It's not common. Usually when you have parents and kids in the same pack."

"So let this be a warning to the rest of you, wolf or not," Cam continues when it becomes clear no one plans on stepping in. "The residents of this camp are not to be harmed. Have I made myself clear?"

Grumbles of agreement rise up from the crowd, and without warning, Cam turns back to Terrence and lands the first blow.

Every muscle in my body tenses as the metal cuts through flesh and blood splatters onto the dirt surrounding the tree. Terrence hunches forward under the impact, but he doesn't make a sound. When the whip falls to Cam's side, it's already slick with blood. Crimson beads well on Terrence's back and seep toward the ground. Barely a few seconds pass before Cam strikes a second time, then a third.

Despite the throbbing emanating from my lip and the rage that fills me as I remember that day in the tattoo shop —the cold cruelness in his eyes—still, watching him bow under the whip and blood run in rivulets down his back brings me no satisfaction.

Because this is for you.

But I didn't ask for this. I don't want this. If he hated me before, it'll be nothing compared to now.

Terrence finally lets out a grunt of pain with the sixth lash. The crowd is silent—no gasps, no conversation. It's so quiet I feel like everyone can hear the short pants of my breath. The sound of metal tearing through Terrence's skin fills the clearing—an ugly, wet sound.

Blood coats Cam's arm and is splattered across the front of his flannel shirt. My gaze drifts to his face, not sure what I'm expecting to find. But he wears the same grim expression he had before he started—his mouth set in a hard line, his eyes cold. He could be thinking anything. Feeling anything.

But his lashes don't slow, the movements precise and strong, like he's done this many times before.

And he probably has.

He has a reputation, Reid had said.

For what?

Cruelty.

But if he's enjoying this in any way, it doesn't show.

Terrence grits his teeth as the eighth lash lands across the raw wounds crisscrossing his back. He turns his head to spit into the dirt as his knees buckle, nearly bringing his shins to the ground. Cam waits for him to pull himself to his feet. The wind picks up, rustling through the trees, and Cam wipes the back of his hand across his forehead, smearing Terrence's blood along his face.

I hold my breath as he finally finishes, and the man from before returns to untie Terrence's wrists. No one says a word as he slumps against the tree. But when the man tries to help him, Terrence growls and yanks his arm away. After a moment, he shoves himself to his feet, steadying himself on the tree.

Cam stands with the whip hanging at his side, blood dripping onto the earth, and gives the man a nod as Terrence turns and shoulders his way through the crowd. His movements are slow, stiff, but I'm surprised he can walk at all. He spits onto the ground but doesn't look at me as he passes. Leif inches closer, and I feel the heat of his body against my back.

"What are you all doing standing around?" Cam barks. "Get back to work!"

He meets my eyes, his face covered in blood and sweat, his mouth in a firm line, before he turns and disappears toward camp.

I'VE ALWAYS THOUGHT I had a high pain tolerance, but I guess that's easy to say when you know it'll only last for a little while. That you're guaranteed to heal.

Each step I take causes pain to lance up my face, the throbbing in my lip never easing as I follow Leif back to camp. My face is swollen and tender, only further accentuated by the sensitivity brought on by the sunlight beating down on my skin. But even if I thought Cam would let me out of working today because of it, I still wouldn't say anything.

I've never sewn anything before, but somehow I ended up in charge of fixing everyone's damaged clothing today. There's something vaguely sexist about it. Or maybe Cam thought I wouldn't be up for anything that caused too much moving around.

Maybe that's giving him too much credit.

I find a place to set up in the trees—close enough to camp that I don't get lost, but far enough that I don't have to overhear conversations, or worse, get pulled into one.

"Shit," I mutter as I stab my finger with the needle for the hundredth time. I stick it in my mouth as blood wells on the surface. The lack of response from my magic serves as an unneeded reminder of my situation.

"Darkmore," Cam's voice calls behind me, close enough that I know he sees me.

I don't respond and tear the thread with my teeth.

"We stop at sundown. Come on. Dinner's almost ready."

I stab the needle through the pants in my hands. "I'm almost done," I mutter.

He says nothing for long enough that I think he's left, but then the brush crunches to my left as he comes closer. I don't look at him.

"You can stop. Those can wait."

"I'm almost done," I repeat.

Actually, with the speed I've been going, even with only a few shirts left, it'll take me at least an hour. But I don't care. It's nice, almost, to have something to do with my hands. Something pointless to focus on.

"What are you trying to prove?"

My hands finally still, and I turn. "I'm not trying to prove anything."

The comment makes me pause though. Am I trying to prove something? That I'm not useless? That I'm capable? That I can handle whatever job they give me?

Cam holds my gaze for a moment. "It'll be too dark to

146

see well enough in a few minutes," he mutters, then turns and heads back for camp.

He's right, but even once the darkness falls and I can barely see my hands in front of me, I wait in the trees as sounds of laughter and a spitting fire trickle through the air.

My stomach growls, but I shove the hunger down and retire to my tent instead. The exhaustion has seeped all the way to my bones, and no amount of food would be worth having to interact with all of them right now. Conversation seeps in as I zip the tent shut and crawl into bed.

I wince as my face hits the pillow. Even lying on my opposite side makes the gash in my lip throb. I don't have a reference point for injuries like this. How long will this take to heal? If it really is cut clean through my lip like it feels, it would take a while, even if my healing abilities were functioning. But without them? Will it be days? Weeks? Longer? I grit my teeth and swipe the back of my hand against my cheeks as tears leak out of the corners of my eyes.

Reid's jacket is right where I left it, tucked between the cot and the side of the tent. I pull it out and bunch it under my chin, closing my eyes and breathing deeply through my nose. The smell of him is faint, fading. How long do I have until it's gone?

How long after that until I forget it completely?

A lump rises in my throat, and I tighten my arms on the jacket, curling my body around it. The sight of him in that body bag burns in the back of my mind, radiating sharper and deeper than the pain in my face.

But worst still is the brief moment—barely the space between heartbeats—where I close my eyes, and the scent of him fills my head, and I forget.

147

I forget about what I saw at the compound, what West-cott told me.

I forget about the coldness of his skin and the stillness of his chest. And think, just for a second, that if I can survive this, if I can hold out for a little while longer, he'll find me. He'll come for me. I'll see him again. I'll get to go home, and all this will be a distant, dark memory.

But I won't. Even if I make it out of here, even if by some miracle I get out of this deal with Westcott and get to go home, he won't be there.

He won't ever flash me that stupid grin of his again. I won't ever breathe in the musky smell of his skin or feel the softness of his hair between my fingers. I won't feel his arms around me as I fall asleep or the pulse of the bond between us as he looks at me. I won't hear his deep, contagious laugh or see his dreams or hold his hand or listen to him breathe while he sleeps or hear him say my name ever again.

A sob breaks free, and I slap a hand over my mouth to stifle it. I press my face into his jacket, ignoring the screaming protest the wound in my face gives, and lie there until I finally cry myself to sleep.

CHAPTER FIFTEEN

REID

WE DON'T MAKE it to the water. Traffic comes to a complete stop a good half mile from the checkpoint, and Connor and I exchange a look.

"This isn't normal, is it?" he asks.

I shake my head and peer out the window. They could be doing searches.

Or they could not be letting anyone through at all.

We could be too late.

Connor drums his fingers against the steering wheel, his growing anxiety palpable. I strain my neck, but the line of cars is too long to see what's going on at the other end. All streets that feed into this one are also at a standstill. If the bridge is this backed up, I'm willing to bet the tunnel isn't any better.

"Get out of this line," I say.

"How the hell am I supposed to do that?" Connor gestures to the traffic packing us in.

He's right, of course. But abandoning the car and running through the lines of stalled vehicles will draw more attention than I'd like.

And yet.

"Grab your bag," I say, already twisting to grab mine from the back seat. I expect him to protest, but he complies and doesn't ask questions as I tug a hat on, low enough to cover my eyes, then pull the hood of my jacket over it. "Keep your head down and follow me."

Rain patters softly on the pavement as we slip from the car, and the glow of red taillights surrounds us. I take off at a jog. A few horns blare, and someone rolls down their window to call out to us, but their voice is lost to the wind.

I head in the opposite direction of the bridge, wanting to put as much distance between us and the checkpoint as possible.

The stopped cars continue the next street over, and the next. *What the hell is going on?*

"Get out of your vehicle!" someone shouts up ahead. I freeze and raise a hand for Connor to do the same, trusting the footsteps that have been slapping against the wet pavement behind me are him.

I squint through the rain and duck into a nearby alley. Connor flattens himself against the wall beside me.

"What is it—?"

I hold up a hand to stop him as I lean into the street. A tall man in a Marionettes uniform is standing beside a silver car with the driver's window rolled down. The woman inside is gesturing frantically with her hands, the rain plastering her short blond hair to her cheeks.

A second man steps up next to the Marionette, taller and with darker hair.

A vampire.

The Marionette's partner, I'm willing to guess.

He smiles warmly at the woman and leans his hands against her open window.

My throat tightens, already knowing what happens next.

"I believe my partner asked you to get out of the car," he says.

The woman blinks, the panic in her eyes ebbing away, and she slowly opens the door and steps out. The drivers of the surrounding cars are staring at the three standing in the rain, but no one intervenes.

Of course they don't.

Not if they don't want to be next.

"What did she do?" Connor whispers.

"Nothing, I'm willing to bet," I murmur. I glance up and down the street, but there doesn't seem to be anyone else patrolling this part.

"Screaming will only make this unpleasant for all of us," says the vampire as he brushes the woman's hair behind her shoulder. She trembles beneath his touch but doesn't try to move away.

I grind my molars together, and I'm surging out of the alley before making the conscious choice to. I barely make it a step before Connor hooks his arm through mine and yanks me back.

"You're going to get us caught," he says through his teeth. "Let's just go down a few streets while they're distracted."

I stare at him for a moment, and rain trails down the sides of his face. I didn't know him when he was a human. Maybe I saw him in passing at the estate, but I hadn't known who he was.

But I'd *felt* how Valerie felt about him. How highly she thought of him.

The selflessness I'd seen in his face when I'd gone to him in the cell.

I can't even ask him *What happened to you?* because *I* did.

"I'm not just going to let her die," I say, pulling my arm out of his grasp.

She doesn't scream as the vampire sinks his fangs into her neck, but she lets out a choked sob. The rain muffles my footsteps so they don't hear me coming.

At least not until it's too late.

I go for the Marionette first. Not knowing what kind of magic he has, I'm not taking any chances. The force I use to slam his head against the nearby SUV isn't enough to kill him, but it'll knock him out.

The vampire hisses as he whips around, the woman still clutched in his arms.

I squint against the headlights, and a gust of wind sweeps over us, shoving back the hood of my jacket.

The vampire's eyes go wide.

Shit.

"Your—Your Highness, we were just...we were going to let her go..."

The woman's eyes are half-closed, her body limp against him. Clearly in no state to walk away from this, let alone get in her car and drive.

"Were you?" I say, my voice light. Blood weeps from the

wound on her neck, mingling with the rain as it drips onto the street.

He swallows audibly.

Connor clears his throat behind me, something I probably wouldn't pay attention to if it weren't for the sudden spike of anxiety in the bond.

I glance over my shoulder to see four figures jogging toward us, backlit by the car headlights.

I can't just leave her here. He'll either finish her off or let her bleed out in the street.

"Give her to me."

"Reid," Connor says under his breath.

"Of—of course, I—"

I take the woman from him and scoop her into my arms, her body lighter than it should be from the blood loss. I meet the man's eyes. "It would be wise for you to reconsider your priorities in the future."

"Yes, Your Highness." He nods vigorously.

"Stop them!" one of the approaching people calls, his voice gravelly and low.

One that I recognize.

Shit.

"Connor." I jut my chin toward the alley. "Go."

He hesitates as his gaze lingers on the woman, but then he takes off at a run. The air whistles near my head, and whatever they'd shot shatters a nearby car's windshield.

I sprint after Connor, the woman unconscious against my chest. The coppery tang of her blood floods my senses, but I grit my teeth, forcing my eyes to focus on the street in front of us.

They wouldn't shoot to kill—even if they don't know

who I am, but I'm willing to bet their urgency suggests they do—so it must be some kind of tranquilizer. How they found us, I have no idea. Someone at the estate could've overheard or seen us leave. Someone here could have called in a report.

It doesn't matter.

"The hell you going to do with her?" Connor asks as we weave through the dark alleys.

I ignore him, scanning the buildings as we pass. A reasonable question for sure, but one I don't have an answer to yet.

"What street is this?" I ask instead.

"Does it matter?" Connor scoffs, but he slows, taking in the surrounding street signs. "162nd, maybe."

"This way." I veer to the left, and he lets out an impatient noise.

"You're going the *opposite*—"

"Just shut up for a minute." I scan the buildings, hoping I'm remembering things right. It's been over a decade since I was here with Quinn. Hell, the shelter might not be here anymore.

The woman stirs in my arms, murmuring something unintelligible.

"You'll be all right," I say quietly.

Her body twitches like she wants to resist but doesn't have the strength, her fingers getting caught in the chain around my neck. My stomach plummets, the breath completely leaving my lungs.

They look nothing alike, her and Valerie.

But for a moment, it's her I see, in that cell, trying to fight back with no strength left in her.

But that hadn't really happened, had it? The scene had been staged. The blood. The body.

What the hell actually happened?

A ping of metal snaps me into the present. It was this street. I'm sure of it.

There.

It's small, pressed tightly between two larger buildings, with a nondescript door and thick curtains covering the windows. If the lights are on inside, I can't tell.

I ring the bell, then knock for good measure. Connor waits near the corner, his leg bouncing as he glances down the street every few seconds, but it's quiet. Maybe we lost them.

For now.

The door cracks open, held back by the chain. A woman with deep wrinkles around her eyes and graying hair peeks through.

"Can you help her?" I ask.

She looks at the woman in my arms, then abruptly closes the door, the metallic clinks of the chain rustling on the other side. By the time she opens it again, Connor is at my side.

"What happened to her?" asks the older woman, a Russian accent pulling at her words.

"Look, no disrespect meant, but we don't have time for this," Connor cuts in. He grabs the woman from my arms and strides into the building uninvited.

The older woman raises a single eyebrow but doesn't protest as Connor lays the woman on the bench in the entryway.

"Connor—" I start.

He pushes me outside and closes the door behind us. "I hope it was worth it," he mutters as he jogs down the steps.

"She would've died back there!"

"Yeah?" He whips around as he reaches the street. "And Val? You're absolutely sure that she's okay right now? That every minute we waste isn't her last?"

His words hit like a punch to the gut. My hand instinctively goes to the chain around my neck.

But it isn't there.

Fuck. It must have broken off when I was carrying—

"Stop!"

Marionettes pour around the corner, all dressed in black, six of them this time. Connor grabs my sleeve and urges me to run the opposite way, but Valerie's ring, it must have fallen off back there.

I head straight toward the group. Connor yells after me, but I don't hear him, my eyes sweeping the ground, desperate for a glint of metal.

"Prince Reginald," says the man leading the group— Davis, one of my mother's preferred members of the Marionettes. Not as bad as running into Rosemarie Darkmore, but not much better. "We've been sent to escort you back to the estate." He pauses a few paces away and folds his hands in front of his body, both covered with black leather gloves. He smiles at me like an obedient dog. "Now, if you'll come with us."

"Get fucked, Davis," I say, stepping around him.

"We will use any force necessary," he adds.

"Yeah, give that a try."

His minions—whoever the hell they are, I don't recognize any—sidestep and follow my movements.

I'm really not in the mood for this right now.

The skinny one in front of me raises his gun, his hands shaky. A newbie, probably. I rip it from his grasp before he has the chance to point it at me and sink a dart into the side of his neck. He lets out a surprised gasp before going limp in my arms.

Voices layer over each other as the others shout and level their guns at me. I hold the unconscious one up as they fire, their darts perforating his chest as I twist around and shoot one of the women in the arm. She crumples to her knees first, then onto her side.

"Jesus Christ, people," spits Davis. But whatever he was going to say next is cut off with a choked garble.

I whip around to see Connor's fangs tearing into Davis's throat from behind. In my distraction, something pinches my right arm. I spin, sending off another few darts, though I can't see where they land as my vision tilts and blurs.

A shout pierces the air as Connor moves on to the last man standing. Hopefully he's just draining them enough to subdue, not kill. I drop the man in my arms and fall to my knees. My vision swims, but I manage to hold on to consciousness. It would've taken a second dart to knock me out completely. I brace a hand against the pavement, and a hint of light reflects off something on the ground.

Thank God.

I reach forward, the knot in my chest loosening at the familiar feeling of the ring in my hand.

"What the fuck?" Connor snaps. "Are you trying to get us killed?" He kneels beside me. I uncurl my fingers, and he stills as he takes in the ring resting in the center of my palm.

He meets my eyes, the hardness in his expression gone. "Are you good to walk?" he asks after a moment.

"Yeah." The skinny man is within reach, so I grab his arm and pull him closer. After a little blood I should be fine.

Connor sighs and wipes the back of his hand along his mouth. "Just give me a heads-up next time, okay?"

CHAPTER SIXTEEN

REID

"WHY THE FUCK ARE YOU WET?"

The rain is pouring in earnest now, but that's nothing compared to the ice-cold water from the river soaking through every inch of my clothing.

Unsurprisingly, Jared hasn't changed. He's looked pretty much the same since we were teenagers, though he finally grew into his nose when we hit our twenties. His dark hair is longer, the curls reaching his chin. He stands in the doorway, the wide set of his shoulders blocking the view of the rest of the cabin as his gaze drifts from me to Connor, and his eyebrows lift until they nearly disappear into his hairline.

"Are you going to let us in or not?" I ask.

Jared looks back to me, and we grin at the same time. He crushes me in a hug and slaps my back twice.

"Good to see you, mate," he says.

The cabin is small but exactly what I'd expect despite never being inside of it. The walls are painted a bright orange, though they're barely visible beneath the various tapestries and woven decorations. The living room leads directly into the dining area and into the kitchen, but somehow, it's a seamless transition between spaces rather than a single, cluttered area. It makes sense for him. The deep woody smell of the place would make me think of him even if he weren't right in front of me. All that space at the estate, the glamour, the extravagance—it never suited him. And I knew he never wanted it to.

Bells chime above the door as Connor steps inside and closes it behind him. Jared's eyes shoot from the fireplace roaring in the corner, to the kitchen, to our wet clothes. "We have a dryer," he says wryly.

"Is Jia here?" I ask as he dips into a door off the kitchen.

"She should be back soon!" he calls before returning with some dry clothes in hand. "I don't see you for five years and you come for my *wife*? Low blow." He grins as he hands me the piles. His eyes flick to Connor before he heads to the kitchen. "I see court life has made you lose your manners."

"This is Connor. He's…" I exchange a look with Connor, debating how much to get into it.

"So what the hell happened?" Jared asks without turning.

I hand half of the clothes to Connor. "You're going to have to be more specific."

"*I'll never be a maker*—were those not your exact words?" He cracks the refrigerator open and pulls out three beers.

Connor meets my eyes before disappearing into the

bathroom to change. Jared's always been exceptionally perceptive. I guess I shouldn't be surprised. He raises his eyebrows expectantly as the door clicks shut.

"It's complicated," I sigh, taking the beer from him.

"How the hell did the two of you get over here?" The floor creaks under his feet as he heads for the couch and drops into the spot on the end. "They've completely closed the borders down."

I sink into the wooden chair opposite him and take a long drink of the beer. So that explains the chaos. But why? I hadn't heard any plans of that before leaving the estate.

Jared's expression sobers as he braces his forearms on his knees and leans forward. When he speaks again, his voice is low. "And not that I'm not glad to see you, but you chose a real shit time to come."

My eyes flick back to his face. "Why?"

Jared shakes his head. "There's been a bounty out for any vampires from the estates or Marionettes on this side of the boundary. A generous amount. Too generous. No one knows who's behind it, but that's my best guess as to why dear old Mom closed the borders. Any one of you who has stepped foot on this side over the past few days hasn't made it back."

"You two are brothers?" Connor asks, returning from the bathroom.

"Half," supplies Jared. "Not public knowledge though. Mommy Dearest never felt the need to claim me like she did this one." His eyes widen for a moment as he glances from the soaked clothes in Connor's hands back to me. "You little shit," he murmurs. "You two swam here, didn't you?" There's nothing accusatory in his voice. Mostly just amusement. The smirk he gives me is all too familiar, the look he'd get on his face when we were young and he'd gotten information he could use against me should it ever come to that.

Not that it ever did. Despite only being a year older, he's always been more protective of me than either of my parents ever were, or our other siblings, for that matter.

The mirth drains from his eyes. "Why the hell did you need to get over here so bad?"

"You mind?" Connor strides to the kitchen, pointing to the remaining beer sitting on the counter.

Jared waves his hand. "Go ahead."

I sigh as Connor turns his back on us and takes a long swig. "That's why I'm here, Jared. I need to speak to Jia. I think her old pack might be able to help me find someone."

"Someone?" he pushes.

"My partner," I say, trying to ignore the dip in my stomach.

Jared nods slowly and leans back in the couch. "I didn't know you'd been paired again."

"It was...recent."

His eyes narrow as he takes another drink, but there's a softness in his expression now. Pity. "Reid, if this is about Graham—"

"It's not about Graham," I snap.

Connor turns back to us, but I don't look at him.

"You can't keep holding on to this guilt forever," continues Jared as if I hadn't spoken. "Anyone in that position would've done what you did—"

"It's *not* about Graham," I repeat, louder this time. It's

been years, but even with that barrier of time passed, the name is still suffocating. I go days without thinking about it now, something I never thought would happen. But for once, this isn't about the guilt.

Not with her.

Jared raises his palms. "All right. All right." He nods at Connor. "How does the baby vampire fit into this? No offense."

Connor snorts, probably wondering how the hell I'm going to explain that.

I focus on the bottle in my hands, the cool condensation along the glass. "He's important to my partner," I say after a beat. "And her final trial was..."

"Fucked up?" suggests Connor.

I flick one of my hands up.

The front door flies open and bangs against the wall. Rain slants in through the open door and splashes against the rug. "Sorry, sorry!" calls a woman's voice as she steps into the house backward, her arms covered in various overflowing tote bags. She shuffles along, then kicks the door shut. "You should have *seen* the line at the—" She freezes as she turns and takes in me and Connor, then slowly lets the bags slide to the floor.

I clear my throat. "Good to see you, Jia."

Her dark eyes narrow. "The last time I saw you, your mother was threatening to rip out my teeth."

I grimace. "Can't choose your family."

She shakes her head and hauls the bags onto her shoulders. "As if one vampire under this roof wasn't bad enough," she mutters as she heads to the kitchen.

"You *married* this vampire," Jared calls, then jumps up and follows to help with the bags.

"And my parents lament leaving China every day because of it." She elbows him in the ribs, but she's smiling. "*Them* I made no vow to." She points a carrot at me and Connor. "You know you have a hefty little price tag on your head, right?"

"So I've heard," I say. "We'll be out of your hair tonight, Jia. But I was hoping you could answer a few questions about your old pack."

She freezes in the middle of the kitchen, scrutinizing me, then Connor. "The fuck do you want with a bunch of wolves? They'd definitely turn you over for the money."

"Does the name Camden Farley mean anything to you?" I ask.

A laugh bursts from her lips. "You're looking for *Farley?*" Jared lays a hand on her arm, and they exchange a look. Whatever she sees in his face makes the amusement drain from her own. "His pack moves constantly," she says slowly. "I could tell you where I saw them last, but they've probably moved on from there. I guess I could point you to my old pack master. She's seen him more recently than I have."

"Any information you have would be appreciated," I murmur.

"Reid...they won't take kindly to a Carrington vampire in their territory."

"I know."

"No, I mean they might kill you on the spot—"

"Can you help us find them or not?"

I blink up in surprise at Connor's voice. For once there's

no anger, no impatience. There's a softness, a desperation in his expression that I'm willing to bet is mirrored in mine.

Jia sighs and leans against the counter. After a moment, she nods. "I just hope you know what you're getting yourselves into."

CHAPTER SEVENTEEN

VALERIE

TIME BLURS TOGETHER. After the incident with Terrence, I keep my head down and pass my days with whatever job Cam gives me, then retreat to my tent at my first opportunity, spending my hours curled in bed around Reid's jacket. I keep waiting for the pain to subside. For the hole inside of me to heal. For his face to stop showing up in my dreams.

But the only thing that changes is his scent fading from his jacket.

The gash in my lip is mostly healed. The skin is raised, textured, though I haven't looked in a mirror to see how bad it looks.

But to my surprise, Terrence hasn't tried anything else. He hasn't spared me a glance around camp on the few occasions we've crossed paths. Not that I plan on getting too comfortable.

Breakfast is leftover stew from dinner. Squirrel. Of all the animal blood I've had to choke down since being here, that was by far the worst. Despite swallowing every last drop from my bowl, the hunger inside of me doesn't subside.

"Here." I blink to see Cam standing in front of me, backlit by the sun. A few others are lingering on the logs surrounding the remains of last night's fire, their breakfasts in their laps. I squint as he extends a blood bag. I can't even hesitate before snatching it out of his hand and rising to my feet.

Cam watches me as I tear into the bag and quickly down the entire thing, then lick my lips for good measure.

"We'll try to get more to keep in stock around here," he says as I wipe the back of my hand across my mouth. "You're in the blacksmith tent today. The others will show you what to do."

I turn, eyes scanning the surrounding tents. I still haven't mastered my way around, especially with so many tents I've never been in. Cam sighs and points to the large one near the center of camp with smoke rising out the back.

"Right." My nose wrinkles as I consider my next words, if it's even worth it, since the answer has been the same every other time I've asked.

"Still no word from Westcott," Cam says, reading my mind. "But there's a good chance he won't reach out before showing up. He doesn't tend to give us much warning."

I nod slowly, not unsurprised, and not disappointed, exactly. But the words settle in my chest heavy and thick just the same.

He'll stop by when he thinks of it, when he has the time. Like

I'm an afterthought or a stray errand instead of his daughter.

"Darkmore," he says before I can walk away, and I lift an eyebrow in question. He scratches the back of his neck, his gaze drifting somewhere over my head. "I spoke to Leif. He thinks maybe you shouldn't be out in the sun during the day. So we can find you some jobs in the shade, at least, moving forward. Or if you'd rather work while everyone else sleeps, we can come up with something."

I grit my teeth. Fucking Leif. "I'm fine," I snap.

A smirk rises to his lips as he finally looks back to my face. "No need to be a martyr, princess. Wouldn't want you to swoon. Don't think anyone around here would be chivalrous enough to catch you."

"You're a prick." The words have little bite to them. They sound small and pathetic, even to me.

The easy smile doesn't leave his face. "Such a filthy mouth. You know, it's customary to speak to your pack master with respect."

I scowl at him. "You're not *my* pack master."

He shrugs. "While you're in this camp, I am."

"Look," I sigh, "I'm doing what you ask. I've been doing my part, but if you want me to pretend like I like you, that I can't do."

He brings his hand to his chest. "And here I thought we were getting along."

I catch sight of a few of the other wolves watching us over his shoulder, and they quickly look away when we make eye contact. I cross my arms. "If you don't want me to call you a prick," I say, "then don't act like one." With that, I turn and head for the tent he'd pointed out.

As I lift the flap and step inside, the temperature increases tenfold. The back is propped open to give access to the fire roaring behind it, and the tent itself is scattered with various metals and tools that I definitely don't know how to use. There are four guys already working, and they scowl at me as I enter.

"You lost?" grunts the short, round one in the back. He's holding a long metal rod, sweat dripping down his face as he leans over the fire.

I jab my thumb over my shoulder. "Cam sent me here for today. Said you'd show me what to do."

The tall bearded one near me lets out a slow exhale, then nods to the side. "Come on. You can finish the cuffs off as we make them."

The cuffs?

He pushes a warm piece of metal into my hand as I step up beside him. A long, narrow table spans this side of the tent, and the surface is covered in identical products. I squint at it, trying to figure out what it is. It's smooth, the band thin and rounded, almost like a bracelet. My gaze slowly trails from the cuff to the shackle around my ankle, though mine is noticeably thicker and clunkier. It also doesn't appear to be made of the same materials at all. This one is lighter, shinier.

"It's nothing too complicated," says the man beside me as he lifts a small bolt and another rounded piece of metal from the table. "You slide this through here." He holds it up so I can see as he slides the bolt through the small opening at the end of the contraption, then wraps the other end around to meet it. "And give it a firm tap." He grabs a hammer, sets the cuff down, and nails the bolt into place.

Something like a smile crosses his face as he lifts it again to show me, then tosses it in a box beneath the table.

I raise my eyebrows. "That's it?"

"That's it."

"Wait, how many do I make?" I ask as he returns to his station.

He snorts. "More than you'll be able to do today. Just keep going until someone tells you to stop."

Great.

The others quickly resume ignoring me as I find a stool and pull it up to the table. The tent is about a million degrees, and a few minutes in, I tie my hair in a knot and roll my sleeves past my shoulders, my shirt clinging to my chest with sweat.

The men drop more parts onto the table as they finish, all of them humming some song I don't know.

"Here you are, boys."

My head jerks up as Terrence rounds the back of the tent with more supplies. He sets the box by the fire, his gaze finding me a moment later. I sit up straighter as a slow smile spreads across his face.

"Need two more hands?" Terrence asks.

One of the other men grunts something I don't catch, and I turn back to my station, trying to brush off the unease prickling my skin. The work might be repetitive and tedious, but at least having something to do with my hands distracts my mind. Sweat rolls down my back as I finish a cuff and hammer the bolt into place. It takes me a few swings instead of the single strike the other guy had managed.

I pause before tossing it into the box, inspecting it. There's silver in it, among other things. What are they? The hairs on the back of my neck rise as my eyes sweep the boxes beneath the table, all filled to the brim.

What could they possibly need so many for?

Whatever it is, I'm willing to bet I won't like it.

"...got us doing fucking slave labor."

Their voices filter to me through the harsh clangs of metal and crackles of the fire. I keep my gaze focused on my work so they don't know I'm eavesdropping. Their voices are low, hushed, to the point where I can't tell who's saying what.

"...been unfit for a long time. We all know it..."

"...but now that he's got that damn vamp, he thinks he's involved in our..."

"...I'm not afraid of a vamp, no matter who he is..."

"...not what I signed up for..."

"...got all the pups in the camp with stars in their eyes..."

"No one offered to help the little vamp over there, did they?"

I stiffen at Terrence's voice, but I don't turn, not even as I hear his footsteps approaching behind me.

"They gave you the most boring job too," he muses. "The least we could do is let you try the fun stuff—"

I smell the burning flesh before the pain registers. I jerk around, a hiss slipping through my teeth as the heat flares up my arm.

"Oh, how clumsy of me! Are you all right?" Terrence steps back, a hot poker in his hand, the end bright red from

171

the fire. The burn is directly across my Marionettes tattoo, a diagonal line marring it. He tsks. "Cam should know how dangerous it is in this tent. Most accidents tend to happen in here. What a shame you walked right into one of the hot tools."

The other four wolves are now pointedly not looking in our direction.

Terrence tosses the poker at my feet, and I jump as it ricochets off the ground, which only makes his grin widen. "Feel free to talk to Cam about it," he says, voice light, then winks. "Worth it."

The other wolves still don't look up as he exits the tent. My arm throbs, but I hold back my wince and return to my stool. He *wants* me to go to Cam, I realize. If he gets whipped again, it'll strengthen the view of me as the enemy for the rest of them. And it'll make me look like the weak little girl running to their pack master for protection. I grit my teeth and pound the next bolt in with more force than necessary.

I roll my sleeve over my arm, wincing as it brushes against the tender skin. It's just a burn. I'll live.

It's not like I haven't endured worse.

———

THE SOUR TASTE of the deer's blood lingers in the back of my throat, killing off what little appetite I had for human food.

Terrence sits across the fire from me, ripping into a raw hunk of meat with his teeth. The flames dance in his eyes as he laughs with the wolves beside him on the log.

I grind my molars. I don't want to be here any more than he wants me here. I didn't ask for any of this. *Any of this.* I might not go to Cam, but I'm not going to sit here and let him torment me until Westcott decides to summon me—if he ever comes back for me at all, something I'm starting to doubt with each day that passes.

But why go through all that trouble to get me just to dump me here?

"You should eat something."

I startle as Leif slides into the spot on my right. He nudges his plate toward me, where a few pieces of cooked meat and vegetables sit. I ignore him, keeping my gaze focused on the fire, the rage inside of me burning hotter and hotter with each passing second.

"If this is some kind of hunger strike…" Leif starts, his fingers brushing my arm, right where the fresh burn is. I jerk back and rise to my feet.

Saying nothing, I turn on my heel and head for my tent. Cam is lingering on the outskirts of the group talking with one of the older wolves, but his eyes follow me as I go, his forehead set in a deep scowl. Probably making sure I'm not trying to run away.

But where would I go? I can't go home. I don't think I can *call* the estate home anymore. There's no one coming for me. No one waiting for me. Hell, this damn mark on my arm might take me out as soon as I stepped foot out of camp.

There has to be an answer. A loophole. A way out.

I'm nearly to my tent when leaves crunch behind me. My shoulders tense, and I whip around to find Cam following. Before I can say anything, he grabs my shirtsleeve and yanks it up. I stiffen as his eyes trace over the burn.

In a perfectly calm voice, he asks, "Who?"

I pull away from him. "No one."

He lets out a short breath through his nose. "I can't help you if you won't—"

"I don't need your help. And I don't want it."

He rubs his eyes, the fire flickering behind him in the distance. The sight of it momentarily steals my breath, my stomach clenching as a memory of another night flashes before me. A different man standing in front of a fire, my blood on his lips, the roar of the party fading to background—

"It doesn't always feel like this."

I blink back to Cam, and his eyes search mine, though there's no warmth there. No softness.

I look away. What could he possibly know about what this feels like?

"Why do you even care?" I mutter.

"I don't," he says immediately, his voice light. "But I'm willing to bet your father wouldn't be too pleased if you starved to death on my watch. So you can either stop moping or I can shove the food down your throat myself."

"Does being an asshole come this easily to you, or do you have to work at it?"

He grins—more showing me his teeth than a smile— and I notice for the first time the plate he's holding. Despite the coldness in his eyes, there's something gentle about the way he holds it out to me and juts his chin at my tent.

"You can eat in there. I don't care. But whatever you think refusing food is accomplishing, it's not. The only person you're punishing is yourself, and maybe that's what you're trying to do." He pauses until I sigh and take the plate from him. His eyes flit over my face before he adds, "The loss hurts now. It always will. Whether it was in vain is up to you."

CHAPTER EIGHTEEN

VALERIE

"Get up. And pack a bag."

I blink at Cam from my cot, willing the sleep to clear from my eyes. The sun lights him from behind as he stands in the entryway for my tent. I squint a single eye. The light is soft, low, like the sun just rose. But he's already dressed for the day—complete with a tan jacket over his T-shirt and hiking boots coated in fresh mud.

"Why?" I ask, my voice coming out scratchy.

"You have five minutes" is all he says before stepping out and letting the door flutter shut behind him.

Groaning, I roll onto my side. It's been a few days since the *incident* in the blacksmith tent, but the burn on my arm is still aggravated. Wincing, I gingerly pull the shirt I'd slept in over my head and replace it with something warmer— one of Leif's old long sleeves.

Pack a bag? What the hell for? And with *what?* It's not like I have too many keepsakes hanging around here. Are we going somewhere for the day? A few days? For good?

Is Westcott...?

I let out an annoyed huff as I grab an old backpack from the floor and start shoving things into it. Cam can be as maddeningly vague as Reid sometimes.

I freeze in the middle of the tent, my throat closing up. *Not now.*

I shove down the thoughts and the tears rising to my eyes. Once I have a reasonable overnight bag—hopefully that'll be enough—I double up my socks, tug on some boots, and pull Reid's jacket over my shoulders. I don't think it's cold enough out there to need a jacket, but I'm not leaving it behind, and I don't want it balled up in the bottom of this bag.

Cam's waiting beside the tent when I step out. He says nothing and takes off toward the edge of camp, apparently expecting me to follow. The rest of the tents are quiet as we pass.

When we reach the end of the clearing, there's an old Jeep waiting. It's as caked in mud as Cam's shoes and looks so old I'm surprised it runs. There are no doors, no roof.

Cam hops into the driver seat, but I pause before climbing in. He sighs. "Do you need me to open the door for you?" He waves toward the open hole of the car's side.

"Where are you taking me?"

He pinches the bridge of his nose with two fingers. "Into town."

Something jumps in my chest at the words. *I'm getting out of this godforsaken camp.* I try not to let the excitement show on my face and narrow my eyes instead. "Why?"

"Christ." Cam shakes his head and starts the car. "It's a full moon tonight, Darkmore."

That excitement quickly turns to lead and drops to the pit of my stomach.

"There's a hotel not far that I'll put you up at. I don't think it's—it's not a good idea to have you stay here tonight. Okay?" His voice holds the usual exasperation he has when he speaks to me, but his jaw is tense.

Almost like he's...concerned.

I climb silently into the passenger seat.

The Jeep lets out an angry grinding noise before jerking forward. I brace one hand on the dashboard and one on the frame overhead as Cam maneuvers through the trees. If he's concerned by the screeching, animal-like noises coming from the car, he doesn't show it.

"I thought weres were still in control once they shift," I say as we finally turn onto a dirt road. It's not much smoother as the car bumps along.

"Some are. It takes a lot of practice and training," he says, his voice surprisingly lacking all its usual edges. "Even then, it can be difficult to hold on to that control at all times. Even the most experienced wolves have slips. And the pack has quite a few newer members...it's not worth the risk."

I peek at him sideways, but he's focused on the road, and I can't glean anything from his profile.

"Do they scare you?" I ask after a moment. "The full moons?"

He says nothing, but a muscle jumps in his jaw.

"That's probably a stupid question," I say. "You've been dealing with it your whole life."

"They terrify me," he says, voice barely audible. "Every time."

I stare at him, but there's no more expression on his face than there was before.

"Even the chance of not being in control, of not knowing what I'll do, of waking up the next morning with no memory of the night before..." He shakes his head.

Goosebumps rise on my arms as a memory swims into view—waking in a field covered in blood, having no idea how I got there. All the blackouts and deaths and being out of control. I can't imagine having to live with that as a regular occurrence. Knowing every month it would come back. A small shiver works its way through me.

"I get it," I say.

He glances at me sideways before returning his attention to the road. His grip on the steering wheel tightens. "Yeah, I imagine you do."

We fall into silence, but it's not uncomfortable. I try to enjoy watching the trees pass us by, feeling the wind in my hair, but being out in the day has my body screaming at me. The sun beats down relentlessly this morning, and I shield my eyes with my hand as they burn and water. Pulling the visor down in front of my face can only do so much.

Cam digs around in the center console for a moment before coming up with a pair of black sunglasses. He hands them to me wordlessly, never taking his eyes off the road.

"How does that work?" he asks after a moment. "The sun. It doesn't kill you like other vampires."

"I don't really know," I admit. "I imagine it might—kill me, I mean—if I were in it for too long. It's mainly uncomfortable. My skin itches. My eyes burn. It makes me really tired, and I get hungry a lot faster if I'm in it for too long."

He tightens his grip on the wheel again but says nothing.

"What's your deal with Westcott?" I ask, full well knowing he'll likely shut me down, but for some reason, he seems rather forthcoming today, and hell if I'm not going to take advantage of it. "He said you owed him a debt."

He snorts out a laugh. "Yeah, your dad's a real prick, you know that?"

"He's *not* my dad."

He lifts his shirt enough to reveal his hip. Along the bone is an all too familiar mark—black webbed veins, the skin discolored and bruised.

"You made a blood deal," I breathe.

He drops his shirt.

"For what?"

He grinds his teeth. "It doesn't matter."

I shift in my seat, wanting to ask more, but the topic is clearly not up for discussion, and if I push it, he'll probably stop talking altogether.

"I've always known he was fond of them, but I'll admit, it surprised me he made one with you."

My fingers brush the mark on my wrist subconsciously. The rest of his sentiment is left unsaid, but it fills the space between us all the same. *That his daughter would be just as disposable to him.*

We don't talk any more, and it doesn't take long for the dirt path to shift to a gravel road—one with actual street signs—though we're still the only car in sight as Cam turns right, drumming his fingers against the steering wheel.

"I doubt anyone will suspect anything with you being in the sun," he says suddenly. "But just in case, this town doesn't take well to vampires. Or Marionettes, for that matter. So if I were you, I'd draw as little attention to yourself as possible."

We come to a break in the road where various bikes, cars, and carts are parked, though the street seems to continue on from what I can see.

"Foot traffic only from here," says Cam as he pulls the Jeep to the side of the road and cuts the engine.

The sun makes my body feel like it's moving through wet cement, but I force myself to keep pace with Cam as I follow him down the path. After a few minutes of walking, the town seems to appear out of nowhere.

It *did* appear out of nowhere, I realize. The dirt and trees that once surrounded us are gone, replaced by tables set up beneath brightly covered tarps, lopsided buildings tightly crammed together, and a lively crowd bustling down the center street, perusing the little shops and talking.

I look to Cam with wide eyes, and there's a hint of amusement in the set of his mouth as he nods for us to continue forward. No one pays us any mind as we weave through the crowds. The town must be enchanted somehow, shielding it from view. Maybe it can only be seen if you get close enough to it, so it can only be found if you know where it is—or happen upon it accidentally. But magic of that scale, and for it to be constant—what kind of witch had managed that? And *how*? There's no way they're upkeeping it, so the spell is somehow standing on its own.

"It's this way," murmurs Cam. He tugs on my sleeve and pulls me down an alley between the buildings, and I realize there are more streets—more shops, more people. How big is this place?

We come to a side door in a dark stone building. Cam looks both ways down the alley before knocking twice. My shoulders tense. He'd said he knew of a hotel, but this seems kind of sketchy.

The door cracks open, not enough for me to see whoever is on the other side.

"Camden Farley," says a raspy voice.

He nods toward me. "Like we talked about."

"My lips are sealed."

Cam hands her a roll of bills. I look between him and the door, unease tingling the back of my neck. It must show on my face because he says quietly, "You'll be safe. Stay here until tomorrow, and I'll come get you in the morning, okay?"

Slowly, I nod. His eyes scan my face for another moment, his mouth set in a hard line, then he nods and disappears the way we'd come.

IT OCCURS to me a bit too late after I leave the room that I might not be able to find my way back. But I wasn't going to sit around in there all night—maybe that would be the smart thing to do—but this is my first taste of freedom in I don't know how long. I'm not going to waste it.

I pull Reid's jacket tighter around my shoulders, hoping no one can hear the clang of the shackle against my ankle with each step. Cam left me with some money, so I start in the market area and grab something to eat—potato salad. After so many nights of mystery stew, it's the best damn thing I've ever tasted.

The streets are overflowing with pedestrians bustling back and forth. The mix of scents isn't quite as overwhelming as it had been at Westcott's compound—not as much variety. There's human, wolf, and a few others thrown in there. I try not to get too close to anyone or linger too long, but I smell enough other witches in the crowd that hopefully my scent won't stick out. Hell, maybe I've been around the wolves long enough that their stench has rubbed off on me. I'm in Leif's clothes, after all.

The sun is bright overhead, and it weighs down my every step, but I push forward, wandering my way through the winding streets, surrounded by smiles and laughter and conversation. Everyone here seems so...*happy*.

My steps slow as I come to a building much larger than the rest. It's shaped like a dome with large pillars framing the entrance. A library? I drift forward. If there are computers in there, maybe I could...

I freeze at the front doors. Reaching out might violate the blood deal. But that doesn't mean I can't look to see what's going on back home, right? Maybe check Roe's and Kirby's social medias, Adrienne's blog...

"You new here?"

I suck in a sharp breath and stumble back a step. A woman stands in the shadows beneath one of the pillars, a cigarette hanging between her fingers. My eyes linger on it a beat too long, and my fingers twitch at my sides. I can't remember the last time I had one.

She's leaning against the building, a foot propped behind her, and she considers me through slitted eyes as she slowly blows out a cloud of smoke. She's a direct contrast to the vivid colors and almost cartoonish smiles of everyone

I'd passed on the way here. She can't be much older than I am, though she has lines etched deep into her face, and her all-black outfit makes her blend in with the shadows all that much more.

She nods toward the doors. "Ain't open during the day."

"Oh," I say. There are no signs on the doors to indicate when they *are* open either.

The heat of her gaze continues to burn against the side of my face, and I take a step away, not wanting to draw any more attention to myself than I already have.

"Here." She digs in her bag, then holds up a second cigarette between two fingers.

I hesitate, and she lifts a single eyebrow until I finally step forward.

"Thanks," I murmur, putting it between my teeth as she leans in to light it with her own.

I inhale, and the moment the smoke fills my lungs, every muscle in my body relaxes, and I lean my head against the building with a sigh.

"You're a long way from home, aren't you?" My eyes cut to her, and she waves her hand. "Relax. I don't give a shit."

Her scent is faint, barely there. But the sweet hint of magic is unmistakable.

"I'm Jamie." After a quick glance around us, she sighs and pulls up her sleeve to expose the tattoo around her biceps.

The red Marionettes tattoo.

She lets the fabric fall back into place just as quickly and takes a drag of her cigarette.

"Valerie," I say.

A half smile curls her lips. "I know. I remember you. I was in your sister's year."

"You knew Calla?" I blurt out, really taking her in now. I suppose there's something vaguely familiar about her features. Maybe I saw her around the academy. But as a freshman, I hadn't known that many of the upperclassmen. Not unless they were close friends of Calla's.

She shrugs. "Of her, mostly. But who didn't? *The golden Darkmore child*," she whispers in mock-awe.

"When did you—how long have you—what are you doing here?"

"So many questions. Could ask you the same thing." She pops her eyebrows and tucks her cigarette between her lips. "Just waiting out the end of the world, baby. No shame in jumping ship. Anyway." She straightens and tosses her bag over her shoulder. "Nice chatting with you."

"Wait. Wait." I grab her wrist, suddenly desperate for her not to walk away. She's the first glimpse of home I've had, no matter how distant. She eyes my hand, and I release her. "I—are you staying here?"

The amusement in her expression remains, but there's a slight softening in her eyes as she sighs and nods to the side. "Come on."

HER PLACE IS down the street, a small studio apartment above a bakery. There's an older woman out front serving a couple beneath a rainbow umbrella, and she smiles at Jamie as we pass and head for the side entrance.

"I heard it was wendigos," says the man at the table as he loudly slurps his drink.

My steps slow, my heart rate immediately picking up.

"Well *I* heard it was a disease, and they have the whole place quarantined now."

"Either way," snorts the man. "Finally getting what they deserve—"

Jamie loops her arm through my elbow and yanks me into the stairwell and out of earshot. She levels me with a stern look as she unlocks her front door. "You're going to have to work on that whole *not drawing attention to yourself* thing."

They had to have been talking about the estate. "They could have…"

"They're drunk gossips. They weren't going to give you anything useful."

I can barely step foot inside with all her stuff. Her bed is a mattress on the floor in the center of the room, covered in blankets and pillows randomly strewn about. Papers and books take up most of the floor, and the windowsills are overflowing with glass jars, crystals, herbs, and plants. There's no other furniture, other than a single chair beside the tiny kitchen counter.

"Sorry. This place isn't really equipped for visitors."

"Aren't you worried about someone finding you?" I ask, thinking back to the woman downstairs. They seemed friendly with one another. Something I'm willing to bet wouldn't be the case if she knew about Jamie's history with the Marionettes.

Crossing her arms and leaning against the door, she pulls on the cord around her neck, and a small glass vial slides out from beneath her shirt. An alchemist then. "Took me a while to find the right combo, but it works well enough. I smell like a human to them." Her eyes narrow. "But not to you."

"I almost didn't notice it. It was really faint."

"Huh." She tucks the vial into her shirt and paces into her kitchen. "Good to know. So what are you doing here anyway? You're not sticking around, are you?"

I ignore the first part of her question. I have no short way of answering that. "No. Just for the night." My eyes snag on the laptop on her kitchen counter.

She follows my gaze and flicks her wrist before opening the fridge. "Go for it."

"Really?"

She shrugs as she sets two beers on the counter.

I all but pounce on the thing, my heart rate skyrocketing in my chest as I pull up the internet browser. Just the sight of the search bar almost brings tears to my eyes. I hadn't realized how disconnected I'd felt until now. How utterly cut off and in the dark I've been.

Jamie pops the cap off one of the beers, but I barely hear it. The rest of the apartment blurs and fades as I pull up Adrienne's social media first.

She hasn't posted anything in months. Not that it's unusual for her, but still. The disappointment sinks into my chest like lead. The one thing she usually keeps up with is her blog, but even that hasn't been updated since before it all went down.

My finger hovers over the message button, my hand shaking. Would this count as violating the terms of our deal?

Would she want to hear from me if it didn't? She almost died because of me.

Swallowing the lump in my throat, I click over to Kirby's page instead, expecting her daily updates.

But her feed, too, looks like it's barely been touched. There's a picture from move-in day a few weeks ago. She and Monroe are standing in front of the building, arms around each other's shoulders, but their smiles are small. No witty caption or anything, either. Just: *Senior Year.*

"You okay?"

I suck in a breath and lean back, the room trickling in around me again. Jamie watches me across the counter, her forehead crinkled in concern. I quickly swipe the tears from my cheeks and clear my throat. "Yeah. Yeah."

I close the laptop. I don't think I could take any more. I thought seeing them might help. Just knowing they're okay.

But it only makes the loss worse. Because I can't go back. I can't let them know I'm okay. That I'm *alive.*

"Here." Jamie digs around in her bag until she finds a second necklace, identical to the one she's wearing, and holds it out to me.

"Oh no, I couldn't—"

"It's my backup." She pushes it into my hand. "And I can make another."

I tighten my fingers around the tiny glass, and it's warm to the touch. "Thank you."

"Are you—I mean." She sighs and cups both hands around her beer. "Are you going to be all right? Do you have a place to stay tonight?"

"Oh, yeah." I wave my hand in front of my face and

stand. She probably feels like I'm a lost puppy who followed her home. "I'm good."

"I mean it. It's a full moon out there. Can never be too careful around these parts."

"I appreciate it, Jamie. Really. I have a room."

She drums her nails against the bottle and nods. "Cool."

"Cool. Well, thanks. And good luck. And I should… yeah." I jab my thumb toward the door.

I'm almost to the door when she calls out again. "Hang on." She holds up the other beer. "I know my apartment is shitty and I don't have anywhere to sit but…have a drink?" I hesitate, and she sighs. "I'm not doing you a favor, Darkmore. You're the first person I've seen from home in weeks."

"Is that how long you've been here?"

She nods.

Weeks. "Was that…?"

"Right after your funeral, actually."

My eyes snap to her face. "You don't seem surprised to see me."

"I was at first," she admits. "Wasn't sure it was you until I heard your voice. But after the shit I've seen, few things surprise me." She gives the beer one last wave, and I finally step forward and take it.

"What was it like?" I ask, my voice all but a whisper. "The estate. Before you left."

She swirls her bottle and considers her words, her mouth set off to the side. "It was weird. After the bunker, it was like they all wanted to go back to normal. Pretend nothing happened. But anyone who was paying attention could tell that wasn't true. It felt off. I had this really bad feeling...so I trusted my intuition, and I left. I've tried checking in a few times since then, but a lot of the usual news outlets haven't been updating as frequently. And I wouldn't recommend asking anyone around here about the estate."

"Right," I murmur as my scalp prickles. How bad would things have to be for the news to stop reporting? They eat that kind of shit up. Nothing sells like violence and fear.

What if everyone's social media has been quiet because—

"The academy seems to be the same as usual though," continues Jamie with a small smile, probably sensing my panic. "Still posting updates on the website about events and everything."

I nod and take a long swig of the beer. "That's good."

"I know you must think I'm a coward."

My eyes snap to her face. "No. I wasn't thinking that at all."

She shrugs, the hint of a blush on her cheeks now. "I wouldn't blame you. I ran at the first sign of trouble to save my own skin."

"Really, Jamie," I insist, hoping she can hear the sincerity in my words. A million memories I've been trying to suppress flood back—the death, the blood, the deal. Maybe things would've been better if I'd run. If I'd left sooner. Before I caused as much damage. "I'm not in any position to judge anyone. Trust me."

CHAPTER NINETEEN

VALERIE

"I'm not going to leave. I'm a very patient man, Valerie. We can do this all night…*or* you can just give in now."

I glare at Leif from my cot. This isn't the first time he's tried this. I've started anticipating his visits like clockwork. As dinner wraps up, every day for the past week since Cam brought me back after the full moon, he's shown up, trying to pull me into whatever he and his friends are doing for the night.

Tonight, however, is the first time he's brought backup. Saint and Jones stand behind him, the three of them taking up the entirety of the tent's opening.

It's the first I've seen of the two of them at the camp at all, actually. They must have left with a later group from the compound or something, though if vans have been coming and going, I haven't noticed.

"We'll drag you out if we have to," Saint singsongs behind him.

My scowl deepens, and I tighten my fist around Reid's jacket on the bed. "Seriously, guys, leave me alone."

"We could bring the party in here," Jones offers.

"Absolutely not. Look, I appreciate the sentiment or whatever, but I can promise you I won't be any fun to hang out with anyway."

"Anyone is fun to hang out with after a couple of these." Saint brandishes a bottle of brown liquid and grins.

"Not if she's a sad drunk," Jones mumbles out of the corner of his mouth.

I hold up my palm. "One hundred percent a sad drunk. So you should all just run along."

Leif walks toward me, and before I can react, he hooks his hand through my elbow, yanks me to my feet, and drags me toward the door. "Great! So you're coming."

Despite the easy smile on his face, his grip on my arm is solid. I couldn't break away if I tried. Might as well save myself the bruises and go along with it—at least until they're enough drinks in to not notice when I slip away. I could use a drink to help me sleep anyway.

A few guys are lingering by the fire, but to my surprise, that's not where they lead me. Instead, we turn and head straight into the trees. The darkness is thicker here, especially once we drift far enough that the fire disappears.

We stop after a few minutes of walking at a smaller clearing, this one also set up with logs in the center for a fire. Judging by the ashes on the ground and the logs already situated around it, they've been here before.

Jones takes a swig from the bottle, then hands it off to Leif so he can get the fire started. Leif swallows a mouthful and offers it to me.

Sighing, I bring it to my nose and inhale. Whiskey. I expect it to burn on the way down, to cringe as the taste fills my mouth, but there's nothing. So I swallow again, waiting for the sting in the back of my eyes, the warmth in my chest.

And still, I don't feel anything.

Or maybe I do. It just feels like nothing compared to everything else.

Leif watches me with an unreadable look on his face as I pass the bottle to Saint and head for one of the logs to sit. The fire starts slowly, gently, barely a flicker at first. Jones feeds some of the surrounding brush to it, willing the flames to grow. They cast an eerie glow around him, deepening the orange hues of his hair and the patches of freckles on his skin.

"So how are you liking the barrens, Darkmore?" Saint falls into the spot next to me, the whiskey sloshing in his hand. "Probably not the accommodations you're used to."

"Saint," Leif warns.

I snort. "I've never been into camping."

"You know what? Me neither." Saint raises the bottle as if toasting me, then downs another swig. "Much prefer the compounds. Stayed as long as I could until they kicked me to the curb."

He hands the bottle to me, but Leif interjects before I can take a sip. "Maybe we should slow down on that, yeah? We have all night." He glances at me out of the corner of his eye. "And you didn't even eat."

Slowly, I lift an eyebrow. "Did you or did you not forcibly remove me from my tent to come drink with you?"

"Well, yeah, but——"

"Just giving you what you want, Leif." I lift the bottle toward him before taking a drink.

He sighs as Jones rises to his feet. "At least save me some! Jesus."

Jones swipes the bottle out of my hand before Saint can go for it and takes it with him to the other side of the fire.

"I think we should tell ghost stories," announces Jones.

"No," Leif and Saint say at the same time.

"He always tells the same one," Saint explains to me out of the corner of his mouth.

"And it's not even a good one," Leif adds.

Jones grumbles something unintelligible and tilts the bottle to his lips.

"You know what? I've actually got a good one," says Saint.

"Don't listen to him. It's not a good one either."

I whip around as Cam steps through the trees. A weird sense of unease washes through me, like I've been caught doing something I'm not supposed to, but his eyes sweep our group, seemingly unsurprised as they gloss over me.

"Well, if it isn't the boss man," calls Jones. "Care to join us?"

Cam laughs and shakes his head. "I'm heading into town. Shouldn't take more than a few hours." He nods at Leif. "Can you keep the others from burning the camp to the ground while I'm gone?"

Leif salutes him. "You got it."

Apparently satisfied, Cam turns back the way he came, not even sparing me a glance as he disappears through the trees.

"*So.*" Saint leans forward and rubs his palms together, his cheeks dimpling around his smile. "About that story…"

IT'S DARKER, colder when I make it back to camp, the moon hidden beneath a layer of clouds. The others are still in the woods, most too drunk to notice I slipped away…or that I took one of the bottles with me.

The fire roars in the center of the clearing, though it's quiet, with no one sitting on the surrounding logs. I hesitate a moment before stepping into my tent, looking around. Usually someone puts the fire out before everyone goes to sleep.

The tent flap rustles in the breeze as I duck inside, stumbling as the alcohol burns through my system. The numbness isn't any more welcome than the kind I'd already been feeling.

Before, alcohol had numbed the bond. Now, it amplifies its absence. It's a limitless, gaping abyss in my chest threatening to swallow me whole. And a big part of me wants to let it.

No amount of Leif and the others trying to cheer me up or alcohol or time or *anything* is going to make this go away.

None of it will fix how irreparably my life has broken.

None of it will ever bring him back. Or let me reach out to my friends or Adrienne. None of it will let me go home.

I slump onto the cot, tossing the bottle of whiskey aside as I search through the blankets for that familiar fabric. It doesn't smell like him anymore. I don't remember when it stopped.

My hand stills, and I sit up straight. I slide my hands across the cot, then toss the blanket to the ground to be sure.

The jacket isn't here.

But I could have sworn this is exactly where I left it—exactly where I've left it every day since I've been in this godforsaken place. A quick search of the ground surrounding the cot also proves pointless.

My breaths quicken. Where could it have gone? There's no way I lost it. There's *no way*—

Laughter sounds somewhere outside deep and low. Mocking. Heat surges through my veins as I rip the tent flap aside and step out.

The fire continues to crackle in the center of camp, though there are now three people standing beside it.

People holding Reid's jacket.

My vision is hazy from the alcohol, but there's no mistaking the tattoo on the face of the man in front, or the way his mouth twists into a sneer as he watches me stumble out of my tent. My gaze zeros in on Reid's jacket, on how close it is to the fire.

The last thing I have of him. The *only* thing.

Something snaps inside my chest, filling every inch of me with blistering heat. I grit my teeth.

"I will kill you," I growl.

The men laugh as Terrence dangles the jacket closer to the fire. "Oh, is this something important?"

I stomp toward him, my hands balled into fists, my nails digging into my palms, and it takes me a moment to remember that no matter how much I bleed, my magic isn't going to answer me right now.

He lifts the jacket out of my reach. "Why don't you ask me for it *very nicely?*"

"How about I just rip out your throat instead?"

His smile widens. "Wrong answer."

In the space between blinks, he tosses it into the fire. I surge forward, my hand extended, not caring if I get burned, but arms grab me from behind and tighten around my waist, holding me in place. I thrash, but my body is weak right now, *useless*. I don't stand a chance.

"Stop!" I scream, my eyes locked on the jacket as flames lick up the sleeves. Tears run down my cheeks. "*Stop!*"

The arms tighten around me, restricting my air, and my mind flashes to when Reid had held me back like this in the hall, trying to stop me from going to see Connor after my final trial.

A choked sob escapes me, and the man laughs.

"That's enough, Terrence," says a low voice. "Stop playing with our food."

Something hard strikes the back of my head as he says it, and then everything goes dark.

THERE MUST BE RUNNING water nearby. It crashes against rocks and roars in my ears. Pain pulses somewhere near the base of my skull, but I keep my eyes closed, listening. I'm on the ground—I know that much. I can smell the dirt pressing into my face. Footsteps sound around me, at least two people, maybe three.

"Anyone see you?" asks a low voice.

A second voice lets out a derisive sound in the back of his throat. It sounds like he's somewhere by my feet. "No one is left conscious by now."

"If Cam finds out you drugged the pack…"

"It's not *drugs*. It just helped them sleep a bit. No harm done. And no one forced it on them. They ate the stew on their own."

The other man grunts. "Where the hell is he?"

"Maybe he chickened out," he mutters. "Who's to say Westcott will even care? He's left her here for weeks."

The sharp sting around my wrists trickles in—rope. My arms are tied behind my back, though my ankles feel free. I won't be able to fight them off, but I might be able to run.

But run where? I don't know where they took me. And even if I manage to make it to camp, there's no guarantee someone there would help me, even if they were awake.

I take in slow, measured breaths, but the panic that once would have filled me never shows.

I'm going to die here.

And I don't think I care.

Footsteps crunch somewhere in the distance, heavy and slow, and I clench my jaw.

I *do* care, I realize. If not for my own survival, just for the sake of depriving these idiots of the satisfaction.

For the sake of making Westcott pay for all he's done. The queen, the estate—all of them. Dying here would make it too easy. Let them wash their hands of me for good now that I've served my purpose. I've outlived my use.

Then the beatings and the trainings and the tests and the deaths and the blood and the staring injustice in the face and having to swallow it silently would have been for nothing.

That was everything I was. Every piece of my identity was wrapped in becoming a Marionette. In being a Darkmore.

Which means *I* would have lived for nothing.

Another witch forgotten. Another name lost. Another complication flushed away so the cycle can continue on and on.

With my friends.

With my sister.

But I am not dying today.

"Wake her up," barks a new voice. Terrence.

Before I have a chance to react, a foot connects with my ribs, forcing an involuntary yelp from my lungs as my body flies to the side and my shoulder cracks against the earth.

Terrence squats in front of me, a long metal poker in his hands, and grins. "Glad you could join us."

I spit at his feet. "He'll know it was you."

His grin broadens. "I'm counting on it."

He nods at someone behind me, and they rip the sleeve of my shirt. I recoil against the dirt, trying to push to my feet, and a second pair of hands pins my shoulders.

The moonlight falls on the bare skin of my arm, at the angry red burn that's already marring my biceps. Terrence flashes his teeth, and he spins the poker in his hand. I struggle against the other man holding me down, and his nails dig into my skin. Terrence takes a step forward, and I twist my head and sink my teeth as deep as I can in the hand restraining me.

"Fuck!" The man rears back. "She bit me!"

I don't hesitate. I scramble along the dirt and push to my feet. The hot, coppery taste of the man's blood fills my mouth as I take off toward the trees, my shoulders screaming and ribs aching.

But I can't think about any of that right now.

I just run.

"Not so fast, you little bitch."

Someone tackles me from behind, his full weight crashing into me as we hit the ground. I wheeze and gasp as it knocks the wind out of me.

"How's the blood magic treating you now?" Terrence growls beside my ear, then presses his knee between my shoulder blades, pinning me to the dirt.

My arms ache from where he landed on them, and something in my wrist burns and pulses.

The weight disappears from my back, and the restraints around my wrists loosen. Then he fists his hand in my shirt and flips me over. My arms are free now, but I barely have time to draw in a breath before he raises the poker and stabs it down, straight through my biceps, right over the Marionettes tattoo.

I scream as pain explodes through my veins, blackening the edges of my vision.

Terrence grins. "Thought you'd be a screamer." He spits onto my face before rising to his feet.

He disappears from my view as he walks toward the others, apparently no longer worried about me getting away. I try to move my arm, but the poker is lodged into the ground beneath me. With shaking fingers, I wrap my other hand around it.

Just pull it out.

Even the slight jostle from gripping the end sends a wave of pain through me so strong that nausea surges in my stomach. Gritting my teeth, I yank hard before I can talk myself out of it. The air whooshes from my lungs as I drop the bloody poker and curl onto my side, every nerve in my body zeroing in on the wound.

Blood seeps down my chest and drips from my elbow as I cradle my arm against me and sit up.

Three men are standing a few feet away by the edge of a lake, seeming unconcerned—amused—as they watch me. Terrence stands in the center, a splatter of my blood running the length of his shirt. Their eyes glow in the moonlight, the grins on their faces more wolfish than anything else.

I'm their prey, and they clearly have no intention of making this kill quickly.

Not without toying with me first.

The one I bit sways on his feet. I recognize the haze in his eyes. So I might not have my magic, and my body may be the weakest it has ever been, but I *do* still have my venom.

I spit as I shakily climb to my feet, and blood splatters on the dirt. "Is that the best you can do?"

Something like annoyance flickers across Terrence's eyes. He wants me to scream. To be afraid.

I crouch to pick up the poker and tighten my fist around it. The movement makes heat flare up my injured arm, but I hold back my wince.

Terrence's eyes darken as I meet his glare.

"Three against one? Too afraid to face me on your own?"

He leans his head to the side, and his neck lets out a loud crack. "I can't wait to hear you beg for your life," he murmurs as he prowls toward me.

He shouldn't be able to hurt me at all after I marked him, not without inflicting the same damage on himself. Either I fucked up the spell, or the connection can't go through with my magic being blocked.

This fucking shackle is really starting to piss me off.

My fingers tense around the poker, but I don't raise it, not yet. With the little strength I have left, I might get one good hit. He swings his arm out, fist flying toward my face, and I duck and shuffle to the side. I lock my teeth together as he throws another punch, and I dodge, my body thankfully retaining the muscle memory from all that training at the academy.

Another man steps toward us, but Terrence holds up a hand to stop him, his eyes locked on me. Now that I've called him out on needing backup, if he lets them step in, it'll be a blow to his pride.

The tattoo near his eye crinkles as he scowls at me, his hands flexing and tightening into fists at his sides. He lets out a growl, and there's nothing human in the noise, then he's a blur of motion. I try to dodge to the side, but his fingers dig into my injured arm. I cry out as he hauls us both to the ground, the poker flying toward the water.

He straddles my hips and pins my arms above my head, his chest heaving with his breaths.

I whimper as he tightens his hold on my wrist—definitely broken—and the hole in my arm pulses.

"You know something, Terrence?" I rasp, my voice barely audible.

"What's that?" he asks, a triumphant smile on his face.

I move my lips, but nothing comes out.

"What was that, sweetheart?" he asks, leaning down more.

Just like I'd wanted.

I whip my head up, my fangs digging into the meaty part of his neck. His flesh tears easily, his thick, hot blood spurting against my face. He stumbles back as I spit the chunk I'd managed to rip off to the side. Blood pours over his chest, and he clamps a hand to the wound, snarling.

So, deep enough to hurt but not enough to kill.

But it'll slow him down.

The others surge forward, and I roll, grabbing the poker off the ground. The pain that lances through my bones as my injured arm hits the ground blurs my vision, and I sway as I try to stand. I swing the poker forward blindly as my head spins from the pain, and I feel like I might pass out. It meets resistance, so it must have hit something.

But then something hits *me*.

The water crashes around me as I hit the edge of the bank on my back. A boot lands against my ribs, hard enough to flip me onto my side. Another foot waits for me there and clips me under the chin. I gasp as blood spurts from my lips, and water rushes into my lungs.

Another kick, this time in my lower back, and it nudges me far enough on the bank that my entire face submerges in the water. A shock of electricity runs down my spine, numbing my legs. I try to lift my neck, but then someone is holding me down by the back of my head. My eyes burn, and I thrash, all the air leaving my lungs as I scream. A foot presses into the center of my back, pinning me in place.

This is it.

This is truly and finally it.

My lungs seize in my chest, clawing at themselves for one last breath. The rest of the pain ebbs away, until it's just me and the blur of water in my eyes, the black rim of my vision rapidly creeping in.

And then there's nothing at all.

CHAPTER TWENTY

REID

THE SUNLIGHT LIMITS how much ground we can cover in a day, but at least with the UV-blocking tent I swiped from the estate, stopping at a moment's notice isn't an issue. Jia and Jared graciously let us stay until the rain cleared, but Jia couldn't offer much more than a name and some coordinates. The campsite is likely cleared out by now, but maybe we can catch a scent or some tracks.

It'll have to be enough.

Despite leaving our bags by the fire while we waited, mine is still damp as it bounces against my back with each step. It's quiet as we trek through the trees, this part of the barrens clearly not frequented by hikers or campers. The path—if there's one at all—isn't visible beneath the overgrown foliage. I check the dying battery on my phone again —down to twenty percent. There's no reception out here anyway, so I turn it off.

"It's not a full moon tonight, is it?" mutters Connor behind me.

"You afraid of a few wolves?"

"Is that not the message your estate has been pushing for decades? The reason your mom banned them from stepping foot in the region? They're far too dangerous, blah, blah, blah?"

His word choice doesn't escape me. *Your estate.* Though as far as I'm aware, he's spent more time there than I ever did. "That is the message, yes," I say. "The reality is a bit more complicated."

Connor makes an unintelligible noise in the back of his throat. "I don't know how Val could stand to be around you all the time," he mutters. "You have a half answer for everything, don't you?"

I smirk, picturing all too well the face she'd make after one of those *half answers.* The way she'd set her mouth to the side, her eyes flat, that damn scrunch in her nose…

I clear my throat. "On full moons, yes, it's best to avoid them. They have no control over the shift. Some have trained enough to be able to remember their humanity even in their wolf forms, but"—I cast a sideways glance at him—"best not to find out which are which, obviously. They can shift during the rest of the month too, but it's more difficult for them, and harder for them to hold on to."

"Why do you know so much about wolves?"

I shrug. "Not all the estates are as unwelcoming as ours. I ran into quite a few of them abroad. Some of the estates go as far as employing them."

"Is it true about the bites?" he asks after a moment.

It's not as difficult to kill vampires as old stories led people to believe. Sure, a stake to the heart is one of the most effective ways. But there are other ways—burning, decapitating.

And a bite from a werewolf, though that's generally believed to be the worst way to go. It would make Valerie's psychosis look preferable.

Her face flashes behind my eyes, this time from the last time I saw her. As she looked at me in that cell, the light completely gone from her eyes, asking me to let her die.

I close my eyes for a moment. "Yes, that much is true."

"So your plan is to hike aimlessly through their territory?"

"Was *your* plan to tag along so you could complain the entire time?" I snap. "No one forced you to be here. Feel free to turn back at any time."

"That would be great for you, wouldn't it? So you can be her knight in shining armor?"

"Enough," I say through my teeth, whipping toward him. "I'm not going to keep doing this with you. You. Weren't. There. I'm not going to feel bad that I was. And I'm not going to apologize for caring for her. You got dealt a shit hand, and I'm sorry about that. I am. But no amount of hating me is going to fix it. So you can either shut your mouth and help me find her, or you can—" I break off and shake my head. Quietly, I add, "You were her first love and her best friend. You think I don't know how this ends once she realizes the change in your feelings wasn't permanent? So for fuck's sake, just shut up."

Connor stares at me. "If you actually believe that, then you really don't know her at all."

A branch snaps somewhere to our left, and I freeze, eyes scanning the area. I sniff the air, but there are no hints of wolves. There is, however, a heavy layer of...anxiety in the air. Nervousness.

I hold up a hand for Connor not to move and strain my ear, listening. The wind rustles through the trees, and there must be running water nearby. A bird chirps a few yards away—but *there*. Heartbeats, likely human.

Behind us.

Their pulses steadily increase the longer we stand here.

Which means these are not hikers or campers we just happened upon. Whoever the hell they are, they've been following us.

You know you have a hefty little price tag on your head, right?

Jesus fucking Christ.

How stupid are these people?

I drop my bag at Connor's feet. "Stay here," I mutter.

I find the first one crouched behind a tree a few yards back from Connor, aiming a gun with tranquilizer darts. He looks to be about a hundred pounds, so what he was going to do with our bodies once we were unconscious, I have no idea. I rip the gun from his hands before he hears me coming, then pin him against the tree by his throat, cutting off his air enough that he can't make a noise to alert his friends.

His eyes bulge as he wraps his hands around my arm, trying to pull himself free.

"How many of you are there?" I ask, voice flat. Red creeps up his neck, but I tighten my grip. "How. Many. And I'll know if you lie."

He holds up four fingers, his hand shaking.

I let out a slow breath through my nose, then lift the gun up so he can see. "Keep following us, and you'll get a lot worse than this, you understand?" Before he can respond, I sink one of the darts into the side of his neck and wait for his body to go limp before releasing him.

The second isn't hard to find either, though he got a little more creative and is crouched in a low branch of a tree. He hears me coming and whips around, gun pointing directly at me. I duck as he lets off a dart, then grab him by the back of his shirt and yank him to the ground. The impact is hard enough that he gasps for air as I kick the gun out of his hand.

I'm about to repeat what I said to the first one, but I pause, my foot coming down to hold him by the chest. "How much did they offer you?"

The man gasps, eyes frantically searching his surroundings for a makeshift weapon.

"I'm not going to kill you," I sigh. "But I *will* if you try this again."

"It's ten thousand for a Marionette," he gasps. "Twenty for an estate vamp. Fifty for a royal."

Fifty thousand? Who the hell has that kind of cash to throw around?

"Who?" I ask.

The man shakes his head. "I—I don't know. I swear. They didn't give a name."

He opens his mouth to keep babbling, but I sink a dart into his thigh and keep moving.

A shout stops me in my tracks, then I take off at a run to where I left Connor. I duck through the brush as another human—this one a woman—goes down in front of him. He aims the gun at me as I approach, and he takes a moment too long to lower it once he realizes it's me.

"You didn't kill her, did you?" I ask.

He scoffs like I've asked a ridiculous question.

"There should be one more," I say, rubbing my eyes.

"Unless they took off after seeing their friends go down."

I try to listen for another heartbeat or catch a scent on the wind, but there's nothing. Grabbing the bag from the ground, I toss it over my shoulder beside my newly acquired gun and jut my chin toward Connor. "Let's keep moving."

IT TAKES LONGER to reach the coordinates than I'd been expecting, long enough that I lose track of the days. Despite not seeing anyone since the bounty hunters the first day, Connor and I have been sleeping in shifts.

"Well, it looks like someone *used* to be here," says Connor.

The remains of a fire are scorched into the earth at the center of the clearing, but there are no other signs that anyone was here.

Except for, of course, the scent. The stench of wolf is so assaulting it tends to linger around longer than usual—or maybe that's just to vampire senses. Maybe our scent does the same for them.

There's a hint of something in the breeze—but it's too sweet to be wolf.

Connor paces forward and nudges the ashes with the toe of his boot, his brow furrowed. I rub my eyes and glance around. There's no telling how long ago they left, how far they could've gotten, if they would've had any helpful information to begin with. I'd really thought Jia would be our best bet, and one I was sure we could trust.

There are others who might have information, but they're affiliated with different estates, and asking them for help could get ugly fast.

"What are you thinking?" says Connor. "Tell me you have a plan B."

Hell, I'd hike through these damn woods until we stumble upon someone, but there's over a *million* acres. They could be clear on the opposite end for all we know.

She could be somewhere else entirely, and we're wasting time.

She could be—

No. She's still alive. I have to believe that.

"They could be anywhere by now," continues Connor. "And—"

"Just give me a minute to think."

He steps into my line of sight, but none of the expressions I've grown accustomed to seeing on his face greet me. There's a calmness there, almost the indifference he'd flaunted around after turning, but not quite. "Just think," he says. "You have to have some other connections—some other way to find them. The barrens might be big, but an entire pack of wolves doesn't vanish into thin air..."

A sharp pain pierces the center of my stomach, and I pitch forward at the waist, gasping. I don't hear whatever the end of Connor's sentence is—I can't hear anything at all. I brace one hand against my stomach and the other in the dirt to keep from falling over, but I don't have to look

211

and see if I've been injured—if those idiotic humans followed us.

Because that pain is very clearly not coming from me.

"Reid? What's wrong?" Connor's voice echoes faintly, thinly, as if from a distance.

The pain strikes again, deeper, hotter.

I fall to the earth this time, my knees hitting the ground hard.

How is this possible? Without the bond…

My chest constricts, and I roll onto my back, desperately trying to pull air into my lungs.

If the aftershocks alone are this bad…

No. *No.*

"Valerie," I gasp.

Connor's face looms above me, his eyes wide. His mouth moves, but I can't make out the words.

I grit my teeth as my fingers dig into the dirt, trying to pull myself up. To go where, I'm not sure. But I can't just lie here. I can't just—

The muscles of my legs seize, and my vision blurs. The strength of my arm holding me up gives out, and the side of my face hits the ground. I cough, my lungs feeling like they're filling with fluid. "Valerie," I whisper.

Footsteps pad softly somewhere to my right, and a brown pair of boots strides into focus a moment before everything goes dark.

SOMETHING IS CHEWING beside my car. The sounds are hard, fast, and...*wet*. I lurch away, and a high-pitched giggle splits the air.

My blood turns to ice in my veins.

Because the sound is...familiar. But that's impossible.

It's dark, wherever we are. Judging by the stone surrounding us, a cave of some kind. I don't turn, not at first.

It could be a dream. I could be unconscious right now.

But I don't think so.

The stench filters in next. The blood. The rot.

The chewing resumes.

She's crouched on all fours, the body in front of her. Human, based on the smell. Blood and gore drip down her chin as she smiles up at me, and the look is so familiar and yet not at all that my entire chest twists.

I swallow hard, silent as she rips another piece of skin from the man's stomach and shoves it into her mouth.

"Quinn," I rasp.

She smiles again, her teeth stained red with blood. Her face is thinner, her clothes barely hanging on to her frame. She waves a hand to the side. "Not safe. Not safe. Not safe," she mutters, then widens her eyes and points at me. "Not for you. Not safe. Not safe."

She keeps muttering the same thing over and over again as she struggles to chew the skin, then licks the blood from her fingers.

I cover my mouth with my hand and feel a tear fall onto my fingers. My chest shakes with my exhale, like it can't decide whether to be horrified or just relieved that she's alive—if that's what she is right now.

But the guilt isn't far behind, sinking into my stomach like lead.

How had I noticed that wasn't Valerie, but I'd never questioned Quinn's death? The woman who was like a mother to me, and she'd been out here all this time, all alone, struggling the same way Valerie had, and I'd been so swept up in—

"Quinn," I say a little louder.

She's alive. She's *alive*. *She's alive.*

A rock shifts on the opposite side of the cave, and my head snaps up. Connor is propped against the opposite wall, watching this all unfold, his expression tight and unreadable.

Quinn stops eating and looks at me, the haze clearing from her eyes. "Offered me a cure. The deal…" She shakes her head too many times too fast. "Couldn't. *Couldn't.* Couldn't hurt you." She blinks, whatever clarity that had fallen over her for a moment dissipating as she bends over the body and starts chewing directly from the source.

I rub my jaw, my other hand tightening into a fist, but I force my voice to remain even. "James Westcott offered you a deal."

She nods, slurping at the blood pooling on the man's skin.

This. Fucking. Bastard.

Taking Valerie wasn't enough? He had to go after *Quinn?* I force in a deep breath through clenched teeth. Killing me—or something of that nature—had probably been the deal.

And she'd said no.

She knew what would happen to her if she didn't take it, but she still said no.

But then why go through the trouble of faking her death? To what end? Had it even been Westcott if she turned him down?

My throat tightens until I can barely pull air in at all. There's a second ache, a dull, bruised kind of feeling, exactly where I'd felt the pain before waking up here. Somehow, I know it's Valerie. I know she's alive. But whatever happened—whatever *that* was—it might not be for long. I need to keep moving.

Apparently thinking the same thing, Connor rises to his feet. When he speaks, his voice comes out rough. "Is she... did you feel her...?"

"She's still alive," I say, my hand unconsciously coming up to rub my chest.

My gaze drifts back to Quinn, and a fist squeezes around my heart. I can't leave her here.

She blinks at me. "Out there"—she points in the same direction as before—the cave's entrance—then points to me—"looking for people like you."

I nod. So she knows about the bounty hunters. "I know."

Her brow furrows. "Why here?"

I clench my jaw, my eyes burning. She tilts her head in the way she always did when she was concerned. I clear my throat, but my voice still comes out rough. "They took Valerie."

She stops chewing and sits up straight. She blinks at me for several moments in silence, and it's like I can see the gears spinning in her head—trying to remember who Valerie is, maybe.

"Valerie," she breathes.

"Valerie." I nod.

The head tilt again. She smiles. "Valerie."

Tears break free onto my cheeks, and I quickly brush them away. She had seemed inexplicably fond of Valerie from the get-go.

The smile drops from her face as she looks at the body in front of her and then back to me. She points between the two of us, and my stomach flips. At first I think she's offering me some of her meal, but then she waves her hands around like she's struggling to say what she wants to.

"He...? He did?"

"He?" I glance at the body. Am I supposed to recognize him?

"No. No. No. No. No." She flaps her hands, harder this time, clearly frustrated now. She points to her own chest. "And Valerie? He did?"

"James Westcott?" I guess. "Yes. He took Valerie."

Quinn scowls—an expression on her that usually makes me laugh, but it's difficult to find any humor in the current situation. She nods understandingly, then tries to wipe the blood from her face with the back of her hand, but that's covered in blood too.

"Here." I pull off my sweatshirt and hand it to her.

She shakes her head, but I wave my hand and push it into her lap. She gives me a small smile that cracks my heart clean in two, then gently dabs the fabric against her face.

"Help," she says, moving on to clean her neck.

"Yes, Quinn, anything you need—I promise—"

"No. No." She points at her chest. "*Help.*"

A small, disbelieving laugh breaks free, and I exchange a glance with Connor. "*You* want to help," I breathe. "You want to help find Valerie."

She nods, determination hardening her features.

I'm already shaking my head. "Quinn, I won't put you in harm's way."

"*Help,*" she insists, glaring at me now. "Valerie."

Well, it's good to see her personality hasn't changed.

I throw my hands up. "We don't even know where she is."

She points toward the cave opening. "Why here then?"

"We were tracking some wolves. I was hoping they might know someone who might know something useful. It's a stretch."

She crosses her arms over her chest. "Seen wolves."

My eyes flick from her to the entrance. "You've seen the wolves?"

She nods.

"You know where they are?"

She raises a single eyebrow. "Help."

I press the heels of my hands into my eyes and sigh. "I've never been able to stop you from digging into my business before," I mutter.

She lets out a triumphant *hmm.*

CHAPTER TWENTY-ONE

VALERIE

THE NUMBNESS GIVES way to cold, then gives way to pain. I figured pain would go away after death. After all, what would be the purpose? But no, there it is. In my ribs, my wrist, my arm, my lungs, my head, my back. I can't feel my legs at all.

I blink, and suddenly I'm not underwater anymore. The stars stare back at me, but then a head swims into view, blocking them.

His face is blurry, dark. Slowly, the features trickle in.

His brow is strained, his jaw set.

Cam?

I try to say it aloud, but my lips don't move.

"Can't stay out of trouble for even a few hours, can you?" he mutters, though the usual humor in his voice is gone. He picks up my limp body like it's nothing, but instead of throwing me over his shoulder like the first time, he brings me against his chest as he turns away from the water and hikes through the trees.

So, not dead then. Because there's no way *this* is what would be waiting for me, or what my subconscious would summon up—however it works.

But judging by the tension in his jaw as the muscle flexes over and over, and the uncontrollable chills racking my body, it's not out of the question yet.

I don't know how long it takes to get to camp. I think I lose consciousness at some point, because one moment my head is lolling against his shoulder, the stars just streaks of light above the trees, the next, Cam's weaving through the tents.

It's quiet, the camp. The fire in the center has been extinguished, and everyone else seems to be asleep.

Drugged, apparently.

And if I'd eaten the stew, I would be too. Maybe that had been their original plan. To grab me unconscious from my tent and kill me before I woke up.

Cam steps into the blacksmith tent, still warm and smoky from the fire earlier.

"You still with me?" he asks as he sets me on the table.

I roll my head to look at him, and apparently that's answer enough, because he ducks away and rummages through the tools at the other end.

I frown as I watch him. If he'd wanted to finish me off, he could've left me there.

He returns with a pair of pliers, grabs my foot, then shoves my pant leg up, revealing the shackle around my ankle. It takes a moment for him to maneuver the pliers between the metal and my leg, and he's shockingly gentle. Gritting his teeth, he applies more pressure until the shackle snaps.

A gust of air fills my lungs, and electricity zips through every nerve in my body as it falls to the floor. The magic warms inside of me, like it's excited to come home, and tears spring to my eyes at the familiar feeling.

The comforting heat burns hotter as my magic fights to heal me, but there's so much damage, and my body is already so weak, let alone I haven't had nearly enough blood since coming here.

Cam rolls up his sleeve, his face pinched together, and holds his arm toward me. "Here."

I shake my head.

"You need it to heal, don't you?"

I swallow hard, trying to find my voice. "It would take more than you have," I rasp.

He sighs and looks from me to the tent flap. "Stay here."

I don't bother telling him I couldn't move if I tried as he ducks outside. I close my eyes. Most of the heat is focused in my chest, trying to heal whatever damage is there first. Broken ribs, at the very least.

I don't hear when Cam comes back, but I smell the blood. The plastic of the bag brushes under my nose, and I open my mouth to wrap my lips around the opening. I'm too fucking hungry to be embarrassed about being hand fed right now.

When I finish the first bag, Cam quickly replaces it. By the end of the second, I finally feel strong enough to sit up. He watches me closely as I take the third from him and bring it to my mouth.

My toes twitch inside my shoes, and I let out a breath of

relief. I'm not sure even my magic would've been able to heal paralysis.

"Are you going to need a healer?" Cam asks quietly.

I shake my head. "I'll be fine."

"Your injuries were pretty extensive—"

"I'll be *fine*."

He lets out a low laugh and rocks back on his heels, still kneeling in front of me. He bumps the discarded shackle on the ground and the metal dings. My eyes shoot to it as he picks it up and twists it around in his fingers, and something I don't recognize flits across his eyes.

"I'm sorry," he says.

I raise an eyebrow.

He gestures to the shackle, his gaze traveling to the scar through my lip. "I should've taken it off sooner," he explains. "But I'll have to put it back on."

I stiffen as he rises to his feet, but he turns away from me.

"I'll take out the lining," he says. "But you'll need to keep it on so the rest of the pack—and Westcott, for that matter—doesn't suspect anything."

I narrow my eyes at his back as he grabs another tool to disassemble the shackle. Why is he being nice to me all of a sudden?

This scared him, I realize. How close I came to dying. Something Westcott wouldn't be too pleased about. Something he'd get blamed for.

"You can relax," I say, my voice still weak. "He probably wouldn't care either way about what happened to me."

"You think I did this because I was worried about what Westcott thinks?"

I raise my eyebrows as if to say, *Well, yeah.*

He shakes his head, his eyes lingering on my face for another beat before he turns back to his work. "I don't wish to see you dead either, Darkmore," he says quietly, almost as if to himself.

I open my mouth, close it.

Silence stretches between us, marred only by the soft sounds of tools against metal as he reworks the shackle. He meets my eyes as he heads over to me, then gestures to my leg.

I nod and hold it out for him.

"I'm sorry about this," he says, voice dangerously quiet as he snaps it into place. The weight of it feels different without the red salt, less suffocating.

"I've gotten used to it."

He shakes his head, still looking at the shackle, then gently tugs my pant leg down to cover it. "You shouldn't have to."

I meet his eyes, just now realizing how close his face is to mine. He has hazel eyes, parts of them gold, parts of them green. Nothing like the pure, deep blue of Reid's.

The thought cuts through my stomach like a knife. The memory of his jacket burning deepens the ache in my chest where the bond used to be.

I don't want to feel like I'm drowning in it anymore. I don't want to think about it. To remember. To cry every night, and then dream about him, then have to wake up and remember he's gone all over again. I just want...

We lean forward at the same time, our lips barely brushing. But then his hands slide into my hair, and he deepens the kiss. He tastes like whiskey and starry nights and fresh air. And there's something soft about it, something beyond the gentle, slow touches, as if he's afraid he'll hurt me. Despite the stubble on his jaw, the calluses on his palms, the gravel in his voice—like this, nothing about Cam feels cold.

Then just as quickly, he pulls back and stands, turning away before I can see his face. "We should get you to your tent," he says gruffly.

I nod and push to my feet, relieved when I don't sway. I could still use a *really* long night of sleep to recover, but the blood helped.

We walk in silence. I should probably ask about what happened to them, the guys who did this to me, but honestly, right now, I don't want to know. I'm too exhausted. He hesitates outside my tent as I pull the flap back, and I glance at him over my shoulder.

He yanks the sweatshirt over his head, revealing his chest, the rigid definition of his muscles clear even in the dim light. His skin is deeply tanned from a life spent under the sun and marred with too many scars to count.

"What are you doing?" I demand.

He juts his chin toward the tent. "You should go in."

"I—what are you—"

He yanks down his pants next, and it occurs to me a beat too late as he goes for his boxers what's happening.

The shift is fast, almost too fast to catch, even with my half-vampire vision. A large, black wolf takes his place, his coat so dark it nearly blends in with the night around us. He settles himself outside the tent and rests his face on his paws. When I don't move, he nods his muzzle to the door.

He's planning on…staying out here.

Like some kind of guard dog.

The thought is irrationally funny to me for some reason, and hysterical laughter bubbles in my stomach. I shove it down and head inside. The fabric rustles as Cam situates himself in the dirt, his tail brushing against it. I sink onto the cot, staring at the shadow he makes against the canvas.

The absence of Reid's jacket fills the tent as I curl beneath the blankets without it, so I press my face into the pillow, trying to silence my cries so Cam doesn't hear them, and wait for sleep to take me.

CHAPTER TWENTY-TWO

VALERIE

My ENTIRE BODY feels bruised and feverish—likely the magic still fighting to heal me. I lie on my back, staring at the roof of the tent as the sun trickles through the fabric. I lift my hands in front of my face, unsurprised to find dirt and dried blood caked under my nails. Gingerly, I prod at the biceps Terrence stabbed the poker through last night. I wince, the wound tender, but at least it's healed enough that the hole has closed. Each breath twinges. The damage done to my ribs—and whatever the hell else in there—clearly has not repaired yet.

It isn't until I force myself to sit up and swing my legs over the side of the cot that the noise outside registers. At first I think it's the wind—it can get pretty loud out here some days—but no, those are voices. Dozens of them, loud and angry and piling on top of one another.

This can't be good.

I stumble out of my tent, and it doesn't take long to locate the origin of the noise. The entire pack is gathered in the center of camp, and my stomach quivers. It looks a lot like the crowd before Terrence's whipping.

I freeze in my tracks, still several yards away. That's probably exactly what this is. I hadn't told Cam who did this—but he'd been the one to get me from the lake, so he must have seen.

Leif, Saint, and Jones are near the edge of the crowd, so I head toward them. When Leif catches sight of me, he does a double take.

"The hell are you doing up?" he whispers.

"What's going on?" I ask instead of answering.

The surrounding shouts drown out his response, and it's so loud I can't make out what any single person is saying. I glance around. They all definitely look more...disheveled than usual, a green tint to their complexions.

The stew. Of course. They're not mad about him attacking me.

But they *are* mad about him drugging them all.

I step to the side, trying to find a window of space to see what's going on at the front.

Terrence isn't bound to a tree like last time, but his wrists are in chains. Two pack members I don't know are holding the chain on each side of him. This time, the crowd doesn't quiet as Cam approaches. If anything, their yells get louder, angrier, egging Cam on.

I can't see his face from this angle, but the tension in his shoulders is clear. He raises a hand, and that's enough to get the shouting to stop.

"Terrence McCullough," he says, voice utterly calm. "Not only did you attack another member of the camp—*again*—but you've also been found guilty of disobeying a direct order from your pack master *and* putting the well-being of every member of this pack in jeopardy by drugging our food source."

I frown and squint, trying to locate his accomplices, but they're nowhere to be seen.

"The punishment for your crimes," continues Cam, "is death."

I gasp despite myself. I don't know what I'd been expecting—another whipping, maybe—but for him to be executed? It's not that I suddenly have sympathy for him. If given the chance, I would've killed him myself last night. I try to gauge the rest of the crowd's reactions. Their expressions are grim, but no one protests.

"You should go back to your tent," murmurs Leif.

"I'm no stranger to death, Leif."

He presses his lips together and shakes his head. "It won't be fast. Every member who was negatively impacted by his actions will get a chance up there if they want it. Cam will go last to finish him off."

"You really are past saving," Terrence growls, his face twisted in disgust as he meets Cam's eyes. "Choosing a vamp over one of your own. You aren't fit to lead this pack. I'm not the only one who thinks it." He spits onto the dirt. "You'll get what you deserve."

There's murmuring in the crowd, but I can't tell if it's dissent or…agreement. Cam's expression remains calm, and he gives a small nod to the man standing at the front—the first in line, I suppose.

He shifts, a dark gray wolf taking his place. A growl rips through the air as he slashes his claws over Terrence's chest.

His shirt tears, and blood wells to the surface. To his credit, he grinds his teeth but doesn't make a sound.

I swallow hard as the wolf snorts and turns away, the next man stepping up for his turn.

"He's always been a bastard," mumbles Leif, "but it's a bad way to go, for sure."

"The others?" I breathe.

"Banished and branded—no other pack will take them now. If they show their faces again, they'll get the same fate."

I glance up and lock eyes with Cam. He's waiting off to the side of the group, arms crossed over his chest, watching me with a frown.

The second wolf, this one a lighter gray and taller than the first, sinks its teeth into Terrence's left thigh and rips out a chunk of his flesh. This time, Terrence does cry out, though his teeth remain locked together, and there's murder in his eyes as he stares down the rest of the crowd.

The wolf spits the bloody piece of his leg—not big enough for him to bleed out, but enough for it to be painful —at his feet and growls. As it turns to go, it kicks at the dirt with its back paws, sending pieces directly onto Terrence's open wound.

"Fuck you too!" grits out Terrence.

"Valerie…" Leif starts.

"I'm not leaving." I don't know why I'm so intent on this, but I'm not going to cower and hide in my tent.

One by one, the crowd thins, the dirt surrounding Terrence becoming more and more stained with blood as the scene turns into a never-ending flurry of teeth and claws and snarls.

When it's Leif's turn, he meets Cam's eyes and shakes his head. Cam turns to me next, and a small jolt goes through my chest. I don't know why I hadn't realized I'd be offered a chance if I wanted one, seeing as I was the person hurt the worst from his actions.

Terrence is barely staying on his feet as I approach. If the guys holding the chains on either side of him weren't there, I suspect he'd fall over. He's drenched in blood, and his head hangs between his shoulders. He stirs as he hears my footsteps though, so he isn't dead yet. He lifts his face enough to see who it is, then lets it drop again.

"Enjoying this, little vampire?" he wheezes, and the liquid in his lungs is audible.

"It didn't have to come to this."

He rolls his head onto one shoulder and grins, his teeth covered in blood. "Of course it did. Go on. Give me your worst."

At one point, I would've jumped at the opportunity. Jabbed a poker through his arm for the poetry of it. But despite the heaviness in my limbs as my body fights to heal itself, despite the new scars on my skin that will never fade now, I shake my head and take a step back.

"I'm sorry for what I did to you before," I say.

Then I turn and walk away. I don't wait to see how Cam finishes it. But the last thing I hear is an animalistic growl, and then the soft thud of a body falling into the dirt.

WHATEVER ADRENALINE HAD BEEN FUELING my body wears off the moment I step into my tent. I nearly collapse in the opening but force myself to make it to the cot before slumping onto my side. More blood would help speed up the process, but unfortunately, even blood magic has its limits, and healing this amount of damage is going to take rest and time.

But I've never been a very patient person.

I glare at the black mark on my wrist, running the pads of my fingers along the raised skin. I'd only made this stupid deal to stop killing people, so no one I loved would get hurt. If it didn't give me that, what was this for?

Tears run down the sides of my face, and I clench my teeth, trying to hold them back, but to no avail.

Despite how acquainted I've been with death all my life, I've never given much thought to what comes after. It seemed a frivolous path to follow. What did it matter what happened when you died? You were *dead*. And whatever the answer was, it's not like you could change it one way or another.

I *felt* the moment Terrence died, the energy in the air immediately shifting. But the images that materialized in my head hadn't been of his body slumping to the dirt.

They were of Reid.

Westcott hadn't given me any details on how it happened. How they did it. Had it been fast? Did he suffer? Was he surrounded by strangers? Had he known it was coming? Had he fought back? Had he—

I force down a deep breath.

The thought of Reid being dead, fully and truly dead— no lingering spirits or presence or afterlife or whatever the hell else it could be—that his spirit or soul is just *gone*...

Gone because he'd tried to come after me.

Because of this stupid choice I made.

My throat closes up, and I fist my hand around the blanket on the bed, willing myself to believe it's his jacket as I close my eyes, but I'd memorized the feel of every inch of that thing, and this blanket is nowhere near the same.

He's gone, and everything I had of him is gone with him.

A part of me hopes there's nothing waiting on the other side, that his presence isn't still with me, because I don't want him to see me like this.

I press my hand against my stomach where the bond used to be, but all I feel is the gaping void of its absence. I don't know how feeling nothing can be so all-consuming, how it can possibly hurt this much. It threatens to swallow me whole.

When I open my eyes, my gaze lands on the bottle of whiskey I'd discarded the night before—before everything happened. I doubt Cam will try to make me work today, but even if he does, I don't care. I snatch the bottle off the ground. There's not much left in it, just a thin line swishing around the bottom, but given the lack of food in my system, my general weakness, and how I'd never had much of a tolerance to begin with, it will be more than enough.

WHEN I OPEN my eyes again, the light filtering through the tent is gone. I roll over, and something cold and hard presses against my ribs—the bottle of whiskey. A bit of the dark liquid lingers at the bottom, so I pop off the cap and swallow the rest of it. My stomach burns and gurgles. How long had I been asleep? When was the last time I *ate?*

I lie on my back and stare at the ceiling, listening to the rest of the camp, but it's quiet outside my tent.

I can't go on like this.

The voice in my head is my own, but it also feels like it's not, like it's coming from someone else. But I know it's right. Reid wouldn't want this for me—to stay curled in bed sobbing over him every night. And after everything I've been through, I refuse to let that be for nothing. For this to be the thing that finally takes me out.

My throat tightens, and tears threaten to rise. The hole where the bond used to be pulses, the emptiness coaxing me to give in to it, to let go.

I sit up straight.

If it weren't for this damn not-bond, maybe I'd stand a chance. But feeling the reminder of it all day, every day. I can barely feel anything else past it.

Insects chirp somewhere in the trees as I make my way across camp. The smell of smoke lingers in the air, though there's no fire. I must have slept through dinner.

I've never been to the tent I'm looking for, but it's easy to find. I would've thought it'd be bigger, but it's the same modest size, just spaced a little farther from the rest. A light flickers beneath the canvas—a candle?

I don't give myself the chance to hesitate before grabbing the tent's opening and stepping inside.

Cam is sitting on the cot in the corner in nothing but a pair of black sweatpants, a book in his hands. His head snaps up, but he says nothing as his eyes roam over me in his doorway, a pinch between his eyebrows now.

I fist my hand in the bottom of my shirt and pull it over my head in one motion. He shows no reaction to the fact I'm not wearing anything beneath it, but his gaze is laser focused on me now, unblinking. A muscle in his jaw ticks.

I slip my thumbs under the waistband of my pants and add those to the floor next, leaving me in nothing but a pair of black panties.

He stares at me, and the silence fills the tent for what feels like an eternity. Goosebumps rise to the surface of my skin—from the chill or him assessing me, I'm not sure. His gaze travels the length of me, starting at my face, then working its way to my feet and back again.

Finally, he rises to his feet and crosses the distance between us. He lets out a slow breath through his nose. But as he leans forward, he pulls the blanket off the chair beside me. He secures it over my shoulders, covering me, then meets my eyes.

"You should go back to your tent," he says, voice husky and low.

My gaze falls to the front of his pants—his body's reaction to me standing here on full display. "Is that really what you want?"

There's a pause, then: "You smell like whiskey."

That would probably be all the whiskey. "Don't tell me you've turned into a gentleman now."

He gives me a thin, humorless smile. "Oh, I'd never be mistaken for that. But the desperation is unbecoming. Go to bed." There's a clear order in his last words, and it makes my cheeks burn. I don't know why I'd thought coming here was a good idea.

I can smell it in the change of his scent, the attraction.

But he's still telling me to leave.

Desperation.

"You're an asshole," I mutter. Swallowing the lump in my throat, I start to turn, but then his hands tighten on the blanket, pulling me to a stop.

I frown up at him, but before I can say anything, he bends, retrieves my shirt from the floor, and yanks it over my head. He grabs my pants next, but when I reach for them, he doesn't move.

I sigh, the embarrassment in my chest tightening into annoyance. "Look, message received. You don't have to be a complete dick about it—"

The last word barely leaves my lips before his mouth is on mine. I gasp and stumble back a step, but his arms cage me against his chest, his touch firm, unyielding. After a moment, I open my mouth, letting his tongue sweep in, and his hand tangles in my hair.

The kiss is rough, hungry, and when I pull away, we're both breathless.

"What the hell?"

"Stop talking." He turns me away from him and guides my hands to hold the chair. "Unless you want to leave."

At first, the words send another flash of heat through my chest, strong enough that I grit my teeth. *Shut up or leave, really?* But he's giving me an out, I realize. Letting me change my mind.

Slowly, I shake my head.

The stubble on his jaw grazes the sensitive spot between my ear and shoulder, his hot breath raising the hair on the back of my neck. My eyes flutter shut as his hand skims my ribs, my hips. I never thought *gentle* would be a word used to describe Cam, but the touch is barely there, his fingertips hardly brushing my skin. But then he hooks his thumbs under the waistband of my panties and yanks them down my thighs, a hand pressing on my lower back to bend me over farther.

His lips start at the inside of my knee, trailing up the back of my thigh. Not kissing me, exactly, just touching.

"Last chance to leave, princess," he murmurs, his voice surprisingly soft.

I grit my teeth at that stupid nickname, but I stay still. Even as he kisses my inner thigh and works higher, I barely feel like I'm in my body at all. Despite the heat of his breath and the pressure of his hands and the gravel in his voice—it all feels…distant.

My breath hitches as his mouth finally finds its way between my legs, and he runs his tongue along the length of me.

But that's the last gentle thing he does.

He sucks my clit into his mouth and between his teeth, the pressure sending an unfamiliar sensation through me. Not pain, exactly. Or maybe it is, and I've grown to like it.

I squeeze my eyes closed as he slides a finger inside of me, then another. His tongue circles my clit before he pauses and murmurs against the back of my leg, "I'll give you one thing, princess. You've got a nice cunt."

My eyes fly open, but he doesn't give me a chance to respond before diving back between my legs. I gasp, my fingers wrapping around the chair hard enough that pain flares up my wrists.

No one has *ever* spoken to me like that. Not even in those painful few months Connor and I tried everything we could to make me enjoy having sex with him more—the dirty talk lasted about five seconds before I quickly realized anything he said just made me laugh.

But right now, I don't feel like laughing.

His hand presses into my back, forcing me to bend over more, then holds me there. I bite my lip, trying not to moan as he slows, teasing me, bringing his tongue farther and farther away from where I want it. My hips squirm, desperately seeking friction, and his laugh rumbles deep in his chest.

He pulls back enough to graze his lips down my thigh, though his fingers are still moving inside of me agonizingly slowly.

"I want to hear you beg for it," he says against my skin.

"I won't ever beg you for anything," I pant.

His hand on my back presses me down farther. "Then we can do this all night, princess."

Without warning, he slaps my ass, *hard*, then sucks my clit between his teeth. I gasp, something between a sob and a moan getting stuck in my throat. His tongue fills me, and a whimper escapes me despite myself as he urges me closer to release then pulls away again.

"Ask me nicely."

"Fuck. You."

"Those really aren't the words I had in mind." He strokes my clit with his tongue again. "You know what?" And again. "I'm feeling"—again—"generous"—again.

I dig my nails into the chair, my body coiled so tight it feels like it will snap in two.

"I'll settle for just one word." He holds his tongue there,

and my hips try to grind against him, and he laughs as he
pulls back an inch.

"Cam—"

"Nope, still not it."

"Fine," I gasp. "*Please.*"

I don't even finish the word before his mouth is back
on me.

Then suddenly, I'm not in the tent anymore. I'm in the
bathroom with Reid, his hands in my hair, his scent filling
my head, his voice in my ear.

Heat builds in my center as he moves faster, harder.

*I would understand, if that's what last night was. If it was just
the situation and everything.*

Is that what that was for you?

No. That's not what that was for me.

I grit my teeth, trying to force the image of his blue eyes
out of my head. The way his hair falls across his forehead.
How much his face lights up when he laughs.

You're the most beautiful thing I've ever seen.

I'm not going to let anything happen to you, Valerie. I promise.

I'll be right back.

My throat tightens, my chest heaving with each breath.
It's like I can feel his skin against me. His lips on the side of
my neck. His hands holding me against him, like he was
afraid to let me go.

God, if he could see me now, he would hate me. He
would think I'm pathetic. And weak. That I hadn't been
worth all the effort he'd gone through to save me.

I hadn't been worth dying for.

Tears burn in my eyes, and the tension in my body

winds tighter, the heat filling every inch of me until I cry out, "*Reid.*"

Hands catch me before I go limp against the chair, and my entire body turns cold as I blink and take in the tent.

I whip around to Cam still kneeling behind me, my eyes wide.

"I—I'm sorry," I stutter.

His expression is utterly unreadable until a corner of his mouth kicks up. "You want to pretend I'm him? I don't give a shit, princess. Well." He claps his hands on my shoulders, then hauls himself up. "You got what you came here for. Best get back to bed before the rest of camp gets up and sees you slip out of here."

He turns away and heads to his cot. I stare at him for a moment, then quickly tug on the rest of my clothes. He picks up the same book he'd been holding when I walked in and flips through the pages until he finds his spot.

I wait for him to say something else, *anything else.* He peers at me over the book, a single eyebrow raised.

"You waiting for a payment, or what?"

My jaw drops, and I let out an unintelligible noise before ripping the tent flap aside and hurrying out.

I swipe the backs of my hands against my cheeks, annoyed at the tears insisting on falling right now. I don't see anyone else as I head to my tent and promptly collapse on my cot.

And yet, as I curl myself around the blanket and close my eyes, somehow the mix of anger and hurt in my chest is better than the gaping hole that had been there before.

CHAPTER TWENTY-THREE

REID

THE SUN RISES NOT long after that, leaving us trapped for the time being. Quinn takes off a bit later, assuring me "Back, back" before heading out into the day. To do what, I'm not sure. There are no belongings or signs that she's been staying in this cave, so where has she been? How has she been surviving out here all alone? I glance at the body lying in the center of the cave, his abdomen a gaping hole. But he's twice Quinn's size. How did she manage to take him down, let alone drag him here? He's in hiking boots and a flannel, so he was likely camping.

He's been dead for at least a few days. I can smell that much. Blood from the vein is nearly inedible once a person has been dead this long, but I need to keep my strength up. Averting my gaze from his face, I lift one of his arms and sink my fangs into his wrist. The blood is thick and clotted and more difficult to bring to the surface now that it's not circulating the body. At least with him on his back like this, gravity hasn't pooled it in places that would be less than desirable to drink from.

When I'm done, I lean against the cave wall, willing the nausea to pass, and rub my hand against that spot in my chest. It's not exactly where the bond used to be. Can she feel it too, whatever it is?

Is it her at all, or am I just feeling what I want to feel?

I sigh, staring off toward the cave's entrance. I should sleep, save my strength. Connor is currently snoring a few feet away. But I feel so useless sitting here and doing nothing. If this lead with the wolves doesn't pan out... I truly don't know what I'll do next other than scouring these millions of acres, one by one.

And even that could be a waste of time.

The wolves could know nothing. She could be far away from here.

I could be too late.

I dig my fingers into my temples and hang my head between my knees. I promised her I wouldn't let anything happen to her. I promised her I would come back.

I promised her. *I promised her.*

The words repeat over and over in my head, layering and morphing together like voices echoing off the walls of the cave. I knot my fingers in my hair, pulling at the roots, trying to silence them, but to no avail. My body is vaguely aware that I've only gotten a handful of hours of sleep for who knows how many days now, but the adrenaline wars with the exhaustion in my veins, simultaneously weighing down my limbs and forcing my eyes to remain open.

I can't just sit here and do nothing, especially not after

whatever it was I felt last night. She could be bleeding out somewhere, or being held captive and—

I pull in a deep breath through my nose, the image of her in the hall outside of my room rising into my mind whether I want it to or not. Her wrists had been raw and bright red from trying to escape the ropes, her hair sweaty and plastered to the back of her neck, blood stuck in the ends. The shadows beneath her eyes were twice as dark as they usually were, and the panic in her face as she tried to communicate, as she couldn't even speak...

I shove up from the wall and pace the length of the cave, then again, and again. The smallest sliver of sunlight streaks across the ground around the bend a few yards away. Even just looking at it has my eyes burning and watering.

"Fuck," I mutter, running my hand through my hair and turning away.

"Are you feeling something from her?"

I jump at Connor's voice. He's sitting propped against the cave's wall now, and he rubs at his eyes as I pace toward him.

"No," I say, then nod at the body. "You should eat."

He makes a face but grabs the man's arm and brings it to his mouth. We lapse into silence while he drinks, and I pull my phone out of my bag and power it on. Still no service, unsurprisingly, but I just need to know what time it is. How much longer we'll be trapped in here.

4:00 p.m. Jesus Christ. The sun won't set for hours.

"You had partners before her, didn't you?"

I turn the phone off and shove it in the bag. "Two," I

say simply, hoping my tone will stop him from asking any further about it.

It does no such thing, of course.

"What happened to them?"

There's nothing accusing in his voice, and I guess I shouldn't be surprised that he's asking. Not that we've been particularly open with one another since he turned, but if the roles were reversed, I'd be curious too.

"Valerie told me they both died," he adds quietly.

I squint at the light seeping in from the cave's entrance and give a short nod. "They did."

A long beat of silence stretches between us, and I sigh. "My first was a woman named Emory. I was thirteen—the age a lot of royal vampires first get paired. She was in her thirties, I believe. And she didn't say much. At least not to me. English wasn't her first language—or her second, or her third—and I was still learning Portuguese, so any conversations we did have were pretty short. I always thought she didn't like me. But then two years later, we were near the Botner estate. There was an attack, and she didn't hesitate to jump in front of me."

Despite that being more than ten years ago, I can remember every detail of that day. The colors, the smells, the sounds. There had been a few attacks from extremist groups around that time, but the humans who'd been following us were more skilled than anything I'd seen. Like they'd been preparing for this, training for this, for years. I blink and clear my throat. "She died instantly."

Connor says nothing, and that weight in my chest doubles in size. As much as I don't like thinking about Emory's death—the sight of her bleeding out on the ground, her graying hair fanned out around her, the way she'd smiled at me right before the light left her eyes. Thinking about what happened next is always worse.

"My second partner," I continue, "came along a little more than a year after that. I was seventeen. He'd just graduated from the academy, so he would've been twenty-two at the time. Where I'd been unsure whether Emory disliked me or not, he made it very clear." I can't help but smile and shake my head. "Saw me as some stupid kid he got stuck with, at least for the first few years. And I don't know when it happened, but somewhere along the way, that changed."

My throat tightens, and I blink hard, trying not to let the memory materialize, but there's no way to think of his death without also summoning the rest of it. The look on his face when he was trying not to laugh, how easily he'd say yes to any plans for the day, no matter how stupid the idea was, the way he'd swear up and down that my company was absolutely insufferable, but if someone so much as looked at me the wrong way, I'd end up being the one holding *him* back from throwing a punch.

"His name was Graham," I say.

"How long were you paired with him?"

"About seven years. He died when I was twenty-four. A few days before he would've turned twenty-nine. He was..." I sigh, debating my next words. "He was my best friend. And I killed him."

I meet Connor's eyes, but there's no judgment there, not even surprise. He says nothing, just waits for me to continue.

"I didn't understand what had happened until afterward. We were at Vasiliev. And one night, he just kept coming at me. I'd thought he was just fucking around at first, but…" I trail off, my arm burning with the memory of the stake he'd stabbed directly through my biceps. If I hadn't pivoted at the last second, it would've gone right through my chest. "I tried to talk him down," I say, my voice coming out hollow. "To reason with him. But it was like he wasn't even in his body. He couldn't hear me. He wasn't him. I wasn't trying to…I was just trying to subdue him. To get him to stop." I pull in a deep breath, feeling the warmth of his blood on my hands all over again. "It occurred to me a few hours later that the reason he couldn't stop attacking me was because he'd been glamoured."

"Shit," Connor breathes. "Did you find who——?"

We freeze at the crunch of footsteps. A second set follows not far behind, these ones heavier, slower.

Maybe more of those humans, but I don't think so. The scent is too hard to pick out from this distance and with the cave walls between us, but something tells me it's not them.

My muscles tense as I strain my ear and wait to see if they'll keep moving, but the footsteps get louder, closer.

Fuck, I really didn't want to have to kill anyone today.

A scent hits me a moment later——sour, rotten.

It's how Quinn had smelled earlier.

But then who does the second set of footsteps belong to?

"No. Stay. Stay. You, stay."

My shoulders relax at Quinn's voice. Her footsteps echo as she makes her way farther into the cave, then stumbles to a stop at the sight of me and Connor.

"Why awake?" she asks.

I glance behind her, but whoever she'd told to *stay* had listened. "Who's with you?"

And with her limited ability to communicate right now, how the hell did she convince them to come here?

She points at the body in the middle of the cave. "Eat?"

"What? Yes, yes, we ate." I let out a short breath through my nose. Even under the circumstances, she can't drop the mothering. "Quinn, what is—"

"Help," she says simply, as if that explains everything, and then heads for the cave's entrance.

"Quinn!" I try to follow but stop in my tracks as she disappears around the corner and into the light. I tighten my outstretched hand into a fist. The daylight thing has always been the worst part of being a vampire, but it's never been more inconvenient than it is now.

Hushed voices sound at the entrance of the cave, but the moment Quinn's companion steps inside, the musky tang of wolf floods my senses.

The woman is taller than Quinn, with broad shoulders and dirty blond hair that barely skims her jaw. Her cut-off shorts and black tank top nearly blend into her skin, considering every inch of her is caked in dirt.

Her dark eyes narrow on me, and she tilts her head upward as she inhales, scenting me, then does the same to Connor.

Quinn chews on her lip, suddenly looking decades younger as her gaze darts from the mystery wolf to me. How the hell did Quinn find her, let alone convince her to come?

"These woods won't be kind to you, *Your Highness*," purrs the woman.

I ignore the sarcasm laced through the words. "So you know who I am. Who are you?"

"Freya," she says simply, as if that explains everything. She nods toward Quinn, though her eyes never leave me. "We struck a deal."

My head snaps to Quinn. "What did you agree to?"

"She stops hunting near our territory in exchange for the information you're looking for," says Freya before Quinn can try to speak.

My brow furrows. Why would she care? And if she did, with presumably an entire pack at her disposal, there would have been easier ways to deal with it than this.

"We're not in the business of killing humans to solve our problems, if that's what you're thinking," says Freya. "That's your kind's thing."

I say nothing, because she's not wrong.

She sighs. "There are rules here for packs. If word gets out about too many missing humans in the barrens, who are they going to look at first? Us. Especially with the...condition of the bodies." She glances at Quinn sideways, a hint of uncertainty crinkling her forehead.

"Who is *they*?" I ask.

"I'm not interested in an interview. If you want my help, you get one question, so choose it wisely."

Despite the hard tone of her voice, there's something tentative about the way her eyes shift, how much she has to force herself to hold her confident body language. Her scent changes—just barely, but enough for me to notice.

The tang of fear.

Whoever *they* is referring to, it's someone with power

over her. But there's no authority outside of the regions, not that I know of.

But whatever that's about, I don't have time for it right now.

"I'm looking for Camden Farley," I say finally.

"That's not a question."

"What information do you have that could help us find him?"

"The golden city."

I scoff and rub my eyes. Why even come here if she had no intention of actually helping?

"What?" Connor asks.

"The city that no one can find," I say, flicking my wrist. "It's just a legend."

"It's real," insists Freya.

"Okay. Then do you know where it is?"

"No." She shrugs. "Just heard Farley's pack's been spotted around there."

"How would you know that if you don't even know where it is?"

She gives me a thin smile. "That's two questions." She turns to Quinn. "I held up my end of the deal. You know the consequences if you don't hold up yours."

I grab her elbow before she can leave, and she bares her teeth at me.

"I know you know more than that," I say through my teeth. "This isn't a game."

"Get. Your. Hand. Off. Me."

All I want to do is tighten my hold, force her to stay until she gives us something useful, but I release her. "Please," I say quietly.

She considers me for a moment and sighs. "There's a town not far from here. I've never been myself, but the wolves I know who have been to the city talked about going there first." She shrugs. "Someone there might know something."

I grind my teeth. She could be lying—and it's barely any more information than we had before—but Quinn grabs my arm before I can respond. At first I think she's trying to avoid an altercation, but it's the look she gives me, the intensity in her eyes, that makes me take a step back. Like she knows something I don't.

Freya doesn't hesitate. The moment my eyes leave her, she shifts, and a black wolf bolts toward the cave entrance.

CHAPTER TWENTY-FOUR

VALERIE

I CONSIDER SKIPPING BREAKFAST, or not leaving my tent at all today—I'm sure given the circumstances, Cam wouldn't fault me for it—but I also don't want him to think I'm hiding because of *him*.

It was a mistake, last night. One I won't make again.

In part it had been to numb the gaping pit inside of me, yes, but there was also a second part to it, one I don't want to admit even to myself.

But a small part of me had actually started to believe Cam cared for me. Maybe not beyond the basic desire to keep me alive, but still, there were rare moments when his cold exterior fell away, and I swore I could see some warmth in his eyes, some humanity.

But he made it very clear last night that I'd been seeing what I wanted to see. I just wish it hadn't taken humiliating myself to figure it out.

But I keep my head held high as I step out of my tent and wind my hair into a ponytail. It seems to be a slow morning—only a few others up, and the sun is barely peeking through the trees.

Cam, unsurprisingly, is sitting on a log and chewing on a piece of meat. He never seems to sleep—always the first person up and last to turn in for the night.

I head toward him, willing my features into a look of indifference. But he's the only person with the blood bags, and my hunger won't be satisfied with whatever disgusting human food they're going to make me scarf down today.

He glances up as I approach and raises an eyebrow, no hint at all as to what happened last night.

A mercy, really.

"Are there any more bags?" I ask.

Nodding, he wipes the back of his hand across his mouth and rises to his feet.

"I can get it—"

He waves me off, then gestures to follow him, still chewing his mouthful of food. My stomach sinks. At first I think he's taking me to his tent—I have no desire to step foot back in there and seeing it will only make the memory resurface—but he veers left toward the one he uses as an office.

It's about the same size as the sleeping tents, and about as minimally furnished, though there's an actual wooden desk instead of some makeshift contraption. I hesitate in the entrance, cross my arms over my chest, and drum my fingers against my elbow, an annoying level of anxiety rising in me the longer I stand here.

"Last one," he announces as he straightens, bag in hand. "I'll have to go back into town." He meets my eyes, and a corner of his mouth lifts as he sees I haven't come any closer. "Afraid I bite, princess?"

That squashes the anxiety. Rolling my eyes, I cross the distance between us and hold out my hand for the bag. I expect him to be a dick about that too—maybe ask me to beg for it like he did last night. The thought makes me swallow hard and my cheeks burn. But he drops the bag into my waiting hand wordlessly.

"Do you *enjoy* being insufferable?" I mumble.

"Oh, you're just mad because I didn't fuck you last night."

I scoff and sputter, hating the heat that finds the tips of my ears, then tear the bag open and turn to go. But then he's standing right behind me, his chest pressed against my back. I curse the skitter my heart does as his warmth washes over me and hate the way my breath hitches even more as his hands land on my hips.

"What are you doing?" I squeeze out. "Someone could walk in."

He hums again, his fingers dipping between my legs and slowly running along my folds. "They could," he muses.

My eyes flutter shut as his thumb works my clit in agonizingly slow circles while his other fingers press against my entrance.

"I guess that leaves me with two choices," he continues. "I could make this fast, or I can make you nice and wet now, then make you wait for later."

Then as quickly as he'd started, he pulls his hands back and steps away from me. I turn to face him, but he's already heading for the door.

"Asshole," I mutter and rebutton my pants.

He waves at me over his shoulder without turning. "See you tonight, princess?" Then he ducks outside.

For the second time, my jaw falls open an inch. *Not likely.* I don't care how my body reacts to him. My downward spiral may have turned me into a bit of a masochist, but *not* to that degree.

I sink my teeth into the blood bag and swallow a mouthful as I shift my weight, hating that he actually made me wet. But we will not be having a repeat of last night.

Never again.

THE DAY PASSES IN A BLUR, and after what happened to Terrence, even fewer people speak to me now. Whether it's because they blame me and hate me for it, or because they're afraid of crossing a line and something similar happening to them, I'm not sure.

All I know is I'm thankful for the peace and quiet. Especially since Cam put me on laundry duty, so I spend most of my day away from the group.

I scowl at the pair of pants from Cam.

The ones he was wearing last night.

I'm tempted to throw them in the lake and feign innocence later—but I wouldn't put it past him to publicly punish me or some shit. Maybe not something as severe as whipping, but who the hell knows? I can't keep up with all the unspoken pack rules around here.

The water laps gently against the shore, and it should be peaceful, comforting. But all it does is bring back memories of that night. Water filling my lungs, the deep ache as I struggled to breathe…

I beat the pants against the rock more forcefully than necessary, my jaw aching from clenching it so hard.

I don't know why I let him get under my skin. Why I let him get under my clothes. *Twice.* It wouldn't be as bad if he weren't so damn smug about it.

But I guess I know why I did it. I just don't want to admit it to myself. Being with him, it felt awful. But the guilt, the shame—it was better than the alternative. It made the pain dim, at least for a little while.

I move with the sun, shifting every so often to keep myself in the shade while I work, and head for camp once the sun goes down. I prepare myself to face Cam, but he's not there as I carry the heavy buckets of laundry to the drying lines, nor once a few guys light up the fire and get dinner underway.

I take mine to my tent but pass on the blood from the animal—a coyote. The bag from this morning was enough to satisfy the cravings, though it won't last for much longer if Cam doesn't restock.

It occurs to me that's probably where he is, somewhere in town. But even as the night comes and goes and people retire to their tents, he doesn't return.

It isn't until several days later than Cam finally strides back into camp as if he'd never been gone at all. The sun is already setting, everyone finishing with their tasks for the day. He barely spares me a glance—just heads from tent to tent, distributing whatever he picked up while he was gone. No one seems particularly surprised or concerned about this, so he must disappear often.

Leif and the only other wolves I like are off on some errand, so I ignore the snickers as I lean over the dead deer beside the fire to feed. I've found that no matter how much I do it, I never get used to it, my fangs sinking into fur instead of human skin.

It's just as gross every time.

Wiping my mouth with the back of my hand, I rise and head for my tent, but even once I'm inside, I can still hear the conversations and laughter by the fire. The animal blood sours in my stomach, killing whatever appetite I would've had for human food. But I've found if I eat the food first and then drink the blood, the nausea is so bad I end up throwing up whatever I ate half of the time anyway.

"Peace offering."

I startle and turn to find Cam in the entrance to my tent. He holds up a blood bag and tosses it on the makeshift table.

I frown, scrubbing off the last of the deer blood from my lips. "You couldn't have given it to me two minutes ago?"

He grins and shrugs. "Maybe I find the sight of you on your knees too appealing."

I make a noise in the back of my throat and roll my eyes. "Thanks for the blood. You can leave now."

He, of course, makes no move to do so. "How were things while I was gone?"

I narrow my eyes, but the humor is notably gone from

his face. "No one tried to kill me, if that's what you're asking," I say flatly.

A corner of his mouth lifts. "While I am glad to hear that, that's not what I was asking."

I throw my hands up and let them slam against my thighs. "What do you want, Cam? I'm really not in the mood for whatever game this is—"

He covers my mouth with his, cutting off my next words. The tension in my muscles loosens, and for just a moment, I let myself sink into it.

But then my pride breaks through, desperately banging on the walls of my mind, and I shove him back by the chest. He pulls away, breathless. His lips are swollen, and I hate how much the sight makes me want to kiss him again.

"What the hell, Cam?" I say, but my voice doesn't come out as strong as I'd hoped.

His eyes never leave mine. He steps toward me, and I step back, my legs brushing the edge of my cot. Slowly, he frames my face with his hands and tilts my head to look at him. There's nothing sweet or soft about his expression, but it's not unkind either. Curious, maybe. Considering.

My breathing quickens as the heat of his hands sinks into my skin, as his scent envelops me—something like fresh air and sunlight and musk. He wets his lips, and my gaze tracks the movement, remembering all too well how it felt to have that tongue on me.

Quietly, he asks, "Do you want me to leave?"

There's an earnestness in his voice that I don't expect. Not taunting, not challenging. If I say yes, he'll do it.

When I don't—can't—say anything, he adds, "I'm not playing a game, Valerie."

I swallow hard, the tangled mess of emotions warring in my chest. Loudest is the confusion, the guilt. Because as I look from his eyes to his lips, I realize I want him to kiss me. A feeling I haven't felt since Reid. Thought I might never feel again.

Even now, his name cuts through me like a knife.

Cam must see the shift in my eyes because he pulls back. "You know I was married?" he says.

My eyes snap to his face, and he nods, then takes a seat on the edge of my cot. I hesitate a moment, then sit beside him. He stares at his hands clasped in front of him and chews on his lower lip.

"Her name was Rea." His lips curl a bit. "We met when we were thirteen."

My stomach drops at his word choice. *Was.*

He rubs his palms together, his gaze still cast toward the floor. "We got married when we were nineteen. Too young to do it—it was stupid—but it would've happened eventually anyway. I was already pack master at that point, so really, what was a little more responsibility? She died when we were twenty-three, so in a way, I'm glad we did it so young. Gave me more time with her."

I stare at the side of his face, unable to speak.

"That was over three years ago, and still, it hits me sometimes out of nowhere. How much it hurts. How much I miss her. How *angry* I am. And then there's these moments when I feel completely fine. Like it never happened. Like she was never here. Maybe those are worse. So anyway." He clears his throat and lifts his head to look at me. His eyes trace my face for a moment, and my skin heats under the scrutiny, but I can't look away. "I just wanted to say I see you. I see what you're going through, and when it happened to me, I had my whole pack around me, and it was still excruciating. For you to be stuck here with us at the same time…" He shakes his head. "Westcott's a real jackass. I can't remember the last time I wanted to be there for someone. Probably not since Rea. And I can't explain why because you get on my *fucking* nerves, Darkmore, and I know you don't like me either, but for some reason, I want to be here for you, okay? So this isn't a game. I'm not trying to be a prick. And I'm not any good at this." He throws his hands up and lets out a long sigh.

"You want to be here for me," I repeat slowly.

He clasps his hands and presses his lips together. Then after a moment, he nods.

I open and close my mouth a few times, but then realize I have no fucking idea what to say. I face forward and stare at the wall of the tent, and the silence stretches between us.

"Huh," I finally say.

He snorts.

I eye him sideways. "I'm not going to, like, hug you or anything."

"Please don't."

"You know, you really don't live up to your reputation."

He chuckles. "Sorry to disappoint. What, exactly, had you been expecting?"

"I don't know," I admit. "I figured the rumors had to be exaggerated. But…" My gaze flickers down his side. "How long ago did you make your deal with Westcott?"

He lets out a slow breath. "Right before Rea died."

"It was for her?"

A muscle in his jaw jumps.

"And she died anyway."

He nods.

I tuck a leg under me and turn to face him. "But then, wouldn't that break your deal? If he didn't hold up his end of it?"

"Technicalities," he mutters. "Every deal has a loophole. It took me a year to realize he'd never intended to help her—this had been his plan from the start. And I'd walked right into the damn trap. Then when I found out the wendigos were *his* to begin with…" He rubs his eyes with his hand. "I'd kill him myself if it wouldn't take me out with him."

"Wait, wait, wait. Wendigos?" I demand.

"Didn't know what was happening to her," he murmurs, a faraway look in his eyes now. "As far as I know, it had never happened to a wolf—never been documented, at least." He waves his hand. "And I'm sure you're all too familiar with what happened next."

"I know it doesn't help at all, but I'm sorry."

He gives me a humorless smile.

I almost don't want to ask my next question, but it slips out anyway. "How long did it take before it started getting better?"

He presses his lips together and slowly shakes his head. "I'll let you know."

CHAPTER TWENTY-FIVE

REID

THERE'S AN ABANDONED rail line not far from the cave, so old that trees taller than I am are growing in the center of the tracks. The woods are quiet. Even when I strain my ear, I can't hear any nearby insects or animals, just the brush crunching under our feet and Quinn's humming as she cranes her neck to look at the moon overhead.

I grit my teeth, something about the forest pulling at my steps, as if urging me to stay. If what the wolf said was at all credible—and it's the only lead we have—then we're looking for some random invisible city that could be anywhere in these godforsaken woods.

The rail line must lead to the town she'd been talking about. That's the hope, at least. I have to trust Quinn knows where she's going. Before, that wouldn't have been a problem. But in her current state? Who knows what effects the psychosis has had on her mentally.

Even as the hours blur together and the temperature noticeably drops with the moon's descent across the sky,

Quinn still doesn't say a word. She keeps humming, a smile on her lips and a skip in her step.

The sight squeezes around my heart like a fist. Because she's somehow simultaneously the woman I've always known and not her at all.

But no. No matter how far she's into the psychosis, how much it's affected her speech and whatever else, she's still in there. I should know that more than anyone else, especially after Valerie. Though in general, it's affecting Quinn differently. Valerie had been perfectly fine most of the time, but when she snapped, she was more animal than human.

Thinking her name makes me skip a step, and I stumble along the tracks. Quinn's humming cuts off, and she glances at me, concern pinching her brow. Connor looks up too. He's been trailing behind us so silently I almost forgot he was there.

"I'm fine," I murmur, quickening my pace.

"Valerie," she says simply.

I tighten and release my fists at my sides.

"How did you get all the way out here in the first place?" I ask.

A small frown appears as a far-off look takes over her face, a look I've become all too familiar with these past few months on Valerie.

She has no idea how she ended up here. Probably blacked out and woke up in the middle of these woods one day.

I startle as her hand brushes mine, softly at first, then she firmly grips my fingers. I glance at her sideways, but she just gives me a sad smile and squeezes my hand once, but she doesn't let go.

Suddenly I'm on the grounds at the estate again, eight years old, following her through the gardens as she pulls me along with one hand and reads from the book she holds in the other.

Her hands had felt a lot bigger then. Now, looking at her, she's barely a ghost of the person she used to be. Her face is too thin, too pale.

I squeeze her hand but can't force any words out past the lump in my throat.

I let her down once. But it's not going to happen again.

AT FIRST I think we're not going to make it before sunrise, but as I slip the pack holding the tent from my shoulders, something swims into view on the horizon. Quinn lets out an excited little squeal and walks faster.

"Quinn, wait." I pull on her hand, trying to get her to slow. We have no idea what we're walking into.

These woods will not be kind to you.

I'd thought she'd meant because of my title, but it could have just as easily been a warning for vampires in these parts. People outside the regions don't tend to think of us very highly.

Connor and I exchange a tense look.

"Okay," says Quinn, tugging on my hand with surprising strength. "Is okay."

At my hesitation, she lets out an impatient huff and drops my hand. She strides toward the entrance like she's done it many times before.

Because she *has* been here before, I realize.

"Is okay," she repeats.

Whatever this place is, it's small. I can tell that much. The gates are made of tree branches, though a barbed wire fence lines the perimeter. As we draw closer, a man steps in front of the gate and lifts his chin. The breeze catches his scent, and it makes me pause.

It can't be.

"What's your business here?" he asks.

Part of it is distinctly human, but whatever his other half is, I can't make out.

"Help," says Quinn as she gestures wildly with her hands.

The man holds his gaze on me and Connor for a beat too long before finally glancing at her, but the moment he does, his entire face softens into clear recognition.

What the hell has she been up to all this time she's been gone?

"Good to see you back!" He steps forward and wraps her in a hug, which she returns immediately. "Who are they?" he asks, nodding at me.

"Reid," she says simply, then gets a small furrow between her eyebrows as she looks at Connor, probably trying to remember his name.

"Connor," he supplies.

The man glances at me, appraising this time. "The infamous Reid."

I lift an eyebrow.

The man cranes his neck back as he releases Quinn, then waves for us to follow. "If I remember correctly, you're needing to get inside somewhere pretty soon here, right?" His eyes flick to Connor, and his nostrils flare as he inhales. "You too, I suspect." He turns and heads for the entrance before I have a chance to respond. "I wouldn't advertise that, by the way," he adds. "But I've got a place for you."

What I'd thought was a town behind the gates turns out to be a modest-sized village with small wooden structures and clotheslines strung between them.

But there's no one else here. No one walking around, but I also can't hear a single heartbeat.

"This way." The man takes us to one of the larger structures on the right, made of thick, dark logs and a door covered in peeling white paint. He shoves the door open with his shoulder and it lets out a low groan as it scrapes across the floor.

"Watch it, Riley!" barks a raspy voice.

"As if the floor is in pristine condition," mutters Riley as he waits for Quinn to step in ahead of him. He meets my eyes as I follow her, though there's nothing threatening there anymore…just curiosity.

The moment I cross the threshold, I pause, focusing on the man behind a check-in counter. His face is barely visible beneath the wiry gray and black beard and matching head of hair that's past his shoulders.

But still. Even now, standing just paces away from him, I can't hear a pulse.

He gives me a slow smile, revealing a mouthful of crooked yellow teeth, as if he knows exactly what I'm thinking.

"Unfortunately," says Riley behind me, "this is the only inn for miles—dozens of miles—hell, maybe hundreds. So you're stuck with old Barney here."

"Who are you calling old!"

"Good to see you." Riley claps Quinn on both of her

shoulders, then slips out the door, letting it scrape across the floor again as he yanks it shut.

Barney's yellow grin widens, his attention on Connor now. "A room?"

"Three," I say, eyeing the lobby around us—if it can even be called that. All the windows are covered with wooden shutters. Though I suppose I should be grateful for that with dawn quickly approaching. It casts a dark, dingy shadow over everything, but I doubt the building would look much better in the light. Dust lingers heavily in the air, thick enough to choke on. And there's a single couch in the corner beneath the windows, the leather ripped and covered in what appears to be claw marks. "If you have the space."

It doesn't look like anyone in their right mind would stay here by choice, but what do I know? If there are others like this old man with apparently no heart, there could be a dozen other people under this roof and I wouldn't know it.

The thought is immediately chilling.

"Anything for you, *Your Highness.* But unfortunately, we only have two available."

So he knows who I am. I exchange a sideways glance with Connor, and he shrugs. I dig my phone out of my bag, figuring there's a better chance of service now that we've found some semblance of civilization—or at the very least, somewhere to charge it.

"I wouldn't waste your time." Barney winks and ducks beneath the counter, popping up a moment later with two sets of metal keys. "Doubt you'll find anywhere around here not affected by the enchantment."

"Enchantment?" Connor asks.

"People don't come to the barrens because they want to stay on the grid," he says as if it's obvious, then heads for the wooden staircase in the back.

Quinn follows him, seemingly unfazed. But the chill forcing every hair on my body to stand at attention lingers, even once we make it to the second floor and he unlocks two doors, then holds out the keys for us to take.

"Hope you'll find the accommodations to your liking," he says as I take the key.

"Thank you," says Quinn, her voice coming out surprisingly clear.

He does a small bow before turning for the stairs, whistling. "There's a bar in the basement if you're thirsty!"

The ugly blue carpeting from the hall continues into the rooms, where two small beds sit in the center. A wooden chair is tucked in the opposite corner, but there's no other furniture in the room.

Thankfully, the single window on the far wall is covered with wooden shutters, but also thick black curtains. I peer into Quinn's room and frown. Hers has the shutters, but not the curtains. A single ray of morning light peeks through the cracks and falls onto her bed.

"What is this?" I ask. "Who are they?"

She smiles at me and squeezes my arm. "Sleep. Talk tomorrow."

"Quinn—"

"*Sleep*," she insists.

I grab her arm before she can pull away, then bring her in against my chest. She lets out a surprised giggle but wraps her arms around my waist as I tighten my hold on her and rest my chin on the top of her head.

"Reid," she says softly.

"Good night," I say, my voice coming out gruff, before releasing her.

Despite the lack of sleep since Connor and I left the estate, I can't feel any of the exhaustion now. I sink onto the edge of the bed, and the mattress springs creak beneath my weight.

Connor hesitates with his back against the door, a deep crease between his eyebrows. "What are they?"

The mattress slopes toward the center as I lie back, the comforter giving off that same odd scent as the man from the gate. In all my traveling—in all the creatures I've encountered, full-blood and halflings alike—how have I never smelt anything like that?

I mean, I haven't heard of creatures without a heartbeat before today either.

What the hell have we stumbled into?

"I don't know," I murmur.

"Quinn seems to know them," Connor adds.

I don't know if that should be a comfort or just confusing. I've always trusted her judgment. In theory, if she feels safe here, we should have nothing to worry about.

But in her current state…

I don't know how much that's affecting her mind. Her decisions. But then she has these moments of clarity, where she seems perfectly herself.

I meet Connor's eyes across the room.

"Maybe we should sleep in shifts," he says.

I nod.

CHAPTER TWENTY-SIX

VALERIE

I'VE FOUND the early morning to be the best time to sneak out to the lake to bathe. A lot of the pack isn't up yet, and the ones who are, for the most part, are up for a reason, so they're busy with their jobs. Still, I hesitate as I reach the edge of the water, glancing around and straining my ear to ensure I'm alone before stripping off my clothes and wading in. The cold water is a shock to my system, but I grit my teeth and keep going until it reaches my shoulders.

Leaning my head back until the water covers my hair and skims over my ears, I close my eyes and let myself relax into the silence.

The sun is starting to rise, so it's uncomfortable against my skin, but not too bad yet.

It used to feel good, the sun. The warmth. Before everything changed. It felt like a shame, even, to be on the vampire timetable and never get to enjoy the daytime.

I scrub at my hair. That line of thinking is just as useless now as it was back then. *Careful what you wish for*, I suppose. Now I've had enough sun to last a lifetime.

A branch cracks somewhere in the woods behind me, and I still. Slowly, I turn, eyes darting from one end of the trees to the other. There's a second crack, and I stiffen, but then Cam steps into view a moment later.

"You scared me," I breathe, pressing a hand to my chest.

He smirks, but it doesn't reach his eyes. "I heard a couple of the guys say they were going to head over here in a bit. You'll probably want to clear out soon."

"You came all the way here to tell me that? How did you even know where I was?"

He shifts his weight and stuffs his hands in the pockets of his jeans. He doesn't look at me, not really. And for some reason, I…want him to. And it's not like he hasn't seen me naked before, but every time his gaze lands on me, he quickly looks away, just a few inches above my head, to the side.

"You're in the blacksmith tent today" is all he says.

I nod, starting to shiver.

He nods too, then heads through the trees. Numbly, I finish up, climb out, and redress. Sure enough, as I trek toward camp, I hear footsteps going in the opposite direction. I veer off course a few yards so I don't have to run into whoever they belong to.

If Cam felt the need to trek all the way there to give me a heads-up, I'm willing to bet they're not the sparse few pack members who can actually stand me.

The others in the blacksmith tent ignore me as I work on the cuffs. Everything about the day passes the same as usual—except I keep catching myself looking for Cam. I never used to pay much attention to his comings and goings before, so I can't tell if it's out of the ordinary for him to be gone so much, but I don't see him all day, not even once dinner rolls around and everyone is wrapping up their jobs.

I scowl at the others gutting a deer, my stomach cramping at the thought of having to drink that. I catch sight of Leif climbing out of his tent and wave him down.

"Have you seen Cam?" I ask.

A weird look crosses his face, and he scratches at the back of his neck.

"I need a bag," I explain, gesturing to the animal carcass as a few others step in to get the fire going. "Otherwise, I have to drink that. Would *you* want to drink that?"

"I wouldn't..." Leif shakes his head. "I wouldn't go see him right now. It's best to leave him alone when he's like this."

"I—like what? Where is he?"

Leif sighs and runs a hand over his mouth. He seems to debate with himself for a few moments before finally nodding to the woods on our right. "Don't say I didn't warn you," he mutters as he heads toward the fire.

He isn't hard to find. He's not far, and I hear him long before he comes into view. The tree trunk is massive, though it barely resembles one at this point. Lying horizontally in the dirt, one side is almost completely hollowed out.

A low grunt fills the space between us as Cam swings the ax over his head and strikes down hard against the trunk, chipping away at it, though there doesn't seem to be a particular rhyme or reason to the cuts.

I stop a few paces away. The stiffening of his spine

implies he knows I'm here, but he doesn't break pace. Sweat drips down the tanned skin of his back, enough that it's clear he's been at this for a while.

"Go back to camp," he says through his teeth without looking at me.

I don't, obviously. "What are you doing?"

"What does it look like?" he grunts, the ax sinking into the tree a little harder this time.

"Like you're having a bit of a meltdown."

He barks out a humorless laugh. "You could say that." Before I can respond, he adds, "What do you want, princess?"

The muscles in his back flex and strain as he brings the ax down over and over.

"What's wrong?"

I don't know who's more surprised by my question—him or me. It certainly isn't what I'd intended to say. He pauses and lets the ax rest at his side, his shoulders rising and falling rapidly as he catches his breath. The intensity in his expression pins me to the spot as he turns. I feel his gaze like a physical touch as it travels across my face, sending a shiver through me.

"Go back to camp," he grits out, his voice more wolf than human.

I take a step closer. "You don't scare me."

He holds my gaze a moment longer, then shakes his head and looks away, his fist tightening around the ax. There's something about the set of his shoulders that makes my next words freeze in my throat.

He isn't angry. He's...sad.

"Cam—"

"Just get the fuck out of here," he snaps.

I cross the rest of the distance between us and hesitantly lay a hand on his arm. He whips around, ax raised, nostrils flared.

I stumble back a step despite myself and look from him to the ax. "Go on then. What are you planning on doing with that?"

I don't know where it came from, this absolute certainty that he won't hurt me. But there's no trace of fear inside me as I stare at the sharp blade. When my gaze finds his face again, his focus is trained on my lips. I stop breathing as he slowly drags his eyes back to mine.

"Today's Rea's birthday."

My heart drops into my stomach. "Oh. I—" I sigh, immediately feeling like an ass as he turns and sets the ax against the trunk. "I'm sorry. I shouldn't have—"

"This is usually the worst day of the year to get through," he says, almost to himself.

That would explain the mangled remains of that tree. Did he do that all today, or is this a regular thing for him?

"And yet…" He lets out another hard laugh and shakes his head. "This time, I didn't even remember what day it was until halfway through."

I can see there's far more that he's not saying behind his eyes as they burn into mine. A look I know far too well. A unique mix of guilt, shame, confusion…and something else.

Something that coils itself tightly low in my stomach.

Something warm and heavy and—

KATIE WISMER

He takes a step back from me, then another. I turn
away at the same time, heading for camp. I focus on my
breath—in, out, in, out—but his footsteps behind me break
through the haze.

"Darkmore," he calls.

I keep walking.

Everyone is preoccupied with dinner when I duck
through the trees and step into camp. The last of the sun in
the sky has faded, the moon beneath a cloud cover, so the
fire offers the only light. I slip into my tent at the end of the
row unnoticed.

And when Cam steps in a moment later, it isn't a
surprise. I say nothing, and neither does he. The hesitation
from before is gone now, but there is the hint of a question
in his eyes as he slowly crosses the distance between us,
giving me the opportunity to say no, to tell him to leave.

But I don't.

The kiss is different this time. Slow. Curious, almost, as
if it's the first time. There's none of the hunger, the desperation, though the way his hands frame my face, his thumbs
gently gliding across my cheeks, sets every inch of my skin
aflame.

It twists in my stomach, how good it feels. How much I
want him to keep kissing me and touching me and
breathing me in. But I swallow the guilt, because it's pointless to keep feeling guilty over a ghost. Maybe it's selfish and
wrong and stupid, but when I look at the past few months
of my life, all there's been is pain and suffering. One thing
after the other after the other.

Is it so unreasonable, just for once, to stop thinking?

I reach for the hem of the shirt he must have thrown on

before running after me as his lips press harder against mine, his tongue sweeping into my mouth. He yanks the shirt over his head, then grabs my face again, his grip stronger this time, his kiss more demanding. His skin is still slick with sweat, amplifying the scent of him—like earth and fresh air and the way it smells just before it rains.

We stumble backward toward my cot, kicking off our shoes as we go.

"Lift your arms for me, princess," he murmurs against my lips, a smirk pulling at his.

"If you call me that one more fucking time," I grumble.

He tugs the shirt over my head, then grabs the backs of my thighs and hoists me into his arms, his lips never breaking from mine.

"You'll what?" he taunts. "I'd like to hear the end of that sentence." His mouth moves to my jaw, my throat, my collarbone. I gasp as his stubble scratches my skin, and he gently scrapes his teeth against the top of my breast.

"You're so fucking smug," I pant as he lays me out on the bed and yanks my pants down my legs.

"And yet..." He dips his head between my thighs to taste me. I shudder at the stroke of his tongue, and I *feel* his grin. "I don't think you dislike it nearly as much as you pretend." He pulls my clit between his teeth, and I gasp. "Otherwise," he breathes, "you wouldn't be this wet for me already."

His lips trail down the inside of my thigh to my knee, but then he pauses as he reaches the shackle around my ankle, his hands stilling on my legs. He looks up and meets my eyes, a hardness in his expression that wasn't there before.

"Cam?"

"Hold on," he murmurs.

I push myself to my elbows as he shuffles through the contents of the desk. He comes up with a screwdriver that must be left over from when Leif slept in here, then kneels in front of me.

His gaze is intent on the shackle as he props my foot on his shoulder and works the screwdriver into the hinge. A few seconds later, it opens, and he sets it on the ground.

I say nothing as he takes my ankle in his hand, brushes his lips where the shackle had been, and starts working his way up my body. He pauses as he reaches my face, his forearms braced on either side of my head.

"Thank you," I murmur.

"Don't." His voice comes out tight. "Don't thank me. Not for that."

We stare at each other, and the intensity sinks into me, completely immobilizing. Something stirs in my chest, something I don't want to acknowledge.

Something that makes me want to kick him out of the tent and forget this whole thing. Because this was *not* what I was looking for with him. A distraction. Even the guilt was preferable over the gaping hole in my chest. But whatever this is—

He covers my mouth with his, his lips hard and sure as he shoves his own pants off. My fingers trail down the muscles of his abdomen as he kisses my jaw, my neck. I pause when I reach his hip, the skin shifting from soft to rough. He pulls back an inch as I trace the mark of the blood deal, his eyes closed.

My hand stills. Is that what this is about for him? Is he

pretending I'm her? I know that shouldn't bother me, especially considering what happened the first night.

But still.

I don't want to see it on his face. I start to roll over, but he grips my hips, holding me in place against the bed.

"If you can't look at me when I fuck you," he says, his voice impossibly low, "then we're not doing this. You're not pretending I'm him tonight."

Slowly, I nod.

He stares at me, as if trying to read my thoughts on my face, before finally kissing me again. His tongue sweeps into my mouth, his hips pressing into mine, and a groan escapes my throat.

I wrap my legs around his waist as he pushes against my entrance, the slickness between my thighs granting no resistance as he glides himself inside of me. We both inhale sharply, and he presses his forehead against mine.

"You feel even better than I imagined," he breathes.

Slowly, he grinds his hips, filling every inch of me. My inner walls contract around him, burning and pulsing and aching—part pain, part pleasure. He gradually increases his pace, each thrust harder. I gasp, my nails digging into his shoulders and my ankles locking together around his waist.

His next thrust knocks the wind out of me, but I don't have time to catch my breath before he pounds into me again and again.

"Fuck," I breathe, my head falling against the bed.

He wedges his hands under my hips, tilting them up to angle us so he grinds against my clit with each thrust. My breaths turn into pants as the sound of our bodies coming together fills the tent, and heat builds low in my core.

Abruptly, he slows, then adjusts his weight so he's kneeling in front of me. I look up at him, breathless, and he gives me a wolfish grin.

"Why are you stopping?" I gasp.

"Because, *princess*"—he tucks both hands beneath my knees and pulls me closer, then works my clit with his thumb as he starts to thrust again, slower—"I'm going to make you come, and I want to watch."

My breaths turn to moans, to whimpers, to noises that have never come out of me before. But as my eyes fall closed, his hand on my hip tightens almost to the point of pain.

"Eyes on me," he orders, "or I stop. Understand?"

I swallow hard and nod, my hips moving with him, desperate and needing more, more, more... He keeps his pace slow, thrusting all the way in, then almost all the way out, hitting exactly the right place until every nerve in my body zeroes in on the contact. On the fire spreading through me. I gasp as he presses his thumb harder, my back arching.

"Not a screamer, huh?" he breathes. "Or do you need me to fuck you harder?"

My eyes roll back, and he grabs my head with both hands, forcing me to look at him as he pounds into me harder, faster. The sensation is ferocious, agonizing, intoxicating, filling me completely, deeper than I thought possible. It's almost too much. Or it is too much. So, so much.

"Touch yourself," he rasps.

My hands go between my legs without a second thought, my entire body desperately seeking its release.

I can't breathe. I can't think. I can't—I can't—

"C-Cam."

"I know," he grits out through his teeth.

"I—I can't—"

"You can take it. I've got you."

"Cam," I gasp, his name apparently the only word my brain is capable of remembering right now.

"You're doing so good, princess. That's it. Breathe for me."

"*Fuck,*" I cry out as I finally crest the edge. He never breaks pace, and I whimper as another wave rolls over me, then another. I grip the sheets, trying to quiet myself, but the noises are coming out of their own accord.

"You can be as loud as you want," he breathes, a smile clear in his voice. "They can already hear you getting fucked out there. Might as well let them know you're enjoying it."

I convulse around him, clinging to his arms as the orgasm tears through me, violent and devastating. He doesn't let up, each thrust just as hard and deep until it feels like it will never end.

"Atta girl," he breathes, slowing as he leans over me, his lips brushing mine, then my jaw, my temple. "You're taking it so good for me."

He releases my head and grabs my hips instead, angling them farther up as he sinks deeper, and my head falls against the pillows with a breathless moan.

A devilish grin appears as he looks down at me. "If you need to tap out, just say the word."

It's like a bucket of ice water. Every muscle in my body freezes, and he must sense it, because he stops, concern pinching his brow.

"Did I hurt you?"

I shake my head, trying to gulp in air, but nothing is making it to my lungs.

It's like I'm not in the tent anymore. I'm in the bathroom. Reid lying next to me with that damn grin, ready to go again.

It's taking every ounce of my self-control not to convince you to stay in here.

"Hey." Cam's face swims into view, right in front of mine.

Understanding lights his eyes, and he pulls out.

He falls onto the mattress beside me. My chest heaves. I don't think I could move—could speak—if I tried. But then his fingers brush my arm.

I glance at him sideways, not sure what I'm expecting in his expression, but the way he strokes my hair takes me by surprise.

"You good?" he asks quietly. I nod, but his gaze is just as intent as he searches my face. "You sure?"

I nod again. His skin is flushed, his hair an absolute mess, and sweat glistens on his chest. I can only imagine what I look like.

"I'll be right back," he says, pressing his lips to the top of my head.

He climbs out of the cot, pulls on his boxers, and disappears through the tent flap. I push myself into a seated position with shaky arms, then tuck my knees into my chest.

I don't know what's worse, Reid appearing in my mind at that moment, or the fact that it had taken that long for me to think of him in the first place. Covering my face with my hands, I order myself not to cry. I don't know why I thought I could do this.

"Hey."

I jump as Cam pushes the hair from my face, kneeling beside the cot now, a cup of water in his hand. I hadn't heard him come back in.

My hand shakes as I take it from him and force down a sip.

"I'm sorry," I whisper, not able to meet his eyes.

He curls his fingers beneath my chin and lifts my face. His eyes are serious, but not unkind. "Don't be."

I shake my head, trying to clear the thick feeling in the back of my throat. "I don't—I didn't—"

"It's all right." He pulls me to his chest.

"I'm sorry," I say again. "You didn't even—do you need me to—I can—"

"No, no, it's okay," he murmurs, and I can hear how much he means it in the tone of his voice, despite this now being the second time things have ended in a less-than-satisfying way for him. After a moment, he adds, "I couldn't honestly expect you not to think about him."

"I wasn't." I'm not sure why I say it, but I guess some part of me wants him to know the truth. "I wasn't," I repeat, my voice barely louder than a whisper. "Not until then. Were you thinking about her?"

He pulls back to look at my face, his hand stroking my hair, the touch gentler than anything I've ever felt from him.

He meets my eyes as he says, "Not until then." A tear runs down my face, and he wipes it away with his thumb. His jaw works, like he's carefully choosing his next words. "I'm…okay. With complicated. If you are."

I blink at him, not sure who's more surprised when I nod.

A small, soft smile replaces his serious expression, and he glances at the bed behind me. "Is it okay if I stay then?"

I lay my hand over his, still cupping the side of my face, and let out a shaky breath. "Yes."

CHAPTER TWENTY-SEVEN

REID

QUINN'S GONE by the time the sun sets. Her room is quiet as I pass in the hall, no pulse or breathing on the other side. Connor rubs his eyes as we head downstairs, still trying to wake up since he had the second sleeping shift. It's quiet when we reach the first floor, the front desk unattended.

"He said there was a bar in the basement," Connor offers. I nod, struggling to shake off my unease as I follow him down the stairs.

"Late sleepers, I see!" Barney calls from behind the bar.

The rest of the room is empty. It's larger than the lobby —if the upstairs can be called that—with three small tables and four barstools.

Barney finishes toweling off the glass in his hand and sets it on the bar. "I'm guessing you're not here for a drink."

"Have you seen Quinn?" I ask.

"She'll be back in, I'd say..." He glances at his watch. "Well, any minute now."

"Where is she?"

He smiles as if the question amuses him and doesn't respond.

"Look, we were told you might have information on the place we're trying to go," says Connor.

Barney's eyebrows slowly climb his face.

"What do you know about the Golden City?" I add.

Barney barks out a laugh. "You have a death wish?"

"Do you know where it is or not?" snaps Connor.

"I know where it is," Barney says, unperturbed. "But you know, I'm not in the business of giving out things for free." He spreads his hands wide. "Wouldn't make me much of a businessman, now would it?"

Of course it wouldn't be that easy. "What do you want?"

His eyes darken, his smile twisting into something sharper. Hungrier. "How important is it to you?"

"You're not making a deal with them."

Footsteps pound down the stairs, and the man from the front gate appears a moment later—Riley, I think his name is. He barely acknowledges me and Connor, his gaze leveled on Barney.

Barney laughs and shows his palms. "Can't blame a guy for trying."

"Come on." Riley juts his chin for us to follow him upstairs, and I cast one final glance at Barney. He's not a witch. I'm sure of that much. The heartbeat anomaly aside, his scent is all wrong. It's not sour, exactly, but sharp, like chemicals.

If he hadn't intended a blood deal...what the hell is he? He shows me his teeth in some semblance of a smile.

"You're looking for the Golden City?" Riley asks,

ushering us past the lobby and out the front door. The rest of the town feels as abandoned as it did when we got here, but something tells me there's much more going on around here that I can't see. The wind picks up, scattering the leaves littering the dirt path, carrying that same sharp smell with it.

"Here." Riley presses a small stone into my palm, but he doesn't release my hand.

I meet his eyes, and he stares back, unblinking. "But I have one condition."

"Okay?"

He tightens his hold on me. "You go alone."

I glance at Connor out of the corner of my eye, his frown mirroring my own.

"Why—?"

"You will not take Quinn to that place," he says lowly. "And I will not have sending *two* vampires past their protections on my conscience. Are we agreed?"

Connor opens his mouth to speak, but I raise a hand to stop him.

"Yes."

Riley holds my gaze for a moment longer before releasing me, then nods at the stone. "It's a simple enchantment. It'll grow warm as you get closer, cold as you move away."

I turn the stone over. It's ordinary in appearance— small, black, dull—but I can feel the power in it. The pulse.

"Don't make me regret this," Riley says lowly.

I nod and tighten my fist around it. "Thank you."

"Reid?" Quinn heads toward us down the dirt path,

wiping at the corners of her mouth. Her hand comes away red with blood.

She must have gone out to feed.

"I don't like this," Connor says. "I'm not just turning around and going back."

Quinn's gaze bounces from him to me, and I grip his shoulder. "You take her to Auclair—"

"I'm not—"

"Listen to me. You take her to Auclair, and you make sure she's safe. My mother has a team who tracks the movements of all the packs close to the region. The head is at Auclair. If this lead falls through, we need a backup. That backup is you."

He sets his jaw, looking like he still wants to argue, but says nothing.

It could take days to get to Canada, and even then, there's no guarantee Ashley would help us. He's a good man, but the last time I saw him was almost ten years ago.

The wind rustles through the trees, and a shiver runs down my spine so violently that my eyes fall closed. There's a vibration in the air, a pull.

Like the forest is urging me not to leave.

Which is entirely insane, of course.

And yet.

"I'll do it," he says suddenly. "Tell me where to find him and what to say, and I'll go."

"It might be another dead end."

He shrugs. "I need to feel like I'm doing something. Just tell me what I need to do."

I tell him what I can about Ashley, about Auclair, what to ask, what to say. It would make me feel better if Connor had at least *been* there before, but until now, he'd never even left the region.

"Tell him I'll owe him a favor," I add, a smirk gracing my lips. "He can add it to my tab. Are you sure you'll be able to find your way back?"

He snorts. "Give me a little more credit than that."

I turn to Quinn, and my chest tightens at the thought of saying goodbye to her again, but she gives me a small smile, like she'd known it would come to this.

"Will you go with him?" I ask, and my voice comes out rough. "He'll keep you safe."

The smile never leaves her face, but she steps forward, places a hand on my cheek, and slowly shakes her head.

"Quinn...you can't come with me."

She shakes her head again. "Stay."

I cover her hand with mine and sigh. "Quinn, I can't. I can't stay."

"No. No. Me. Stay." She points to her chest, then to our surroundings.

"Quinn, no, you don't have to stay here."

"Want," she insists and squeezes my hand. "Want to stay." She shrugs. "Family."

I slowly look from her to the buildings around us. Riley disappeared without me noticing. But she can't mean...

The look in her eyes is all too knowing as I find her face again. She nods. "Family."

"Reid..." Connor starts behind me.

I tighten my hold on her hand, a million thoughts whirling in my head. On the implications of this. What this could mean. But we don't have time for the questions, and I don't know if she'd be able to answer them. "You're sure you'll be safe here?"

She nods and pats my cheek. "Go. Valerie."

My breath comes out shaky, and a tear breaks free. I lock my jaw and pull her against my chest. Connor meets my eyes over her head, and I nod.

"Go. I'll try to get ahold of you when I can. Do you have everything you need?"

"I'm good." With that, he turns and heads toward the entrance.

He's nearly out of view when I call, "Just...be careful. I didn't save your life just for you to die now."

He smirks at me over his shoulder. "Careful. Might think you're actually starting to like me."

CHAPTER TWENTY-EIGHT

VALERIE

CAM'S GONE the next morning. I don't know if I should be surprised, but I sure as hell shouldn't be disappointed. And yet, as I roll over and find the cot beside me empty, a heaviness settles in my chest. I slowly push myself into a seated position and am immediately taken aback by the soreness between my thighs. That doesn't usually happen with how fast I heal. It must be because I haven't been feeding enough. And last night hadn't been particularly...gentle.

My face heats as I glance at the entrance to my tent. The light coming through the canvas is faint, but several sets of footsteps pound against the earth, voices carrying from somewhere in the distance. There isn't usually this much activity this early.

After yanking on the first clothes I can find and pulling my hair up, I duck out of the tent, my eyes stinging as the sun hits them. No one pays me any mind as they hurry back and forth, their faces pinched together in what looks like...worry.

"Leif!" I flag him down before he can disappear into the trees. "What's going on?"

He nods for me to follow him but doesn't wait, so I have to jog to catch up.

"The funny thing is, Cam's probably got the worst reputation of the pack masters on this coast," he says, though I don't know if he's actually talking to me, seeing as he's still hiking through the trees at a pace that's nearly impossible to keep up with and he hasn't checked behind him once to see if I followed. "But Nina?" He blows the air out of his cheeks. "I don't use the word lightly, but if anyone deserves to be called a psychotic bitch…"

"Leif!" I grab his sleeve, fully out of breath now, and tug him to a stop as we reach the top of a hill. "Who is Nina? What are you talking about?"

His eyes search my face, then he swears under his breath. "Cam hasn't talked to you yet?"

I raise a single eyebrow. "Would I be chasing you through the woods right now if he had?"

Leif sighs and runs a hand through his hair. "You should go find him—"

"Why are you being so weird and secretive?"

"Nina's the master of a different pack. They're usually down in Georgia, but we got word this morning that they're on their way here to see Cam."

"What, why?"

"Your guess is as good as mine." Leif shrugs, and his expression darkens. "They're not the type of pack you want to associate with. And they definitely aren't the type that'll take kindly to you being here. If you thought we were bad…anyway. I'm sure Cam's gonna want to put you up in town again or something. You should go find him before they get here."

With that, he turns and resumes his trek.

"Wait! When will that be?"

Leif throws his hands up but doesn't turn. "Who the hell knows?"

———

CAM ISN'T easy to find. I circle the entire camp—checking his tent, his office—until finally giving up and heading for my own. If he wants to speak with me, he can find me, I guess. But when I shove back the flap to my tent, he's already standing in the middle of it.

"Where the hell have you been?" he barks.

I flinch, and the hardness in his face softens. I'm unable to stop my brain from summoning images of last night as he meets my eyes. "I—Leif said I should find you. I was looking for *you*."

"Sorry." He rubs the bridge of his nose with two fingers and squeezes his eyes shut. "I thought..." He shakes his head. "You and I are leaving. Now."

I notice the bag at his feet for the first time, already packed and ready to go. "Are you going to give me an explanation, or...?"

"In the car," he says, yanking the pack off the floor and tossing it to me. "We're heading into town."

I don't move, even as he brushes past me for the exit. "Because of this Nina person?"

He lets out a low growl that sounds a lot like *Leif*, but when he turns to me, there's something almost pleading in

289

his eyes. "Please, Valerie," he says quietly. "Just come with me."

It's the use of my first name more than anything that gets me to follow. Even when he isn't being an ass and calling me *princess*, he's only ever used *Darkmore*.

The camp is full of activity as we step out—everyone is awake and moving by now.

"Cam—" calls a voice.

"Not now, Ledger," he says through his teeth, his hand curling around my arm as he pulls me forward.

"*Cam*—"

Cam lets out a frustrated breath through his nose. "I *said*—"

Something crashes into us from behind, and the impact throws me into the dirt. The inhuman growls are deafening as I push to my knees, wincing at the rocks imprinted in my skin. A gust of wind sends my hair flying around my face, and I shove myself back as I take in the two wolves in front of me. One I recognize immediately as Cam from the night he slept outside my tent. But the other—a smaller, longer white wolf with something inherently feminine about it— I've never seen.

Judging by the way Cam is snarling and the hair on his back is standing on end, it's Nina.

The white wolf paws the dirt, her lips curling back from her teeth, but then just as quickly, the wind picks up, and she shifts into her human form.

She's tall, taller than Cam even. Her orange hair almost reaches her hips, but it's not enough to cover her nakedness. Not that she seems remotely self-conscious about that. She stands tall, hands on her hips, as she looks at me over her nose, a small, curious smile on her face.

Cam shifts a moment later and takes a not-so-subtle step between us, but that just makes her smile widen.

"Well," she purrs, "are you going to introduce me to your guest?"

"Nina," Cam all but growls.

She sniffs the air, and her smile drops. "What the *fuck*?" She squints at me, still splayed in the dirt, but I'm frozen in place.

Maybe it's a primitive instinct, but her gaze sends a spike of panic through my veins, every nerve in my body screaming at me to *run*. Maybe it's my vampire half—if werewolf bites can kill vampires, I don't know if my witch half would be enough to save me. And yet, even in all my time surrounded by wolves at this camp, I never felt fear like this.

"Is it a pet?"

"You are in *my* camp, and she's with me. That's all you need to know."

Nina's eyes turn to slits, and Cam takes another step to the side, cutting off her view of me. "Maybe we should continue this conversation in private," he says.

The rest of the camp is crowded around now, lingering on the outskirts, looking like they'd jump in at a moment's notice if Cam asked them to. It's more than just our camp, I realize. There are far too many people for that.

It's clear who belongs to Nina and who belongs to Cam. There's something protective about the way they watch their pack masters, how their bodies are all perfectly in tune, like a different kind of gravity connects them together.

"Leif?" Cam says without turning.

"Yeah?" Leif steps beside me and helps me to my feet.

"You know where to go?"

"Yes, sir."

Cam nods once and tosses Leif the car keys, his eyes never leaving Nina. Leif grabs the bag from where Cam dropped it and throws the strap over his shoulder. Cam still doesn't turn, instead gesturing for Nina to follow him to his office.

"Come on," Leif says lowly, tugging on my arm. I stay frozen until Cam reaches the tent and finally turns around and meets my eyes. Every line of his face is tense, and he gives me a quick nod before he steps inside.

CHAPTER TWENTY-NINE

REID

I'VE HEARD of the city in whispers, rumors. But it had always seemed more fiction than fact, a fairy tale, almost. And should it exist, it certainly wouldn't be a place that welcomed people like me. It isn't too far from the town. It only takes me a few days. But it's a lot of time alone with my thoughts. I hadn't particularly enjoyed Connor's company most of the time, but I can't help but notice his absence now.

Between the fears about this being a dead end, about me being too late to find her, and the doubts about whether leaving Quinn behind was the right thing, I barely notice the physical toll, though it's been far too long since I've fed. I try with a few animals along the way, but it doesn't satiate the hunger the same.

The stone pulses in my hand, growing warmer and warmer, almost to the point of discomfort. I have no idea how close I am until, suddenly, it appears around me.

I half expected whatever charm covered the area to

stop me from stepping foot inside, but I pass by with ease, the endless forest in front of me materializing into a bustling town from one heartbeat to the next.

The rain hammers down the hardest it has since the day I left the estate. I pull my hat lower over my eyes and hunch my shoulders as I weave through the crowd, trying not to draw attention to myself. I don't know how much truth there is to the stories about them rounding up vampires and burning them in the town square, but I'm not going to take any chances.

Everyone is scurrying by with their heads down, shielding themselves from the rain. Maybe the weather will work in my favor today and it'll be easier to get by unnoticed. Despite the rain, the shops along the streets are still set up, their tables covered with tarps and tents. Colorful umbrellas flood the space as patrons browse, clearly accustomed to weather like this.

I push through the exhaustion weighing on my shoulders and ignore the growing hunger in my chest.

With this many people living here, maybe there's actually service…

I fish my phone out of my bag, cringing as I power it on and see I'm down to five percent battery. But after a moment, a string of text messages appears.

I nearly drop the phone when I see Connor's name. He made it to Auclair much faster than I would've expected.

Here.

Ashley said he's going to kick your ass.

But he also reserved a room for you. Said there should be blood stocked in the fridge.

I tap on the final message—the hotel's address—and let

out a sigh of relief. What are the odds this thing can hold out long enough to give me directions?

I slip through the narrow alleys between buildings. The concrete beneath my feet is old, cracked, the buildings weathered and worn. How long has this city been here?

I squint around, but there don't seem to be any street signs. So finding this place should be interesting. Worse comes to worse, I suppose I could glamour someone for information, but with the risk of getting caught...

"You Reid?"

I freeze in my tracks as a figure steps into the alley in front of me. A woman, I'd guess, by the tone of her voice, but I can't see her face beneath the hood.

"Ashley said to expect you."

The tension in my shoulders eases, and I give a quick nod.

"Follow me." With that, she turns and disappears around the corner.

Maybe I've completely lost my mind and trusting a complete stranger in a city where allegedly everyone wants to kill me isn't the best idea, but I break into a jog so I don't lose her. She doesn't turn to see if I'm following, and she certainly doesn't take it easy on me. For such a short person, her pace is *fast*, and she zigzags through the streets with ease, turning so many times I'm convinced we've gone in a circle.

But then she stops at a nondescript door, unlocks it, and walks away without a word. I peer inside. From first glance, it looks like an average motel room. She left the key in the lock, so I pull it out and store it in my pocket.

"Okay then," I murmur and head inside.

THE SUN RISES NOT long after that, leaving me with limited options since I can't leave the room. True to his word, there are a dozen blood bags in the fridge, and I immediately down three of them. Despite finally having reception, it isn't the saving grace I'd hoped it would be. I can't very well find information on the secret city no one can find on Google.

I try to rest, but it's mostly tossing and turning and checking the time on my phone every few minutes until, finally, it's the next night.

I don't let myself think about how this could be another dead end. More wasted time. But if I'm going to get information about Farley and his pack, I need to be smart about this. He hasn't stayed hidden this long for no reason.

I try to find my bearings among the many curving streets, especially after looping around so many times yesterday. The rain pounds against the pavement, but the paths are less crowded today, even as I reach the market on the main street.

I squint at each building as I pass, trying to locate an identifier. A woman with a large red umbrella glances at me, frowning. I turn away and quicken my pace, hopefully looking like I know where I'm going. I wonder how often they see visitors around here, or if any new face sticks out.

Something in my chest twinges, and I rub my fingers against the bone, wincing. It's been happening more and more since I got here. With each step forward, the ache increases, almost to a painful degree. I pause and try to pull in a deep breath.

Another man glances my way, his gaze lingering a moment too long. I turn to the booth beside me, the table covered in multicolored fruit. I busy myself with one of the apples and give the woman a thin smile as I hand over a few coins. She takes the money and gives me a small nod.

When I look up again, all the air leaves my lungs at once.

The apple falls from my hand.

It can't be.

There's barely anything recognizable, especially with the rain. She's turned away from me, talking to a woman at one of the booths. The jacket is far too big for her, nearly swallowing her entire frame whole.

But a single piece of dark hair escapes her hood, and there's something about the way she tilts her head when she talks…

I stand there staring at her for a moment, willing her to turn to the side enough for me to see her face. Just to prove to myself that I'm being ridiculous.

The apple rolls across the wet dirt and bumps into the side of her boot.

She bends to retrieve it, and I catch myself holding my breath. The hood obscures her face as she twists the apple in her hand, but then she finally glances up, trying to find where it came from.

Her gaze locks on me.

And the rest of the market disappears.

Her face is thinner, the hollows of her cheeks more pronounced, and there's a scar running through her lips that wasn't there before. Rain drips down her face, collecting in the few strands of hair poking out of her hood.

297

The confusion on her brow quickly softens as her eyes widen and her lips part.

The expression threatens to crack my heart clean in half.

But then she grabs the large tote bag from the table and quickly turns away.

I don't dare call out for her, but I'm not about to lose her in this crowd. I quicken my steps into a jog, keeping my gaze locked on her as she turns for one of the alleys.

Even the way she walks is different—her shoulders hunched around her ears, her steps shorter, and there's something about them that almost looks...*pained*.

My throat tightens.

I glance over my shoulder as I turn into the alley, ensuring we're alone.

"Valerie," I call, my voice low. "Wait."

Her back stiffens, but she keeps moving.

"Valerie." I grab her arm, trying to pull her to a stop. Even through the fabric of her jacket, the touch sends a jolt of electricity through me.

It's her. I know it is.

She lets out a noise I've never heard come out of her before—something between a sob and a yelp. I yank my hand back. Did I hurt her?

"Valerie?"

"*Stop.*" She whips around to face me, her voice choked with tears. Taking in her face hits like a punch to the chest all over again, the details coming into focus. Her cheekbones look sharper than I remember them being, though the freckles across her nose are the same. The way her lips part, somehow looking delicate and gentle despite the hard way she's looking at me right now. They're her eyes, her chin, her cheeks, her skin.

It's her.

All I want to do is reach out and touch her, but I hold back. Because she's clearly not feeling the same relief exploding in my chest and stealing my breath right now. Her entire body trembles as she looks up at me, and the set of her jaw is tight. Angry.

Angry with me for not coming back? For letting this happen to her when I promised—

"Okay? Whoever you are, you had your fun. You had your laugh. Now leave me the hell alone."

I stare at her, unable to respond. *Whoever you are.*

"Who sent you?" she demands.

"I—it's me, Valerie. It's Reid."

"Reid is dead," she practically spits, then turns away.

Dead? *Dead?* "Valerie, wait—"

She rips her arm away when I grab her, but this time, I don't let go. I can't. I push her against the side of the building. She gasps, trying to wrestle herself free. "Let me go!"

But I can't let her slip through my fingers now. Not after all this. *Dead.* Why would she think...?

"They showed you my body, didn't they?" I demand, the desperation making the words come out so quickly they nearly trip over each other. But she can't—*I* can't let her walk out of this alley. I can't lose her again.

Tears stick in her lashes as she blinks, her expression still closed off as her eyes search every inch of my face, but after a moment, she nods.

"You know that they faked your death? Had a funeral for you with an open casket at the estate and everything?

You really think if they could fake yours so easily, they couldn't do the same for mine?"

There's nothing in her expression that tells me whether she believes me. I keep talking before she can pull away. "Valerie, it's *me*. I can prove it to you—*I can prove it to you*." I rack my brain, trying to think of something—anything— that will get through to her.

"When we got paired in Coderre's office, the first thing you said to me was *You can't be serious.*" I let out a small, pitiful laugh. The look she'd given me that day wasn't too far from the way she's looking at me now. Full of suspicion and unease. "Then after our first task, even though you had no reason to trust me, no reason to think I wouldn't turn you in, you risked it to help a human. And that's when I knew I could trust you."

I search her eyes, desperate for a sign of recognition, for the wariness to ease from the tension in her body. But I can see in her eyes that it's not enough. I loosen my grip on her arms but don't let go as I lower my voice. "And that night in the bunker...I wanted to tell you that I love you. But I thought it would be too soon. And I've regretted not saying it every day since." I swallow hard, the image of her sitting in the kitchen as they took me away all too clear in my mind. The panic in her eyes.

And I'd let them take me away. I'd let them leave her there.

I meet her eyes again, and they're clouded with tears. Her body shakes beneath my hands like she's holding back sobs, but she doesn't say anything. Gently, I touch the side of her face. She closes her eyes and lets out a shuddering breath, but she doesn't pull away.

"I know you can't feel me anymore," I whisper, "but I need you to *see me*. What do you need to hear to believe me?"

She says nothing for a long time. But then, finally, she whispers, "If they showed you my body, how did you know I wasn't dead? How did you know it wasn't me?"

Her voice comes out so small and low it's nearly inaudible—nothing like how she usually sounds. And the more I look at her, the more differences I notice. She's so fucking *small*. It makes me grit my teeth. For her to lose this much weight in just a few months, she must have been starving. My hand trails to the back of her neck, but she keeps her gaze lowered, and the sight of it—the heaviness in her that wasn't there before, the desolation—it tightens around my chest like a fist.

Because I know her, and whatever's happened in our months apart to have her looking like this, I can't even imagine it.

"I had a feeling, even after finding the scene they left in the cell," I murmur. "When I felt the bond break, it was so sudden. If you had been in pain, or scared, or dying..." I break off and shake my head. "I know I would've felt more of that first. But then at your funeral—" I swallow hard, trying to force the image out of my head. The pale skin, the stillness. "I don't know how they did it. She looked exactly like you. Enough that I started to doubt myself. I thought maybe I was believing what I wanted to, that I was in denial. And they had almost every detail on her right." I take her hand in mine and trace her fingertips. My knees threaten to give out as I feel the scars there—just small, barely there lines. My next words come out in a whisper as

I tighten my hand around hers. "But she didn't have these."

She says nothing and stares at our hands. A tear falls from her face onto my wrist. Slowly, she tilts her head up and meets my eyes, the tears running down her cheeks in full force now.

We stare at each other in silence, until finally, she whispers, "Reid?"

I have her against my chest before the word fully leaves her mouth. Her body trembles beneath my arms, and I tighten my hold as she presses her face against the side of my throat. As small as she looks, she feels even smaller, like she might break in my arms. The smell of her floods my senses, and my eyes fall shut.

"I've got you," I whisper. "I'm right here."

"Reid," she chokes out. "You were—dead. You were dead."

"Shh, it's okay. I'm right here. I've got you. I'm right here."

Her chest shakes with a silent sob, and I try to loosen my grip so I'm not hurting her, but I can't force my arms to relax.

"I've got you," I whisper into her hair as I breathe her in.

Despite my certainty at the funeral that she was out here somewhere, the longer it took to find her, the more space there was for doubt to trickle in.

But she's here. She's real. She's *alive* and breathing and *here.*

My throat aches and water drips down my face—rain or tears, I'm not sure. I glance over my shoulder, making sure we haven't drawn any attention to ourselves, but the alley is empty. Once the shaking in her body starts to settle, I pull back enough to see her face. The sight of those dark eyes looking back at me makes me try a few times before I manage to get the words out. I'd dreamt of her a million times, but I could never get her eyes just right. They're so dark sometimes they appear black, but if you look close enough, the smallest hints of dark blue sneak through the brown.

"We need to talk," I say. "But not here. Will you come with me? It's not far."

She chews on her lip for a moment before nodding.

I wrap my arm around her shoulders and bring her into my side, trying to shield her from the rain. Her breaths come in small gasps as we wind toward the room, like she might still be crying. In shock, probably. I am, too, but I've spent the last few months looking for her, certain she was alive out there.

She's spent all this time believing I was gone. Believing everyone thought she was dead. That no one was looking for her. That no one was coming.

I tighten my arm around her, not knowing how I'll ever convince myself to let go again.

CHAPTER THIRTY

VALERIE

EVERYTHING inside of me is numb as I follow Reid to a motel room not too far from mine.

Reid. Alive. Pacing back and forth in front of me as I sink onto the edge of the bed, barely able to keep myself standing anymore. He rifles through drawers and a duffel bag he has sitting on the TV stand, something almost frantic about his movements.

All I can do is stare.

Because he's alive. Alive and breathing and here and not in that body bag they showed me…

A laugh bursts out of me unbidden.

He straightens and turns to look at me, his brow furrowed.

Once the first laugh is out there, the floodgates are open, and I can't hold them back. He kneels in front of me, the confusion in his eyes shifting to concern as I wrap my arms around my stomach and hunch over.

"Valerie?"

"Can you believe," I gasp between laughs, "this is the second time—this has happened to me?"

He tentatively reaches for my hand. "What do you mean?"

"You, coming back from the dead. You're the second now. Oh, God." I cover my eyes and try to pull in a deep breath. "I'm losing my fucking mind. This is a dream or a hallucination, isn't it? I'm gonna wake back up in that goddamn tent—"

"Valerie, shh." He grabs the sides of my face and forces me to look at him, and God, his eyes are so wide and blue—my dreams could never get them exactly right. "Look at me," he whispers. "What do you mean the second time?"

"Calla," I murmur. "She's been with Westcott this whole time. None of it was real."

He blinks and sits back on his heels but doesn't let go of my face. "Are they here too?"

I let out a small, pitiful laugh. "It's a long story."

One side of his mouth curls into a smile, but there's nothing happy about it. "I imagine it is." His eyes flick over the length of me, that concerned pinch between his brows returning. "Are you hurt? Are you okay?"

I shake my head. "I'm not hurt," I say quietly.

"And is anyone going to come looking for you? Is you being here going to be a problem?"

Another shake. "Not until tomorrow night."

He nods a few times, seemingly to himself. "Okay. Okay. Here's what we're going to do." He rises to his feet and pulls something out of his bag. I don't realize it's a blood bag until he pushes it into my hand.

I shake my head. "Reid, I don't want to take your stash."

"Valerie, I don't care if you drink every last one I have. Please, just take it. Drink that. I'm going to find you some dry clothes," he says, turning to the bag. "The bathroom's that way if you want to take a shower or something." He nods to my right, then lays some clothes on the bed next to me. "And I'm going to go get you some human food, then we can get into the long story, okay?"

"You don't have to do that. I'm fine."

"No, you're not." He kneels in front of me and takes both of my hands in his. "I'll be right back."

I swallow hard and meet his eyes. He winces like he's thinking the same thing I am. The last time he said that to me…well, that was the last time I saw him.

"It won't take me long," he amends, voice softer now, and squeezes my hands. "I'm just going down the street. Okay?"

I want to tell him no because the idea of watching him walk out that door after all this time is impossible, unthinkable. As if the moment he leaves my sight, the fantasy will shatter. Waking up from the dreams of him have been bad enough. But this? Nothing has ever felt so real, so *alive*. If I wake up only for this to be another delusion—

He cups the back of my head with one hand, bringing our faces just inches apart. "Lock the door behind me, and don't open it for anyone."

Swallowing hard, I nod. His eyes search my face, and a small smile appears.

"What?" I murmur.

He shakes his head. "Nothing. It's just—you have no idea how good it is to see you."

"You too," I whisper.

His smile grows, and I can't help myself. I throw my arms around his neck and yank him against me. He hugs me just as tightly and smooths a hand over my hair.

The scent of him fills my head as my eyes fall shut, and all I can think is, *I thought I lost this. I thought I'd lost this forever.* "I can't believe you came after me."

"Of course I did. I told you I'd come back." He smiles ruefully as he pulls back and tilts his head to the side. "Just ended up taking a bit longer than expected."

I laugh and brush away the tears leaking from the corners of my eyes. "Yeah, you really took your sweet time, huh?"

The amusement in his expression fades. "Valerie, I pledged myself to you in that throne room, and I meant it. Bond or no bond, you're my partner, no matter what." His hand drifts to the side of my face, then he gently taps beneath my chin and rises to his feet. "I'll be right back."

I let out a shuddering breath and stare at the door for several moments after he's gone. I'm not sure which is racing faster, my mind or my pulse. I make short work of the blood bag, leave it on the counter, and take the clothes with me to the bathroom.

The silence is thick as the door clicks shut behind me. I turn the water as hot as it can go and strip off my wet clothes and toss them in the sink. I'm about to turn for the shower when the movement of my reflection in the mirror catches my eye.

There's no preparing myself for what I see looking

back. I'd known it must have been bad, not just from the look on Reid's face when he saw me, but also from experiencing it. From feeling the weakness in my body, the pain from the scars that I know are there now.

But God, I didn't realize it was as bad as this. The girl looking at me in the mirror, she barely looks like me. Her face is so thin it's changed the entire shape. My eyes now look disproportionately big compared to the rest of my features. The scar through my mouth is jagged, the skin raised, but it's not as bad as I thought it would be.

I've never been that big or small. My body has always fallen somewhere in between. No matter the physical conditioning and training at the academy, or the food that I ate, nothing really made a difference. My body liked to be the size that it was. Being self-conscious about its softness and curves always seemed a waste of time. But now looking in the mirror at the absence of them, it makes my chest feel hollow. For the first time in my life, I can see my ribs, my hips, the definition of my abs, my collarbone.

My chin wobbles, and I clench my jaw and force myself to turn away and step under the water. But it doesn't clear away the feelings clogging my throat like I'd hoped. I don't even know what they are, exactly.

I've never considered myself to be a vain person, so I don't think it has much to do with my appearance. Or maybe it does. But it feels like a loss. A death. The girl I was before all this. I guess I never really considered what it would feel like to grieve yourself.

The water turns brown as it collects at my feet, and I avert my gaze as it catches on the shackle around my ankle.

After a few minutes of scrubbing at my skin, I switch the water off.

The cold air makes every hair on my body stand at attention as I step out and towel myself dry. Reid's clothes smell like him as I pull them on, and the tension eases from my shoulders. Ever since I lost his jacket, his scent has faded more and more from my memory. It was something I thought I'd lost entirely.

When it comes time to button the trousers, unsurprisingly, the waist is too big, and they immediately slide down my hips. I try folding them over a few times to no avail.

I let out a frustrated whimper, and my head falls back. Stupidly, tears burn in the backs of my eyes.

"Valerie?"

I straighten at the light knock at the door. When had Reid gotten back? I sniffle and quickly wipe my hand under my nose.

"Are you all right in there?" he calls.

"Yeah." I curse my voice for shaking. "It's just the—I can't get the—" I sigh. "They're too—"

"Can I come in?"

"Yeah."

He cracks the door open. I gesture vaguely to the pants, not wanting to speak again in case my voice decides to do something else weird.

"Well, that's an easy fix," he says, his voice gentle. Before I know it, he's ripping a strip off the bottom of his T-shirt. He snakes the piece of fabric through my belt loops, his arms wrapping around me. "How high do you want them?" He positions the pants on my waist, and I nod. "Is this too tight?" He knots the fabric, snug, but not uncomfortable.

I shake my head.

He doesn't release me, not at first. I can't quite meet his eyes, especially now that I know exactly what he sees looking back at him.

"You didn't have to ruin your shirt for me," I say.

He chuckles, then steps back and gestures for me to pass. "Looks better on you anyway."

He has a few meals in paper trays spread out along the bed. I'm not sure what kind of meat it is. All I know is it's warm, the sauce is sweet, and it's broken into little bite-size pieces. And it's not so raw that it's impossible to chew.

Reid sits quietly as I finish the first and immediately pick up the second tray. Now that my body has remembered what it's like to have an appetite, my stomach feels like a bottomless pit, the monster inside of me gluttonous and unsatisfied no matter how much I put in my mouth. Or maybe I'm using it to stall because I know once I'm finished, he's going to ask. He's going to want to know what happened to me, where I've been, and I don't even know where to start. How to possibly explain the last few months.

The thought makes me pause. I finish chewing and meet Reid's eyes. "How long have I been gone?"

Something in his expression softens. "About three months."

I nod, slowly processing this. Somehow the answer makes complete sense. But it's also entirely foreign. I only spent a few days at the compound with Calla and Westcott, and who knows how much time was lost getting me there in the first place or transporting me here with the wolves while I was unconscious?

But still, that means the majority of that time has been spent in these woods. It's been all too easy for the days to blur together, for everything to look the same. I've spent my time keeping my head down, doing the job they gave me for the day, and sleeping as much as I could—on the off chance that I wasn't spending my nights crying into my pillow.

But *three months?* Three months of my life just gone up in smoke. I don't think I could pick out a handful of moments that are memorable enough to describe. None of them that are good, at least.

I can remember almost dying. I can remember the claws ripping through my face. I can remember Cam—

The thought makes ice flood my veins. Cam.

I lower my gaze from Reid's face as if he'll somehow be able to see what happened between us in my expression. The guilt is immediate and sharp in my stomach.

He probably wouldn't judge me for it. I know that. But *I'm* judging me for it.

We hadn't made any promises to each other. We'd never established whatever was going on between us, but if the roles were reversed, even if he'd been thinking I was dead, I think I would still be hurt.

"What's going through your head?" he asks.

I blink, the spiraling thoughts quieting for a moment. "A lot," I admit.

"Why don't you start from the beginning?" he suggests, his voice achingly gentle, and for some reason, it makes me clench my jaw. I want to scream at him that he shouldn't be so nice to me. So understanding. So careful. That I don't deserve it. I didn't deserve for him to spend the last three months looking for me or for him to risk being in this city. He must know its reputation. Its feelings toward vampires. What would happen if he were to get caught?

"What happened in that cell after I left?" he asks.

That part, at least, is easy enough. So I tell him as best as I can recount about Westcott shifting not once, but twice. The deal he offered me.

Reid's expression doesn't change, but his eyes flick to the black mark on my wrist. "What were the terms?"

I press my lips together, not knowing how to respond. I know I didn't have a choice, but I still don't want to admit it out loud.

"What did you agree to?" he demands.

"To be in his service until he releases me," I say quietly. "The other terms were I had to leave with him, fake my death, break my bond with you, and I couldn't return to my old life or try to leave unless he approves it. I don't really know where the line is, to be honest."

"But you're here with me, and it's not…" He presses his lips into a tight line and studies my face.

"Maybe because *you* found *me*—I didn't seek you out. I don't know. What did they leave? In the cell. What did you find when you went back?"

He winces and swallows hard. I know there must have been a body. He told me as much earlier. There had been a funeral with an open casket and everything. How they achieved it, I'm not sure. Was it some kind of glamour? Dark magic? Hell, maybe a skinwalker, since clearly I don't know as much about them as I thought I did.

"You—" he starts, then shakes his head. "The body was on the ground. There was blood everywhere." His voice gets a far-off quality to it. I know he's seeing it all over again in his mind. He takes a deep breath, and his next words come out calm. Distant. "Her throat was slashed."

"Oh," I say, because what else am I supposed to say?

"The guy in the cell next to you," he adds, almost in an offhanded way, "I tried to glamour information out of him, and there was a block in his mind. A lot like Madison's. That was probably the best hint Westcott could have left behind. Which makes me think he did it on purpose. That he wanted me to come after you."

I nod, thinking to that first day at the compound and that conversation I'd had with Calla. "They'd wanted me to kill you. When I was under the psychosis, they were hoping I would take you out."

"Did he tell you why?"

I shake my head, though I've run through a thousand possibilities in the meantime. Why Reid, specifically? If he was after the estate, wouldn't the queen be a better target?

He meets my eyes, a furrow to his brow now. "After the cell, after he broke the bond, what happened next? Where did he take you?"

"I don't know where, exactly. I just woke up in a bed. Some compound in northern Canada. That's what they told me, at least. It was huge, Reid. And according to them, it's one of many."

"A compound," he repeats. "But if you were in Canada, how did you get all the way down here?"

I laugh a little. "I didn't make the best impression there."

It seems easier to explain when I'm not looking at him, so I focus on my hands in my lap as I work my way through what happened at the compound. Things I haven't let myself think about. Like the body I'd left in the control room. How much easier taking a life has become for me. How I hadn't given it a second thought until now.

I tell him about Cam and getting sent to stay with the wolves while Westcott is off doing God knows what. How I've been there killing time and waiting to see when—if—Westcott ever comes for me. "So I think that's why I can be here even though Westcott's not. He put Cam in charge of me while he's gone, and Cam sent me here."

The light brush of his fingers on my face makes me jerk my head up. He traces the scar over my lips with his thumb. "What happened?" He frowns and meets my eyes. "Why didn't it heal?"

I sigh and slowly lift my pant leg. His entire expression shifts into one of fury in the blink of an eye.

"What the hell is this?" He kneels and takes my leg in his hand as if to remove the shackle.

I gently extract myself from his hold. "It's fine."

"It sure as hell is not fine."

"I can't take it off—"

"I can get it off," he insists.

"No, I mean." I sigh and run my hands through my hair. "I have to keep up appearances, but it's not…" I wave my hands. "It used to have red salt in it so I couldn't use my magic. But it doesn't anymore. I just need all the wolves to think that it does."

He stares at me for a moment. "But it still did when that happened." He nods to the scar on my face.

My hands drift up to cover my lips almost subconsciously, but he takes my hand and pulls it away.

"Who did that?"

"It doesn't matter, Reid."

"It matters."

"He's dead. The guy who did this, he's dead. And honestly, it was my own fault. Picking a fight with a wolf my first day at camp was not my smartest moment."

He doesn't laugh at my joke. He doesn't even smile. If anything, he looks angrier.

"They knew if they took this off you, you would heal, and they just let you suffer."

When I don't respond, he tightens his fingers around mine. "You almost died too, didn't you?"

A flash of that night appears—my head under water, the darkness edging into my vision as my lungs screamed for air. My eyes shoot to his face. "How'd you know that?"

His frown deepens. "I felt it."

"What do you mean, you felt it? We don't—"

"Have the bond anymore, I know." He rubs the center of his chest—I don't think he's even aware he's doing it. "I felt it," he repeats. "There were a couple of times I thought I felt something from you, but that one was definitely the strongest."

Something about the words makes reality filter in. I run the pad of my thumb along the black mark on my wrist, and the relief, that awe and hope from seeing him again, turns hollow in the pit of my stomach.

Because it doesn't matter that he's found me. It doesn't matter if he's alive. It matters, but not for me. Because it doesn't change anything. I can't leave. I can't go with him. I'm pretty sure I would drop dead if I tried.

The silence in the room feels thick enough to choke on. I should tell him to go home. To get out of this city because it's not safe for him here. It would be selfish to ask anything else of him, but still, a part of me—the very large, raw, vulnerable, desperate part that feels more like an injured animal than the person I used to be—wants to beg him to stay. To not leave me here.

"All blood deals have a loophole," he says.

I meet his eyes, but that horrible feeling in my chest doesn't change. "Not for this one, I don't think," I say softly.

"We're going to get you out of this deal."

"Reid—"

He kneels in front of me and takes both of my hands in his. Nothing in his expression invites any kind of debate. "I'm not leaving here without you, so one way or another, we're going to get you out of this thing. I don't care if it takes tracking Westcott down and killing him myself. I'll do it if that's what it takes."

"I have no idea where he is," I whisper.

"You've been with Farley this whole time?"

I try not to flinch at his name. I nod.

"He has a deal with Westcott?"

"*Deal* would be exactly the right word," I murmur, fingers still tracing over the mark.

Reid follows the movement and quirks an eyebrow. "He made a blood deal with him too?"

I nod.

"You think he would know where he is?"

"Possibly, but you can't very well go ask him, Reid. He's

got an entire pack of wolves out there. And I doubt they would greet you too kindly. They're definitely more the kill first, ask questions later sort. And they'll be expecting me tomorrow night."

His eyes snap to mine, a hint of unease there now.

I stare at him, the gears in my head churning. He can't go to that camp. But I can. I have to. And I'm not under any delusion that what Cam and I have is any more serious to him than some meaningless fling. But at the same time, there have been rare moments when I've seen some humanity behind his eyes, some compassion. At the least, he's saved me from dying. I don't know if he'll help me, but asking him is the only chance I've got.

"Give me a chance to go talk to him," I say.

The corners of Reid's mouth tighten. He clearly doesn't like the idea, but he doesn't argue. Probably because he knows we're short on other options. "They're not here in the city, are they?"

I shake my head. "They're about half a day's ride out."

He nods slowly, almost as if to himself. Then his head pops up like something just occurred to him. His eyes slowly travel from the shackle around my ankle to my face. "You have your magic back?"

I nod and a slow smile spreads across his face.

"Well, if you're feeling up to it, do you want to try this again?" I frown, at first not understanding what he's talking about, but then he adds, "I never thought I would miss having you in my head all the time, but I do."

The loss of the bond almost felt like its own kind of grief. Apart from thinking he was dead, the lack of its pres-

317

ence was a wound inside me that never healed. And just the thought of having it back, of feeling him again...

"Me too," I whisper.

"What do you say? At least then I'll feel a little better about sending you back there. I'll know if you're okay. I'd be able to find you if this doesn't work."

"You got the ultimate Get Out of Jail Free card, and you would willingly tie yourself back to me?" I tease, but my voice comes out small.

A single corner of his lips curls. "I already told you. I won't give you up to someone else that easily, Darkmore."

I agreed to break the bond, but Westcott hadn't said anything about re-creating it. Maybe since I couldn't try to escape and he'd planned on killing Reid anyway, he hadn't thought it necessary.

I reach for my middle finger, the muscle memory strong though the ring has been missing for months. "I don't have a—well, I guess you could just bite me now."

His brow furrows.

"Calla," I explain. "The whole venom addiction was her cover story when they faked her death. That was never real."

"I still don't have to," he insists. "And anyway..." He reaches beneath the collar of his shirt and pulls out something on a thin chain.

I stare at it for a moment, not understanding what I'm seeing. It somehow looks smaller when it's around his neck rather than on my finger. But it is undoubtedly mine.

"Where did you get that?" I whisper.

He slips the chain over his head and holds it out to me in the center of his palm. "They had it on the body he left in the cell, but I grabbed it before they could take her away."

My vision blurs with tears. "You've held on to it all this time?"

"Well, I figured you might want it back."

I start to reach for it but pause. "I can't take it to the camp. If they see it..."

He nods and closes his fingers around it. "I don't mind holding on to it for a little while longer, but you can still use it now to make the cut."

The thought of the alternative, despite knowing what I now know, twists in my stomach the way it always has. But I steel myself. "I don't want to be afraid of it anymore."

He holds my gaze for a moment before nodding. I push my hair over my shoulder to reveal more of my neck. When he leans in, the heat from his breath skates across my skin, making every hair stand at attention. His hand finds the side of my face, and he meets my eyes, just inches away from me now. "Are you sure?"

I nod and start to murmur the incantation under my breath. Once the last word leaves my lips, his fangs sink into the delicate skin of my throat. A small sound escapes me, but the sting fades almost immediately as he drinks. A glowing warmth floods my veins, and a moment later, he pulls back. He doesn't let go of my head as his eyes search my face.

I nod to let him know I'm okay. The bite was short, brief, so I doubt much venom got into my system. Not as bad as when Connor bit me after my trial.

Reid sits on the bed beside me and tugs the collar of his shirt down. I lean in, my eyes involuntarily fluttering shut at the smell of him. After saying the incantation a second time, I sink my teeth into his neck. One of his hands finds my waist while the other holds the back of my head, and I barely manage to swallow a mouthful of blood before I feel it. Like an animal coming back to life after hibernation, the string between us stretches and pulls so intensely that all the air leaves my lungs and I have to grip his shoulders to keep from falling over. He lets out a strangled breath too.

And for a moment, neither of us moves. We just cling to each other, breathing heavily, and that spot in my core blazes and buzzes with energy.

His forehead falls against my shoulder, and almost too low for me to hear, he whispers, "There you are."

God, I feel like all I do is cry these days, but the back of my throat burns. I gently hit him in the chest, my head still pressed against his shoulder, and mumble into his shirt, "If you ever fake die on me again, I'll kill you myself."

"That's fair," he murmurs. "But if we're keeping score..." He pulls back and smirks. "You've been kidnapped on me twice now."

I let out a small laugh and reach up to wipe the tears from my cheeks, but he beats me to it, cupping both sides of my face with his hands and running his thumbs gently across my skin.

I close the rest of the distance between us, covering his mouth with mine, and his grip tightens on me as if he's afraid I'll slip through his fingers.

I don't think I realized how different things with Cam felt until now. Because when Reid kisses me, all the static in my mind fades, the tension in my body evaporates, and in one perfect, blissful moment, I stop thinking altogether. All that matters is his lips and his hands tangling into my hair and his body beneath mine as I throw a leg over his and slide onto his lap.

He tucks my hair behind my ears and pulls back enough to see my face.

My cheeks heat under the scrutiny, the intensity in his eyes. "What?"

He gives me a half smile. "I just spent three months trying to find you. Is it so hard to believe that I just want to look at you?"

My returning smile grows of its own accord. I push the hair away from his forehead. "Your hair is a lot longer," I murmur.

He breaks into a full grin. "Is this your way of telling me I need a haircut?"

I laugh and run my fingers through it. "No, actually. It looks good."

"Ah, so this is what it takes to get a compliment out of you."

I hit him lightly on the chest. He catches my hand and holds it there, and his heart beats evenly beneath my palm. I meet his eyes and open my mouth to respond, but something stops me. Something about the smoldering blue of his eyes. Something faint and thin like a shadow. It's warm, the heat steadily growing alongside Reid's increasing heart rate beneath my hand. The need. The *desire*.

He seals his lips back over mine, his movements fast, hard this time. I sigh into his mouth and lock my legs around his waist and my arms around his shoulders. There's something about the way his body fits with mine that's inherently easy. Like a familiar blanket. Everything about it feels safe and warm.

He lifts me into his arms and twists us to pin me against the bed, his weight pressing into me. I arch against him, moments from that night in the bunker flashing through my mind and mingling with his movements now.

But then just as abruptly, he stops.

I blink at him, breathless, as he braces his hands on either side of my head, a deep line carved between his brows.

"What's wrong?"

"Nothing. I just—I can't do this."

I have the urge to cover myself, though we're both still fully dressed. He must have been able to feel the difference in touching me. The edges where there used to be softness. Maybe he doesn't—

"Valerie, there's nothing I want more right now than you," he says, his voice low. "But if we do this, I'm going to feel like I'm saying goodbye. Like I'm sending you back to those wolves tomorrow and—" He breaks off and takes a deep breath. "But that's not what's happening here, okay?" He leans down until our noses brush, his eyes searching mine. I don't blink. I don't *breathe*. My heart feels like it's trapped somewhere in my throat. "We're going to get this all sorted out, and then you're going to come back to me, and I'm going to take you home. And I will wait until I can have you in my bed, do you understand?"

If his words were meant to defuse the situation, they had the opposite effect. Heat pools low in my core, and my gaze trails from his eyes to his lips.

"Then you have to stop looking at me like that," I murmur.

"Believe me, I'm trying."

With a long breath, he rolls onto his back beside me, and we both lie there staring at the ceiling. His fingers brush my hand, then slowly interlace with mine. I close my eyes, focusing on the warmth of his skin, and he tugs on my arm, pulling me closer. I roll onto my side and tuck myself against his chest.

"Try to get some sleep." His hand runs up and down my back as he kisses the top of my head. "I'll be here when you wake up."

I knot my fist in his shirt, my chest constricting. Because what if this all really is a dream? A hallucination? What if the next time I open my eyes, I'm in that tent, and he goes back to being dead?

"You promise?" I whisper.

His arms tighten around me. "I won't make you any promises I can't keep. But trust me when I tell you, I am not going anywhere without you, Valerie."

CHAPTER THIRTY-ONE

REID

I<small>T'S WORSE</small> than the scar on her face. She's asleep on her back, her sleeve shoved up from all her tossing and turning throughout the night. At first, I'd thought it was the scar she's had since I met her, but no, that one's there too—lower, beneath the crease of her elbow, faded with time, but thick enough that whatever caused it must have been deep. This one is fresh. It's directly over her Marionettes tattoo, so it was clearly intentional. The skin is puckered and white like a burn.

Jesus fucking Christ. Even in her sleep, her forehead is crinkled like she still can't relax. What the hell else happened out there that she left out?

Her eyelids flutter as she turns her head against the pillow. At least she'd managed to fall asleep. Judging by those shadows under her eyes, she was more than exhausted. I don't know if I ever did fall asleep. If I did, it wasn't for long. My brain was far too occupied going through every possible scenario, trying to come up with an alternative plan for today before she woke up. Sending her back to those animals cannot be the only option.

"Can you at least save the worrying until after breakfast?"

I blink back to the room, and Valerie smiles up at me, just a soft, small curl of her lips, her face half tucked into the pillow. And God, the sight of it makes me feel like someone punched me in the chest.

"I'm not worrying," I say automatically.

She rolls her eyes, still smiling as she turns onto her back and stretches her arms overhead. "It's all over your face."

"If you feel even a little unsafe going back there, we can come up with something else—"

She sits up and squeezes my shoulder. "I'll be fine. I'm not worried about it. As strange as it sounds, I trust their pack master, if nothing else. He won't let anything happen to me." She gets a weird look on her face as she says it, but I can feel the truth of her words in my chest.

I don't bother reminding her that he did, in fact, let something happen to her. Her arm and face are proof of that—and I'm willing to bet there's more I can't see, not to mention how much weight she's lost.

"I should get going," she says. "It'll take me a while to get back. I don't want them to suspect anything."

"I'll come with you."

She gives me a look almost like I'm being a difficult child. "You can't—"

"I know I can't go all the way with you," I say, "but you

said it's half a day away. I can at least take you most of the way."

She takes a deep breath, seeming to consider this. I know she's more than capable of making it there on her own. She's survived this long. So I'm not sure why I'm insisting. Maybe it's because I want to spend more time with her. The twelve or so hours we've had hasn't been enough. I'm not ready to say goodbye. I'm not ready to watch her walk away.

Something softens in her expression like she knows exactly what I'm thinking. Or maybe she feels it. I can never tell exactly what she's picking up through the bond.

"Fine," she says, "but you're not getting anywhere close enough that there's a chance the wolves are going to catch your scent."

"Deal."

I shove the rest of my blood bags in her sack when she's not looking. She can be annoyed with me later, but at least I'll have some peace of mind that she has that much.

She nearly has all her belongings collected when my spine stiffens. It's not the sound of footsteps outside our room that sets me off, but the smell. Wolves, at least a dozen of them by the smell of it. But why? She said they weren't expecting her to head back until the sun went down.

She notices a moment later because her hand stills, her bag only halfway zipped shut. We exchange a silent look.

Sending her out alone won't fool them. They've already smelled me in here.

"Little baby vampire," singsongs a female voice.

Valerie goes rigid. I'm at her side in the next moment,

and I position myself between her and the door. I grab her arms and force her to focus on me.

Teleport yourself out of here.

Her eyes widen, so I know she heard me.

I—I don't think I'm strong enough right now to take both of us—

It's okay. Just go.

She shakes her head. *I'm not leaving you here.*

The door bursts open and cracks against the opposite wall. A single woman stands in the doorway, though the rest of her pack is flanking her in the alley.

My hand tightens around Valerie's wrist, pushing her behind me, though I know it's pointless. A few of them I could've taken on my own.

An entire pack?

"Well, isn't this interesting?" muses the she wolf—their pack master, if I had to guess. She looks more lion than wolf with her puffy orange hair, and the glint in her eyes as she grins at us is purely animalistic, like she's eyeing something she'd like to eat. "A vampire mate for Cam's little pet." She sniffs the air. "Does he know? Wait." Her eyes narrow on me and she cocks her head to the side. If possible, her grin grows wider. "You've got to be kidding me."

Valerie stiffens and steps around me before I can stop her. "He has nothing to do with this."

I have no idea who the woman is, but if she leads this pack, then she's not with Farley.

But she clearly knows Valerie.

The woman raises her eyebrows and gestures to the room around us. "Well, that's obviously not true. Imagine our surprise passing through on our way out of town when we smell not one, but *two* vamps. What can I say? Curiosity got the best of me." Her smile darkens. "And what better way to start this new alliance off than with a show of good faith?" She juts her chin ever so slightly, and her pack immediately stands taller. "Take them."

PART III
VALERIE

CHAPTER THIRTY-TWO

My HEAD HURTS when I wake. The back of my skull is tender, a bump forming there now. As I blink and my vision clears, I realize I'm in a tent. The pack of goons who dragged me here is nowhere to be seen.

Neither is Reid.

"You have no authority here," Cam growls.

I lie still, trying to gauge my surroundings without letting them know I'm awake. A cot is beneath me—I've slept on one enough to know what it feels like. And squinting a single eye open confirms my suspicions. We're in Cam's office.

"You should be thanking me," Nina scoffs. "Do you have any idea how it makes you look that you can't even keep this tiny girl under control? It's bad enough she was meeting up with a vampire, let alone the fucking prince of the Carrington estate. You are the master of this pack. They look to you for leadership and guidance. And right now, you look weak."

"How I run my pack is none of your business," Cam snaps.

"Maybe not mine," she says, "but they all saw us bring the two of them into camp, and they're looking to you to see what you do next. How do you think they'll react? I have my theories."

Cam doesn't respond.

"I guess you should hope no one is interested in becoming pack master. This would be the ultimate opportunity to challenge you with a lot of support from the other members. It's your move, Farley."

"Get out."

"Gladly. I have a new toy in the cellar to keep me entertained."

My spine straightens. Reid. "If you touch him, I will kill you," I say through my teeth.

Nina lets out a startled laugh, though she looks unsurprised to find me awake. "I'd like to see you try, baby vampire." She glances at Cam over her shoulder. "Don't worry, Farley. We'll stick around to see how this unfolds. We might even do you a favor and step in if things get a little too...*aggravated*. What are alliances for, right?"

Again, Cam says nothing. He glares at her until she ducks through the tent flaps, then focuses on me.

I stare back, the pieces slowly clicking into place in my mind. "Did you know?" I whisper.

He lowers his gaze.

"You knew he was alive," I say, louder now.

He gives a slight shake of his head and braces his hands on his desk. "Not for sure."

"But you suspected?" I demand, rising to my feet. "You —" I break off, my throat getting tight.

He let me talk to him about Reid. He saw the grief, the devastation, and he pretended he could relate, all the while knowing all he had to do was say a few words and my pain would go away.

But he let me suffer instead. Not only that, he used my grief to relate to me, to bond with me, to get me to trust him enough to let him into my bed. My skin crawls, and I suddenly feel exposed. Something in my chest hardens until I can't feel anything at all.

"Well, get on with it then," I say, my voice coming out hollow. "You going to execute me now too?"

A muscle in his jaw jumps. "I don't like this any more than you do. But you've put me in this situation."

I throw my hands up. "I didn't plan any of this! How could I?"

"If someone challenges me," he says, his voice impossibly low, "and they win, they would be in charge of what happens to you. I can't let this slide, Valerie. They won't allow it. Intent or not, it won't matter. You know that."

"I already said get on with it. If you need to keep justifying it to make yourself feel better, I don't want to hear it."

"You just walked into my camp with a vampire who has a huge bounty on his head! Half the guys want to turn him over for the money, half want to turn him over to Westcott, and all of them would be all too happy to have him served up right here. You might not see yourself as part of this pack, but as long as you're here, with our laws, you are. And since you've benefited from the protections that grants you, they'll go ballistic if you don't get the other side of the stick too. They see him as a threat. And you know too much about this camp, how things work, what we've been doing here. They see you being found with him as a threat to the pack's safety. So what, exactly, would you have me do here?"

The tent flaps rustle, and I expect Nina to waltz in, but my stomach flips as I meet Reid's eyes. He's breathing hard, and I have a feeling Cam is going to find whatever wolves were supposed to be guarding him unconscious somewhere.

Cam sighs, probably realizing it too, though he sounds more exhausted than concerned.

"This wasn't her fault," says Reid. "She had no idea I would be there."

"It doesn't matter," I say softly, though I keep my gaze on Cam. If he's going to do this, he's going to look me in the eye while he does. "So what'll it be, pack master?"

His expression is almost pleading as he searches my face, but then he hardens his jaw, and the look in his eyes grows cold, detached. "For you, they should be satisfied with ten lashes. I'll try to talk them into letting me take him to Westcott myself."

My heart drops. If Westcott gets his hands on him...
"No. You can't—"

"I won't actually take him there," Cam says quietly.

I try to read his expression, but I can't. He stares stonily back at me. I don't want to trust him. But what other choice do I have? What other chance does Reid have of getting out of this camp alive?

"Fine."

"*What?*" demands Reid. "You see how small she is right now? She might not survive that."

"He knows that," I say, holding his eyes. "And you'd need to put the red salt back so no one sees me healing."

Cam's jaw flexes.

"Absolutely not," says Reid, stepping in front of me. "You want someone to blame for this? Fine."

"What? No." I grab Reid's wrist.

"Take me as a proxy. That's in your laws, is it not?"

"It is," agrees Cam, looking at Reid now.

"Stop." I try to step around Reid, but he holds out an arm to stop me.

"They won't be satisfied with ten lashes for you," Cam says.

"*Stop*. I'll take them. *I'll take them*," I insist, but neither of them is listening to me.

A gust of wind cuts through the tent as a few other wolves flood inside.

"Cam, I swear to God—" I start.

He nods at someone over my shoulder, and they pin my arms behind my back. I yank against them, but Cam and Reid are already heading outside.

"Valerie," Leif hisses in my ear. "You've gotta stop fighting."

"Leif." My voice cracks around his name. "Let me go."

"He won't kill him."

"You don't know that—"

"I do. And I also know if everyone out there sees you trying to stop it, they'll want to see it happen to you too. So I need you to calm down. You can't stop this, Valerie."

I have my magic now. I could try.

But there are not one, but two entire packs out there. Even at my strongest...

"It'll be okay," Leif murmurs, nudging me toward the tent's opening.

I whip around to search his face, not sure which betrayal would be worse—his or Cam's. "Did you know too?" I demand. "That he was alive?"

"Of course not," he insists, but I don't know if I can trust the incredulity in his eyes.

I don't know if I believe him.

The energy in the air is palpable as Leif leads me toward the crowd. It's the same spot they took Terrence the first time, though now there are twice as many people with Cam's pack and Nina's. Reid and Cam are at the front. No one's restraining him or dragging him. Reid walks alongside Cam, cooperating despite the wolves he passes sneering and spitting at him.

Tears cloud my eyes, and even once we find our spot on the side to watch, Leif doesn't let me go, though he goes from pinning my arms behind my back to restrain me to an embrace that's holding me up. Laughter and shouts fill the air as Cam rips Reid's shirt and ties his wrists around the tree trunk. His mouth is moving, but I can't hear anything he's saying over the roar of blood in my ears.

Everything inside of me is screaming, *This is wrong.* I can't just stand here, especially not now that I have my magic. Now that I can do something. Would it be that smart or successful? Possibly not. But at least I tried. If the roles were reversed, if that was me up there, he would do something.

Leif tightens his arms around me. "I know what you're thinking. Don't. He'll be okay."

The whip is in Cam's hands now. Silver can kill vampires. If he hits hard enough, and in the right places—

"Cam knows where to aim," Leif adds. "He won't kill him."

The tears break free and run down my cheeks. Reid keeps his focus on the tree in front of him. He doesn't react to the ugly things being shouted at him. He stands perfectly still, waiting.

A light sensation trickles through the bond, almost like fingers skimming along skin. He's trying to comfort *me* in this moment.

I shake my head and clench my jaw. He barely flinches as the first lash hits his back high across the shoulders. But I can tell he's in pain because the bond shuts off, like he doesn't want me to feel it. Cam strikes a second time, and Reid clenches both of his fists but doesn't make a sound.

"How many are they doing?" I whisper to Leif.

He doesn't answer at first, and the third and fourth lashes come in quick succession. "Twenty, I believe."

All the air leaves my lungs at once. *Twenty?*

At some point, I lose count of them, my vision blurry with tears. Reid's back is now a mess of blood. I might not be able to stop this, but that doesn't mean I can't do *anything*. It's more difficult without physical contact and being this far away from him. It's also something I've never tried before. But if I can manipulate other people's body chemistry enough to teleport them, and if I can create barriers of protection around myself, how different would combining the two really be?

It would be too obvious to heal what has already been done. Instead, I focus on his skin. I might not have a physical connection to him, but I have the bond. I concentrate on the place it is in my chest. Even if he's trying to cut me off from what he's feeling, that string tying us together is still there. With a deep breath, I try pushing my magic down it and imagine it coating his back. Not all the way—if they can't see any evidence of the lashes, they'll know something's wrong—but enough where they won't do too much damage. So he won't feel too much pain.

Sweat breaks out on my hairline, and my breath comes in short and shaky.

"Valerie?" Leif's voice echoes as if from a distance, but I grit my teeth and keep pushing the magic down the line between us. It's just a little light-headedness. I'm fine.

I know the second it works because Reid's head lifts, just an inch, like he's surprised. Another lash lands across his back, and he scans the crowd. He stops when he finds me, his jaw clenched and eyes wide.

Leif's grip tightens, and I realize I'm starting to go limp in his arms.

Don't. Reid's voice appears in my mind. *Whatever you're doing, stop.*

Cam must be nearly done now. Twenty lashes can't take that long. I can hold on for a little while longer.

Valerie, please stop.

Finally, Cam drops the whip, slick with Reid's blood, to the dirt, and I release the hold on the bond. The moment I let go, it's like that connection had been holding me up too. My knees buckle. Leif catches me before I can hit the ground, and I hear voices around me, muffled as if I'm underwater. I feel hands on my skin, more than two.

"What the hell happened?" asks Cam.

"She just went down. She was, I don't know, acting kind of weird the whole time. Almost like whatever he was feeling, she was feeling too."

Hands brace on either side of my face, and Cam's eyes swim into view a few inches away. His face is...ashen. Stricken. "Why the hell didn't you tell me that would happen?"

I don't have time to respond before the darkness pulls me under.

I'M IMMEDIATELY ASSAULTED with déjà vu when I wake in the same spot in Cam's office. This time, Cam is sitting near my feet, his elbows braced on his knees and his head hanging between his shoulders. He straightens when he hears me stir, and he rubs a hand across his mouth.

"How are you feeling?"

"Like you care," I mutter and push myself into a seated position.

"Valerie—"

"Where is Reid?"

"Why didn't you tell me?" he says quietly. "I never would have done that if I'd known."

"You were going to do it to me, so what's the difference?"

He shakes his head and presses his lips together. "I was never going to do it to you."

"But you said—"

"I just hadn't come up with a different solution yet."

We stare at each other for a moment, and I so desperately want to hold on to the anger in my chest. Although his expression cracks the foundation a little, all it takes is picturing his arm coming down across Reid's back for it to return full force.

"Where is Reid?"

He sighs and pushes to his feet. "Can you stand?"

"Yeah." I sway but manage to keep myself upright. It looks like he wants to reach out for me, but he doesn't. "I'll take you to him."

The camp is quiet as he leads me through the tents and into the woods in a direction I've never gone. I don't ask where everyone is because I don't care. I only care about one thing right now.

It's hidden within the trees, and it blends in well with the moss and vines growing across the stone surface. The foundation is crumbling, enough that my confidence it won't collapse on us as we follow the concrete stairs into the earth isn't too high.

The cellar, Nina had called it.

The darkness is thick, especially as we get farther away from the opening and the moon isn't enough to light the way anymore. If I didn't have my half-vampire vision, I wouldn't be able to see in front of me at all.

There are various cells lining both sides, some with missing doors or stones caved in. He takes me to one of the last rooms. Saint is leaning against the wall beside it and nods as we approach.

Cam hands me a tote bag I hadn't realized he'd been carrying. It's empty save for a few blood bags.

"That's all we have right now," he says, then turns and

leaves the cellar without another word, gesturing for Saint to follow.

When I peer into the cell, Reid is lying on a slab of concrete on his stomach, his bloody back exposed. I tighten my fist around the bag's straps. If he's asleep, maybe it's best to let him rest.

"What the hell were you thinking?" he whispers.

"What was I thinking?" I demand, crossing the distance between us. If he didn't look so pathetic and injured right now, I'd be beating the shit out of him myself. I kneel beside his head. "I'm so mad at you."

He gives me a half smile, his cheek still pressed against the cement. "I know."

"I would have been fine," I say, my voice coming out choked.

"I know," he murmurs.

"You didn't have to do that."

"I know."

I stare at his back. It looks even worse than I thought up close. The cuts are deep, jagged, the surrounding skin angry and red. Had my magic helped at all?

"Valerie, I'll be fine," he breathes, then takes my hand. I tighten my fingers around his, finally prying my eyes away from the grisly display. "There have been so many things I haven't been able to protect you from, but this was one thing I could do. Can you give me this one thing?"

"You could have been killed," I whisper.

"But I wasn't. I would rather take a hundred of those lashes than let you get a single one."

I scoff and swipe away a stray tear on my cheek.

"You're such a martyr." He smiles and squeezes my hand. I nod at his back. "At least let me heal you."

"I'll be fine after some blood. Really." His eyes search my face. "Neat little trick you learned there. How'd you do it?"

"I don't know. I think I might have only been able to because of the bond."

"Are you okay? You didn't…*feel* that, did you?"

"No. It was just tiring." I pull two of the blood bags out and hand one to him.

Reid lets out a sigh as he rips it open. "Your guard dog's coming back."

A moment later, footsteps echo through the corridor.

I set the remaining bags on the concrete beside Reid and mutter a quick "I'll be right back" before heading out of the cell. Cam holds up both palms when he sees me, as if expecting a confrontation, then waves for me to follow him farther down the cellar. He's being oddly quiet. It makes me feel like I need to be too, as if someone's listening.

"You two need to get out of here before the sun comes up," he says. His voice is low, detached, and I can't gauge much from his face either.

"He won't leave without me," I say quietly, "and I can't —" I clasp my hand over the mark on my wrist.

"Nina's pack isn't leaving. I might be able to keep mine under control, but hers…if the sun comes up, and he's still here, I can't guarantee his safety. They're getting antsy out there, and a lot don't agree with taking him to Westcott."

My chest tightens. But I know it's a useless endeavor already. That information won't change anything for him. He won't leave.

"There's more than one way to get out of a blood deal," he says.

"I know, I know. Everyone's always talking about these loopholes. But finding anything helpful has been harder to come by."

He nods slowly, an odd look on his face. "Not just loopholes. If you kill the other half of the deal—"

"I don't even know where Westcott is."

"That's one way," Cam finishes. "But you can also give it away."

Give it away? "What do you mean?"

"You can pass the deal to someone else. But that other person has to accept it willingly."

I throw my hands up. "Well, no one's going to offer to sell their soul for me."

"Give it to me."

I blink, momentarily speechless. "Why would you...?"

"I'm already in his debt. I'm already locked into a deal with him. Your terms are no worse than mine. It won't change anything for me."

"Except he'll know you let me get away. And he'll...I don't even know what he'll do. Won't he...I don't know, feel me give it away?"

"He would. But by the time he gets here, you'll be gone. And I'm too valuable for him to kill me," he says, but there's something about his face that tells me he's not entirely sure. Even with how angry I am with him, how much I know in my bones I will never forgive him for what he did to Reid, or how used I feel after he lied to me, if I do this, I'm condemning him and letting him pay for my choice.

"Cam…"

"It's up to you, but the sun will rise in a few hours. We'd have to leave now to get you out in time."

I glance from him back to Reid's cell. If I say no, if I turn down what he's offering, if I can't protect Reid during the day, if they got him out in the sun…

I can't lose him. I won't.

I turn to Cam. "What do we have to do?"

Cam rolls up his sleeve without hesitation, bites down on his hand until he draws blood, then holds it out to me. "With that one," he says, indicating my wrist with the black mark.

Not having a blade on me, I do the same as Cam, sinking my teeth into the meaty part of my palm, and slowly reach for his hand, giving him the chance to pull away, to change his mind.

But he grabs my hand, his grip firm, and our hot blood pools and mingles between our palms. Heat surges up my arm, his energy dancing across my skin like electricity.

"What now?" I whisper. "If there's an incantation, I don't know it—"

"There isn't. It's not magic that transfers it." The intensity of his gaze freezes me in place, and for a moment, the rest of the cellar disappears. "Ask me if I understand the terms and if I'm willing to accept the deal. Use my full name."

I swallow hard, the blood seeming to grow hotter between our hands. When I manage to speak, my voice comes out rough and low. "Do you, Camden Farley, understand the terms of my blood deal, and are you willing to accept the transfer to yourself?"

His fingers tighten around mine, and he holds my gaze as he murmurs, "Yes, I, Camden Farley, understand the terms of Valerie Darkmore's blood deal, and I accept the transfer to myself. I take on full responsibility and release Valerie Darkmore from her debt."

I gasp as the blood between our hands burns white hot, then just as fast, runs cold as ice. Cam holds firm on my hand, and the energy buzzing on my skin grows, almost to an unbearable degree. My teeth lock together, and my ears ring.

But then the black mark in my veins moves like something alive, the branches slithering down the back of my hand, my fingers, growing and stretching until they reach the point where my skin collides with Cam's. I can tell when they finally bridge the gap by Cam's sharp intake of breath, and I stare, mesmerized, as the black veins web their way into Cam's hand, then continue upward, crawling and snaking around his forearm until they disappear beneath his shirtsleeve.

But he never breaks my gaze, never lets go. Until, finally, he exhales, loosens his grip, and the energy surging between our hands quiets.

"One more thing," he whispers.

His other hand cups the side of my face, then he brings his mouth to mine.

I gasp, my lips parting for him like they have a mind of their own, and I fall back a step, then another, until my back meets the wall. He weaves both hands into my hair, but his lips are gentle against mine, his movements slow, measured. After a moment, he pulls away, his eyes just as intense as before.

"Was that part of the transfer?" I ask, though I already know the answer.

His gaze travels from my eyes to my lips and back again before he murmurs, "No," then turns and walks away.

CAM PICKS us up from the cellar in a car I've never seen before, this one a small, black sedan. I help Reid into the front passenger seat. Despite his assurances that he's fine, there's a sway in his step and shaking in his hands as he reaches for the car door.

The blood bag hadn't chased away the postmagic exhaustion as much as I'd been hoping anyway, so I take the back to lie down. The inside of the car is quiet as he drives, save for the small hum of the air conditioner. I curl onto my side and close my eyes, my fingers running over the spot on my wrist, something that's become an unconscious tick. But now the skin is smooth, no trace of the mark that had been there hours before. Almost as if it never happened.

I can't dwell on the guilt brewing inside of me. This was the best choice. The only choice.

Wasn't it?

How long has Cam known you could give deals away? With how long he's had his, I guess that left him plenty of time to go looking for answers.

My throat tightens as something occurs to me. He'd implied his deal was because of his wife, that he'd done it for her.

Was his deal even his to begin with?

Cam mumbles something I don't hear, his voice low. But Reid's response is clear—a simple word: "Why?"

I squint an eye open, trying to see Cam through the seats. His hands tighten around the steering wheel.

"She never should have been here," he says.

"You care about her."

Cam shifts in his seat. "Don't read too much into it."

"You took on a death sentence for her."

"Look, if you're marking your territory or whatever, you can save it. I'm not under any delusions about what this was for her."

My stomach drops at the following silence. I knew I was going to have to tell Reid about Cam at some point. This is definitely not how I wanted to do it.

The bond is quiet, so I can't feel how he reacts. I wait to see if he'll say anything else, but he doesn't.

When I open my eyes again, it looks like dawn is threatening to approach on the horizon. Then the car jerks to a stop as Cam parks.

"I'll get us a room," says Reid, and he quickly slips out of the car.

As he walks toward the motel, I stare at his back through the window. When Cam had said he'd take us into town, I'd assumed he meant the same area as before, but nothing about this is familiar.

"I'll leave the car here," he says without turning around. "I can shift and make my way back."

"Thank you, Cam," I say, though it doesn't feel like nearly enough. "For everything. For looking out for me." I wring my hands together in my lap. "Why did you?"

"Is it not enough to not want someone dead on my watch?"

I think we can both hear how flatly the words fall, how little weight there is to them. But I don't push it. "I guess."

He leans his head against the seat and sighs. "That night at the compound, I admired your loyalty to him. How you put yourself on the line. You were willing to risk everything to save him. I just…I understood. And you deserved better than what you got. You didn't know me when I lost Rea. I was…useless, to say the least. And while you've been here, even at your lowest, you still had this fire inside you. You kept fighting back." I catch a glimpse of his faint smile in the rearview mirror. "Even if it was just at me."

"Is this your way of saying you were being a dick to me on purpose?" I mean for the words to sound light, but they, too, fall flat.

"A little bit, yeah." His smile fades. "I think a part of me was afraid of what would happen if I stopped. If you didn't have something to be angry at. It's a lot easier to come back from anger. Once you lose that…"

The silence stretches between us, and I feel like I should say more. This might be the last time I see him. He's saved my life more times than I can count. And somewhere along the way, I'd started to think of him as a friend. Or something more, maybe, even if I didn't want to admit it to myself. As someone I could trust.

"Cam…"

"It's all right," he says quietly. "This was always a place-holder for you. I knew that."

Reid reappears from the office and nods his head to the side, indicating I should follow him. With one last look at

Cam, I climb out of the car. He follows suit and heads for the woods behind the motel. Just like that. The sight of his back, of him walking away…

"Cam, wait!"

I hurry after him and throw my arms around his shoulders as he turns. He lets out a surprised breath, but after a few moments, he hugs me back.

"You were never a placeholder," I murmur beside his ear. "You weren't."

His face is unreadable as I pull away. He studies my face, and a slow smirk curls his lips. "Don't worry, princess. You'll see me around. Just…take care of yourself."

With that, he takes off into the dark. I stare at the place he disappears through the trees, still stuck in this goodbye, but also afraid to turn around and face the conversation I'll have with Reid.

He's waiting at the door for the middle room when I approach. The light overhead flickers as he unlocks it and lets me head inside first. The air is stale, musty as I cross the threshold and take in my surroundings. There's a single bed with a dark green floral comforter, a lamp on the nightstand with a broken bulb, and a TV that looks like it's a hundred years old.

"You should get some sleep," he says. "I'm going to see if I can find something to eat before the sun comes up."

I sit on the edge of the bed, picking at my nails in my lap. "Reid?"

I can't remember the last time his face looked this distant with me. Probably when we were first paired. When he didn't know if he could trust me. And the fact that he might be feeling the same way now, that he might not trust me anymore, makes my heart feel like it's splitting clean in two.

"Can we talk?"

He takes a deep breath. "We don't have to. I know we weren't... You don't owe me anything, Valerie."

I'm shaking my head before he's done. "No."

"It's all right."

"It's not. I can tell that you're upset."

He pauses, still facing the door. And for a moment I think he's going to leave without another word, but then, quietly, he asks, "Do you love him?"

My shoulders deflate. "No."

He nods to himself and runs a hand along the bottom of his jaw. "Do you want to be with him?"

"No," I say, louder this time. He's still not looking at me. All I want is to beg him to *look at me*, but I hold my tongue.

"Whatever happened between the two of you, does that change things for you? With us?"

"No." I sigh and fold my legs underneath me. "Can I explain—"

"You don't have to."

"I want to, if you'll listen."

He finally meets my eyes and gives a single nod. It's not the tension in his face or the distance in his eyes that cuts at me the most.

It's the uncertainty.

"Things with Cam...it wasn't ever...it wasn't like that. Reid, I thought you were dead. I thought you were dead and that it was my fault. And you—you don't know what that did to me." I wet my lips and shake my head, fighting back the lump in my throat. If I start crying now,

I won't be able to stop. And I need to explain. I need him to understand. "That was one of the worst things that had ever happened to me," I whisper. "When the bond broke, I felt this hole in my chest, and it never went away. And staying at that camp, I just, I couldn't see a light at the end of the tunnel, you know? I thought everyone thought I was dead. That no one was looking for me. I could never go home. I had no idea what Westcott was going to do to me when he came back. It all just felt... hopeless. And I wanted to feel something other than that emptiness. Even if it was something bad. I don't know how to explain it. I know it doesn't make sense. I guess..."

I let out a frustrated breath and shove away the hot tears in my eyes before they can fall. "I know we never talked about this before, but it never would've happened if I'd thought you were alive. I just want you to know that."

The silence between us grows heavy, but then his footsteps thud against the floor and he gets on his knees at the end of the bed.

"I know we didn't have time before," he says and brushes my hair behind my ear. I hold my breath and meet his eyes. The distance behind his is gone now, but the uncertainty remains in the way he bites the inside of his cheek. Or maybe it's something else. Maybe it's...resolve. "And we didn't have a chance to figure out what was going on with us. But let me make myself very clear now. I'm yours, Valerie. Completely." My chin wobbles—the relief crashing through me violent and breathtaking—and I clench my teeth to hold back a sob. "And I'm hoping that you want to be mine, and only mine."

I finally release the breath, and a tear falls down my face. "I already am, Reid," I whisper.

He cradles the side of my face with his hand and pulls me against his chest. I wrap my arms around his shoulders, hugging him as tightly as I can.

"I'm sorry."

"You don't have to be," he murmurs.

"I never wanted to hurt you."

"I know that."

I squeeze my eyes shut and fist my hands in his shirt like I'm afraid he'll change his mind and let go at any moment.

He strokes my hair and sighs. "There's something I need to tell you too. I should have told you before."

I pull back, but I don't let go of his arms. "Okay?"

He presses his lips together, his eyes flicking over my face before he says, "It's about Connor."

A jolt goes through my body. That was the last thing I expected him to say. "Is he—?"

"He's all right," he says quickly. "He was actually helping me look for you. Valerie, he…the changes in his personality after he turned, they seem to be wearing off."

I stare at him, his words somehow making complete sense and not registering in my brain at all simultaneously. "What do you mean?"

"It means he's still in love with you, Valerie. It means he wants you back." He wets his lips and glances at the floor between us before meeting my eyes. "And if that changes things for you, I understand."

Connor. I swallow hard. Oh, God. He's…him again. Or closer to it, at least. Months ago, that's all I wanted.

I try to picture what would happen if I tried with him.

He's different now that he's turned, but that's not the only thing that would be different. *I've* changed. How could I not after everything? I'm barely recognizable as the girl he loved. That relationship with him, that friendship, it was everything to me growing up. But the idea of trying it back on now…

Somehow, I already know it wouldn't fit anymore, and more than that, as I look into Reid's eyes, and the thought of not having him, of losing this with him, I can't bear it.

"I'll always be your partner," he says. "No matter what happens between you and me, we're still partners. I don't want you to worry about that."

Even after all of this, all the ways I've hurt him, he's trying to comfort me. To reassure me.

I lean forward and kiss him. He stiffens for a second, surprised, but then he kisses me back, slowly, softly. Like he's waiting to see if I change my mind. My lips brush his as I whisper, "I already told you, I'm yours."

He seals his mouth over mine before I finish the sentence. Kissing him feels like finally filling my lungs with air after being underwater for too long, but as much as I want to lose myself in it, let the thoughts of anything else drift away, I know I can't.

I pull back and rest my hands on each side of his face. "He's going to find out I'm gone. Cam said he would feel me give the deal away."

"I know."

"I don't know what to do now," I whisper.

"Well, I say first, we get you home, then we'll go from there. I'm sure there's a lot of people there who will be relieved to see you alive."

353

My breath catches in my throat. Monroe. Kirby. Daniel. Adrienne. My mom.

Months have passed. Have they already moved on? Are they okay? Have there been more attacks in the region? Since Reid's been out here looking for me this whole time, he wouldn't know any more than I do about the current state of things.

He gently brushes his thumb over my forehead, easing the tension there. "One thing at a time, Darkmore."

CHAPTER THIRTY-THREE

REID SLEEPS LIKE THE DEAD. Literally. Maybe it's a vampire thing. The stillness is almost unnerving.

But then I look at his face. He's lying on his side, his features soft, lacking their usual intensity. His hair is mussed, the pillow creating a crease on his cheek, and the warmth that floods my chest momentarily makes my throat tight.

Two days ago, I'd thought he was dead. That I'd never see him again. I'd never have a moment like this with him. And now that I do, I'm terrified it'll slip through my fingers.

I know what it feels like to lose him.

I don't think I could survive it again.

The sheets rustle, and his fingers trail along my forearm.

"Come here," he mumbles, eyes still closed.

I scoot closer to him on the bed, and he tugs me against his chest and presses a kiss to my temple. I close my eyes, his warmth wrapping around me as he tucks his face between my shoulder and neck.

He lets out a low sound in the back of his throat and murmurs, "I missed the way you smell."

My stomach clenches, and I wind my fingers into his hair, not wanting him to move. Never wanting him to move. His hand trails down my arm until he reaches my hand and threads his fingers through mine.

"What were you dreaming about last night?" he asks.

I let out a surprised laugh. "I don't know. I never remember them." *Unless they're nightmares.* "Why?"

He pulls back and shakes his head. His eyes are still hazy with sleep, his hair a mess. He searches my face for a moment, amusement tugging at the corners of his lips. "You were smiling in your sleep."

"Oh, so you were just lying there watching me?"

His smirk grows. "Like you were doing just now?"

I sputter, my face warming. "I was not. You—you look like a corpse when you sleep, you know that? I was making sure you weren't dead."

"Mm-hmm." He presses a light kiss to the corner of my mouth.

I chew on my bottom lip as I realize how dark the room's gotten. There was a hint of sunlight coming through the curtains when I'd started watching Reid sleep, but it's gone now.

We can't be that far from the estate—not more than a day's drive. Which means we'll be there in a matter of hours.

I suppose I should be excited by the prospect.

A glint of metal catches the light as he runs his hand

through his hair. I reach forward, my fingers slipping beneath the chain around his neck and tugging out the ring.

"Guess it's time to give this back, huh?" he murmurs.

"Thank you for holding on to it for me. Really."

Maybe it's dumb to be attached to something so small, so easily replaceable. It's one of the few things I've carried with me for most of my life. Something that feels like *mine*.

Now, it feels foreign in a way it never has before. It belonged to a different version of me—a different time, a different life. Slipping this on and waltzing into the estate like nothing's changed won't make it true. Considering the way I left, they might not even let me in the door. Or worse, they'll throw me in a cell or execute me just to be safe.

Those people you gave your entire life away to, they would've put you down like an animal.

Westcott is the last voice I want in my head, the last person I want to listen to, but he wasn't wrong about that. His methods aside, he wasn't wrong about a lot of things.

You seem to be fine with your queen making those kinds of calls. Is that any different? I doubt her sentencings have gotten any more humane in my absence.

I squeeze my eyes shut, but I can see the throne room in my mind's eye, the blood beneath the glass swirling from anyone who dared to cross her, no matter how big or small the indiscretion. Whether it was proven or not.

Has she run out of room in that crown of hers yet?

The pleading looks the prisoners would give the Marionettes, as if any of us would help them. As if any of us would disagree.

You might not have worn the same uniforms as the humans, but make no mistake, you were no more important.

The smile on my mother's face as she pried out their teeth or stopped their hearts. It was all a game. An amusement to them.

Can't you see that it's a tyranny? They make these grand claims of safety and protection to keep you all in their grasps, but protection from who? From them?

At any sighting of a werewolf, I'd never seen the queen sentence anything other than an execution, no questions asked.

I picture Leif's tight smile as he told me about his parents, how he ended up in Cam's pack in the first place.

They're not interested in reform. Why would they be, when they have all the power?

"You know I won't let anything happen to you, right?" Reid says.

My eyes fly open, and I clear my throat and let the ring fall against his collarbone. I don't correct him even though the emotion warring in my chest isn't the fear he thinks he sees on my face. Or maybe it is, in part.

But it's easily consumed by something hotter, sharper.

"Maybe I shouldn't go back."

"This wasn't your fault. None of this has been your fault," he says, his voice firm. "This is something that happened *to* you, not something you did. And I will make sure everyone sees that. Valerie." He takes my face in his hands and forces me to meet his eyes. "If you don't want to go, we won't. But not because you feel like you can't or you don't deserve to. We'll smooth things over. I promise."

I don't even know what that would look like, *smoothing things over.* If it's possible.

If I'll ever be able to forget what happened there. What is *still* happening there.

If I'll ever be able to forget what they all let happen to me.

But I don't say any of that to Reid. How can I when all I see in his eyes as he looks at me is hope?

"How were things when you left?" I ask instead.

His lips press together in a grimace, the confidence in his voice wavering. "Strange. After the wendigo attacks at the estate, there was a big increase in security and reaching out to the other estates for aid. They hadn't come to any conclusions yet for a plan of action, though my mother was quite enthusiastic about planning a counterattack." He rolls his eyes. "Difficult to do when you don't know *where* the enemy is. But the borders were chaotic when we left. I think people were trying to get out, but they weren't letting anyone through."

"Why?" Have they ever shut down the borders completely? To let people enter, yes. But trapping everyone inside?

"I don't know. There's a bounty on this side of the border for vampires and Marionettes, so at first, I thought maybe it had to do with that, but they weren't letting humans through either..." He trails off, then blinks, his eyes refocusing on me. "My point is, they have a lot of other shit to deal with right now."

My head spins. They might not even let us through if the borders are down then—though I suppose they'd make an exception for Reid. I manage a small smirk. "So you're saying I'm old news?"

He grins as he takes my face between his hands. "Very, very old news."

THE CAR IS silent for most of the drive to the estate. I try to imagine walking through those doors. Coming face-to-face with the people I never thought I'd see again. But whenever I try to think about my mother, all I remember is the last time I saw her. The sneer on her face as she peered at me through the bars. The way she left me there, promising she wouldn't come back.

That I was dead to her.

These past few months thinking I was dead, that's exactly what she wanted. I can't kid myself into thinking she'll be happy to see me. Maybe no one will be.

The bond has been quiet for the most part, but as we edge closer to the border, a hint of anxiety trickles through, making my own pulse spike.

"What is it?" I ask.

He shakes his head, eyes still trained through the windshield. "I don't know." Worry lines his forehead. "It seems quiet."

"Is that bad?"

"I don't know," he repeats. "It was chaotic when I left. The streets were packed. And now…"

I hold my breath as we pull up to the entry point at the bridge. Before all this, I had never been on this side of the boundary before. But still, I can imagine it doesn't usually look like this. There's no line. No crowds of people. No noise.

Reid lowers the window as he pulls up to the small structure beside the gate, but there's no one inside. The anxiety pulsing through the bond heightens.

"That's not normal," I say. It isn't a question this time.

"No," he responds, his voice tight.

I glance around, wondering if whoever works this station is just slacking off and taking a break. But there's no one around.

Reid pops the door open and climbs out of the car. He reaches into the structure and hits a button that lifts the gate. It lets out an earsplitting shriek that echoes in the silence.

As he pulls forward to cross the bridge, there are no other cars in sight, and we find a similar scene on the other side of the border. No cars waiting to cross in the opposite direction. And no one manning the post.

A knot forms in the pit of my stomach. Reid keeps driving, but as we venture farther into the city, the streets don't get any more crowded. It's like a ghost town. No cars on the road. No people milling about. No lights in the windows of the buildings.

What the hell happened here?

Reid lays his hand on my leg, his thumb gently brushing my knee as he heads toward the estate. The line of his jaw is hard as he stares straight ahead.

What if we find something similar there? If it's deserted too? The only thing I can possibly imagine would cause this is we were too late. Westcott, whatever his plans had been, he'd already gone through with them. Which would mean the estate had fallen. And everyone inside…

"Oh, God," I breathe.

"We don't know anything yet," Reid says quickly.

"Have you ever seen anything like this?"

He presses his lips together. "No."

Even before I'd gone with Westcott, when I'd been under the influence of the psychosis and going on a rampage through the city, there had been an emergency order for people to stay home, and the city had been the hollowest I'd ever seen it.

But the emptiness around us feels different. The energy in the air.

Something happened here.

There are no guards stationed on the grounds of the estate when Reid pulls up to the gate, but when he speaks into the intercom and presses the button, it lets out its usual buzzing sound and lurches open.

He glances at me sideways before pulling forward and heading for the garages in the back. My nails bite into my palms as I clench my fists and stare out the window, waiting, willing, *begging* to see a sign of someone else. Anyone else.

The garage is full of the estate's other cars. I can't decide if that's a good or bad sign. Reid takes my hand, his grip firm, as we head inside. I barely make it one step through the door before a gust of wind slams me against the wall. Reid lands next to me, fangs bared, but the hold on us releases almost instantly.

I manage to steady myself against the wall so I don't hit the ground, and Reid steps in front of me, but his posture relaxes a moment later.

"Prince Reginald," says a low voice. "You're—you're back."

A tall, dark-haired man in a Marionettes uniform stands

a few paces away, taking in Reid with wide eyes. They widen further as he focuses on me.

Reid smooths his shirt and shoves his hair out of his eyes. "What the hell happened here?"

His gaze lingers on me for another moment before he finally manages to peel his eyes away.

"Long story," he says, his voice distant. "Mostly everyone was evacuated to the other estates."

"Did my—" Reid starts.

"Your mother got out." He glances at me.

"Yes, obviously I'm not dead," I say.

He blinks and offers a small, embarrassed smile. "Sorry, we haven't had anyone new in here in weeks."

"Why are you still here if everyone else was evacuated?" Reid asks.

"Some of us stayed behind to keep an eye on the place. Report back."

"Some of us meaning Marionettes?" I ask.

He nods. "There's about a dozen of us."

"And that's it?" Reid asks.

He shakes his head. "Some of the humans decided to stay behind. Families in the city and whatnot."

"What about the academy students?" I ask.

"They've been staying up in York. The school's been on lockdown."

My shoulders relax. Just a bit. "The city looked cleared out too," I say quietly.

He presses his lips together and doesn't respond for a moment. "It would appear that way."

My brow furrows. What the hell does he mean by that? Before we can ask though, he tilts his head to the side and starts to walk down the hall, gesturing for us to follow him.

"When did they evacuate?" Reid asks.

"About a week after you left. Most of us don't buy into it, but I should tell you, there have been rumors about the timing. You leaving and the attacks of the estate getting worse. Some people think you might have known more than you let on and left early to save yourself."

"What?" I demand. "That's ridiculous."

"I know that," he says quickly. "I just thought you should know."

Reid's expression is unreadable. "The attacks, do you mean the wendigos?"

The man nods. "Among other things."

"Other things?" I press.

"I'm assuming you've noticed the borders are down."

"What does that have to—"

Reid lays a hand on my arm, and I shoot him a questioning look. "If the borders are down," he says quietly, "anyone or anything could have come into the region."

A chill runs down my spine. *Anything.* It reminds me of the conversation I'd had with Connor all those lifetimes ago about him wanting to leave the region, and I couldn't fathom why he'd want to with all the uncertainty about what else is out there.

My head snaps to the side. "Connor—" I start, my voice choked.

"He's fine," Reid says. "I can feel him, and I sent him to Auclair, so he probably hasn't been back here. I also let him know I found you."

I nod, though my heart is still pounding in my throat.

And a trickle of guilt works its way through my system. I think it might always now when I think of Connor.

"Have there been any other attacks since the evacuation?" Reid asks.

The man sighs. "That is a complicated answer. We can talk down here." He leads us to the throne room and holds the door open as he waits for us to step inside. "We've been staying in the bunker," he explains. "Just in case."

Every muscle in my body tightens at the sight of the door propped open in the middle of the floor. I don't know if I can go back there. Not with the memory of what happened last time clinging to my skin like dried blood. The scream as I sunk my fangs into a pulsing vein. One that I now know belonged to Adrienne.

"I'll wait here," I say as Reid heads for the ladder. His brow furrows and he looks at me over his shoulder. I nod and try to plaster on the most encouraging expression I can muster. "I'll be fine."

He stares at me for a moment, but then something shifts in his eyes. Understanding, probably. And he nods as he follows the other Marionette into the earth.

CHAPTER THIRTY-FOUR

CONNOR DIED RIGHT THERE, on the same floor where countless others have, while everyone in this room watched like it was entertainment. I stare at the glass, now polished and smooth, no trace of what happened all those months ago.

I don't know what I'd expected to feel when I got to the estate. Relief, maybe? Safe?

But nothing about this place feels like home. Not anymore.

I can't remember the last time I had my phone, but I wish I had it now more than ever. All I want is to talk to my friends. But if they're locked down at the academy, I might not be able to see them. To let them know I'm alive. To make sure they're all okay.

I can't stay in this throne room for another second. I can't keep looking at that floor. I can't keep looking at the dais where my mother stood by and watched. Where Reid glamoured me.

Given we have no idea what's been going on out there, I know better than to venture far. Maybe if I were feeling strong, I'd feel differently, but in my weakened state, I'm not going to push it.

I'll just wait outside. Yeah, outside the room will be fine. But when I step into the hall, my eyes lock on the bench I'd waited at during Connor's review. I'd leaned my weight on it for a few moments after my final trial, too, waiting for the dizziness from the venom to pass before making my way upstairs.

I squeeze my eyes shut, my neck burning with the memory of Connor's fangs, not just puncturing skin, but tearing and ripping through my flesh as I'd tried to pull away.

"Fuck," I mutter, shaking my head. I have to get out of this hallway. I won't go far. I can't breathe. I can't *think*.

I force myself to stop walking when I hit the pool room, my breaths coming in small gasps.

The sky is dark through the windows, the moon barely visible behind the cloud cover. The garden seems so much smaller than I remember. Maybe it's because the plants are starting to wilt and brown, their leaves curling in on themselves.

The garden used to be one of the few places at the estate where I felt peace, just for a few moments. But looking at it now, I feel nothing of the sort. The feeling in my gut is just a heavy, hard dread.

"You ready to go?"

I jump at Reid's voice and whip around. He's standing with his head cocked as he watches me, his hands in his pockets.

"Go where?" I ask.

"The sun will be up soon, so we'll have to stay, but the team here is alerting the academy and my mother that we're here. Sounds like they're at Auclair right now."

"What did they tell you? Down there?"

He rubs his hand along the bottom of his jaw. "Everything they know so far, which isn't much. The wendigo attacks have been a problem, but not as much as the people from the estate attacking each other."

My eyes snap up to meet his. "You mean..."

"That sounds like Wendigo Psychosis? Yeah."

"How many people?" I whisper.

He shakes his head. "Infected? I don't know. I told them as much as I could about Westcott. About what I'd found in my research. It sounded like it wasn't just at the estate too."

"The city."

He nods. "They evacuated about a week ago."

I rub my hands up and down my arms, suddenly cold. "So we're going to Auclair?" I ask, my voice distant and hollow. "We don't have to wait until tomorrow. I can take us."

"Valerie..." he starts, and I hate the worry in his voice.

"I can do it," I insist. "I'm feeling stronger already."

"Which is why I don't want to push it."

"At least let me try."

He meets my eyes, and though the set of his mouth is hard, he doesn't protest.

"Teleporting you should be easier than anyone else anyway," I add.

His eyebrow lifts. "Why's that?"

I shrug. "I don't know. It was the same when I was

trying to heal you at the camp. Because of the bond, probably. Usually, trying to manipulate someone else's body
chemistry takes a lot of power and a lot of concentration.
But with you...honestly, it almost felt the same as doing it to
myself."

His expression turns soft, thoughtful. I suppose with the
bond connecting us, it would make sense that my magic
sees him as an extension of myself.

"At least let me get you some food and blood first."

It's chilling, the silence in the estate. It crowds in around
us as we head for the kitchen, and his hand tightens around
mine, his shoulders tense as if preparing for a threat to
appear around any corner. But all that follows us is the
echoes of our footsteps.

A small smile pulls at my lips as I lean against the doorjamb and watch him rifle through the cabinets the same
way he had the night that changed everything.

The night he gave me his blood and I turned.

Back then, all I had to worry about was getting through
initiation, and now...

He finds some pasta and throws it into a pot on the
stove. He stands with his back to me as he stirs, and for
some reason, a lump rises to the back of my throat. I cross
the distance between us and wrap my arms around his
waist, resting my head against the center of his back.

He straightens and stops stirring, then his hand comes
to rest over mine, his thumb gently rubbing back and forth
on the inside of my wrist.

"Valerie..."

"Sorry." I release him and take a step back, my eyes a
little watery. "I don't know why I—"

He turns and grabs my face with both hands, his mouth covering mine before I finish the sentence. My hands fist in his shirt and we stumble a few steps until my back hits the counter. His lips don't break from mine, even as he grips the backs of my thighs and hoists me to sit on the edge. My legs wrap around his waist, pulling him against me as his hands find the small of my back.

The low groan he makes in the back of his throat sets every nerve in my body on fire.

The kitchen timer beeps behind him, and he lets out a long breath before pulling back from me, but there's a shadow of a smirk on his face as he meets my eyes and taps the underside of my chin, then turns to the stove.

I THINK my magic missed me as much as I missed it. Teleporting to Auclair should have been exhausting, nearly impossible. The distance alone would've been a challenge for me on my best day, but today, I barely feel it. My magic sings and buzzes inside of me, overjoyed at being used, like it's been waiting for an opportunity to try something big again.

Instead of feeling on the verge of collapse as I open my eyes, I feel...*wired.*

Maybe if I hadn't spent that time at the compound before being sent to the camp, I would have felt more excitement about seeing the Canadian estate. A few months ago, I'd never been outside of New York. Now, my experience of the world has expanded considerably. Unfortunately, none of the experiences being good. But at the very least, it's a relief when we arrive at the estate and there are people all around us. Granted, they're pointing weapons and staring with hardened, suspicious expressions. But after driving through the entirety of New York City as a ghost town, I'll take what I can get.

The Marionette who approaches us is small, a full foot shorter than I am, with her gray hair yanked back in a slick bun. All the other witches, however, a dozen standing behind her, look to her with respect, waiting to see what she does first.

Her eyes flicker from me to Reid and back again. "I had a feeling you two weren't dead" is all she says before she turns and struts to the gate, apparently expecting us to follow.

The similarities between here and the Carrington estate are almost eerie. I wonder if all the estates look this similar or if it's because these two were built a few years apart and they're pretty close location-wise.

Snow-tipped mountains line the horizon, but the building itself has almost exactly the same architecture as in New York, down to the security instruments located at the front of the gate. The woman presses the button and leans her head down so the camera can see her, and it lets out an eerily familiar buzzing noise as it lurches open.

Reid takes my hand as we walk, the heat of his palm comforting and familiar. It doesn't occur to me until we're halfway up the lawn what might happen when we step through those doors.

The Marionettes of the Carrington estate had said both of our mothers were here, and despite everything she did, despite everything she said, I still can't hate her. I still can't help the tiny hope that burrows itself deep into the walls of my heart that maybe time away has changed her mind. That maybe thinking I was dead softened the anger she had toward me. That maybe this reunion will be different.

I shake my head at myself, hating that line of thinking. It's like I'm perpetually a child seeking my mother's approval. Even when, logically, I know I'm never going to get it. When I shouldn't need it. Why should I care about a woman who doesn't care about me? Who left me for dead? Who's done nothing but berate and abuse and hate me my whole life?

Reid's hand squeezes mine. I force the thoughts away, hoping he didn't hear any of that down the bond.

We step through the doors, and even the foyer is eerily similar, to the point where I have a brief, disorienting moment like I can't remember where I am.

"I suspect Queen Carrington will want to speak with you," says the Marionette without turning to look at us. "She's in the guest quarters. I can take you to her."

Whatever disorientation I'd felt earlier quickly evaporates at the thought of the queen in a guest room. But of course, this isn't her estate.

Human servants bustle past us as we follow the Marionette down the hall, all going about business as usual. They experienced a wendigo attack shortly before the Carrington estate did, and yet, they're still operating. Everything seems to have gone back to the way it was before.

So what made what happened in New York different? Why does it seem like that was so much worse than it was here?

The Marionette leaves us outside a white door with gold accents before turning and heading the way we'd come.

I can feel Reid looking at me out of my peripheral vision, but I don't turn my head. My heart is beating so hard it feels like it's in my stomach. If his mom is behind that door, there's a good chance mine is as well, if not close by.

The queen is standing by the floor-to-ceiling windows when we step inside, her back to us. She's wearing a floor-length red silk robe, her hair braided and hanging down to her lower back. But there's no sign of her crown or usual jewels.

"I've been wondering when you'd come," she says without turning. The door clicks softly behind us. "We have much to discuss."

"We can talk about anything you want," says Reid. "But let Valerie go rest—"

The queen finally turns, an almost gleeful smile on her face. "I was speaking to Valerie, actually. You can go, Reginald." She cocks her head at him and blinks, her smile too sweet, when he doesn't move. "Is that a problem?"

A muscle in his jaw jumps. "Of course not."

"Fabulous!" She grins at me as if we're in on a secret.

I'll just be out in the hall, he says into my mind as he slips through the door.

"So," she says, "from what I understand, you've spent this little vacation with your father."

She knew.

I don't know why that's surprising, considering her relationship with my mother, but if she'd known who Westcott was while he was at the estate, there's no way she would have let him get away with being free right under her nose. Not after what Reid told me about her condemning him decades before.

I guess that explains the fire behind her eyes. This is personal for her. Maybe even as personal as it is for me.

But then...she'd known I was alive. Known where I was.

"I wouldn't call it a vacation," I say tightly.

She gives me a humorless smile. "I imagine not. Am I to believe you've come here willingly?"

"What do you mean?"

She gives me a long, considering look but doesn't answer my question.

"You think I'm some kind of spy for him," I realize.

She shrugs. "Blood runs deep. I could hardly fault you for it."

"I have no loyalty toward that man."

"That remains to be seen. Please, have a seat." She gestures to one of the velvet chairs by her window. There's a small table between them with a tea tray. She takes a seat across from me and picks up one of the teacups.

"Thirsty?"

"I'm fine," I say.

She pours me some anyway, and I immediately smell the blood. I take the cup, frowning at the contents. It's clear like tea would be, but there's definitely blood in it.

"It's not poison," she says. "That's your mom's forte."

My eyes shoot to her face, but her expression is perfectly innocent, as if she could be referring to anything. My mother's fondness of poisons is no secret. She could very well be talking about anything at all. How could she know about the perfume? Unless she was somehow in on that. It would help if I knew why my mother had done it in the first place.

I take a sip of the tea. The warmth soothes the back of my throat, the blood satiating the hunger lingering there.

When I look up, her gaze is intent on me, like she's waiting for something.

"So you are cured," she finally says.

I blink. "I—"

"The tea," she explains. "It's laced with a few herbs my Marionettes concocted—Zanthinum, that kind of thing. It detects the psychosis."

I swallow hard. The last time she saw me she had me locked in a cell and left to rot. Even if she believes I'm not under the influence of the psychosis anymore, I still broke more of the estate's laws than I can count—attacking estate members, killing vampires.

"No need to be so tense, Valerie," she admonishes. "You are far more valuable to me alive than dead. If it's your previous indiscretions you're so concerned about, consider yourself pardoned."

The words don't bring nearly as much comfort as they should. I stare at the cup. "If you're wanting to know what the cure is, I don't know how he did it."

"So you wouldn't mind if we had a quick look through then?"

Look through. She's never performed the spell on me, but I'd seen it done a few times during interrogations at the estate. My stomach rolls at the idea of anyone being inside my head and combing through my memories, but I know I don't have a choice.

But to do that, she'd need...

The door opens behind me, and every muscle in my body goes rigid.

High heels tap faintly on the floor as she circles to the queen's side. Slowly, I raise my eyes to meet my mother's. I expect to find coldness, distance. The same look she'd given me through the bars of the cell before she'd left me to die.

And there's a little of that, the impassiveness. But there's also a crease in her forehead, a tightness in the set of her mouth. She's not looking *through* me, as she so often does. She's studying me, taking in every detail of my appearance.

If the queen had known I was alive, does that mean she did too?

All this time, I'd felt so hopeless that no one was looking for me because no one knew I was alive. But the possibility of them knowing and just choosing not to cuts so much deeper.

She says nothing and gestures for me to give her my hand. Her touch is strikingly gentle as she takes my wrist, then presses into the center of my palm with the razors on her nails, drawing blood. She pricks her own finger and smears our blood together before clasping my hand in hers.

She meets my eyes, and I force in a deep breath as her energy flows through me. Images and memories flash behind my eyes—me collapsing after the blood exchange with Reid in the kitchen, him stopping me from attacking Beth in the woods, him ripping Candace's throat out in the hall. The wendigo's claws ripping into my chest, the terror in Dr. Kapoor's face when she said she couldn't help me, waking up in Central Park covered in blood. Reid feeding me in the cell, begging me to drink, seeing Calla for the first time. Rome's dead body at my feet in the control room, Terrence shoving my head under the water, Cam smoothing his hand over my hair until I fell asleep.

Seeing Reid for the first time again in the market.

Cam offering to take my deal.

I don't move, not a single muscle. When she's done, she pulls back an inch and meets my eyes. Her face is more pinched together than before. I hold my breath. If she shows those memories to the queen…me turning…

She takes an abrupt step back, then repeats the ritual with the queen, joining their blood in the palms of their hands, then closing her eyes as she transfers the memories to her.

A slow smile curls the queen's mouth. "Seems you enjoyed your time at the wolf camp after all."

My face burns. Jesus Christ. How much of that did she see?

"Thank you for your help, Valerie. You've given me a lot of useful information. We'll talk again soon," she says, a clear dismissal.

And a threat.

But that's all she says.

I set my barely touched tea on the table, my eyes flickering to my mother.

The movement is so small, it's nearly undetectable, but she nods. I head for the door, my feet stumbling, my energy off after that spell. The last thing I hear before stepping into the hall is the small laugh the queen lets out.

CHAPTER THIRTY-FIVE

REID PUSHES off the opposite wall the moment I step outside.

Are you all right? I felt your anxiety, and then your mom went in...

I nod, and his eyes flick from me to the door, then he wraps his arm around my shoulders and leads me down the hall.

What happened in there?

People stare as we pass, and they give us plenty of space, their expressions wary. Because of me. Not that I can blame them, considering everyone probably heard about *The Golden Darkmore* child having a complete breakdown and going on a murdering rampage by now.

Or maybe it's the coming back from the dead bit that's freaking people out.

They looked through my memories.

He stiffens and offers a tight smile to a servant as they pass.

How much did they——?

I don't know.

His thumb rubs up and down my shoulder, and he gestures to a door on our left. Another guest room, by the looks of it.

"Did she say anything else?" he asks after he closes the door.

I wrap my arms around myself and shrug. "She thought I might be spying for Westcott, then gave me some tea that apparently weeds out Wendigo Psychosis."

He frowns at that, but the door bursts open before he has the chance to respond.

It's like seeing a ghost, and based on the look on his face, seeing me feels the same. Connor crosses the distance between us and throws his arms around me before I can utter a word, his grip unyielding, his face pressed against my hair.

"It's you. It's really you," he breathes.

Shock freezes my body in place for a second before I manage to hug him back. Reid telling me he was getting his emotions back and seeing them firsthand are two very different things.

"Are you hurt? Are you okay?" He steps back and frames my face with his hands as his eyes trace every inch of me. His thumbs brush away the tears on my cheeks that I hadn't noticed falling, and I realize someone else is standing in the door behind him.

My stomach bottoms out as I meet Adrienne's eyes, an overwhelming hurricane of emotions warring inside of me. Guilt. Relief. Anxiety. Fear. The last time I saw her...

But then she's walking toward me. Her arms wrap

around my neck even tighter than Connor's had been, and I loop mine around her waist, closing my eyes as her familiar scent washes over me.

Her chest shakes like she's crying, and I squeeze her tighter, my own breaths coming in short and fast.

I meet Reid's eyes over her shoulder, my vision cloudy with tears, and he gives me a small smile and nods toward the door.

I'll give you some space.

Adrienne pulls back and holds my face the same way Connor had, tears dripping from her chin. "You're here. You're really here."

I nod. "Adrienne, I'm so sorry. I'm so sorry."

She shakes her head. "I don't blame you," she whispers. "Of course I don't blame you."

A sob breaks loose, and she gathers me into a hug. I hadn't realized how desperately I'd needed to hear those words. Connor lingers behind me, his hand rubbing up and down my back.

"I wish you'd told me what was happening," she says. "Maybe I could've—I could've helped or—"

"There was nothing you could have done."

"I thought I'd lost you both," she gasps, her nails digging into my arms. "I thought it was just me left."

I stiffen. *Calla.* It's not that I haven't thought of her since leaving the compound. Our last conversation has appeared in at least half of my dreams. *You're dead to me.*

That was the last thing I said to her.

And despite everything—despite Reid being alive—that anger and betrayal in my chest hasn't extinguished, at least not completely. Because for all she knew, he was dead. And she'd still chosen to turn her back on me, to side with West-cott. Whatever she is now—*whoever* she is—she's not the Calla we grew up with.

But Adrienne has a right to know. "I have to tell you something."

"Okay."

Adrienne sniffles as she releases me, and I force myself to maintain eye contact as I say, "Calla—" I nearly choke on her name and clear my throat. "Calliope's alive."

"What are you...?" Adrienne blinks slowly, then stumbles back a step. "What?"

I run my hand over my mouth and my fingers tremble. "They faked her death the way they did with mine. I —Westcott"—I wince, having no idea how to explain this —"is our dad. She's been with him. He's the one who's been doing all this. He's the one who—" My hand trails over my wrist where the mark of the blood deal had been.

Which just brings thoughts of Cam, and an entirely different ache spreads in my stomach.

Adrienne keeps backing up until she reaches the bed, then slumps onto the edge like she can't hold herself up anymore. "And that's where you were? With him?"

I nod—not quite, but it's an easier explanation than getting into everything with the wolves right now. She fixates on the scar through my lips, her expression harden-ing. "Did he—did he *hurt* you? Is he hurting Calla?"

I resist the urge to cover it with my hand. "No, this— this wasn't him. Um—werewolf." I shrug, then let out a small, humorless laugh, as if anything about this is remotely funny.

She nods, her eyes wide now and looking a lot like she's on the brink of hysteria. "Right."

"What are you even doing here?" I ask. "Shouldn't you be at the academy? I thought they were on lockdown."

"Yeah, Mom pulled me out when the attacks started getting worse and they moved everyone here." She pauses as if something just occurred to her. "Did she know? About Calla? About you?"

"I don't know. The queen did though." I all but collapse beside her on the bed, the exhaustion catching up with me. Exactly what my body's been through. Maybe I'd been running on adrenaline before.

I must show it, because she squeezes my hand and says, "You should rest. We can talk more later."

I nod and squeeze her hand before she gets up to leave.

Connor lingers behind, a muscle in his jaw working as the door clicks shut. We stare at each other, and the look on his face...he looks like him again. None of the coldness or distance that was there before I left.

"Reid told me that you were starting to feel...better."

He nods and puts his hands in his pockets, though he doesn't come any closer.

"Val, I—" His voice breaks, and he looks at his shoes. "I can't tell you how sorry I am—"

"Connor, don't. I knew—I know that wasn't your fault."

He shakes his head, his jaw flexing. "I still can't believe some of the things I said to you. It's unforgivable."

"But I already forgave you."

Finally, he meets my eyes, a sadness weighing his down. "But that doesn't change anything, does it?"

I know what he's really asking. I thought maybe once I

saw him, the certainty I'd felt when Reid asked me the same thing wouldn't be as clear. But the clarity doesn't make the next words I say any easier. "Connor, I will always care about you."

He nods quickly and presses his lips together. "But you're in love with him."

"Connor—"

The tears in his eyes twist like razors in my chest, but he blinks them away before they can fall. "It's okay."

"I never wanted any of this to happen," I whisper, and my crying turns into a choked sob. "I know that you did this for me. You were willing to give up *everything* for me. And I—"

"Hey. It's okay." He kneels in front of the bed and gives me a pained smile, though the tears are flowing freely down his cheeks now. But *him* trying to comfort *me* when I'm the one breaking his heart only makes me cry harder. "I will always be your friend. We were friends before this. We can survive this too."

"I'm so sorry," I choke out, and he pulls me against his chest like he's done so many times before. For the longest time, he was the only person who comforted me. The only one who was always there, even before we started dating. I fist my hand in his shirt, pulling him as tightly against me as I can. "I never wanted to hurt you."

"I know." He smooths his hand over my hair, and his voice is thick as he asks, "Does he treat you well?"

I sob against his shoulder and nod once. Even now, he's trying to make sure I'm okay. That I'm taken care of.

"Okay." He smiles as he pulls back and brushes the tears from my cheeks. "Then that's all I care about."

I touch the side of his face and smile back, remembering the words he'd said to me when he'd been the one breaking this off for good.

I think I'll always love you, in some way. And I'm sorry it can't be in the way you need anymore.

I hadn't understood what that felt like, not really. Not until now.

I wipe the tears from his cheek with the pad of my thumb. "I want you to be happy, Connor. I'm really glad you're doing better."

"Me too." He lays a hand over mine, and I can see in his eyes that there's so much more he wants to say, and a part of me wants to beg him not to go, but I know how selfish it would be. Because I also know that I won't change my mind. So instead, I say nothing as I watch him walk out the door.

———

REID STAYS with me for a while, I think. I fall asleep pretty quickly, so I can't be sure. I wake a few times as I toss and turn and find a note on the bedside table letting me know he got pulled into a meeting, but he'll be back.

The second time I wake, there's a glass of blood and a plate of food beside the bed. I down them both immediately, curl myself deeper into the blankets, and promptly fall back asleep.

But no matter how much sleep I get, the exhaustion never leaves. I can't bring myself to care enough to get up. It seems odd that I've managed to push myself to keep going all this time, despite the circumstances. But now that

I've finally gotten what I wanted, now that I'm out of that camp and people know I'm alive, now is the time when my body decides to stop functioning. It doesn't make any sense.

I don't know how many hours pass, maybe even days, before a gentle knock on the door jolts me awake. I sit up as it opens.

Reid's head appears. "Hi," he says softly.

"Hi."

He places fresh blood on the table and takes a seat at the foot of the bed. "How are you feeling?"

"Better," I lie, slide the cup of blood off the tray, and cradle it between my hands. It's in a mug today, and it's warm. I take a small sip.

"Would you feel up to more visitors?" he asks, a strange look on his face.

I raise an eyebrow. "What kind of visitors?"

"The kind you'll like, I think."

So that weeds out my mother. I narrow my eyes, trying to feel out what he's thinking through the bond, but he's purposefully cutting me off.

"Right now?"

He nods. "They're waiting in the hall."

When I don't protest, he goes to the door, and I catch myself holding my breath as the visitors step inside.

The tears are immediate. From me, and from them. I nearly spill the blood in my haste to set the cup on the table and shove the covers off me. Kirby and Monroe stumble into the room, and a sob rips through Monroe as she throws her arms around me. I can't say anything through my heaving breaths, so I cry and hold them both against me as tightly as I can. Which seems to be okay with them, because they're both crying as hard as I am.

Once I finally catch my breath, I peek at Reid waiting by the door. "How…?"

He gives me a small smile. "The academy is still on lockdown, but I called in a few favors."

Kirby wipes the tears from my face.

"Thank you," I whisper.

He winks. "I'll come back in a little bit."

"I couldn't believe it when we got the call," Kirby says, sniffling. She holds me at arm's length as she looks at me, like she's trying to convince herself that I'm really here.

Monroe gently punches me in the arm. "You asshole."

I let out a small laugh. "I'm sorry."

"Fuck." She throws her arms around my shoulders and crushes me against her. Kirby piles in on the other side, sandwiching me between them.

"I missed you guys so much," I whisper. "I don't even know how to explain—"

"Reid did, or he tried to," says Monroe. "Don't worry, I'm going to yell at him next for not asking us to come with him to look for you. *God*, did no one offer you anything to eat around here?" She frowns as she examines me.

"I'm fine, Roe—"

"I think some hamburgers are in order," she decides and hooks her arm through mine like nothing's wrong, like nothing's changed. Like she didn't think I was dead yesterday.

"I could go for some food," Kirby agrees, linking her arm with mine on the other side.

"You don't have to baby me," I say, but I can't hold back my smile.

"You still look hot—" starts Monroe.

"Obviously," supplies Kirby.

"But you're also missing half of you. So shut up and let us take you out for lunch... Well, they won't let us leave the estate, but we can take you to the kitchen!"

"And you just came back from the dead," says Kirby. "You owe us."

I know arguing with them is pointless—and truth be told, I could eat—so I let them guide me into the hall. Monroe tugs us to a stop after a few paces and whips around to point a finger at Reid, who's still standing by the door.

"We're not done with this conversation," she says.

He folds a smile between his teeth and nods. "Bring her back in one piece!" he calls as they resume whisking me down the hallway.

Kirby flashes me a conspiratorial grin. "No promises!"

———

OTHER THAN A FEW members of the Auclair staff, the kitchen is empty.

The wary glances and people leaving plenty of distance between us continues through the hallways, but no one says anything to me.

"What are you in the mood for?" Kirby asks, her tone overly chipper, even for her.

I catch Monroe watching me in my peripheral vision

like she's waiting for me to fall over or burst into a million tears at any second.

Sighing, I take a seat at the small table tucked in the corner.

"And don't tell us you're fine or *just anything*," Kirby adds.

I throw my hands up. "A grilled cheese, I guess. And some blood."

Kirby beams and practically skips to the refrigerator. "Coming right up."

Monroe's studying me doesn't stop, even as she takes the seat next to me.

"Roe," I sigh, but when I glance at her again, there are tears in her eyes. "You can't start crying. Because if you do that, I will. And I swear that's all I've been doing for the longest time."

She presses her lips together and nods too many times too fast. "I missed you, kid," she says quietly.

"I missed you guys," I manage to squeeze out through the lump in my throat. "You have no idea how much." I exhale loudly and force a smile onto my face. "So tell me what I've missed. I want to know everything. How's senior year going?"

Kirby and Monroe exchange a look.

"Is everyone okay? With the attacks and everything. I heard the academy's on lockdown. Daniel, Wes, Beth—"

"They're all fine," Monroe says quickly. "We told them the news before we came here. As you can imagine, they were insisting they should come too."

I smile a little.

"I believe Reid's exact words were *This isn't a field trip,*"

Kirby calls from across the kitchen.

My smile grows at that too. That does sound like him.

"So." Monroe drums her fingers against the table, her eyebrows lifting. "Are you two, like, a thing?" She's smiling by the end of the sentence, and despite the inflection, we both know it isn't a question.

Still, I humor her, hating the way my cheeks are burning as I roll my eyes and murmur, "Yeah."

"I knew it!" shrills Kirby, pointing a finger at me. "I *knew* it from before you two even made it to the pairing ceremony. Didn't I call this?" She looks at Monroe.

I clear my throat. "Anyway. The attacks. What's been going on? We went through New York and the Carrington estate before we got here, and it was like a ghost town."

Kirby's expression sobers. She tosses the bread into a pan. "We were back in York by the time things got bad, so we only know as much as they told us, and you know how that is."

I bite my tongue, because I do know exactly how that is from my experiences last year trying to get information out of Coderre when the attacks started.

"There were some more attacks on campus," Monroe adds. "Like the vampire who attacked Daniel during initiation. No wendigo sightings or anything like that, that I know of. But they locked the campus down a couple weeks into the term before anything got too bad, more as a preventative measure."

Kirby flips the sandwich in the pan, and it sizzles as she eyes me. "The psychosis...your dad...was all that true?"

My stomach tightens. I nod.

Monroe reaches over and squeezes my knee. She'd been

in that bunker with me, seen the bloodlust in my eyes. I'm just thankful she wasn't one of the people in the room when I snapped.

"How are you doing?" she asks. "Really? Reid filled us in a little on what happened, but I imagine he left a lot out."

"I've been better," I admit, "but I've also been worse."

She gives me a humorless smile. "Yeah."

"Here you are." Kirby slides two grilled cheese sandwiches on a plate in front of me, then adds a mug full of microwaved blood. "Does that change the taste of it?" she asks, pointing at the cup as she takes the seat across from me. "Nuking it."

I shrug and take a sip. "All bagged blood tastes a little off to me. It's not the same as drinking it from the source, but…" After months of drinking dead animal blood, I'm certainly not in a position to complain, and drinking straight from the vein, no matter how much better the blood tastes…I don't think I'll ever be able to do it again. Not without remembering all the lives I took.

"You can talk to us about what happened, you know?" Monroe says quietly. "We're not going to judge."

"But you also don't have to," Kirby adds quickly.

"Of course not," agrees Monroe.

"Whatever you need." Kirby nods.

"Guys." I set the sandwich on my plate. "Can we skip past the walking-on-eggshells-around-me phase and just try to get back to normal? *That's* what I need."

"Fine," says Kirby, sitting up straighter, and I know immediately from her smile that I won't like whatever she has to say next. "Then back to Reid…"

CHAPTER THIRTY-SIX

THE NEXT FEW days pass in a blur, but my strength starts to come back faster than I could have hoped for. I've still been sleeping at least twelve hours a day, though, and spending every waking hour with Kirby and Monroe, who are staying at Auclair for the week.

Reid's face is the first thing I see when I wake. His smile instantly turns sheepish.

"Sorry. I was trying not to wake you."

He's lying on top of the covers on his side, and I raise an eyebrow at the fancy black suit he's wearing, then lift it even farther as I spot the dress draped over the chair at the end of the bed.

"You and I have plans tonight," he says.

"Oh, do we?" I laugh.

He nods seriously, though he looks like he's trying not to smile. "Your friends tried to fight me on it, but they can have you tomorrow."

"What's so urgent about today?"

A strange look passes over his face, and he pauses. "Today's October 21."

I blink. "Oh."

His smile softens as he brushes a strand of hair behind my shoulder. "Happy birthday."

I guess it shouldn't be surprising. I'd left toward the end of the summer, and Reid said I've been gone for three months. The possibility that my birthday was coming up hadn't crossed my mind. Not that a twenty-second birthday is all that significant to begin with, and not like birthdays have ever been something I looked forward to, but still. To forget it completely?

"I don't even know your birthday," I murmur.

"Should be pretty easy to remember." His fingers rub absently along my arm. "Exactly one month after yours."

"November 21?"

He nods.

I nudge him in the chest. "What will that make you then...fifty?"

His smile twists into a smirk. "Twenty-six."

"Oh my God." I throw my head back as dramatically as I can. "You're *old*."

He grabs my waist and pulls me tighter against his chest. "You know, I'm going to remember that when your twenty-sixth comes around."

His words warm something in my stomach. "You plan on still being around then?" I murmur against his shoulder.

He takes my hand and threads his fingers through mine. "Unless you manage to get rid of me before then. But I'm pretty persistent."

"I've noticed. I mean, damn. Can't this guy take a *hint?*"

He snorts and tucks his face between my neck and shoulder, his lips pressing against my skin. "Are you coming with me or not?"

"Well, what do you have planned?"

He shakes his head. "You'll see."

I pull back a few inches and eye the dress again. "But I have to wear that?"

"Yep."

It's far fancier than anything I own, and I'm not familiar with the area, but from everything I've heard about the Auclair estate, it's kind of in the middle of nowhere. A small town, at best. So unless he's planning on going farther out into British Columbia, I can't think of a single thing that would warrant a dress like that.

"You'll like it," he says. "I promise."

I narrow my eyes at him. "I don't like surprises."

But that only makes his smile widen. "I know."

———

THE DRESS IS A PERFECT FIT. I don't know how he managed it or where he even got it from, especially given the recent weight loss. It's a deep red and a silky satin material. It hangs just past my knees with a slit all the way up the left thigh and a low back with crisscrossing straps.

After living in Leif's secondhand clothes for weeks on end and being constantly caked in dirt, the sight of myself in the mirror with high heels and smooth hair is disorienting. But I can't deny the smile that forces itself onto my face. Not that I dressed up like this regularly before, but there's something about it that makes everything feel a little more normal.

After applying some lipstick, I meet Reid in the hallway. He's in the same suit as before, his dark hair pushed back from his face. It almost reminds me of the night of our pairing ceremony.

We take one of the estate's cars, but even once we're on the road, Reid still won't tell me where we're going. I watch the streetlights through the window as we drive past the small town and hit an expanse of secluded woods. But eventually city lights appear, and this is where the driver makes an exit.

I shoot Reid a questioning look, but he offers no details, looking far too pleased with himself. The city is buzzing with life when we climb out onto the sidewalk, people milling past, all the shop windows filled with light. It's such a stark contrast to what we saw in New York that it almost feels like I've stepped into another life. Another time.

Reid offers me his arm as he leads me toward the looming dome of a building in front of us. But he doesn't take me to the row of shiny front doors. Instead, we head around the corner.

"You better not be breaking us into this place," I mutter.

"Don't worry," he muses as he props the back door open and waits for me to pass. "I didn't forget about your goody-two-shoes conscience."

I scowl and step inside. It smells like rich wood, and lights flicker on overhead as Reid hits the switch on the wall.

I let out a small gasp. We're standing at the back of a

stage of an auditorium, which, thankfully, is empty. There are, however, dozens of chairs set in a semicircle, prepared for a show. An orchestra, if I had to guess, by the stands set up for music sheets. There's one chair situated where the conductor should be in the center with a music case resting against it.

Reid's footsteps echo as he heads toward it.

"Reid."

He picks up the case, the perfect size for a violin, and holds it out to me. I look around, waiting for someone to shout at us to get out of here.

"Whose violin is that?" I finally ask.

"It's yours."

I squint at the case and cross the distance between us. It's shiny and brand-new and nothing like the shabby case I've had all my life.

"Reid—"

"Sit down." He gestures to the chair.

I sigh, knowing all too well he's not going to give me any information before he's good and ready, so I sink into the chair. He kneels in front of me, resting the violin case on my lap.

"I know he's taken a lot of things from you," he says quietly. "And I know yours was originally his." He meets my eyes. "But you're good at this, Valerie. Better than good. And I know that you love it." He flicks open the clasps and tilts the lid up. "So now, this one is yours. And only yours. Something that has never been his."

All the air escapes my lungs in an audible whoosh. The maple wood is gorgeous and warm. I run my fingers over the grain, itching to play and see how it sounds. It's in excellent condition for an antique—it must have cost a fortune.

I blink, my eyes threatening to fill with tears, and he gently places his fingers under my chin and forces me to look at him. "Don't let him take this from you too."

I let out a shuddering breath and glance to the violin in my lap. I've never owned anything this nice before.

"If you don't like this one, I had no idea what I was doing. We could get you something new—"

"It's perfect," I whisper. "Thank you."

"I do have one condition though," he adds after a moment.

I snort. "It's not really a gift if there's a condition."

"Play for me."

"Right now?" I glance around the empty auditorium. It looks like there's about to be a concert.

He gives me a crooked smile. "You can't tell me you don't want to hear how it sounds in here."

My eyebrow lifts a little. The acoustics are probably better than anything I've experienced.

He takes a few steps back, grabs one of the chairs, and points it to face me as I pull the violin from its case. I quickly tune it, and somehow, despite never holding it before, as I rest it under my chin and let the first note hang in the air, there's something about it that is immediately familiar and comforting.

I let out a slow breath as my fingers fly over the strings and the music swells around us, rich and complex in a way that I've never heard it before, each note brassy and warm. It feels like filling my lungs with air for the first time in weeks. My fingers ache, not used to the strings anymore, but I keep playing, not wanting it to end, this feeling in my chest or the music surrounding us.

When I finally open my eyes again, I find Reid watching me. He's not smiling anymore. Just watching.

"I'm a little out of practice," I say.

That gets him to smile. "You're perfect," he murmurs.

My cheeks burn, and I busy myself returning the violin to the case. "We should probably get out of here before the show—"

"It doesn't start for a few hours. However, if you want to stay, I have a couple of tickets for us."

My eyes snap to his face. "You want to sit through an orchestra concert?"

"Is that a yes or no?"

I swallow the lump in my throat as I secure the clasps of the violin case. My voice comes out barely audible as I say, "Yes."

I'VE NEVER BEEN to any kind of musical performance. I went through a period when I was younger of searching for videos online, especially when I was first teaching myself how to play. But those recordings are nothing compared to watching it live.

The music itself is one thing, but what's even more captivating is how the musicians are so in sync. How they work together like a well-oiled machine, seeming to communicate with each other silently. It's mesmerizing to watch.

My heart feels full in a way I don't know if I've ever

experienced, and in the back of my mind, a quiet voice whispers, *I want that.*

I've never considered myself to be much of a performer. I don't even let anyone listen to me play. But suddenly, I can picture myself up there.

I jump at the pressure on my hand as Reid slides his fingers through mine and squeezes. I can't help the stupid grin on my face as I look at him and then back to the stage.

"Are you bored to tears right now?" I whisper.

His eyes flicker from my eyes to my mouth. "I'm exactly where I want to be."

WE GRAB dinner at a nearby restaurant after the show, and Reid even orders a human entrée, though I know he doesn't need it. But he can still appreciate the taste. A candle flickers on the table between us, casting a glow to his face as he thanks the waiter, and the man nods and turns away, not even a flicker of recognition in his face for me or Reid. I hadn't realized how much of a relief that would be until now. How *normal* it feels.

The pasta is probably the best thing I've ever tasted in my life, but that also might be the wine talking. We've already made it through an entire bottle.

"This has been fun," I murmur.

He smiles and takes my hand across the table. "So, a good surprise then?"

I laugh and roll my eyes. "I suppose."

He laughs too, and I lean my cheek into my hand, trying to keep my head up. I was a lightweight to begin with, but I didn't account for how much harder the wine would hit me at my current weight.

"Maybe I should get you home before you pass out on the table."

"I'm fine."

He gives me a knowing smile, but says nothing, even as he has to support my weight as we head outside to the car waiting for us by the curb.

The ride back to Auclair feels like it passes much faster than the way into the city had, but I'm a bit more sober by the time we make it upstairs. Enough to notice how much these shoes dig into the sides of my feet. Or maybe I'm not used to wearing heels anymore.

I plop on the bed once we reach the room and start fighting with the straps.

Reid laughs and kneels in front of me. "I'll get it."

"I'm not drunk," I insist. "These shoes are just impossible."

Reid tugs on the clasps, but it doesn't come undone for him either. He grits his teeth as he wrestles with it for a few moments. "Jesus Christ," he mutters.

He stands abruptly, slides his hands under my hips, and moves me farther onto the bed. I let out a surprised laugh as I fall onto my back, and he kneels, my foot in his hand so he can see the shoe better.

"Once we get these things off, we're getting rid of them. I'll get you some new ones."

I giggle as he finally manages to force the strap open. He tosses the shoe aside, then promptly collapses on top of me. His breath tickles my neck, and his fingers slowly weave into my hair as his lips trace my shoulder, then up to my jaw. I grab his face and bring his mouth to mine. He kisses me slowly, deeply, until I pull back an inch.

"Reid?" I whisper, and my lips brush his.

He hums.

"You only got one shoe."

He groans and presses his forehead to my chest before rising to his knees and taking my other ankle in his hands.

"These aren't just going in the trash," he mutters. "We're burning them."

I laugh as he ducks to inspect it and his hair falls into his eyes. He smashes his lips together, his face creasing in concentration. I smile, shaking my head as I watch him, and my heart feels twice as large as usual—so big there's probably not enough room inside of me anymore to fit the rest of my organs.

"Aha!" He rips the shoe away from my foot and tosses it to the floor. He leans over me, bracing a hand on either side of my head, and his eyes flicker over my face. "What's wrong?"

"Nothing," I say, trying to clear the emotion from my throat. My next words come out small and barely audible. "I love you. I—I probably should have told you that sooner. But I—I love you."

He doesn't say anything for what feels like a long time, but I don't break his gaze. I can't take the words back now, and I don't want to.

I've said the words before, plenty of times. To friends. Family. Connor.

But never, not once, did it feel like this.

And I don't think anyone has ever looked at me the way Reid is right now.

"I love you too," he says, his voice low and rough.

I smile, a nervous laugh bubbling in my chest, and he smiles down at me, the kind that reaches his eyes. The kind that makes everything else in the world okay, as long as he keeps looking at me like this.

I unbutton the jacket of his suit, but he takes my hands in his and pins them over my head, interlacing our fingers.

"What's wrong?" I breathe.

"Nothing at all. I just—I want to take things slow tonight." His lips curl into a crooked smile, but it softens as he looks from my eyes to my lips. "Let me make love to you the way I should have the first time."

I feel his next kiss down to every nerve in my body. It burns away all the shadows lingering inside of me, instead filling my veins with light. His lips move slowly against mine, and I let out a small moan as he deepens the kiss, his hips pressing me into the mattress. I wrap my legs around him, pulling him closer, completely consumed by the feel of his body, the warmth of his presence surrounding me.

I think it's always been there, this magnetic push and pull between us, at least in part. But now that I've finally leaned in, let myself completely and utterly fall into it, it's like the world has tipped on its axis, and there's just this. There's just him.

His lips trail to my jaw, then down my throat. I tilt my head back, giving him better access, and my eyes close.

"From now on, no one gets to touch you like this but me," he murmurs against my skin. "Do you understand?"

"Yes."

"Say it to me."

A shuddering breath passes my lips as his teeth graze

my collarbone. "It's only you, Reid. No one touches me but you."

His fingers trace down my arm, then my ribs, until he reaches my hips. "Tell me what you want, Valerie."

He kisses down my chest over my dress, working his way lower, and I tangle my hands in his hair.

"I want to know what you like," I breathe.

He lets out a low laugh as his hands glide up my dress, his fingers slipping beneath the waistband of my underwear. "I just got you back," he says as he pulls them down my legs. "Don't make me scare you away now."

"Why do you think it would scare me away?" He doesn't respond, so I push myself up and lean forward until our faces are a breath apart. "Why do you assume I won't like the same things you do?"

He searches my face, and I straddle his lap. He cracks half a smile as I tug the suit jacket off his shoulders, and he tosses it onto the bed beside us. Something in his expression shifts as he winds his fingers into my hair and tightens his fist around it at the nape of my neck, pulling my head back as he leans in and brushes his lips up my jaw toward my ear.

"You want to know?" he asks.

My breath halts as his other hand slides up my thigh. I nod.

"If I had my way with you," he murmurs, "I'd tie you to this bed and touch you and lick you and fuck you until you come so many times you physically can't anymore."

My stomach clenches, my breaths coming in shorter and faster as his lips continue carving their path along my throat to my other ear.

"Would you like that?" he whispers.

"Yes," I gasp.

His hand around my hair tightens. "Would you let me tie you to my bed?"

"Yes."

His hand on my thigh finally reaches my hips, but he goes in the opposite direction I want, his hand gripping my ass instead and pulling me against him.

"Will you do as I tell you to?" he asks, a raw and rough quality to his voice now.

"Yes," I say, panting for breath already.

I hit the mattress on my back, his full weight pressing into me as his mouth crashes against mine. I rip at the buttons of his shirt, trying to pull it off as he hikes up my dress.

"Taking it slow?" I ask with a breathless laugh as he leans back on his knees and pulls his tie over his head.

He gives me that damn crooked grin. "Next time."

Our movements turn frantic, trying to peel off the remaining layers between us. The moment I'm naked on my back, he ducks his head between my legs, his arms wrapping around my hips and pinning me to the bed by my stomach. The first stroke of his tongue is enough to make me moan and squirm, desperate for more friction, but he takes his time. He licks in slow, careful movements, working his way around my thighs, inching closer, but never where I want him.

"Reid," I whimper.

Slowly, he dips his tongue inside of me and trails it up to my clit. My skin feels like it's on fire, my heart threatening to burst out of my chest. I fist my hand around his hair, pushing it back from his face. He looks up through his lashes to meet my eyes, a smirk tugging at his lips, and *fuck*, the sight of it. He knows exactly what he's doing to me too, because he winks, then murmurs, "You taste even better than I remembered," before his lips close around my clit and suck.

I moan as his tongue works faster, harder. My back arches off the bed, my feet pressing into his shoulders.

His arms tighten around me, one holding me in place, the other grabbing my hand and lacing his fingers through mine. The noises coming out of me are breathy, animalistic, as his tongue circles my clit over and over, never breaking pace.

I cry out as the orgasm rips through me, my hips spasming against the bed. But he doesn't stop, not until the very last of it ebbs away, and he slows along with me. His arm loosens around my hips but doesn't let go as I close my eyes and catch my breath.

"You're so goddamn beautiful," he murmurs, his voice low. Gently, he presses a kiss right above my hips and lays his head against my stomach, and I run my fingers through his hair, pushing it back from his eyes. "Roll over."

I do, and he grabs my hips, pulling me toward him, his chest pressing into my back. His knee urges one of mine up until I'm flat on my stomach, and he grabs a pillow to prop under me.

His lips trail up my spine, then he grabs both of my hands and interlaces our fingers, pinning them on either side of my head.

He kisses the side of my face as he slides inside of me,

inch by inch. We gasp at the same time as he fills me all the way to the hilt.

"I could spend the rest of my life inside of you"—he slowly pulls out all the way, then sinks back in—"and it still wouldn't be enough."

I don't even bother trying to quiet my moans as he picks up the pace, each thrust harder than the last. I can't breathe. I can't *think*. There's just his body against mine and his heart pounding against my back and his breath on my neck. He groans deep in his chest, and the sound travels through every vein in my body.

"God, Reid, don't stop," I gasp.

"Right there?"

"Yes." I tighten my fingers around his, and his face presses against my shoulder, his breaths as short and strained as mine are.

One of his hands slides under my hips, holding me to him as my moans turn breathy, desperate.

"Reid," I whimper, and his hand slides higher to my breasts. It doesn't take long for me to finish a second time, but when I do, he flips me onto my back and slides inside of me again, his forehead coming to press against mine.

"Tell me if you've had enough," he breathes.

I moan in response, my nails digging into his back.

"Fuck, do you have any idea how much I love the sounds you make?"

I pull his mouth to mine, wanting him closer somehow, even though there's no space left between us.

"I love you," he whispers against my lips.

"I love you," I breathe.

"Hands above your head."

KATIE WISMER

I do as he says, and he wraps his tie around my wrists and gives it a small tug. "Too tight?"

I shake my head.

"Good." He kisses the corner of my mouth and presses my wrists into the mattress. "Keep them here."

I nod, and he grabs my thighs and angles my hips up, sinking in deeper. My head tilts against the pillows, a moan getting caught in my chest.

He braces his hands beside my face, and I lock my ankles around his waist, lifting my hips to meet him each time. Holding my gaze, he wraps his fingers around my neck, like he's gauging my reaction, then puts pressure on my throat, just a little at first. I nod, and he presses harder on the sides, cutting off my air as his other hand trails between my legs.

The muscles in my legs shake as he thrusts into me harder, his thumb on my clit keeping a slow, steady pace.

"That's it, baby," he murmurs. "Just like that."

I fight to keep my arms where they are, but all I want to do is touch him. To run my fingers along the muscles flexing in his back, his chest, his arms.

Heat builds, consuming every inch of me until I feel like I can't survive another second of it, and my back arches off the bed. My mouth opens in a silent scream, and my muscles trembling as wave after wave crashes into me and I can't tell the end of one orgasm from the start of another.

Reid releases my throat as the shaking in my body dies down, his lips replacing where his fingers had been, tracing kisses up and down my skin. My body feels limp, boneless beneath him.

"I could watch you do that all night," he says, his voice

rumbling deep in his chest as he undoes the tie around my wrists.

"I want to watch you come," I whisper.

His breathing is as hard as mine is as he leans back on his knees, and it's almost shocking to see the size of him after he was just inside of me. He holds my gaze as he takes himself in his hand. His eyes are hooded and dark, darker than I've ever seen them.

I try to hold his eyes, I do, but it's transfixing, every movement of his hand, the flex of his abs, the veins standing out in his forearm. I wet my lips, unable to look away as his chest rises with his breath, a low moan rumbling deep between his ribs, his jaw hardening as he gets close.

His brow creases, a hint of uncertainty creeping in, like he's asking me for permission.

"Come on me, Reid," I breathe.

The groan he lets out makes every hair on my body stand at attention—a sound I could listen to again and again and still never get enough.

He finishes on my stomach, then slumps on top of me.

"Valerie," he murmurs on an exhale, almost too low for me to hear.

I tighten my fingers in his hair, and he slides his hands under my ribs. His heart pounds against his chest as he rests his head on my breasts. It feels different than it had the first time in the bathroom. There's no uncertainty, embarrassment, panic. I don't feel the urge to flee, the confusion about what this means.

His thumbs caress my sides in small strokes, and I let out a shaky breath as my eyes fall closed. I'd known coming back would feel different. That I wouldn't feel welcome here, comfortable.

But that feeling I've been searching for, that inexplicable warmth, it's this. This place might not—maybe no place ever will—but Reid feels like home.

"You've ruined sex for me," he says. "I'll never want that with anyone else."

I tug on his hair, fighting back the sudden emotion clogging my throat. "Good."

He lets out a low laugh and kisses my collarbone. "I can promise you that much, Valerie. I've never touched anyone the way I touch you." His lips press a little farther up my throat. "Never kissed anyone the way I kiss you." Beneath my jaw. "Never fucked anyone the way I fuck you." He slides his fingers through mine as his lips find my mouth. "And I've definitely never loved anyone the way I love you."

"How do you do that?"

"Do what?"

I smirk. "Always know the right thing to say."

His returning smile is slow, warm. He seals his mouth over mine, the kiss gentle, soft. "We should get you cleaned up," he whispers. "But I'm not ready to let go of you yet."

"Me neither."

He falls onto the bed beside me and tucks me into his side. "Just another minute then."

I nod, my arms wrapping as tightly around him as I can manage. "Just another minute."

CHAPTER THIRTY-SEVEN

"Rise and shine, bitch!"

The bed jerks, and my eyes fly open to find Kirby and Monroe standing on it and looking down at me.

"Jesus Christ," I breathe, my heart in my throat.

Then Reid's body against my back registers, his arm wrapped around my chest.

My naked chest.

"Guys!" I whisper-scream.

The blankets are covering everything, but *still.*

Reid stirs, his arm going rigid around me as he realizes we're not alone, but then he relaxes a fraction once he sees who it is.

"We're kidnapping you," Kirby says simply.

Monroe points at Reid. "A deal's a deal."

He groans and buries his face against my back. "Can you give us a minute?"

"Nope," she says cheerily. "You had your day yesterday. Your time is up."

"I'm regretting bringing you here," he mumbles.

"No you're not," Kirby singsongs.

"Can you at least let me get dressed first?" I mutter.

"You can have five minutes." Monroe narrows her eyes at Reid. "If you two start having sex, we *will* walk in on it."

Reid keeps his face pressed against my back and waves a hand for them to leave. I can't help the small giggle that slips out as the door closes behind them.

"Lock the door before they come back," he whispers.

I giggle again and tap his arm. "You have to let me get up."

He pulls me tighter against his chest. "No."

"They're just going to come back."

He lets out a low growl in the back of his throat but loosens his grip.

I slide out from under his arm, and he lets out another noise of protest. "I'll see you later," I say, planting a quick kiss to his forehead.

He blinks up at me with a sleepy smile, his eyes half-closed. "I'll wait here."

I snort and head for the closet. The human servants stocked it with some things in my size when we got here, and though they might not be my style, they're far better than the options I had at the camp.

Reid groans from the bed. "If you want me to let you go, you've got to stop walking around in those."

I cringe wondering who had been put in charge of acquiring clothes for me—and why they thought black satin panties with mesh detailing were a necessity—but the look on Reid's face definitely makes it worth it, like he'd very much like to add them to the pile of the rest of our clothes on the floor. I grab a black sweater off a hanger and yank it over my head. "You'll survive."

"You're torturing me."

I roll my eyes as I dig through the jeans until I find a pair I think will fit. Reid's eyes never leave me as I shimmy into them. My hair probably looks like a disaster from sleeping on it wet after a shower last night, so I yank it into a ponytail.

"Sixty seconds, Val!" calls Monroe's voice.

Reid sighs and flops onto his back.

"Bye!" I head for the door, but he catches my hand as I pass. "Reid…"

He stands and takes my face in both hands. "Have fun with your friends," he murmurs, then kisses me lightly on the forehead.

"Time's up!" announces Kirby.

Reid winks and disappears into the bathroom as the door flies open.

"Is the blindfold really necessary?" I mutter.

"Yes!" Kirby chirps, and I jump, her voice closer than I expect. Her hands land on my arms a moment later, steering me to the left. "We're coming up to some stairs in three, two…"

"Where the hell are you taking me?"

"Would you quit trying to ruin the surprise?" Monroe calls from somewhere up ahead.

I reach out blindly for a handrail and slowly shuffle my way up the stairs, counting them in my head. Kirby holds on to me the whole time, humming some song I don't know under her breath.

A loud metal screech fills the stairwell, followed by howling wind.

"The roof?" I say.

Kirby nudges me forward. "Stop trying to guess."

"Start with her over there!" Monroe calls.

Kirby steers me to the right as we crest the top of the stairs and cool wind whips around us. The metal door clangs shut with a bang, and after a few feet, Kirby stops and spins me to face the other way.

I inhale deeply and scrunch my nose. "Why does it smell like fire?"

"On this day—well, yesterday—twenty-two years ago," Kirby starts in an announcer voice, "Valerie Josephine Darkmore graced the world with her presence."

"Oh, God," I mutter.

Someone finally tugs off the blindfold from behind, and I blink, waiting for my eyes to focus. Monroe stands a few paces away, grinning. We are on the roof, as expected, the night sky clear overhead, exposing the faint glow of the stars. The rooftop itself is littered with its own light—lines of candles and two firepits closer to the edge. And along the wall leading to the stairs is a line of photographs, strung together with twinkling lights.

"Four years later was the best thing that ever happened to Valerie," Kirby continues, skipping to my side as she turns me to the first picture. "She met her best friend, Kirby."

I snort, though it comes out kind of choked as I take in the photograph. We must be four, Kirby and I, grinning in the estate's pool room, our smiles full of missing teeth.

"*Actually*," cuts in Monroe, "the best thing happened six years later..." She hooks her arm through mine and pulls me to the second photo—the ten-year-old versions of us on the estate's grounds. We're huddled together in the grass, Monroe's arm stretched as far as it can go as she tries to take the picture. All of our cheeks are pressed together, but Kirby's face is still cut off halfway.

I can't help but laugh—Monroe's bangs that don't fit her face at all, the glasses I'd insisted on wearing that entire year even though I didn't need them, Kirby's horribly smudged pink eyeshadow. She'd just started wearing makeup that year and used her fingers instead of brushes.

They take me down the rest of the line, pointing out each picture and the memory attached to it—the year Connor and I finally started dating, Kirby's sixteenth birthday when we all got wasted and Adrienne let us sleep on her floor so Mom wouldn't find out, our first day at the academy.

By the end, I stop bothering to try to hide the tears running down my face, but judging by the sniffles happening on either side of me, I'm not the only one.

"Where did you get these?" I whisper.

"After your..." Kirby wipes her hand under her nose and clears her throat. "After the funeral, your sister let us go through your things to see if there was anything we wanted to take with us." A strange look passes over her face, and she hesitates before adding, "She also let us into your mom's room."

"My mom?"

My mother had never been one for keepsakes or senti-ment. We never had photobooks or art projects kept from when we were children. Maybe a few family portraits framed on the walls, but that was all.

My eyes gloss over the pictures again—so many moments and memories I'd all but forgotten. "She...kept these?"

"There were more too," Monroe says quietly. "Adrienne helped us go through them. She said she'd never seen them either. But your mom left them out for us in this big box on her bed."

I have no idea what to say to that. What to think. Some of the pictures have lines down the middle, like they were folded and unfolded time and time again.

"Anyway," says Monroe behind me in a forced-chipper tone. "I'd like to propose a toast."

I turn to find them both holding champagne flutes, and Kirby grins as she hands one to me, tears still shining on her cheeks.

"To our best friend in the whole world." Monroe holds her glass up. "Don't you dare ever put us through some-thing like that again, you bitch. We love you. Happy birthday."

"Hear, hear!" cheers Kirby, and I laugh as we clink the glasses together.

"Thanks, guys, for doing this. Really."

Monroe grimaces. "It's totally lame. But they wouldn't let us take you anywhere, so our options were kind of limited—"

"It's perfect. I promise."

"Good!" Kirby huddles up next to me and links her

arm through mine, immediately tugging me toward one of the fire pits. "But we also have…"

I snort at the cake laid out on the table, still in the plastic from the store. The top is covered in basketballs and rocket ships.

"It was the last one the store had," Monroe explains.

"Is it chocolate?" I ask.

"Yes!" Kirby grins and pries the lid off.

I shrug, grab one of the plastic forks, and dig out a bite —directly in the middle of a basketball, naturally, to get the most frosting. "Then I don't give a fuck," I say as I shove it into my mouth.

"We—we had candles!" Monroe sputters. "We were going to sing!"

"Then sing," I say, digging out another basketball.

"Oh, let the girl eat her cake," says Kirby.

"You've always been so impatient," Monroe mutters, but she's smirking as she takes the seat beside me and holds her hands out to the fire.

"I just like cake," I say around a mouthful.

She meets my eyes, and the heaviness that's been behind hers since the first time she saw me again is still there despite her smile. I have a feeling she sees the same thing looking back at her. But still, she just sighs and waves a hand. "Are you going to hand me a fork, or are you planning on eating the entire thing yourself?"

"Are you going to tell us what Reid needed you the *entire* day for yesterday?" Kirby asks as I hand Monroe a fork.

"We just went into the city," I say, sipping my champagne, the taste mingling perfectly with the sugar-loaded frosting. "There was an orchestra concert, then we got dinner."

"Oh my God, look at her face," says Monroe.

"You're blushing!" shrills Kirby.

"I am not." I try to scowl, but my face seems to be permanently stuck in a stupid grin.

"I'm guessing that only describes about ten percent of your night," Monroe mumbles into her glass.

"You guys have boundary issues. Do you know that?"

"Yeah, Roe. Stop picking on her." Kirby leans against my shoulder and adds in a hushed tone, "But, like, on a scale of one to ten, how good was it?"

I swat her away with my fork, my face burning as I focus on the fire crackling in front of us. It makes the entire rooftop smell like roasted marshmallows, a smell I'd probably found comforting at one point, but now anything that reminds me of camping just makes me think of the wolves.

I push the frosting around on the edge of the cake but don't take another bite.

"So, does this mean you're coming back to York for second semester?" asks Monroe. "After all of this gets cleared up, obviously."

I blink and lean back in my chair, grateful for the change in subject, but also thrown. *School.* The idea is almost ridiculous. I can't even picture it. Being back at the academy. Sleeping in a dorm room. Sitting in a classroom. Like none of this ever happened.

"...I'm sure they'd work something out for you," Kirby is saying, but I'm not really listening.

Because it's not just the mundane routine that wouldn't fit me anymore—it's everything. Going back to York would mean continuing the vampires' curriculum, learning how to best serve my partner as a member of the Marionettes. To maintain peace in our society, to uphold the laws, the way things are right now.

Plenty of things hadn't sat right with me before, but it was simply the way things were. There was nothing I—or anyone else—could do to change it.

Except...

I picture Westcott's compound. The hundreds upon hundreds of followers under that roof, and that was presumably only one of many locations.

But is he really any better? The wendigos, the attacks, the deaths...

"Val?"

Monroe's face swims back into view, half illuminated by the fire. Her brow pinches in concern as she watches me.

I could smile and shrug it off. Fake a laugh, throw back the champagne, make a joke about not getting enough sleep because of Reid.

Instead, I say, "Do you ever question it? The Marionettes. What we're doing..." I trail off, not knowing exactly what I want to say. How to explain this feeling in my chest.

But to my surprise, Kirby whispers, "All the time." Taking my hand in hers, she laces our fingers together and sighs. "All the time."

"I know we haven't really asked about everything that happened while you were gone," Monroe adds, sliding her chair closer to mine. "We just didn't want to push you. But if you want to talk, Val, we're all ears."

Kirby nods her agreement as Monroe takes my other hand.

I smile at my two best friends, their touch warming me from the inside in a way the fire can't. Despite everything else in my life changing, I know without a doubt in my mind that this never will.

I squeeze their hands. "I might need another glass of champagne first."

418

CHAPTER THIRTY-EIGHT

I DON'T KNOW how late it is when I stumble back to the room, but it's a different kind of exhaustion than what's been keeping me in bed the past few days. The kind that has me smiling like an idiot as I open the door, my heart full.

I've spent so many months thinking I would never see my friends again. Just a single night with them repaired so much of that damage inside of me.

The room is quiet, so it must be later than I'd realized if Reid already went to sleep. I don't want to wake him, so I turn on one of the lamps by the door instead of the overhead light. At first, my brain can't process what I'm seeing. I freeze in the doorway, everything inside of me going numb.

Reid is on the floor on his back, and a hysterical laugh gets caught in my throat when I think, just for a moment, maybe he's asleep.

The stake protruding from his chest would say otherwise.

The blood on his white shirt is a bright red. Fresh. But there's enough of it that it's soaked through to the carpet beneath him.

He's not moving.

Finally, something inside me kicks back to life, and I stumble into the room. I don't say anything. I don't think I could even if I tried. I fall to my knees beside him, grab his shoulders, and shake them as hard as I can, trying to get him to wake up. Because he has to be asleep. He has to be. There's no other option.

His head lolls to the side, his body limp beneath my hands. This isn't happening. This can't be happening.

I don't know anything about CPR, but I yank the stake out of his chest and pound on it with my fist instead, urging his heart to beat.

"No, no, no," I say through my teeth. "Reid." I grab his head, forcing him to face me. His eyes are closed. "You can't do this to me. You can't do this to me. You promised."

An image from a lifetime ago blurs together with the scene in front of me. His body on a table in the middle of a room. The arms around me as they carried me away before I could help.

But this time, there's no one to stop me.

I dig the blade in my ring into both wrists, deep enough that my head swims, and then press them against the wound in his chest. I squeeze my eyes shut, visualizing him opening his eyes and taking a breath.

I remember the bird launching into flight from the field and the rabbits I saved when I was a child. This won't be any different. This won't be any harder. I can do this just the same.

I reach for the bond to hold on to like an anchor and pull him back, but I can't find it.

"You're not doing this to me again." The room spins around me, the edges of my vision getting darker and darker. I dig my nails into his chest, holding on as the blood runs down my arms. I can do this.

What is the point of having this power? What is the point of having all this magic if it can't do this?

My breaths shorten, each one more of an effort than the last. My arms start to feel weak, the muscles threatening to give out, but I don't let go. I don't stop.

I picture every ounce of my magic as white light flowing out of me through my hands into his chest. Everything muffles around me, the room getting darker and darker, my breaths getting shorter and shorter, when something moves beneath me. The floor, maybe. But it's enough to knock me off whatever balance I had left, and I hit the floor on my side. I don't feel it though. I roll onto my back, and my eyes fall shut.

I don't feel much of anything at all.

Something touches my arm. My face. There's a voice, but I can't make out what it's saying. It's slowly getting louder and rising above the buzzing in my ears. It repeats the same thing over and over until finally my brain can make sense of the word.

"Valerie. Valerie."

Reid's face swims into view above me. His eyes are wide, wild.

I didn't do it. I guess if he's dead, then I'm dead too. I

couldn't do it.

"What did you do?" he asks through his teeth.

I try to pull in a breath, and it gets stuck somewhere in my throat. I try again and again, but I can't force them down. They come out as wheezing gasps.

"Valerie." His voice shakes around my name. "What do I do? How do I help? Tell me what to do."

I blink as more of him comes back into focus. His face, his throat. The blood staining his shirt. His skin is paler than usual. Like he's on the brink of death.

I part my lips, trying to force my voice out.

"What are you saying?" He leans down, bringing his ear as close to my mouth as possible.

The two words I finally manage to gasp out are something I never thought I would find myself saying.

"My mother."

I DON'T KNOW how much time passes. Reid's arms disappear for a bit, and several voices fill the room, but then a soft surface replaces the floor beneath me, and the warmth of Reid returns. His arms wrap under my back and knees, holding me against his chest, his chin resting on the top of my head. He keeps repeating the same thing, and it takes me a moment to understand the words.

You're okay, you're okay, you're okay.

"What the hell happened?"

The voice goes through me like an electric current, but I can't manage to pry my eyes open.

"She—" Reid clears his throat. "She...brought me back."

There's a beat of silence, and then: "Lay her on the bed."

Reid's arms disappear for a moment, but then his hand returns, lacing his fingers with mine.

"Can you help her? What's wrong with her?"

Cold fingers tilt my chin back and forth and force my eyelids open. Each breath passes through my lips small and strained.

My mother mutters something under her breath, but her touch is surprisingly gentle as she examines me.

"Necromancy is a dark magic," she says quietly. "She doesn't have practice with it. She doesn't know how to do it properly. My best guess is she didn't draw on her power to do this."

"What do you mean?" Reid demands. "What would she have used then?"

"Her own life force."

"I—then give it back! Take it back!"

"It doesn't work that way."

Reid's hand tightens on mine. "You have to do something. There has to be something you can do."

She sighs. "I'll need some time to look through some books and collect some materials—"

"Look at her!" Reid's voice rises with thinly contained rage. "She doesn't have *time*—"

"She won't get any worse," my mother says, her voice strikingly quiet. "She won't get any better, but she won't get any worse than this."

Reid either doesn't respond, or I can't hear what he

423

says. But I do hear the door click shut across the room, so she must have left. Reid smooths a hand over my hair, and his lips brush my temple.

"What did you do?" he murmurs.

I try to lift my hand, try to give him some kind of reassurance, but it's all I can do to keep pulling each breath into my lungs.

My mother said it seemed like I'd used my life force instead of my magic, and somehow, I immediately know she's right. That white light I'd envisioned pouring out of myself and into Reid—I've never experienced that when using my magic before. The feeling of that was entirely different than my magic. I'd felt it draining me, but big spells feel similar enough to that exhaustion that I hadn't thought twice about it.

But even still.

Even if she can't fix this, if she can't help me, I would still do it again.

"You can't do this to me," he whispers. "Not again, Valerie."

I try to wet my lips, and my voice is hoarse and barely audible as I rasp out, "You're...the one...died...twice...you asshole."

He lets out a startled laugh and presses his forehead to mine. "Did you really have to even the score?"

The corners of my lips quirk up.

"You'll be all right. I promise. You'll be all right." He rubs his thumb gently up and down my arm, and the motion threatens to lull me to sleep.

Or maybe it does, because the next thing I know, when I open my eyes, my mother is carving a line into the inside of my wrist. I barely feel the bite of the blade, and the incantations she chants don't even sound vaguely familiar to me. I've learned a lot of healing spells over the years, but none of them ever sounded like this.

Reid holds my head up as she tilts a small container to my lips.

I meet her eyes. Why is she doing this? Why is she even bothering to help? She told me I was dead to her.

Her lips are pressed together in a hard line. She could be thinking anything right now. Feeling anything.

The liquid is thick and chalky, but I swallow it down. And it isn't long until sleep pulls me under.

CHAPTER THIRTY-NINE

I'VE NEVER FELT BETTER in my life. I wake up refreshed, energized, my body feeling stronger than it has in a long time. My eyes fly open, and it takes a moment to remember what happened, where I am.

Reid's lying in the bed next to me, but he's not asleep. Judging by the exhaustion on his face, he hasn't slept at all. He's on his side, watching me. I try to give him an encouraging smile, but the worry on his forehead doesn't lessen.

"Hi," I say.

His smile is soft, sad. "Hey, how are you feeling?"

"Good. Honestly, really good."

But even this doesn't seem to lift his spirits. He nods. "That's good. You look better. There's color in your face again."

I touch my cheeks, and everything comes crashing back. The sight of Reid's body on the floor lifeless and still.

"You were dead," I whisper.

The crease between his eyebrows deepens. "I know."

I sit up straight in the bed. "Do you remember what happened? How did—?"

He shakes his head. "I can't remember, exactly. Trust me, I've spent all night trying. It was dark when I got to the room, and something smelled off. Then there was this pain in my head. God, it was like my brain was exploding. And my vision was blurry. Then…" His brow furrows, his focus on his fingers as they press into his chest where the stake had been. "I couldn't see who it was. They were tall, maybe. Taller than me. I don't think they were alone. I could sense someone behind me too."

I gently touch his arm, and he blinks, coming back to himself. "How do you feel now?"

He offers a tired smile. "Alive, thanks to you."

"You know what I mean."

He tucks a strand of hair behind my ear. "I'm fine. I promise."

I bring my hands to my chest, feeling my heart beat steadily beneath my palms, my lungs pumping oxygen through my body with ease. "My mother…"

His expression noticeably darkens, but not in the way it used to when talking about my mother. He just looks more concerned.

"What is it?" I ask.

He sighs. "She's gone, Valerie. She left after she helped you."

That's not particularly a surprise. I'd be lying to myself if I said I wasn't disappointed that she hadn't even bothered to stick around afterward. But I'm honestly more surprised that she'd showed up to help in the first place.

"Valerie…there's something you should know."

"What is it?"

He rubs a hand under his jaw and sighs. "I could tell that it took a lot out of her to heal you, but it wasn't just that. When she was done, her scent changed. I'm sure you've noticed different creatures smell a little different—witches, wolves, vampires." He pauses before adding, "Humans."

I nod, still not sure where he's going with this. "Yeah, I've noticed."

"When she was done, she didn't...she didn't smell the same. She smelled the way humans do."

I blink, trying to process his words. "What are you saying?"

He shakes his head. "I honestly don't know. She didn't say anything. But she didn't just leave the room, Valerie. She left the estate, and no one's seen or heard from her. Not even my mother."

"Where would she have gone?" She's never gone against the queen's wishes. Never just disappeared.

"I don't know," he says quietly. He presses a hand to the side of my face. "You're sure you're feeling okay?"

"Yeah, I'm fine," I murmur. "If somebody did that in this room, it means they could be anywhere in the estate. You—"

"I know. I spoke with King Auclair. They're launching an investigation. Doubling security, glamouring the human servants for information. He assured me that this will be taken seriously."

"Did you tell him about..."

"You? No, of course not. I told them there was an attack in the room. Not that whoever it was...you know."

I let out a slow breath.

"Don't worry about it," he says.

I let out a surprised laugh. "*Don't worry about it?* I just found you dead in the middle of the floor."

He offers me a humorless smile. I point a finger at him before he can say his next words. "Do not tell me that you'll take care of it."

He grins and kisses the center of my forehead. "You know me too well. Why don't you go back to sleep? I'll get you something to eat."

"So all it takes is bringing you back from the dead for you to bring me breakfast in bed?"

"Please, for the love of God, never do that again."

"I mean, if you stop dying on me, I wouldn't have to."

He pats my leg a few times before climbing out of bed and heading for the door.

I bury myself deeper into the covers, but sleep doesn't take me as easily as it has the past few days. I keep eyeing that spot on the carpet where I found him. The bloodstain is smaller than I remember it being when I first came in here.

Who would want to kill him? And why here? Why like that? If they wanted to get away with it, why not take the body with them? We all probably would have assumed he'd gone missing for a couple of days. And how did I not feel it through the bond? Surely I would have felt his death.

I close my eyes, trying to force the tension out of my shoulders. I don't know much about the Auclair estate, but they've always had a good relationship with the Carringtons. Reid, especially, has been sitting in on their meetings and offering them aid for years. I can't imagine why anyone here would want to hurt him. And how many people outside of Auclair even know he's here?

Then there's the whole situation with my mother...

I can't even wrap my head around it.

Despite the new energy strengthening my body—my mother's magic?—the exhaustion is still there. All my energy has been going toward repairing my body, so I suppose some more sleep would do me good. After a while, my thoughts finally stop racing enough for me to doze off.

———

FINGERS BRUSH MY SKIN, and I groan, now groggy from being in the middle of a sleep cycle. He moves my hand.

"Can you let me sleep? I'll eat later," I mumble into the pillow.

"Это не может ждать."

My eyes fly open. The man is close to my face, so close I jerk my head back, but that just makes his smile widen.

"Pleasure to see you again, Valerie," he says, his Russian accent as strong as I remember, and his voice turns my blood to ice. I try to sit up, but something tugs at my wrist.

Hot, sharp terror immediately grips my throat. They used Reid's tie to bind my left wrist to the headboard.

I blink, and I'm back in that windowless room, hands tied behind my back. The knife in my stomach... The snake...

"Mikhail," says the one near my face. "Другая."

I whip my head around, and the second man—Mikhail—grabs my right hand. I try to pull away, and he bares his teeth at me.

"I would not fight if I were you, blood girl," says the man next to me—Viktor, if I'm remembering his name correctly. "His patience is small."

"What do you want?" I demand, but as soon as the words leave my lips, I freeze. *It must have been them who killed Reid. They've been here all this time.*

But how? And where have they been hiding? How did they get past Auclair's security?

Unless, for some reason, they let them in…

Mikhail ties my other wrist to the headboard with rope that digs into my skin.

I yank against it, and Mikhail grunts and grabs my hand. Before I realize what he's doing, he grabs my pinky finger and yanks it to the side. The bone snaps, and I gasp, the shock registering far before the pain.

"I did try to warn you," croons Viktor as he paces toward the foot of the bed.

I grit my teeth against the pain flaring up my arm. Blood rushes to my hand, pulsing and pounding, every nerve zeroing in on the injury as my body fights to heal it— which it can't do, not without resetting the bone. "Why are you doing this?"

I curse my voice for shaking, for the fear probably evident on my face. But it's like my body remembers the last time I was around them, even if I'm forcing my brain not to think about it.

But I am not helpless. It doesn't seem like they injected me with the drugs they used to dull my powers last time— or like they've done anything really to prevent me from fighting back.

Why would they take that risk?

I dig the nails of my uninjured hand into my palm, drawing blood. The magic buzzes along my skin—

—but before I can use it, Mikhail is at my side, and he breaks the next finger on my hand.

I choke on my scream, and Mikhail holds my gaze, his hand still on mine, as if daring me to try something again because he still has eight fingers to work with, and I'm sure he'll get creative if he runs out.

"Are you done with this game?" Viktor asks.

"What do you want?" I ask through my teeth.

"Right now?" Viktor lifts his eyebrows and glances at his wristwatch. "We're just waiting for your boyfriend to show up."

As if on cue, the door opens behind him, and it's not until then that I realize there are others in the room— another two men waiting by the door.

"No, Reid, don't!" I shout, but he barges inside just the same, grabbing the closest man and ripping his throat out with his teeth.

The room turns into a blur of motion, everyone moving so quickly I can't keep up. I yank against my restraints until blood runs down my wrists.

Mikhail pins Reid against the wall by the throat, and I focus on Mikhail's hand, his muscles, the blood pumping through his veins, and force them to all freeze.

Reid's eyes dart to me, just for a moment, before he grabs Mikhail's arm and knocks him back. But Viktor and the other vampire are there, one of them holding a stake.

"Stop!" I shriek, but Mikhail appears in front of my vision.

I hear the stake sink through flesh, then thud into the wall.

"Stop!"

Mikhail grabs my arm, this time not bothering with my fingers, and snaps the radius of my forearm so viciously that it pierces through my skin.

The pain explodes inside of me, and I might scream— I'm not sure. Everything goes quiet for a moment. Nothing exists but the fire in my arm. I duck my head to the side, empty the contents of my stomach over the edge of the bed, and desperately gasp for air.

Reid lets out a roar somewhere across the room. *He's not dead.*

"Just let her go," he growls. "I'm the one you want, and you have me."

"That's where you're mistaken, friend," coos Viktor. "You're not the one we want at all."

My vision swims as I lift my head. They have Reid pinned to the wall with four stakes—one in his abdomen, one in each arm, and one in his left thigh—but none of them look fatally placed. Just meant to subdue.

Reid's nostrils flare as he looks from Viktor to me, his jaw tightening as he locks in on my arm.

"You see," continues Viktor, and he spins another stake around in his hand, clearly waiting for either of us to give him an excuse to use it. He points it at Reid's chest. "We'd heard rumors about your little witch here. No one believed me at first. So, I decided to test it."

My breath catches. They didn't kill Reid with the intent of him staying dead.

They wanted to see if I could bring him back.

"Why?" I whisper.

He grins like he's so glad I asked and paces to the side of the bed. Reid struggles against the stakes, gritting his teeth, and blood drips from the wounds.

Viktor tsks, wraps his hand around the exposed bone in my arm, and twists.

There is no hiding my scream, the agony flowing through every inch of my veins. Reid shouts something, but I can't make out the words. My ears ring, and Viktor waits a few moments for me to come back to myself before he places the stake under my chin and tips my face up to his.

"Because you're going to bring back someone very important to us."

Bring back…?

The story Reid told me after they showed up the last time comes flooding back—what happened at Vasiliev right before he left. The reason they came after me in the first place.

Their brother.

The one who's been dead for…a year now? Maybe longer?

Bringing Reid back—someone who was still warm— had nearly killed me. I can't. Even if I wanted to, that's beyond even me.

Viktor grabs my chin between his fingers, his nails digging into my jaw, and forces me to look at him.

"It's your choice," he says. "You can help us, and then you'll never see any of us again. Or both of you can die right now."

He rolls up his sleeve, and the other man I don't know heads toward us. He pulls a knife from his pocket and carves a line in Viktor's forearm, then points the blade at me like a question.

He's a witch, I realize, not a vampire.

A witch who's offering to perform a blood deal.

"What are the terms?" Reid grits out.

"She revives Sacha and does not try to interfere or change our plans. Then we leave the two of you alone. It's that simple."

Take the deal, Reid says into my head.

Reid, I can't—

Trust me. Do it now. Don't hesitate.

"Deal," I gasp.

Viktor whips toward me, grinning. "I knew you'd see reason."

The moment his witch completes the deal, the web of black veins grows up my wrist, the sight of it sinking into my stomach like a rock.

Again. How did I find myself in this position *again*?

"We leave tomorrow," says Viktor, and taps his stake beneath my chin. I pull my head as far away from him as I can manage. "See you then, love."

A shudder rolls through me as the three of them retrieve the body Reid left by the door—apparently disposable if they're not upset by his death—and their witch teleports them out of the room.

Reid yanks at the stakes securing him to the wall the moment they're gone.

"Reid—" I start, but he manages to pull his arm free,

the stake moving all the way through, but he doesn't make a sound.

He grits his teeth and lets out a slow breath through his nose as he yanks the others free, one by one. When he's done, he collapses to his knees, his chest heaving with his breaths.

I pull against the restraint on my uninjured arm feebly, my entire body leaden from the pain.

"Don't—don't. I've got it," he rasps as he stumbles to the bed. "Look at me."

I do, and he gently takes my chin in his hand. "Let me glamour you."

I blink. "What?"

His face softens, his eyes flickering over mine. "I won't do it without your permission. Let me glamour you so you won't feel it when I fix your arm."

As he says it, the pain breaks through the barrier of shock. Slowly, I nod.

He looks into my eyes, and after a moment, my body relaxes.

"You won't feel any pain. You won't feel this arm at all until it's healed."

"I won't feel any pain," I find myself echoing.

He winces, then presses a quick kiss to my lips and murmurs, "I'm sorry," before releasing my uninjured arm from the tie.

"Reid, I can't do that deal," I whisper as he gets started on the rope.

"I know. You won't have to."

"Reid—"

He meets my eyes as he carefully brings my hurt arm

onto his lap. "They said you couldn't interfere with their plans. They said nothing about me." I start to look down, but he grabs my chin, stopping me. "Don't watch. Just close your eyes, okay?"

If I see that bone sticking out of my arm, I'll probably be sick, so I comply. "You can't take all of them at once," I whisper. The loophole is obvious. Too obvious. "That's probably just what they want."

"Give me a little more credit than that, Darkmore."

I inhale sharply as he puts pressure on my arm, and he freezes.

"Does that hurt?"

"No...it just..." I don't know how to explain it. "Feels... odd, I guess."

"I'll be fast."

I squeeze my eyes shut tighter, trying not to think about the fact that he's literally shoving a bone back into my arm. After a minute, he moves on to fixing my fingers.

"Are you all right?" he asks in a low voice. "Are you hurt anywhere else?"

"I'm okay."

"You can open your eyes."

His face swims into view, his expression still pained.

"You need blood," I say.

"So do you." He tucks the hair behind my ear, then leaves his hand cradling the side of my face. Though his voice comes out softly, there's nothing forgiving in his expression. "They're never going to touch you again."

I want to tell him no, that he could get himself hurt— get himself *killed*—but I can see it in his face, feel it through the bond, that nothing I say or do will stop him. He

437

searches my face, as if checking for other injuries, then pulls me against his chest, his grip almost too tight. His heart pounds against his ribs beneath my ear, his breathing still uneven.

"We're going to end this with them for good. I promise."

CHAPTER FORTY

WE FIND a note the next day with a time and an address for a tarmac with a private plane waiting.

Two words are scrawled at the bottom. *Come alone.*

Reid refuses to tell me anything about his plans, not wanting me involved in the slightest in case it affects the deal. But he's oddly calm as he helps me climb into one of the estate's cars and gives the driver the address. Or maybe he's trying to appear that way for my sake.

He hesitates, just for a moment, beside the open car door, one hand braced on the roof as he leans down and peers in at me. I'm sure my nerves are clear on my face. My hands won't stop shaking in my lap. But he gives me a half smile, leans in, and presses a soft kiss to my lips. "I'll see you soon" is all he says, then closes the door.

The driver says nothing as he takes off, a low song playing on the radio filling the car. I stare out the window, rolling through the possibilities in my head of what Reid could be planning.

KATIE WISMER

How can he be so confident, especially after what happened last night? Maybe he's not planning on coming alone. But who could he possibly pull into this?

The thought makes my blood run cold. He wouldn't...

There's no way he asked Kirby, Monroe, or Adrienne. He wouldn't put them at risk like that.

But who else do we even know who's currently at the Auclair estate? Someone who would care enough about me to risk their own life? I can't think of anyone.

God, I hope he didn't pull Connor into this.

It doesn't take long to reach the destination, or maybe it does. No amount of time would have felt like enough. The car idles beside the curb, and the moment I step out, the driver pulls away without a word.

There's a chain-link fence along the sidewalk, and I follow it until I find the opening of the gate. A few lights dot the path, and there's a small plane waiting in the darkness.

I wrap my arms around myself like I'm cold, but the chill is coming from inside of me, not the weather.

"Glad to see you can follow orders," says Viktor.

I pause in the middle of the tarmac, trying to find the origin of his voice.

Movement flickers in my peripheral vision on the right, and Viktor steps out of the shadows a few yards away.

I have no idea how long Reid needs for his plan, if I should stall. I don't want to set Viktor off. I don't want him to suspect anything. At the very least, I want to give Reid the element of surprise.

"Where are your friends?" I ask him.

He cocks his head, considering me. He doesn't answer

440

my question and lets out a long sigh. "You know, Valerie, I really was hoping that no one would have to die today."

I keep my expression perfectly neutral. "I don't know what you're talking about."

"You know what I'm talking about."

"I mean, here I came, alone, just like you asked. So let's get on the plane and go."

He gives me a mocking smile, then something wraps around my throat from behind. I gasp, and the arm tightens, putting pressure on my windpipes and crushing my back against their chest.

I dig my nails into their arm, trying to pry myself free, but they don't budge. My skin burns where he touches me. A scent I'm all too familiar with floods my nose. Vexillium.

"Reginald, why don't you step out now and let's get on with it," calls Viktor.

A growl rips through the air, very clearly not human.

I stiffen against my captor.

He didn't.

There is no way—

There's a blur of motion. First, on my right. And then on my left.

If Viktor's surprised, I can't tell because I don't have a chance to see his face before a wolf as black as the night emerges from the shadows, sinks its teeth into his throat, and tears him in two.

The vampire holding me back—Mikhail, probably—lets out a low, rumbling growl, and more bodies flood down the stairs from the plane. Mikhail hauls me toward it, his arm cutting off my air. My feet drag along the ground, trying to find purchase, but he's stronger than I am. I dig my nails into his skin, drawing blood, but my magic keeps slipping through my fingers like smoke.

My head is swimming from the lack of oxygen, my vision starting to blur. We're almost to the plane now. If he gets me in there and closes the door, this will all be over.

A gunshot rings out once, twice. Mikhail's grip loosens on my throat enough to let me pull in a breath, and I look around desperately as the sound of a body hitting the earth fills my ears. Too heavy to be Reid. A wolf? How many are even here? I thought I saw at least two, but everything is moving too fast, and my vision is too blurry.

I finally spot Reid. He's on his stomach on the ground, his face pressed against the cement. There's a vampire on top of him, their foot pressing on the back of his neck. He bares his teeth and flips the other vampire onto his back, but every time he tries to break away to get to me, the vampire wrestles him to the ground.

I thrash in Mikhail's arms as he pulls us up the stairs. It can't end like this.

More gunshots ring out, more sounds of splattering blood and falling bodies and growls and tearing skin. It's dark and loud and there are too many blurs of motion and I still can't *breathe*.

We're two steps away from the inside of the plane. One. My body starts to go limp, and his arms tighten, my feet dragging along the stairs. I claw his arm, my lungs screaming for air.

"Well, hello there," says a light, feminine voice, her words tinged with a Russian accent. I don't know who she is, but she must be working with them. She's going to close the door on us. She's going to—

Mikhail's body tenses against mine at the sound of her voice, and we lurch forward. He lets out a wet gurgling sound by my ear, then hot blood gushes over my shoulder. It takes me a moment to realize it's not mine. We collapse onto the stairs. I manage to catch myself, but his body rolls all the way down to the concrete, a gaping hole in his back where his spine used to be.

I frantically suck in air as I turn and take in the woman who just saved my life. She smiles, blood coating her arm from the elbow down, a chunk of Mikhail's spinal column in her hand. She tosses it aside carelessly, and it thuds against the pavement below with a sickeningly wet smack.

Lights from the plane's interior cast an eerie glow around her, almost like a halo, only further accentuated by her golden hair and eyes.

I've definitely never seen her before, and if she's not with them, then who…?

"Who are you?" I gasp.

She cocks her head to the side in a small, delicate movement. "You must be the Marionette."

"Who are you?" I repeat.

She lets out a soft hum and crosses the distance between us, squatting so we're on the same stair. The smile never leaves her face as she inspects me like I'm the most curious thing she's ever seen. "My name is Anya. I'm Reid's fiancée."

SEE WHAT HAPPENS NEXT & A BONUS SCENE

Thank you so much for reading *Bloodless Ties,* and thank you for your reviews! It's appreciated so much and really helps the books. Continue with Valerie's story in the fourth book in the series, *Ruthless Ends,* coming 2023, now up for preorder.

Can't wait until then? Good news! I have a bonus scene **from Reid's point of view**, available through my newsletter. Find out why Valerie and Reid were *really* paired together in book one.

Download it for free here:
https://BookHip.com/FNRVCLZ

Looking for more bonus material? Every hardcover in the series has its own exclusive content. (Bonus scenes, character art, annotated chapters, letters from the author, and more!) Available at most online book retailers.

ACKNOWLEDGMENTS

First and foremost, thank you to my readers for being so patient waiting for this book. Eleven months between book releases isn't unusual, but I know all too well that feels like *forever* when you're left with a cliffhanger. That wasn't very nice of me. I mean, I'll 100% do it again, but at least I'm evil and self aware.

A huge thank-you-isn't-enough thank you to my beta readers and critique partners for helping shape this into the story you see today—Naemi, Lydia, and Jessi. Some of you saw some *rough* drafts of this. Thanks for not running away screaming.

To Mama Wiz, forever my biggest supporter. I 100% got whatever creativity and talent I have from you. I told you not to read this one, but I know you did it anyway. Let's just not talk about it, kay?

Thank you so much to everyone who helped make the audiobook version of Bloodless Ties possible with the Kick-Starter campaign. Audio is one of my favorite ways to experience books, and I will never get over hearing narrators bring my characters to life.

Amanda Edwards, Emily McCosh, Sherill Reynolds, Jamie Rice, Hannah Rush, Ainslee M., Ashley Brown, LeeAnn Logan, Tandia Remmenga, Samantha Bourbon, Erika Gudino, Jordyn Roesler, Courtney Shapiro, Paige, Bonnie Minatra, Makenzie Bell, Laura Schmidt, Ashley Bettencourt, Alexis McCoy Lupinski, Jovanah Watkins, Maiken Hansen, Clair johnson, minato, Ann, Shaughnessy Duke, Megan Puthoff, Amy Hall, Kylie Rodriguez, Hannah, Kirstie Fredrich, and Derek Murphy—you're all honorary Marionettes in my book. (Though you may not want to be after reading this one…oops.)

Huge thanks to Aaron for joining the team and bringing Reid's voice to life with the audiobook, and Stef for nailing Valerie's narration yet again. To Beth, my fabulous proofreader, and Stef, my amazing cover designer.

And of course, my social media fam. I love taking you guys along for the process with each book, and I'm so blown away by the love you've shown this series this year. (I'm looking at you, TikTok.)

I'm nowhere near done with this world, so I hope you aren't sick of me yet.

xx Katie

ABOUT THE AUTHOR

Katie Wismer is a freelance editor and author of romance (sometimes contemporary, sometimes paranormal) and poetry books.

When she's not writing, reading, or wrangling her two perfect cats, you can find her on her YouTube channel Katesbookdate.

You can sign up for her newsletter at katiewismer.com or check out her instructional videos on writing and publishing on Patreon.

patreon.com/katiewismer

instagram.com/katesbookdate

goodreads.com/katesbookdate

bookbub.com/authors/katie-wismer

facebook.com/authorkatiewismer

amazon.com/author/katiewismer

twitter.com/katesbookdate